Resounding praise for
DAVE DUNCAN
and
The King's Blades

"Swashbuckling adventure doesn't get much
better than this."
Locus

"For panache, style, and sheer storytelling
audacity, Duncan has few peers."
Kirkus Reviews (*Starred Review*)

"He explores heroism, betrayal, and sacrifice,
all within the context of breakneck
adventure . . . But in a Dave Duncan story,
'rollicking' should not be mistaken
for 'insubstantial.' "
Calgary Herald

"Just the sort of marvelous yarn that lured
me into reading fantasy."
New York Times-bestselling author Anne McCaffrey

"One of the leading masters of epic fantasy."
Publishers Weekly

"Dave Duncan has become a master of fantastic
adventure, and nowhere is that more obvious
than in the The Tales of the King's Blades."
Edmonton Journal

By
Dave Duncan

THE KING'S BLADES
GILDED CHAIN
LORD OF THE FIRE LANDS
SKY OF SWORDS
PARAGON LOST
IMPOSSIBLE ODDS
THE JAGUAR KNIGHTS

THE KING'S DAGGERS
SIR STALWART
CROOKED HOUSE
SILVERCLOAK

DAVE DUNCAN

IMPOSSIBLE ODDS

An Imprint of HarperCollinsPublishers

This is a work of fiction. Names, characters, places, and incidents are products of the author's imagination or are used fictitiously and are not to be construed as real. Any resemblance to actual events, locales, organizations, or persons, living or dead, is entirely coincidental.

EOS
An Imprint of HarperCollins*Publishers*
10 East 53rd Street
New York, New York 10022-5299

Copyright © 2003 by Dave Duncan
ISBN: 0-06-009445-1
Excerpt from *The Jaguar Knights* copyright © 2004 by Dave Duncan
www.eosbooks.com

First Eos paperback printing: October 2004
First Eos hardcover printing: November 2003

HarperCollins® and Eos® are trademarks of HarperCollins Publishers Inc.

Printed in the U.S.A.

10 9 8 7 6 5 4 3 2 1

To the memory of Rudolf Rassendyll,
who showed the way

D' Ye Ken John Peel?

D'ye ken John Peel with his coat so gay,
D'ye ken John Peel at the break of day,
D'ye ken John Peel when he's far, far away,
With his hounds and his horn in the morning?

For the sound of his horn brought me from my bed
And the cry of his hounds which he oft times led.
Peel's "View Halloo!" would awaken the dead
Or the fox from his lair in the morning.

Yes I ken John Peel and Ruby too,
Ranter and Ringwood, Bellman and True,
From a find to a check, from a check to a view
From a view to a death in the morning.

Then here's to John Peel with my heart and soul
Let's drink to his health, let's finish the bowl,
We'll follow John Peel through fair and through foul
If we want a good hunt in the morning.

—JOHN WOODCOCK GRAVES

This is a stand-alone novel,
set during the reign of King Athelgar,
two years after the end of *Paragon Lost*.

◆   ◆

Contents

Contents

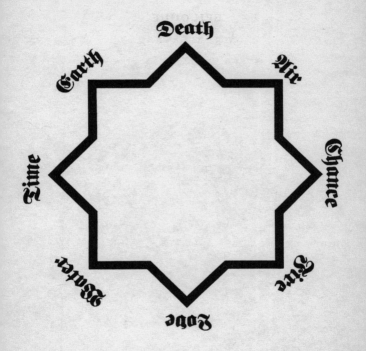

IMPOSSIBLE
ODDS

PROLOGUE

Awaken the Dead

$\mathcal{T}$he night was unusually dark. The day had been hot and clear, but heavy clouds had rolled in after sunset to blot out the stars. There was no moon. In Chivial such nights were called *catblinders*.

The guard changed at midnight. In pitch darkness Mother Celandine, Sister Gertrude, and their escort paraded through the grounds of Nocare Palace. Nocare's gardens were deservedly famous and especially lovely now, at the start of Eighthmoon, except that they were totally invisible. Although Trudy was catching enough scents of night-flowering plants—stock, evening primrose, possibly moonflower—to tell her what she was missing, the lanterns carried by the two footmen leading the way illuminated only the paved path underfoot and mere hints of shrubbery.

The four men-at-arms of the Household Yeomen marching noisily at the rear she considered an unnecessary precaution, because any evil-intentioned intruder who glimpsed her and the majestic Mother Celandine in their voluminous white robes and steeple hats was likely to run screaming off into the darkness, gibbering about ghosts. Besides, one of them was wearing a talisman that jangled her nerves like a tortured cat. In the few days since she had arrived at Court she had been appalled by the number of people who put their trust in such quackery. Good luck charms would attract bad luck as often as good, because chance was elemental. Educated people ought to know this. Other than that, midnight prowling was rather fun. Sour old Mother Celandine must not be finding it so, for she had barely spoken a word since they met.

The White Sisters were rarely required to use their conjuration-detecting skills in the middle of the night. Nighttime security was normally a male sport—the Yeomen guarding the gates and the grounds, the Blades patrolling the inside of the palace—but now the King was entertaining an important guest and either he or someone in his train had been tactless enough to include conjurements in his baggage. Anyone else would have been reprimanded and made to turn them in, but a Grand Duke had to be humored. So the White Sisters' help was required, and Sister Gertrude was the most junior Sister in attendance at Court. Tonight Mother Celandine would supervise and instruct. Thereafter Trudy would have the night honors all to herself.

It was only a formality.

Two lights came into view and soon resolved themselves into torches set in sconces on either side of an imposing doorway, the entrance to Quamast House. The Grand Duke had been lodged a long way from the main palace, and Sir Bernard had assured Trudy that this was the Blades' doing. Most visitors were bunked in the West Wing, but the Blades never took chances with unidentified spirituality.

Under each sconce stood a pike man in shiny breastplate and conical steel hat. The one on the right stamped his boots, advanced one of them a pace, lowered his halberd, and proclaimed, "Who goes there?"

That was a very stupid question when he knew the answer already. The Royal Guard scorned such folderol as passwords, Bernard had told her, because they all knew one another and because they tried to do nothing the Yeomen did, or at least never in the way the Yeomen did it.

"The nightingale sings a sad song!" Sergeant Bates proclaimed at Trudy's back. That was not true, because nightingales had finished singing back in Fifthmoon, and he said it loud enough for any skulking trespasser to overhear.

The man-at-arms resumed his former position, slamming the butt of his halberd on the stone. "Pass, friend."

One of the footmen opened the right-hand flap of the double door. As Trudy followed Mother Celandine through it, she caught a startling whiff of . . . of she was not sure what. She did not stop to investigate.

She found herself in a pillared hall that must take up most of the ground floor of the building. A very inadequate light was shed by a pair of enormous bronze candelabra standing at the foot of a showy marble staircase set in the center of the hall, which seemed an inefficient use of space. Much vague sculpture loitered in the shadows along the walls. The marble floor supported some random rugs and a few ugly sofas and chairs, poorly arranged.

A voice at her elbow said, "Good chance, Trudy."

She jumped and turned to meet his grin. "Bernard!" He had not told her he would be here!

He smirked. "A last-minute roster change."

Obviously he had arranged this so he could surprise her—and embarrass her! Mother Celandine was frowning, and three other Blades had emerged from the darkness to leer. All Blades looked much alike—lean, athletic men of middle size, mostly in their twenties. The conjuration that bound them to absolute loyalty to the King showed to her senses as an ethereal metallic glow, which she found very becoming.

"He's a fast worker, our Bernie," one said.

"Gotta watch those rapier men."

Horrors! Her face was on fire.

"That will do!" The fourth Blade was a little older and wore a red sash to show that he was in charge. He tapped the cat's-eye pommel of his sword. "Good chance to you, Mother Celandine."

"And to you, Sir Valiant."

"Do you know Sir Richey? Sir Aragon? And our expert breaker of hearts, Sir Bernard?" The men saluted in turn.

Mother Celandine nodded crisply to each salute. "This blushing maiden is Sister Gertrude."

Jealous old hag!

"Known as Trudy to her friends," Aragon remarked in an audible aside.

"We asked for White Sisters, not red ones," Richey countered.

Mortified, Trudy caught Bernie's eye. He winked. She realized that he was showing off. The others' crude humor was a form of flattery. She winked back.

"Why don't you have more lights?" Celandine demanded, peering disapprovingly at the gloom.

"Blades see well in the dark," Sir Valiant said, "but the real reason is that the visitors took every candle and lamp they could find upstairs with them. The Baron said something about liking lots of light. We'll make sure we have more tomorrow."

The old lady sniffed. "Well, let's get it over with. Carry on, Sister."

Trudy led the way back to the door to begin. The lantern-bearing footmen followed, and the Blades retreated to the staircase in the center, so their bindings would not distract the Sisters. Trudy closed her eyes and listened. She inhaled, licked the roof of her mouth, queried her skin for odd sensations . . . did all the curious things that promoted her sensitivity to the spirits, tricks she had been taught at Oakendown. She missed Oakendown and all her friends there, although it had been seriously deficient in boypeople, who were turning out to be just as much fun as she had dreamed.

"Nothing here, Mother." She began walking around the edge of the hall, stopped at the first corner. "There is something above here, though! Mostly air, some fire and water. And love." Except for trivia like good luck charms, conjurations were forbidden within the palace.

Celandine stifled a yawn. "Then we're under the Grand Duke's bedroom. He wears some sort of a translation device."

"It's a seeming, surely? I mean," Trudy added before the old harridan could take offense, "it's more like a seeming than anything else I've met."

Mother Celandine pursued thin lips, wrinkling them more than ever. "I do believe you're right! Yes. That's good. We missed that possibility. But it's harmless, you agree?"

Maybe, but the rules said . . . Trudy had been reprimanded twice already that day for talking back. The Prioress was threatening to post her to uttermost Wylderland if she did not learn proper respect for her seniors. "Yes, Mother." She hoped the King did not sign anything when he was near that enchantment.

With the footmen in attendance, Sister and Mother paraded around the ground floor, through deserted kitchens, a dining room, an office. Trudy detected nothing untoward until she was almost back where she had begun.

"There's something here! Upstairs, I mean." This one was much harder, and she struggled for several minutes, but the jangle of elementals defied analysis. "There's more than one conjuration. I can't make them out. A lot of them, all mixed up." Her skin crawled. "I think we should go up and have a close look at that!"

"It is Baron von Fader's medicine chest," Mother Celandine said. "Or, at least, that was what they were in when they arrived. He is His Grace's physician, as well as his Foreign Secretary and Treasurer and spirits know what else. We scanned it carefully. The Prioress decided not to ask for the chest to be opened."

"Why not? There's death in there!"

"Sister! There's death in almost anything, as you well know. Were you never taken to an apothecary's when you were at Oakendown? Many drugs and simples are dangerous in large amounts. And Grand Dukes are entitled to the benefit of small doubts. Now, have you done?"

"I am uneasy about this one, Mother," Trudy said stubbornly.

"It was approved only this morning. But remember it carefully. If you sense any change in it tomorrow, or any other night, then tell the Guard right away. Don't be afraid to ask for my help if you're in doubt. Come!"

She led the way back to the waiting Blades.

"You wish to go upstairs now?" Valiant asked.

"No, we are satisfied. Anything really dangerous we could detect from down here. Of course we located the Baron's medicine chest and the seeming His Grace wears, but we were already aware of those."

"Are they dangerous?" Valiant demanded.

"Not unless you swallow an overdose of purge or sleeping draft."

"His Nibs wears a seeming? What does that do?"

"Makes him attractive to blushing maidens," Trudy said. That was probably all it was for, but the medicine chest still bothered her. Any job half-done bothered her.

Mother Celandine was not amused. Mother Celandine wanted her beauty sleep. "You know where we are if you need us, Sir Valiant."

As they headed for the door, Bernard pulled another of his

tricks. Right behind Trudy's ear, but loud enough for everyone to hear, he said, "Breakfast as usual, Trudy?"

"Of course," she shot back. "My place this time."

Sir Aragon said, "Oooooh, Trudy!"

"We will come and chaperone you, Trudy," Sir Richey added.

She had never had breakfast with Bernie. She had never been to bed with him, either, although tonight after dinner had been a very close call. If she had not had to go on duty, who knew what might have happened?

She did, of course.

But only by hearsay.

So far.

Before her face could even think about blushing, she followed Mother Celandine into the dark vestibule, then outside. She went down one step and stopped so suddenly that Sergeant Bates almost slammed into her. She looked inquiringly at the guard who had challenged them on their arrival. He was playing statue again, but . . . but . . .

"Something wrong, Sister?" Bates asked.

"I'm not sure." She was sensing something. "Are you all right?" she asked.

"Answer her, Elson!" the sergeant said.

The sentry was very tall and had an untidy blond beard. He blinked down at her stupidly. "Right? Yes, mistress, I mean, Sister."

Trudy shivered. She recalled noticing this same oddness on the way in, and now it was stronger. Very strange. Nothing familiar. Air? No fire. No love or chance. Time, no water. Death. Yes, definitely quite a lot of death.

"What is it?" Mother Celandine had returned. "Mm? Oh, that. Are you wearing an amulet, soldier?"

Elson shook his head vigorously, as if trying to dislodge his helmet. "No, Mother."

"How about a ring, mm?"

"Er, yes, Mother . . ."

Mother Celandine laughed harshly and took a firm hold of Trudy's arm to lead her down the steps. "He's a young male, Sister."

Trudy resisted the opportunity to say she had guessed that much because of the beard. "I don't understand, Mother."

Bates barked commands; the procession formed up as before and began moving along the path.

"Conjured rings are a common form of—*ahem!*—family planning, dear. Rings don't get in the way when you take everything else off. I admit that Man-at-arms Elson's is unusual, not a formula I recall ever meeting before, but you'll find such devices all over the palace."

"I'm sorry." She had made a fool of herself.

"I like your young Blade, Bernard."

Trudy gasped. "Er . . . thank you."

"It must tax a girl to keep up with that sense of humor."

"I've managed so far."

"I noticed."

"Bernie's fun. But you shouldn't refer to him as *my* Blade."

"He thinks he is." The Mother sighed. "I used to lust after Blades quite absurdly, but their bindings always gave me a headache at close quarters. Still do. Even tonight, just those few minutes with them."

If she had an aversion to Blades, why had she accepted a posting at Court? It was no excuse for skimping on the inspection.

"Bindings don't bother me," Trudy confessed, trying to imagine Mother Celandine forty years ago, a demure maiden fresh in from Oakendown. *Lusting?* The mind reeled. "I quite like it, in fact." It was sexy.

"Then you're lucky. You do understand that other young

men will stay well clear of you if you date a Blade? And everyone will assume you're sleeping with him?"

"I do not *sleep* with Bernard! I mean I do not, er, *lie* with him!" Just *sitting* beside him was quite dangerous enough.

"Then you're about to," Mother Celandine said firmly. That was not a question. "Unless you drop him completely, right away." That was.

"I don't want to do *that*," Trudy said.

"Then let's talk about rings and things, dear."

When a stupid twigger asked you if you felt all right, the first thing that happened was that you started *not* feeling all right. Think about it for a while longer and you began to feel all *wrong*. As the night passed, Junior Pike Man Elson grew steadily more unhappy. He was cold. He was sweating. His eyes hurt. He had a flea, and fleas inside a breastplate were worse torture than the rack. He was really mad at his idiot wife for starting another baby so soon. Already he couldn't afford to feed all the gaping mouths that greeted him whenever he went home.

Every quarter hour or so, Corporal Nolly gave the signal that meant, count three, then stamp feet together, shoulder halberd, take one pace forward, turn inward, and so on. It ended with the two of them having changed sides. That was better than being reported for fainting on duty, but it hardly classed as an exciting evening.

It was the glare of the torchlight that made Elson's eyes hurt.

His new girl was probably balling that redhead in Blue Company right now.

Every hour or thereabouts, Nolly gave the other signal, so Elson shouldered his halberd and marched around to the back door to relieve Blaccalf. Then he was all alone and could shiver all he wanted. He could keep his eyes closed so that torchlight didn't pain him. He could run on the spot to try and warm up. He could scratch for the flea. At least the mosquitoes seemed to have taken pity on him. He decided it was no great honor to guard Grand Duke Whosit of Wherever, who was no doubt swiving some cute blonde in a featherbed upstairs. He was screamingly mad at Sergeant Bates.

Tramping boots announced the return of Blaccalf.

Elson went round to the front and took up his position. Just when had the spirits decreed that he must stand out here freezing in the dark to guard some rich foreign slob he had never met, a stuck-up slob who wouldn't ever give him as much as a nod of thanks? That same slob was upstairs right now swingeing some slutty twigger! Why didn't Nolly just tell him to go off home, or go off and find his girl, whatever bed she was in?

Nolly gave the signal again.

Count three . . .

For variety this time, as they were about to pass in the middle of the step, Elson pushed his dagger into Nolly's left eye. Nolly dropped his halberd. He didn't fall down. He just leaned forward and made little whimpering sounds as he watched the thin stream of blood trickling off the hilt of the dagger and splashing on his boots.

The overhead light was too bright for the next bit. Elson walked unsteadily down the steps. Then he swung his own halberd horizontal and held it with both hands so he could cut his throat. The process was not as painless as he had hoped. He should have kept the edge sharper.

Nolly stopped trickling and stopped complaining. He stumped down the steps and headed around to the back of the house, looking for Blaccalf.

Elson finished dying and walked back up, then in through the front door.

*   *   *

The Blades approved of Quamast House because they knew that any questionable guests billeted there would not go sneaking out any secret passages. No assassins were going to sneak in, either. When it had been built by King Ambrose, the Guard Commander had been the great Durendal, now Grand Master, and he had made sure that it was built right. With the outer doors and windows securely barred, as they were, Valiant and his little squad had nothing to do except stay awake at the bottom of the staircase. From there they had a clear view of the upstairs balcony and the doors to all the bedrooms.

It was an easy chore and tonight they even had a rookie with them, who must be introduced to some of the fiendish dice games the Blades employed to while away their stints. No charge for instruction. IOUs accepted without limit. Some recruits needed years to pay off their initiations.

Of course Cub Bernard first had to be baited about that slinky White Sister he had acquired. It was unseemly that a freckle-faced tyro, not two weeks into the Guard and barely through his orgying lessons, should collect something like that when better men hankered in vain. They quickly discovered that young Bernard was not the average run-of-the-mill Ironhall innocent. He could see that they were all as jealous as stags with glass antlers. He gave back as good as he got, inventing much lurid detail.

Abandoning that game as unwinnable, Valiant, Aragon, and Richey got serious. They found a massive oaken dining table and, with some difficulty, dragged it to the bottom of the stair. They tried to move the two colossal bronze candelabra closer to it—however exceptional a Blade's night vision, in monetary matters he liked his brothers' hands well lit. Finding the monsters immovable, they settled for the existing illumination and got down to concentrated instruction.

"You know Saving Seven, of course?" Valiant asked.

The kid said he didn't, so Richey demanded to see the color of his money and Aragon produced a bag of eight-sided dice. Each face represented one of the elements, he explained, and you rolled them four dice at a time. The object was to roll seven elements but not the eighth, death. Roll a death and you had to start collecting from the beginning.

"First player has a slight edge," he added, "so we'll give you the honor. After that the winner starts the next one. Put a farthing in the pot and roll four."

On his first try the kid rolled two airs, a water, and a chance, so he counted three. Sir Richey paid his farthing and rolled two deaths, which put him out of that game altogether. The other two scored four elements apiece.

"Just keep going," Richey said. "You can fold, pay the same price as the last man, or double it."

Nobody doubled on that round, which saw the kid roll love, time, and fire, while Valiant and Aragon added one element each. Being ahead with six, lacking only earth, Bernard doubled the price, but failed to improve his score. The others paid when their turns came, with the same lack of progress, so he doubled the price again. He had spirit. With the pot starting to look interesting, he rolled a triple death. Valiant and Aragon exchanged angry glances. Richey guffawed.

Bernard brightened. "What does that mean?"

"It means you win," Richey explained quickly, before the other two could invent a new rule for the occasion. "Roll a *quadruple* death and everyone who was in the game at the beginning has to pay you the final amount of the pot. That's called the 'massacre.' Another game, Freckles?"

"Why not?" Bernard raked in the coins.

It is regrettable that skill, virtue, and experience are no match for fickle chance. The brat won four games in a row, two of them with triple deaths. The next game turned out to be a never-ender, where everybody kept rolling single deaths and no one could reach the magic seven. With the pot growing enormous and three sharpies' reputations at stake, the betting grew desperate, until eventually they had the kid cornered. They were all sitting on winnable arrays and he was back down to two. All three of them in turn doubled the bet, expecting to price him out of the game. Perhaps he was too dumb to see that he could not win from there in a single roll. Or perhaps it was just that he was playing with their money and they were all writing IOUs. He not only stayed in, he doubled yet again.

Then he rolled a quadruple death.

The appalled silence was broken by a yell from Valiant, who had his back to the staircase and was facing the main door. He leaped to his feet, whipping out his sword. "Intruder! Richey, get him. You two come with me." He ran seven or eight steps up and turned to survey the hall.

"You're seeing things!" Aragon said, but he went to join his leader, blocking the way to the guests above. So, to his credit, did Bernard, who might reasonably suspect a trick to cheat him out of half a year's pay.

Sir Richey strode forward to the main entrance carrying his saber, *Pain*, at high guard. The little vestibule was dark, but when he reached the line of pillars, he shouted, without turning his head, "The door's still barred!" He stopped. "I can smell blood! There's blood on the—" Something standing behind the nearest pillar lurched out at him. Possibly the stains on the floor had distracted him, but he parried the halberd thrust admirably, caught hold of its shaft in his left hand, and swung *Pain* at his assailant's neck.

A Blade had little to fear in such a match, and Valiant wisely did not send him reinforcements. The staircase was still the key. He said, "Aragon, waken the Duke and the Baron and get back here." Aragon went racing up the stairs.

Richey, having almost decapitated his assailant, let go of the halberd. That was a mistake, for the intruder did not drop. Instead he swung the halberd at Richey's midriff. Richey leaped back, parrying. His opponent shuffled after, repeatedly stabbing at him. As they came closer to the stairs and the light, Bernard cried out in horror. Now it was clear that the intruder was a walking corpse, for its head hung at an odd angle and it was soaked in dried blood from cuirass to boots. The gaping wound Richey had made in its neck was almost bloodless, but there was another, a crusted black gash. Its throat had been cut twice, and it was still fighting.

Nearer still, and Richey, incredibly, started to laugh, albeit shrilly. The apparition continued to thrust at him with the point of its halberd, which he parried effortlessly, as if it were made of stiff paper. He tried a few cuts of his own, knocking the apparition aside like straw. It kept coming back, but was obviously harmless.

"It's only a mirage!" he shouted.

Upstairs, Aragon was yelling and beating on doors.

Another Yeoman wraith came into view around the staircase, from the kitchen quarters. It moved with the same awkward walk and it had a dagger hilt protruding from its left eye. When it reached the table it dropped on all fours and crept underneath.

"Leave it alone," Valiant said. "Ghosts can't hurt us."

Richey had almost reached the stairs and his opponent was transparent, barely visible at all. He was letting its clumsy strokes go, for they passed clean through him as if he were not there. Likewise, *Pain* whistled through the shadow without effect.

The table tilted, spilling dice and money. Valiant and Bernard watched in amazement, for all four Blades together had barely managed to shift that monstrosity. For a moment it stood on edge, then tipped over, impacting one of the candelabra. They went down together with a crash that shook the hall. Most of the candles winked out. Darkness leaped inward.

Richey screamed as his opponent's halberd impaled him. *Pain* went skittering off across the marble floor. Richey fell; the corpse withdrew the halberd and stabbed him again. Then again. The second intruder clambered off the fallen table and went lurching toward the other candelabrum with both arms held across his eyes.

"Save the other candles!" Valiant yelled. He and Bernard went plunging back down the stairs.

Bernard got there first with a couple of giant, reckless, ankle-risking strides and made a spectacular lunge, thrusting his rapier into the armpit gap in the side of the dead man's cuirass. He did not stop there. Sword and Blade together went clean through the smoky figure. Bernard hit the floor in a belly flop and slid past Sir Richey and the thing that kept stabbing at him. He lay as if stunned. His heroics had been unnecessary, for the corpse he had been attacking had faded to almost nothing beside the candelabrum.

Upstairs, doors were flying open. Unfortunately, the light pouring out of them did little to brighten the deadly gloom below.

Valiant took station under the remaining candelabrum, parrying the efforts of the second shadow to throttle him until he realized that it could not harm him. A third intruder shuffled in from the kitchens, completely enveloped in a heavy carpet. Valiant waited until it was close and then charged it, thrusting *Quietus* through the rug and feeling her jar against a steel cuirass inside. The occupant retaliated by tipping the carpet over him and body-checking him. He was thrown over backward by the weight of a big man in half armor, but by the time he hit the marble, the load on top of him was no more than that of the rug alone.

He struggled free of it. Now two of the wraiths flitted around him, struggling to injure him with no more success than he would have fighting mist.

Voices upstairs shouted that help was on the way. Out in the shadows Richey lay on his back, obviously dead. Bernard sat up. The first Yeoman corpse swung its halberd at him. Bernard rolled nimbly aside. Steel rang on stone where he had lain. His move put him within reach of his rapier, *Lightning*. He grabbed hold of her hilt, but was not quite fast enough getting back on his feet. Still off balance, he parried the halberd aside with his left hand and drove *Lightning* through the corpse so that two-thirds of her stuck out of its back. That stroke would certainly have ended any living opponent, but the dead one ignored it and fell on top of him. They went down together, with the corpse clawing at his throat.

Valiant reached him, swinging *Quietus* like a broadsword. He chopped the thing's head off with one stroke, executioner style. The helmeted head hit the floor with a clang, but the decapitated corpse paid no heed and continued its two-handed throttling of the boy.

The third wraith was going up the stairs, at first flitting like flying ash, gradually slowing and growing solid as it reached the darkness. Aragon and the fat Baron were coming down to meet it, brandishing candlesticks and lanterns, and it faded back to harmless, flickering shadow.

Struggling to save Bernard from strangulation, Valiant went to work on the monster's arms. He had almost cut through one when he was hurled to the floor. He looked up to see the corpse with the dagger in its eye. It lashed out with its boot. He tried to roll away and it followed, kicking him with bone-breaking impacts. He couldn't breathe; he was as good as dead.

Then Aragon and Baron Fader brought their lights and it again faded to smoke.

"Quickly!" the Baron shouted. He was a gruesome apparition himself, with a voluminous white nightgown billowing around his great bulk and spikes of white hair and beard sticking out in all directions. "Before they escape! We must pen the shadowmen in here. Come, come!"

"Bernard?" Valiant croaked, gasping at the pain in his ribs.

"Bernard's dead!" Aragon shouted. "Can you walk?" He had both hands full of lanterns, four of them.

"Hurry, hurry, hurry!" the Baron screamed in his squeaky voice. "They will escape. They will attack the palace! Hurry!"

Bernard was starting to rise, his eyes like blank white pebbles. Valiant struggled to his feet and recovered *Quietus*. He tottered back to the stair between the other two men. The shadowmen followed, five ominous, barely visible shapes at the edge of the brightness, one of them headless.

Wrapped in a heavy red robe, the Grand Duke was struggling to overturn the candelabrum. His two manservants were coming down, half naked, but bringing more light.

"Stop!" Valiant shouted.

"No!" the Baron retorted. "This must go." He threw his great weight into the argument. The candelabrum shivered. Only when Aragon joined in did it rock and then topple, hitting the ground with a noise like a falling smithy and snuffing out most of the candles. The Baron stamped on the others, dancing grotesquely while waving his many-branched candlesticks, in danger of going up in flames himself. Then the six living men hurried up the stairs together, leaving the lower floor to darkness and the dead.

They piled into the ducal bedroom and slammed the door. The Baron slumped down on a chair, which creaked alarm-ingly. The Grand Duke fell on the bed and buried his face in the covers.

"We must warn the Palace!" Valiant whispered. His bruised chest was an agony.

"No, is all right!" Baron Fader proclaimed, wheezing after his exertions. "*Schattenherren* are deadly in darkness, but then they cannot pass through walls."

"Can't they just open the doors and walk out?" Aragon demanded.

The fat man shrugged. "Hope they won't. They want us and will stay close to us. Of course if someone else comes or goes by too near the house . . . then they might. Daylight comes, they will die."

Richey had died. Bernard had died. Valiant wished he had.

Sister Trudy would breakfast alone.

I

At the Break of Day

♦ 1 ♦

€nter!" Grand Master said.

Sir Tancred did so and closed the heavy door behind him, moving with the feline grace of an expert fencer. He had changed out of his mud-soaked traveling clothes into fresh, crisp livery, and no one could have known from the look of him that he had spent the better part of a day and night on horseback. His silver baldric marked him as Deputy Commander of the Royal Guard; his presence here at Ironhall, far away from Grandon where the King was, meant that something was seriously awry.

"All bedded down?" Grand Master inquired dryly.

"My charges are. Your two are falling all over themselves getting dressed." Tancred's thin smile was a formality, not denying the underlying worry. "Unless they decided I was just a nightmare and went back to sleep."

Grand Master grunted and turned back to stare out the window at the first glow of sunrise on the wild crags of

Starkmoor. Early-morning chill dug into his bones, making him shiver and pull his cloak tight about him, yet in fact his study was still warm from the previous day's heat. Tancred was not even wearing a cloak over his jerkin, and that display of youthful vigor made Grand Master feel old. He *was* old, Lord Roland, although he rarely had to admit it, even to himself. He was too old to be dragged out of bed in the middle of the night, too old to deal with unexpected, unwelcome visitors, and too old to tackle a monstrous problem created by a fool of a king.

"I regret that I brought such trouble," Tancred said quietly. This was their first chance to talk privately.

"Not your fault." It was Grand Master's fault. Yes, the King was being totally unreasonable and Leader was a worrywart, but the responsibility was Grand Master's. If his duties required him to refuse direct orders from his sovereign, then he should be prepared to do so and take the consequences. It was guilt that gnawed at him this morning, not age. In a long life of service, he had rarely known such a sense of failure.

"Exactly how many warm bodies does His Majesty expect me to produce?"

"Beg pardon . . . the warrant." Sir Tancred stepped closer to hand over the baleful paper, a single sheet that might dispose of many young lives. "He left the number blank. He said to tell you at least one, but he knows you don't like to assign less than three private Blades at a time. No more than three, he said."

"How considerate of him! As soon as possible, I assume? Ram the swords through the boys' hearts and throw the lot of them on the first ship out of country by this time tomorrow?"

"Even sooner!" Sir Tancred smiled, although he must be shocked to hear such sarcasm from a man renowned for his discretion.

Idiot king! Athelgar certainly knew that Ironhall had no boys ready to graduate as Blades, because it was only two weeks since he had made his semiannual pilgrimage to the school to harvest the latest crop of seniors, binding them to absolute loyalty with the ancient, arcane ritual. Grand Master had wanted to release six candidates and had reluctantly included another three to please Sir Florian, who was anxious to build up the Guard's numbers. The previous Commander, Sir Vicious, had preferred to keep it lean—as Grand Master himself had, back in his own time as Leader, forty years ago. Florian saw safety in numbers, which was his privilege.

But then, just a week later, the King had decided on impulse to appoint a new ambassador to Baelmark. The hapless designate, Lord Baxterbridge, had arrived at Ironhall with a warrant for three Blades. Grand Master should have dug in his heels then, but how could he condemn a man to go off to that nest of bloodthirsty pirates without adequate protection? Diplomatic immunity carried no weight in Baelmark. Only steel and the skill to use it mattered there, and the season on ambassadors never closed. So Grand Master had released three more candidates, very much against his better judgment.

And today another warrant. It took five years to turn an outcast rebel boy into a Blade and even Prime Candidate Ranter had been in the school for less than four. Not since the worst days of the Monster War, forty years ago, had Ironhall suffered such a dearth of trained, competent seniors.

"*Eagle* did look somewhat sparse," Tancred remarked caustically.

Eagle was a dormitory with a dozen beds and only three occupants—Ranter, Ringwood, and Goodwin. Two of them had not been billeted there a full week yet. A moment ago Grand Master had been feeling sorry for himself because he had lost half a night's sleep. How much worse this morning's awakening must have been for Ranter, being shaken awake by the Deputy Commander! He would have known instantly that his stay in Ironhall was at an end, his adolescence over. Ringwood could still hope that he would not be needed, but both of them had reasonably looked forward to another year of security and instruction, time to mature personally and physically, to perfect the deadly skills they would need as Blades. They were entitled to all that, and Grand Master had failed them.

He realized that Tancred's comment had really been a question about Candidate Bellman, who was none of his business. Bellman was another worry, but this mess had nothing to do with him.

"Goodwin didn't waken?" Grand Master asked.

"Still snoring when I left."

After a moment, Lord Roland's anger erupted again. "Tell me, Deputy, was Leader not consulted about this warrant? Did he not remind His Majesty that Ironhall presently has no candidates ready for binding?"

Tancred squirmed and avoided his eye. "I'm sure he did, because I was sent to fetch your most recent report on the seniors. What you wrote about Ranter was—"

"I know what I wrote about Ranter! I am not in my dotage yet, thank you." *I have promoted Candidate Ranter to senior. He is physically mature and shows promise with the heavier weapons. His horsemanship is above average.* Nothing about his use of the rapier or his social skills, which were nonexistent. Nothing about brains, ditto. "Has His Majesty never heard of damning with faint praise? Did Leader not point out that when I wrote those words there were a dozen boys ahead of Ranter in the senior class and he was a full year from completing his training? Did he not explain that there is a lot more to a Blade than superlative swordsmanship?" Tactical thinking? Political savvy? Working with other people? "Surely Leader knows that what I said about Ranter implied that he is destined to be a face in the ranks, a carrier-out of orders from above, not the leader of a private guard expected to make decisions and win the loyalty of subordinates?"

"I was not present when Leader advised His Majesty," Tancred said stiffly. "My opinion was not asked."

"Or volunteered, I gather!" Grand Master snapped.

A good Commander must sometimes talk back to the King. There had been instances in the Blades' long history when the Guard had literally kidnapped the monarch to move him to safety. When Grand Master had been Commander Durendal, he had argued fiercely with King Ambrose a few times. Sir Vicious had stood up to Athelgar when he had to. Perhaps that was why the King had chosen a yes-man to succeed him. No, that was too hard on Florian. He would learn in time, but other people might have to pay for his lessons.

Ranter had been a borderline admission. Grand Master had made a mistake accepting him. Chance had turned minor error into major disaster.

Knuckles rapped on the door again, unnecessarily hard.

"Enter!" Grand Master turned and forced a smile to greet two scared faces. "Good chance, gentlemen. I think you can guess the subject of this unexpected meeting."

The traditional wording was: *His Majesty has need of a Blade; are you willing to serve?* and only one answer was acceptable.

Ranter's homely, stubborn face was reddened by the summer sun, which had bleached his normally sandy hair to tow. At nineteen he was hefty by Blade standards, but his strength and agility were combined with the social skills of a mollusc. Popularity was often a reliable guide to a boy's potential. The finest Blades Ironhall produced—men like Beaumont, say, or Kestrel, or Ivor—were almost invariably worshiped by the youngsters following them. Ranter's acid tongue and clumsy, even brutal sense of humor had brought him very few friends.

Ringwood was the exact opposite: personable, often witty, dark and lean, with intense, whittled good looks. As Second he was responsible for discipline and had made a good start in the last few days, in spite of his youth. Lacking Ranter's beef, he favored a rapier, and was developing remarkable speed with it. Given the extra year he deserved, he might become one of the finest fencers in the Order, which effectively meant in the whole of Eurania. And yet, closing the door, he tangled his sword in it. Grand Master knew he could never justify binding a mere child under the present circumstances.

And he would not trap Ranter without warning him what lay in store.

"Make yourselves comfortable," he said, going to his favorite chair by the empty fireplace, "this may take longer than usual."

Unlike other masters and the moldering old knights in Ironhall, Lord Roland was independently wealthy, and he had refurbished his study with quality and comfort, with style and fine art. After all, this was where he had expected to spend the rest of his life. When he gathered the seniors there on winter nights for strategy lessons—when there were seniors to gather—the second-best chair, in blue leather, was traditionally reserved for Prime. Now Ranter made a beeline for it, perhaps with the thought that this would be his only chance to sit in it. He should properly have left it for the Deputy Commander.

Grand Master did not rebuke him. There were much worse worms in the salad than mere bad manners. "Sir Tancred and ten other members of the Guard arrived here a few hours ago, escorting a distinguished guest. Will you list the visitors, please, Deputy?"

"His Grace the Grand Duke Rubin of Krupina, Baron—"

"Krup what? Where's that?" Ranter demanded.

"It's not my job to know," Tancred replied smoothly—a nice riposte implying that it might soon be Ranter's. "He is accompanied by his aide-de-camp, Baron von Fader. His Nibs prefers to be addressed as 'Your Royal Highness,' but the King refers to him as 'His Grace,' so that's what he is around Court. He is a distant relative of the Pirate's Son."

"Nothing wrong with 'Your Grace,' " Ranter said. "We say that to the Pirate's Son."

"Prime!" Grand Master barked. "The Guard may refer to our sovereign lord in that disrespectful fashion. You are not so privileged." And never would be.

Ranter glowered. "Beg pardon, Grand Master."

"And if you had paid attention in protocol classes, you would know that you always begin with 'Your Majesty.' Only after that is 'Sire' or 'Your Grace' permissible."

"Yes, Grand Master."

"Carry on, Deputy."

Tancred leaned back on his inferior chair and crossed his ankles. "Wherever Krupina may be, or however His Nibs is addressed, he has been overthrown by his uncle, Lord Volpe, and has been scouring the courts of Eurania to find backing for an attempt to win back his throne. Or at least rescue his wife and child. So far without success, apparently."

Ringwood and Ranter exchanged dismayed glances. In Ironhall, appointment to the Guard was regarded as first prize, because a guardsman dwelt in royal palaces and was dubbed knight and released after ten years or so. A private Blade remained bound until he or his ward died, so being bound to anyone except the King ran a distant second. No catalogue of desirable wards could ever include a dispossessed, penniless noble from some unheard-of foreign fleapit dukedom.

Grand Master gave them a moment and then said, "I fear there is even worse news than that, Prime. Deputy, will you please summarize the events of two nights ago?"

Tancred's expression turned flinty. "Sad events. The usurper, Volpe, is both a skilled spiritualist himself and commands many others. He has been sending evil enchantments against the Grand Duke. I am Returning two swords on this visit, Prime. The night before last, His Grace was attacked right in Nocare Palace. Five men died, three Yeomen and two Blades. Sir Richey and Sir Bernard."

Dismay turned to horror. Richey they knew as a member of the Guard, but Bernard was one of theirs. Just two weeks ago he had been fencing with them, walking the halls, eating at the seniors' table.

While listening for the second time to an account of the disaster, Grand Master planned his response to the King's absurd demand. Ranter would never have been Grand Master's choice for Prime, who should be a role model for all the other boys. Only seniority had landed him in this predicament. Grand Master could not like him, but he felt pity for him. His youthful face was ashen as he listened to the account of the walking dead and the murders in Nocare. He would refuse binding, of course. He would be insane to accept this assignment.

By the rules, the question must then be put to Second, which was why Second had to be present. If he also refused, the process must continue until a candidate accepted, but Grand Master had no intention of binding a boy as young as Ringwood. He had to sacrifice Ranter, but after that he would tell this incompetent Grand Duke that there were no qualified candidates available and send the man back to Nocare with Tancred. Grand Master must submit his resignation at the same time, of course, and Athelgar could decide then what to do with him. It would not be the first time Lord Roland had seen the inside of a dungeon in the Bastion, and his would not be the first distinguished career to end in disgrace.

Tancred had almost finished. "Yesterday morning the five corpses were found heaped together in the darkest corner of the hall, where they had taken refuge from the dawn's light. Two Blades and three Yeomen. The Baron said we were fortunate that Quamast has no cellar. Getting shadowmen out of cellars is almost impossible, he says. Questions?"

Ranter's face was a death's-head. "You say this was not the first attack?"

"The fourth or fifth since the Grand Duke fled Krupina, apparently. Not all by the same means."

"And he didn't warn anyone?"

Tancred nodded grimly. "Yes, he did. He warned the King that there might be more attacks. The King warned Leader. Leader warned me. I warned Sir Hazard and Sir Valiant when I assigned them. Somewhere in that chain the warnings became diluted, Prime."

"Diluted?" Ranter snarled. "What the piss does that mean?"

The Deputy Commander bristled. "It means there will be an inquiry and everyone is kicking dirt over whatever they dropped. In the end no one will get blamed. It was no one's fault! First, these shadowmen only appear on extremely dark nights and we rarely get those in summer. Secondly, this is a very long way from Krupina, and whatever foul enchantment is being used must originate there. Thirdly, they're not dangerous in bright light. I'm sure the Grand Duke played down the threat because he came seeking refuge. Perhaps someone didn't listen properly or explain properly. Spirits,

Ranter! You think I'm happy to have two men die like that? I'm sick as a dog. It's a damnably imperfect world."

Silence.

Ranter shot a terrified look at Grand Master. Here it came, the terrible decision. Yesterday he had been strutting around Ironhall as Prime, lording it over the juniors. Now his world had crumbled to dust.

"Prime," Durendal said, "our Order is rarely involved in military matters. This case is exceptional because His Majesty and Grand Duke Rubin are distant cousins. The King is distressed that a member of his family should be in such danger. He offered him help and protection." More likely meddlesome Queen Tasha had talked him into it, for Athelgar was rarely moved by generosity.

"I know you have not been introduced to foreign politics." Master of Protocol inflicted those lectures on the seniors in Twelfthmonth. "So you will not have heard of this Lord Volpe, who heads the Vamky Brotherhood. I have. He not only commands fearsome enchanters, he himself is reputed to be one of the greatest warriors in Eurania. In all fairness, I will say this. I have been Grand Master for eleven years. Even before that, the Blades have been my life, directly or indirectly, since I was fourteen. I admit that I have never heard of a man offered a harder posting than this one, but our King has commanded and we must all do our duty.

"There is nothing personal in this, you understand. I cannot pick and choose. Nor can His Majesty. It is for this very reason that the Charter insists every candidate will leave Ironhall in the order he was admitted. Only the fickle elementals of chance have chosen you for this burden instead of someone else."

Grand Master sighed and rose to his feet. Ringwood sprang up at once, followed an instant later by Ranter. Tancred stayed where he was, watching glumly.

"Prime, His Majesty has need of a Blade. Are you willing to serve?"

Ranter licked his lips. "What choice do I have?" His voice was a croak.

"You were told the rules when you came here," Grand Master said coldly. "For four years you have eaten the King's bread. He has given you shelter and the world's finest instruction in swordsmanship, not to mention asylum from any legal action that was outstanding against you. Now he expects you to fulfill your side of the bargain." *He offers you an impossible assignment.*

"Or the moor?"

That was the official alternative for quitters. In practice expulsion was not the death sentence it seemed, as Ranter must know. Some victualer's wagon would find him on the road and give him a ride into Blackwater or Narby, but he would evermore be a man without a lord, an Ironhall reject, and everyone knew what sort of boy was admitted to the school in the first place. There would be no dancing at court balls in Ranter's future. The best he could hope for was life as a stablehand, but horse owners were wary of thieves, so sailor, mine worker, or farm laborer was more likely.

Ranter glanced at the equally pale Ringwood standing rigid beside him.

"How many? Just me, or both of us?" Solitary Blades often went mad trying to guard their wards twenty-four hours a day.

Grand Master said, "I will not answer that question until you have answered mine. Shall I put it again, or do I take your silence to be refusal?" This was torture and he hated it, but he must play by the rules the first time.

Strategy, Rule One: *The most probable outcome of any plan is total breakdown.*

Ringwood said quietly, "If Grand Master asks me, too,

Prime, whether you've accepted or not . . . I just want you to know that I will accept."

That little speech should have been cause for Ranter to hug him and weep tears of gratitude down his neck. Instead he curled his lip in scorn. "Of course you say so! If I refuse he's certain to ask you. If I accept he may or may not want you as well, but then you'll at least be one of a pair, won't you?"

Ringwood shrugged. "I suppose so. Wasn't what I meant, though."

"Prime, His Majesty has need of a Blade. Are you willing to serve?"

Ranter swallowed hard. "I will serve," he whispered.

Tancred jumped up to thump him on the shoulder. "Bravo!"

Astonished, Grand Master almost shouted, *Weren't you listening, you young fool? I was telling you this mission is suicide!* Instead he said, "Well done! Very well done! That is one of the bravest things I have ever heard of. I did not expect you to accept." He offered a hand.

Ranter ignored it. "I'm just stupid!"

Even if he was, no cell door would slam on Grand Master now. In spite of his best efforts, he had the Blade the King had ordered, so the problem was solved.

Except that Ringwood had volunteered. All eyes turned to him. Nobody in the room would tattle back to the King if Grand Master refused his offer, but ever since his own terrible experience as a private Blade, he had always insisted that three was the absolute minimum number for a private guard. Even two was infinitely better than one alone.

He owed Ranter a partner.

Ringwood was waiting for the question with eyes shining, like a dog straining at a leash.

He was not old enough to make such a decision.

"Second . . . this is difficult. Because we are so short of seniors just now, His Majesty left it up to me whether I would assign one or two Blades to the Grand Duke. I do appreciate your courageous offer, but it isn't necessary. If you wish to withdraw it, you can remain here as—"

"That's not fair!" Ranter howled. "Why should he get that choice when I didn't?"

"Be silent! He tried to help you and you insulted him. He gets the option because I have the option to give in this case. I did not in yours." Grand Master turned back to Ringwood and saw dismay. "Candidate, this is an exceptionally difficult and dangerous assignment."

"Shadowmen?" The boy flushed. "I'm not afraid of shadows! If Bernard and the others had been told about lights, they wouldn't have died!"

True, but what in the world was going through his young head? Lord Roland glanced at Tancred, who shrugged, and then at the unfortunate Ranter, scowling as he waited to hear his fate.

"Apart from the shadowmen, the Duke has lost his dukedom. He is dispossessed. Powerful enchanters are trying to kill him. You would be bound for life to an exile. Another year in Ironhall and a stint in the Royal Guard is a much better proposition, lad."

"With respect, Grand Master," Ringwood said in shrill and not very respectful tones, "it sounds like the Duke needs me more a lot more than the King ever will. Maybe I'm not as good a fencer as I could be a year from now, but I'm a demon by anyone else's standards. Sir Bowman told me that yesterday!" He did not have much of a chin yet, but what he had he stuck out stubbornly.

Unquestionably two half-trained, half-taught boys would be better protection for the Grand Duke than one. Grand

Master also had a duty to defend the reputation of the Order itself, because that reputation was the first line of defense. Reputation alone would often prevent a fight from starting. If word got around that some Blade guards were incompetent, others would face more challenges in future.

"Very well. *Candidate Ringwood, His Majesty does have need of a Blade, but if you do not want this posting, you may refuse it.*"

Ringwood grinned wildly. "I will serve!" It was almost a cheer. "Thank you, my lord!"

"Death and fire!" Tancred said. "You shame us."

"He's incredible," Grand Master agreed. "They both are. I am very proud of you both. You are living up to the finest traditions of the Order!"

He offered a hand to Ringwood, who beamed and pumped it. "I will always try to do that, Grand Master."

"Just two?" Ranter sneered. "You always told us a guard needs three. Why not give me Goodwin, too?"

Grand Master resisted a desire to bark. He was in debt to this lout and the least he could offer in return was patience. "Goodwin is too young."

"He's a month older than this one."

"I know." Grand Master paused to wonder how Goodwin would cope as Prime; there must be twenty candidates older than he. And how would Ironhall manage with no competent seniors to give the juniors good practice? Goodwin was a better fencer than Ranter.

"Your future ward is resting, gentlemen, but the binding will take place tonight and he has been advised of the need for meditation. Ringwood, find Master Armorer and tell him, please. I don't think he's even begun making a sword for you. If he needs the Forge, we'll find you somewhere else to meditate. Ranter, break the news to our new Prime, please. Then I suggest you both go straight to the Forge, so the juniors don't pester you. I will bring His Grace to meet you later. Ironhall will follow the King's lead, but you two have my permission to address him however he wants.

"And finally," Grand Master said with feeling, "I thank you on behalf of the King, and again I congratulate you on your courage and sense of duty." He could not bring himself to wish them luck.

"Come and meet your doom, jackass." Ranter led the way to the door.

Ringwood followed, but he paused halfway out and looked back uncertainly. "Grand Master? Er . . . Candidate Bellman? . . ."

"Mind your own business! Bellman is not your concern."

"Yes, Grand Master. Sorry . . ." Ringwood vanished, closing the door.

The morning bell began tolling. Prime Candidate Goodwin would waken to find himself alone—very much so from now on, poor lad.

Sir Tancred was regarding Grand Master with a wry, quizzical expression. He did not say, "Chance smiles on you this morning, my lord!" or "How could you do that to those poor kids?" He did say, "Bellman's still around? The healing failed?"

Grand Master scorched him with the glare he had perfected when he was Lord Chancellor. It had worked then on everyone except King Ambrose, and it still had power to make a Deputy Commander flinch.

"We shall deal with the Return right after the morning meal, Sir Tancred."

"Certainly, Grand Master."

✦ 2 ✦

𝕿he bell tolled. Bellman opened his eyes.

The usual chorus of complaint erupted all around him. *Falcon* was normally one of the seniors' dorms, but there were thirty-two candidates in the fuzzy class now, and they had overflowed their own dorms, *Pard* and *Lynx*. Beardless were being promoted to fuzzy all the time, but no one could move up to senior until Bellman did. Bellman never would, because promotion, like binding, was based on seniority and fencing skill, and he fenced like a palsied turtle with its shell on backward. He was the oldest candidate in Ironhall, but that mattered not at all.

He sat up and stretched, steeling himself for another day, another round of ignominious failure. His ordeal must end soon. Grand Master had been incredibly patient, but he could not turn a blind eye forever. The logjam must be broken and Candidate Bellman's feet set upon the long road over the moor.

The door flew open and crashed against a wall. Candidate Mark was short of stature but long on volume. *"THE GUARD'S BACK!"* he shrilled. *"THERE'S GOING TO BE ANOTHER BINDING!"*

This announcement was greeted with a barrage of boots, pillows, and youthful vulgarities, but Mark was already gone to spread the word elsewhere. Bodies piled up against the window, and yes, a pair of blue-liveried Blades were walking across the quad. Where there were two, there would be more.

Fierce debate broke out. Would Grand Master allow even one senior to be bound when he only had three of them? Fuzzies were fanatical at keeping track of every candidate's fencing skills and they knew Ranter was still mediocre by

Blade standards. He couldn't even beat Sir Lewis, the worst lubber in the Guard. Ringwood was Ironhall's best, but Ranter must take precedence.

Nobody mentioned the utterly inept Candidate Bellman, but there would be no new seniors as long as he still ate the King's bread. Seniors were very grand; they wore swords. Fuzzies salivated at the prospect. They dreamed of it all night long.

This had to be the end, Bellman decided. He rose and pulled his better hose from the hamper beside his cot. He would shave, wash, and make himself as respectable as possible for the final, painful interview. The agony of waiting had gone on too long. If Grand Master did not kick him off the cliff today, he would do the honorable thing and jump.

Free! Free at last! Ringwood had trouble not breaking into a run as he went in search of Master Armorer. He found him right away, stoking up a fire in the Forge. The big, echoing crypt was the mystic heart of Ironhall. Eight anvils stood around the walls, each with its own hearth and a water trough fed by the Forge's own spring. Here the magnificent cat's-eye swords were made, and this was where Blades were bound, on the ninth anvil, a coffin-shaped block of steel at the center of the octogram inset in the rocky floor.

Tonight at midnight Ringwood would sit there with his shirt off so his future ward could ram a sword through his heart. The thought gave him shivery feelings in his belly, but they were exciting shivery feelings. He'd seen lots of bindings and nobody ever died. Release! Four years' imprisonment ending.

Master Armorer was a cheerful young giant with a blood-curdling Westerth accent, two apprentices older than himself, and more skill at swordmaking than any other armorer in the entire world. He was clad, as usual, in a pair of boots and knee-length leathers that exposed arms and shoulders speckled with ancient burn spots. His muscles were the envy of every boy in the school, and his swords a state treasure. He frowned on hearing the news.

"Prime are no hitch," he declared, running massive fingers through his hair. "Give him an ax will do he. Ain't given little thought to you yet, pecker. You promise me you warn't not be going to grow none more?"

"I hope I do. Grow, I mean. Have you made a sword for me yet?"

"Narn. Give me a hint."

"Rapier? I'm not much good with a broadsword."

"You're not bad with sabers. I seen. You comes with me, pecker." Master Armorer set off across the Forge.

At the far side he unlocked a chest and threw up the lid to reveal scores of rapiers and slender thrusting swords. He rummaged, taking them out one at a time, unwrapping them to inspect them, then replacing them. "See if one of these might do. Call 'em 'blacks' on account of this." He pointed to the pebble forming the pommel of the one he was holding. "Same weight as a cat's-eye. Try an' this fellow, pecker."

Only Master Armorer ever called anyone "pecker." After tonight people would call Ringwood *Sir* Ringwood, although he wouldn't be a real knight. Never mind, he was more interested in that sword. Thin, straight, and incredibly beautiful! The blade was double-edged near the point, single-edged otherwise. It was not much heavier than a rapier and had finger rings for control. Even now he could manage the extra weight, so he wouldn't lose very much agility, and having an edge would be good if he ever had to hack pieces off a shadowman. *(Gulp!)* He tried a few lunges, a cut or two. To have this for his very own! Forever! Or as long as he lived, say a couple of weeks . . .

Master Armorer took it from him and offered a rapier.

"No," Ringwood said. "I think I need something with an edge after all. My ward has trouble with walking dead."

Master Armorer raised his eyebrows at that, but said only, "Try this 'un, then."

In a happy daze, Ringwood tried out more than a dozen swords. Time passed unheeded; he wasn't allowed to eat today anyway. Always he came back to that first one. Finally he raised it and kissed the blade.

Master Armorer's eyes twinkled. "Love at first sight, pecker? She's a hair long f'r ye."

"I'm still growing."

"What's her name to be, then?"

"Bad News!" Seeing the armorer frown at this insult to his precious work, Ringwood explained, "Sir Tancred woke us up this morning and said he was bringing bad news. Ranter thought so, too, but I thought it was wonderful news if it meant I was going to be bound. So this sword is good news to me and very bad news to my ward's enemies." He'd thought of that on the way to Grand Master's study.

The big man laughed. "I like it! You know what that Ranter wants on his?"

"Invincible."

The chest boomed shut, echoing through the Forge. The armorer scowled. "Then you'll be telling me a good way of spelling that, pecker?"

Under the sky of swords in the hall, a white-faced Goodwin sat all alone at the seniors' table, so the whole school knew what was happening. Ranter good riddance, but *Ringwood*? He'd been a senior less than a week. The hall buzzed like a jostled hive.

Bellman went over to wish Goodwin luck and shake his hand. He also asked him to tell Grand Master that Bellman wanted to see him—meaning Goodwin would have company at the table soon. Goodwin wished him luck, also.

And then the Returning. That ceremony was usually only a formality, for most Blades lived to a mellow antiquity and octogenarians' deaths meant nothing to healthy, overactive youngsters. It happened every week or two. But when Deputy Commander Tancred spoke Bernard's name, it was greeted with cries of shock. Everyone had liked Bernard. The sobs were not restricted to the soprano tables, and Tancred's brief account of the shadowmen was certain to inspire many nightmares in the near future.

Bellman had been close to Bernard, so he was as moved as any, and felt a burning anger as he strode out of the hall. There had been a lot of very odd ends left untied in that yarn about these so-called shadowmen. It did not make sense.

A finger poked in his ribs. "Want to talk with you."

He turned to view the gap-toothed grin and antler mustache of Sir Hazard, notoriously the worst gossip in the Guard.

He returned the grin. "Absolutely forbidden to tell you! What about?"

"But you will exchange hints?"

"I don't have anything to trade." Bellman could think of no scandal he knew that Hazard wouldn't. But Hazard would certainly be his best source of information about the deaths. "Ask me."

They found a quiet corner in the quad and sat on grass browned and crisped by the summer heat. The visiting guardsmen were trying to organize some fencing lessons, but most of the inhabitants were standing around in solemn groups, discussing the bad news. Even masters and knights were gossiping.

"Now," Hazard said intently. "A few months ago there was talk of you being our next champ. We'll need someone to keep those awful garlicky Isilondians at bay when Cedric gets senile. I even laid a little far-out money on you for King's Cup in 408 or 409. I won't tell you the odds I got, but I was planning on buying a farm."

"I was never that good," Bellman protested. "I was just older than most when I was admitted."

"Then Grand Master must have seen something special in you," Hazard said triumphantly.

What he had seen in Bellman had been a very early death, but that was another story and certainly not one to share with Lord High Trumpetmouth. Age had helped, though. Bellman had never been one of the boys and by his beansprout year even the knights had been speaking to him as an adult.

"Then there came talk that you were slipping," Hazard went on, "but the last time you and I crossed steel you beat me silly. Two weeks ago—they left me at home to clean the crown jewels, you may recall—they had a big inquest over you, here in Ironhall. Leader, Tancred, Cedric, Grand Master, the whole gang of scoundrels. Now there's whispers on the wind that you're going to be puked for stumblebummery, but nobody's talking! Why? What's the matter?"

Bellman laughed. "Is that all?" It was no secret around Ironhall. "My fencing stopped getting better, yes. Then it started getting worse. Much, much worse. And nobody could understand why. That's the only secret—they're all ashamed to admit that they missed something so obvious." Including himself, who did not like to feel he'd been stupid. "Cedric the Invincible? Grand Master, the greatest ever? Master of Rapiers, Master of Sabers. Some of the old knights were great in their time, you know. They were all there. They worked me over the whole day."

"And?"

"And it was Cedric who finally saw it."

"Saw *what*?" Hazard demanded, the ends of his mustache quivering.

"Why I could still do well against some of the Guard but just about nobody above soprano in Ironhall."

"And why was that?"

Bellman heaved a deep sigh. "I'm not allowed to say. Now, what's all this about these shadowmen?"

"The King is an idiot," Ranter proclaimed, "giving us away like a brace of partridge to a threadbare tinpot parasite! What good will that do for Athelgar or Chivial or the Guard? He has the brains of a fungus. They cover for him all the time, you know. He used too many nails putting his crown on." He continued to pace restlessly around the Forge.

If he talked like this about Athelgar now, how was he going to rant about their ward after they were bound? Ringwood was sitting on the floor, leaning against the great anvil, which was chilly against his backbone. The Forge was never cold, because of the hearths, and in Eighthmoon it was snug going on cosy. The thought of cold baths in those water troughs had a lot of appeal. That was part of the ritual. Master of Rituals joked that it was a test of courage for candidates being bound in Firstmoon, but of course the whole purpose of the ritual was to give a man enough loyalty and courage to die for his ward.

He wished Ranter would shut up and sit down. They were supposed to be meditating. Meditating, for example, about the wonderful prospect of freedom, of seeing something other than stone walls and moorland all day every day, of not having to sleep in the same room every night. Travel. Adventure. Bearing a sword and guarding a ward. Making his life mean something, as Dad had wanted.

"And what sort of Grand Duke loses his throne and then gets chased all the way across Eurania by evil conjurers?" Ranter continued bitterly. "What does he expect the Pirate's Son to do about it? March the Yeoman over there and arrest that Volpe swine? The most he could do would be to give him money, and Baels don't do that. He won't give the Duke the time of day."

"Grand Duke. Yes, he will. Now he will. Not much, but he's going to toss him a purse of gold and ship the whole gang of us out of Chivial so fast our feet won't touch the ground."

Ranter kicked at an anvil, not hard enough to hurt his foot, but enough to scuff his boot. "Doesn't want any more shadowmen, you mean? I suppose so. I ran into Sir Lewis on my way over here and he says Krapina is two hundred leagues east of Fitain and smaller than Dimpleshire."

"That's *Krup*ina, not *Krap*ina."

"Shut up! I'm your leader now, sonny, and I won't have you standing around correcting me all the time."

Ringwood looked up in alarm. "What?"

"Every guard must have a leader!" Ranter leered. "That's a Blade rule. The ward chooses, although his Blades can elect another if they disagree. This Duke can pick a man or a boy. Which do you think he'll want?"

Ranter as his leader? For the rest of his life? *Vomit!* Ringwood didn't want to meditate on that.

Once again the quad rang with sounds of steel. Fencing lessons were under way. Bellman lay on his back, staring up at fake battlements against cloudless blue. Farewell to good times. This was the last day of the happiest days of his life. Maybe soon his last day, period. How much of a start would they give him?

"That's him," Hazard said. "On his way to see Grand Master, methinks."

Bellman sat up. Four men, two of them guardsmen, were crossing the quad, heading for First House. Activity stopped as they went by the fencing pairs, leaving a trail of staring eyes behind them.

"The fat one?"

"No. The fat one's Baron von Fader."

"Just as well," Bellman said. "I'd hate to think of that butterball shimmying down a rope of bedsheets. How did Rubin escape from Evil Uncle Volpe, anyway?"

"Not yet." Hazard's dark eyes gleamed. "First you tell me what was wrong with your fencing that Cedric saw but everybody else had missed?"

Bellman sighed. "He noticed I cocked my head to one side."

Hazard peered at him, copied him. "Mm. Like this, you mean?"

"Right. So then they tested my eyesight."

"Blood and guts!" The gleaming black mustache curled up in horror. "What's wrong with your eyes?"

"Nothing wrong with the left one, and I can still see quite well with the right one. I can even read with it, after a fashion. But bits are missing. It makes my reactions too slow. The change happened so slowly I never noticed." No one else had, either, but as he had gradually learned to compensate for the loss, so had the rest of the school. Without realizing it, all the people he fenced with regularly—fencing masters, knights, candidates—every one of them had instinctively started taking advantage of his blind spots. The guardsmen, who visited only rarely, had not known about it, so he had done better against them, which was against all normal experience.

"But what caused it?" Hazard cried.

"Rank stupidity. Mine. I came off a horse and banged my head. I saw double for a week or so. I'd been fooling around and I was one of those real tough kids who never complain and never need help, see? So I never told Master of Rituals and he never gave me a healing. Until two weeks ago, but that was far too late."

"Horrible!" Hazard seemed genuinely concerned.

"I can see better to my left than my right," Bellman continued. "So Grand Master suggested they try making a southpaw out of me. He's been enormously helpful and supportive. Everyone has, but it didn't work." Two weeks of hell.

"Just a silly little bang on the head?"

"Even chance can make justice."

Hazard pricked up his ears and the horns of his mustache. "What does that mean?"

Bellman cursed under his breath. The man had the instincts of a wolfhound. "Just a proverb."

"No, really." Hazard peered at him suspiciously.

"Really just a proverb. Tell me about this enchanter who can hurl curses across the whole width of Eurania."

"His Royal Highness prefers to be addressed as such," Baron von Fader huffed, still breathless after climbing the stairs to Grand Master's study.

Grand Master bowed to him also. "I trust your brief repose was refreshing, my lord?"

Baron von Fader was one of the fattest men he had ever seen, waddling behind a grotesquely overhanging belly. His rubicund face had sagged into pouches and sulky folds, his beard and hair were white, wispy, and longer than Chivian fashion allowed. He bore a cumbersome saber on a baldric, which he had to remove before sinking into his host's favorite chair, bulging out of it in all directions. How had he ever managed the long ride from Grandon? How had his mounts coped?

Grand Duke Rabin was less extreme: middle-aged and portly, but not fat, with a face unprepossessing rather than ugly—eyes well bagged, mouth sensual, goatee streaked with gray. The fingers he had offered to be kissed were smooth and uncalloused, and he was unarmed. His jerkin and hose were simple in cut but of impeccable quality, his only jewelry being a gold signet. Invited to sit, he chose one of the lesser chairs, which let him sit very upright, knees together and hands clasped, as if relaxation did not come easily to him.

"I cannot offer you refreshment other than water, Your Grace," Grand Master said, "because you are required to fast before the ritual."

"It is of no matter." The Duke's voice was light and tuneful. "Your King is being most generous in assigning me Blades of my own. You have found me some? Sir Tancred hinted that you were short of suitable candidates."

"I can spare only two, I fear, Your Grace. They have not completed the normal course of training, so they cannot match our usual superlative standards in swordsmanship. We expect a Blade to take on two ordinary opponents at the same time. I would not ask that of these men, but one-on-one they will have little to fear."

"How about against *Schattenherren*?" growled the Baron. His voice had the timbre of busy millstones.

"I was informed that a few candles are adequate defense against them," Durendal said coldly. "Your Grace, the binding ritual is dangerous and we insist on following it exactly. The actual binding will begin at midnight and last about half an hour. Until then you are required to fast, to meditate, and to take ritual baths, as Master of Rituals will direct."

The Grand Duke nodded. "I understand."

"I shall be present, sire," said the Baron.

"You may witness the binding," Grand Master said, starting to bite his words. "But you will not be admitted during the preliminaries. Your Grace has been informed regarding your own part?"

"Sir Tancred told us," the Baron said before his liege could open his mouth, "on the way here. I will read over the text beforehand."

"That will not be permitted, but you may discuss it in general terms with Master of Rituals. Have you any questions, Your Grace?"

Rabin seemed more amused than annoyed at the way his underling was being trampled. "Sir Tancred answered most of them, my lord. Except he could not tell me about names. I understand the candidates swear an oath to me personally. My full name is Rabin Hans Ludwig Irmtrude Burhard Achim Lammert von Krupina und Vargschloss. We should write it down for them? And all my titles?"

Lord Roland said, "Considering the strain the ritual puts on the boys, we settle for just one name and omit titles. The name is unimportant. What matters is whose hand holds the hilt of the sword." And the hand in this case looked as if it never had held one before. That was a worry Grand Master had not anticipated. He had assumed that any minor nobleman from the wilder side of Eurania would be a warrior, like the wicked uncle. "It is essential that the sword penetrate the candidate's heart. They like you to put it right through them, but that is not required."

"Why?"

"Why what? Oh, just that they like to have two scars, front and back. It impresses girls." Grand Master himself had four and had bragged about them shamelessly in long-ago days.

"I will see what I can do to oblige them," Rubin said with no sign of amusement. He kept his face and voice under firm control.

"Master of Rituals can demonstrate the stroke. If Your Grace wishes to practice, we can string up an animal carcass in the kitchen."

"That is an insulting suggestion!" barked the Baron.

"But a very sensible one when two men's lives are at stake," the Grand Duke said softly. "Please do that, Grand Master."

Stringing up Baron von Fader would be an even better idea. Roland said, "I have a brief homily on the care of Blades, which I recite to every new ward, Your Grace. Ringwood and Ranter will not be your servants. They serve King Athelgar by guarding you, even at the cost of their own lives if necessary. His Majesty expects you to provide them with food and clothes . . ." And so on.

The first of the victualers' wagons came rumbling in the gate. Bellman glanced at the shadows and was amazed to see he had been gossiping to Hazard for over an hour. He had many more good-byes to say.

"Must go." He scrambled to his feet.

"Go where?" Hazard followed him up and brushed grass off himself.

Bellman nodded at the wagon. "Catch the stage to Blackwater."

The Blade's eyes narrowed. "You got a job waiting?"

"No." A job was the lesser of his problems. "I know some of the farmers."

"We'll find you better than that. You'll ride the King's horses back to Grandon with us and the Guard will set you up with something worthwhile."

For a moment Bellman feared a cruel joke. "You really mean that?"

Hazard laughed. "You expected a smock and wooden shoes? You're not being puked or running away, friend. Yours is what the Yeomen call an honorable discharge. The Blades will see you land softly. Don't worry about a thing. You prefer blondes or redheads?"

"Virgins," Bellman said, still adjusting to this sudden reprieve.

"They're extinct in Grandon. Some post in the palace? You fancy heraldry? A clerk in treasury? Conjury?"

"There is a complication."

Hazard's eyes gleamed. He twirled the points of his mustache in delight. "Let me guess. You arrived here two steps ahead of the law?"

Bellman nodded. "Barely one step. The charter decrees an automatic pardon on binding. Otherwise Grand Master has to send word to—"

"Forget that bit! It doesn't happen. Ever. Forget your old name, too. You can be Ethelbert Bellman or Bellman Meadowbucket and they'll never find you. Everyone here has a past, even Grand Master, although I never did manage to . . . What's yours?"

"Can't say."

"I killed one of the King's beasts," Hazard said hopefully. "A nice five-point stag."

"Worse than that. If you want to help me you mustn't know."

Hazard's scowl said he would find out one day if it killed both of them. "Was I imagining the horrible apparition?" he asked loudly, gesturing with a thumb over his shoulder at a skinny fourteen-year-old, who was clutching a pair of foils and staring at his back like a demon of vengeance.

"That is the dreaded Candidate Mark," Bellman said. "He believes he is entitled to a fencing lesson from a Blade of the Royal Guard and he will call down a terrible curse upon your descendants unto the seventh generation if you do not satisfy his expectations. He's not bad."

"I'll spit him, you go and get an apple to put in his mouth." Hazard clapped Bellman's shoulder. "You'll ride with the Guard when we leave."

• 3 •

𝕿he Forge was starting to prey on Ringwood's nerves. He wanted to be out in the sun and fresh air—on the open road to anywhere and taking forever to arrive, as Dad had always said.

Ranter was ranting again, still pacing. "It's not right! We were promised five years' training. We got less than four. They shortchanged us. Then I was threatened with death by starvation on Starkmoor. What sort of a choice is that? Grand Master himself has always told us a guard needs at least three men . . ."

And on. And on.

Ringwood, sitting glumly on the edge of a stone water trough, was tempted to tell him to put his head underwater and take three deep breaths, but then Ranter might slap him around a bit, as he often did candidates smaller than himself. That very first day four years ago, the day Dad had brought Ringwood to Ironhall, Ranter had been the Brat, big even then. Once Ringwood was accepted, of course, and Dad had gone away forever, then he had become the Brat and Ranter had been free to choose his new name. He had insisted on "Champion." That name was not on the list, so Master of Archives had sent him back to ask Grand Master, who had approved it.

The sopranos and beansprouts had not. *Ranter,* they had named him, and Ranter he had been ever since. Reminded of that now, he might decide to be Champion again for his binding, so it was better just to ignore him. All those one-time sopranos and beansprouts were gone now. Gone to the Guard, or Baelmark, or wherever. Just as he, Ringwood, was going! Who could say where he might be next week at this time?

Dead, like Bernard?

"Girls!" Ranter said. "Women! 'Course you're too young to care."

"Am not!"

"You wait until puberty gets up to your chin, boy. Girls is what being a Blade is all about. Women can't resist bound Blades." He leered. "Love 'em and leave 'em and onto the next one!"

That seemed a strange definition of love, and he couldn't know any more about girls than Ringwood did, which was nothing. A lifetime working for Ranter was an appalling prospect, but to back out now would look like cowardice. Worse, it would be going back on his word, and Dad had always listed that as a major breach of honor. So did Grand Master.

In a merciful reprieve, the door at the top of the steps opened, spilling more light into the crypt. A harsh voice was shouting. Grand Master's cut it off. Ringwood stood up. Ranter sat down.

An elderly man came down, followed by Grand Master, who shut the door firmly behind him. The newcomer peered around at the eight hearths, the troughs, anvils, and octogram, as he waited for his eyes to adjust to the dimmer light. He was pudgy above the waist, with oddly skinny legs. Not glamorous or virile. Ringwood had been imagining a much younger, warrior monarch.

Grand Master gestured angrily for Ranter to rise. "Your Grace, I am proud to present your future Blades: Prime Candidate Ranter, Candidate Ringwood."

Ranter bowed. Ringwood made a full court bow, which was more elaborate and definitely called for here. He sensed Ranter's angry glare on him; he caught Grand Master's nod of approval. "Gentlemen, meet your future ward, His Grace Grand Duke Rubin of Krupina."

"I am deeply honored by your offer of service," the Grand

Duke said quietly, "and humbled by your display of courage." He offered fingers to be kissed, first to Ranter, then Ringwood.

"The honor is entirely ours, Your Royal Highness," Ranter said. At least he got that bit right.

"And a pleasure, sire," Ringwood added.

The door opened again. Grand Master swung around angrily, but the man who came trotting down was Deputy.

"Pray excuse the intrusion," Tancred said. "Your Grace, the Guard has fulfilled its mission, which was to escort you safely here and see you provided with Blades. Our duty now lies back in Grandon. Will Your Grace grant us leave to depart, or do you prefer that we remain to escort you back with us?"

The Grand Duke smiled. "I shall consult the gentlemen who have assumed responsibility for my future safety. Candidate Ranter?"

Ranter shrugged. "Naw, we don't need them. You'll have to rely on the two of us from now on and Chivial's a lot safer than Krupina or any of those foreign places."

That seemed a wrong decision. Why turn down a gift horse?

The Grand Duke said, "Candidate Ringwood?"

"I'd say if Sir Tancred could spare even a few men, Your Highness, they would be a comfort for two beginners still learning their duties. Ironhall is short of seniors, so they can help the juniors with their fencing while they wait for you."

The Grand Duke chuckled. "Diplomatically phrased! Sir Tancred, I am very grateful for your service to date and shall be more grateful for any escort you feel you can reasonably leave here to see us safely back again."

"I'm sure the absence of five or six will not jeopardize His Majesty." Tancred saluted and departed.

"Master of Rituals will be here shortly," Grand Master said. "Otherwise you will not be disturbed."

"After the events of the last two days, a peaceful interlude is welcome." The Grand Duke dismissed him with a nod. He went to sit on the center anvil and waited until the door had closed before he spoke.

No, he was not what Ringwood had expected. His manners were those of a cultured nobleman—as described by Master of Protocol—and not those of a crude robber baron, which was what came to mind for a tiny state in backwoods east of Fitain. His command of Chivial was faultless, but that could be acquired by conjuration. He was soft-spoken, but too decisive to be called a fop. His voice was almost feminine in its softness, but that was a real beard on his chin. He was tense, but he had good reason to be so.

"Be seated, gentlemen. We have much to discuss over the next few days. Perhaps we should begin by getting to know each other. I am aware that Ironhall admits only the low-born, and I promise you that I do not hold that against a man. Or a woman, either, for my wife is not of noble birth. Courage and honor are what matter, and your willingness to be bound by this drastic ritual proves that you have both in abundance. Ranter, will you tell me a little about yourself?"

"That's all forgotten when we are admitted," Ranter said. "The charter says so. New name, new person. And I'm not lowborn! My grandfather had blue blood in his veins and was knighted by King Ambrose on the Field of Wyldburn. That's all I'll say."

Idiot!

Grand Duke Rubin stared at him in silence until he dropped his eyes.

"How about you, Ringwood?"

"I'm as lowborn as they come, sire, but I'm no criminal. My father was a tinker. He went around with a donkey, mending pots for a living. I know nothing about my mother. He never discussed her, so now I wonder if he was really my father. But

I know he didn't steal me, or anything, because he was honest! Very, very honest! He always said his reputation is all of himself a man can leave behind when he goes back to the elements. Honesty and honor, he said, courage and grace. Those four are what make a man. That's what he taught me, sire."

"He sounds like a father to be proud of. Mine used to say much the same. What happened to him?"

"He died." Ringwood felt a sudden prickling under his eyelids and blinked hard. He must not cry! That would be a baby thing to do now. Trouble was, he'd been thinking a lot about Dad today. Meditating, hoping Dad would have approved of what he was doing. "He got sicker and sicker, coughing and spitting up blood. He said I wasn't old enough to do what he did by myself and the donkey was too old. So he brought me . . . brought me here."

Ringwood had wept when Grand Master said, "He's good. He has great promise, but he's too young. Can you bring him back in the spring?"

Dad had just said, "No, sir," and all three of them had known what he meant.

"The weather's turning nasty out there. You want to stay with us until it blows over?"

"No need to drag it, your lordship." So the tinker had given his boy a last hug and gone off with the donkey into the snow and the moors. Ringwood had never heard any more of him. He had cried then, but he would not cry now.

"He told me, sire, that Ironhall would teach me to be a real man, so my life might be worth more than just a lot of mended pots, however good the patches."

"Pots matter," the Grand Duke said. "Any job well done brings honor to the doer. So far I think Ironhall has done well by you, but we'll see, won't we? Now it's my turn."

He thought for a moment. "You probably never heard of Krupina before today—"

Ranter said, "No."

"I expect Chivial has bigger counties. At one time the area was part of the Great Holy Empire, and the Emperor Carlus IV created the duchy for a son-in-law. So my ancestors held Krupina from the Emperor, but since the Empire is no more, they have held it against all comers. Fortunately it has very defensible borders."

He put his fingertips together. "Imagine a fertile plain, a triangle like this. My hands are two mountain ranges and the Asch flows down the middle, emptying into the Siril Lakes in the south, where my thumbs are. Siril is more swamp than lake, even in wet years. There are two towns, both on the river. Krupa is the capital, and quite central. Zolensa is near the lakes, in the south. City folk mostly speak Fitainish and country people Bohakian.

"The dukes have always claimed to rule the hills and swamps as well as the plain, but they were usually satisfied with a token allegiance, rather than wasting money trying to tax those outlying areas by force. This works both ways. The people who live in the marshes don't want foreigners intruding on them and mountain folk everywhere are doughty fighters. Foreigners have usually decided there isn't enough left over to justify a war of conquest. And that's not even taking Vamky into account. The Vamky Monastery defends Pilgrim Pass at the north end, the apex of the triangle, where the Asch emerges from the mountains.

"That's my homeland. It's small—you can ride from Vamky to Zolensa in a few hours. It's insignificant and tries to stay that way, but it is beautiful. It raises cattle and horses. It exports conjurers, fine wines, and even finer fighting men, which is better than importing someone else's. It belongs to me and my son after me, not my uncle. I want it back."

"We'll help you, Your Highness," Ringwood said.

"Thank you." The Grand Duke smiled approvingly. Or

was he laughing at a loudmouthed boy? What could a couple of half-trained Blades hope to do? "How much do you know about the Vamky Brotherhood?"

Ranter said, "Nothing."

Ringwood said, "Sire, Grand Master mentioned it as one of the famous spiritualist orders."

"The oldest in Eurania. They are great warriors as well as great conjurers, and the monastery itself is a major fortress. Unfortunately my Uncle Volpe rules Vamky."

Speaking of conjurers . . . The door squeaked and sunlight threw a doughty shadow down the steps. With a distinctive sound of slapping sandals, Master of Rituals descended, clutching a pile of white towels to his paunch. Unlike other masters, he was not a knight in the Order, but an adept of the Arcanes. His chubby form was enclosed in a full-length gray robe of heavy wool, although spirits knew how he stood it in summer. His bald head was burned crimson by the sun, hedged in a horseshoe of salt-and-pepper hair, and his face was even redder and shinier. He was the most constantly happy person Ringwood knew, always humming little songs.

"Bath time!" he chuckled. "If Your Grace will forgive my saying so. Better now than Firstmoon, mm? The order is very important. Start here . . ." He dropped a towel by one of the troughs. "Then here!" He crossed over to another and dropped two. "Here . . . and finally, here!" He spilled the rest of the pile and clasped his soft, plump hands. "A complete immersion in each is necessary, but splash around as long as you like. Take all day if you wish. We shall assemble in the hall and then come to join you just before midnight." He beamed. "Any questions?"

"Are you suggesting," Grand Duke Rubin inquired icily, "that I bathe in concert with these youths?"

For once Master of Rituals's happy smile faded. He

blinked. "His Majesty . . . King Athelgar has never objected, Your Grace."

"How about his mother?"

"Queen Malinda?"

"Does he have other mothers?"

Grand Duke Rubin was displaying some grand-ducal temper for the first time. That was his privilege and almost welcome, because it showed he had spark. His reasons did not matter. Ringwood was much more worried by Ranter's stupid leer. He was already unlacing his shirt to prove he was manly enough not to have scruples about stripping in front of other men. Any minute now he would do or say something appalling.

"M-mothers?" Master of Rituals stammered. "Not so far as . . . I believe there are some screens in the cellars that are brought up whenever a lady binds—"

"Surely, Master," Ringwood said, "if our ward wishes privacy, Ranter and I can wait outside? And he can go outside while we bathe in our turn?"

The tubby man was flustered now. "You are supposed to remain in the Forge until the binding!"

"If your ritual is as fragile as that," the Grand Duke sapped, "then I want no part of it."

"Er . . ."

Ranter dropped his shirt on the floor.

"The porch at the top of the stairs is part of the Forge," Ringwood said hastily. "We shall wait in there until Your Highness summons us. By your leave?" He turned Master of Rituals around and pushed him toward the steps. *"Ranter!"*

Ranter scowled and pulled his hose up again.

The stable was hot, acrid, and loud with the drone of flies. The hands were being ostentatiously busy, pretending not to eavesdrop, but even the horses had their ears pricked.

"You may inform Leader," Durendal said, "that I shall send him a report on the new seniors class within the week." He spoke softly, adding a glare for emphasis.

Sir Tancred, who had been checking his mount's girths, leaned an arm on its neck to pat it and nodded warily. "Yes, Grand Master."

"And you may tell him privily that there will be no more bindings until I report that we have suitable candidates available. That will be at least a year! Any request before that, even an informal inquiry, will be answered with my resignation."

Deputy nodded vigorously. "Certainly, Grand Master."

"Good chance to you."

Tancred would tell Leader, but would Leader tell the King? Not unless he had to, likely. Grand Master stalked out into the sunshine and headed for First House.

The new Prime, Goodwin, fell into step beside him. "Beg your pardon, Grand—"

"How many?"

"What? Promotions? I thought twelve?"

"I think fifteen. Fourteen if you have doubts about Sparman. Not Bellman, of course."

"Of course, Grand Master."

"Tell them to move their kit. They'll have to wait until tomorrow for swords. Go!"

And there was Bellman, waiting patiently by the steps for him, surrounded by sorrowful boys saying good-bye.

"Come," Grand Master said, not stopping. "We need to talk."

He felt old as he climbed the stairs. Lack of sleep was making him dull, fogging his wits. Perhaps he could rest for an hour or two, because the binding could not start until close to midnight. The royal guest was out of the way and Master of Rituals had orders to keep the odious Baron occupied. Everything was under control at last. Almost everything. Bellman flowed along beside him in respectful silence.

"Sit!" Grand Master said when they reach his study. "You'll have some wine with me." Yes, he would certainly take a nap. His gray hairs had earned it.

"Thank you, Grand Master."

He handed his guest a glass and sat down facing him. "I drink to better chance in your future, Bellman."

"Thank you, my lord. I blame no one but myself and my own folly. I am deeply grateful for your patience."

"The folly was mine. After all these years I should have seen right away you had a problem. You are a great loss to the Order."

Bellman acknowledged the compliment with his usual grace. Wavy brown hair, hazel eyes, a deeply tanned face that few people would call handsome—craggy or strong, perhaps, certainly not a face to be trifled with. Broad-shouldered and imposing, he stood taller than Ironhall preferred and had done so the day he arrived. Conjuration had stopped his growth but not reversed it. He had stood out from the herd for years because of his greater maturity. He made Ranter seem like a sulky child, although they were the same age. One look at him and you thought *competence.*

"I have scanned the charter and the precedents," Grand Master said, "and I can find no loophole, no way I can bend the rules to let you stay. Nor can I give you a cat's-eye sword when you leave. But we will find you worthy employment. I am not without influence, even yet, and I will give you the strongest possible recommendation."

"You are very kind, Grand Master. Can you recommend a murderer?"

"I can recommend you."

Bellman sipped wine without taking eyes off him. "On

the day I arrived, you told me you had known a lot of applicants to arrive with the law on their tails, but you had never had to close the gates on a lynch party before."

A wolf pack mob of young louts who'd thought they had an excuse to hang someone? "They were fools if they expected to find a tree on Starkmoor."

"You threw coins for me to catch and I missed half of them."

"You *caught* half of them with a noose waiting outside the gate if I refused you. That was good enough for me. But tell me if you wish." Obviously the boy wanted to get it off his chest, probably to test Grand Master's reaction.

Bellman smiled wistfully. "It is a brief, sad tale, my lord. I was apprenticed to my father, the locksmith in Camford. He was called upon to repair a jammed lock at the Sheriff's house, so he sent me to remove the lock and bring it to his shop. The Sheriff had forgotten or not been told, so he saw a man trying to force open his daughter's bedroom. Not impossible, I suppose—I was fifteen and had designs on every man's daughter. The first I knew was this wild old man in a nightshirt screaming and dancing and striking at me with a cane. I jumped up and tried to take it from him. I did not hit him, but he fell and did not rise. I ran for help and was met on the stair by people coming to investigate. He was dead and they thought I'd been running away. Which I then did."

"He'd had a fit?"

Bellman sighed. "I think he banged his head on the edge of a table. Just a silly little bump on the head. One got me into Ironhall; another is taking me out. Even chance can make justice."

"I know a very reliable witness who says it was an accident."

"There were no witnesses."

"There was one."

Bellman smiled. "Thank you."

"You would repeat your story before an inquisitor?"

The youth's eyes brightened. "Certainly I would!"

"I can arrange that," Lord Roland said. Commander Florian would be due to retire in six or seven years, and this boy would have been his logical successor if a certain Grand Master had not been so incompetent as to overlook an obvious injury. Alas! Now that could never be. "So . . . Employment? I am confident that you will succeed at anything you try. Is there any particular field you fancy? You handle people well. You could be a steward, running an estate. Master of Rituals is very anxious to see you enroll in the College to study conjury. Something more vigorous? A royal courier, if you enjoy travel."

The boy looked down at his hands and the goblet. After a moment he said softly, "The enemy of my enemy is my friend."

Flash!

That was Roland's secret name for the lightning bolt of opportunity, the momentary gap in your opponent's guard when your foil streaks in for a hit. He had seen those flashes many times in his days as a swordsman. As Lord Chancellor he had sometimes experienced the same flash of recognition in meetings when a logjam could be broken and a deal made. He had never met it here in Ironhall, where the problems were almost always routine.

Even Ringwood had seen this one, and he had slapped the boy down.

So it had not been old age niggling at him all morning. It had been frustration, awareness of a problem he could do nothing about. Old age was always frustration, but frustration was not necessarily old age. Maybe he could do something about this one after all. Or Bellman could. Cancel the nap . . .

"What do you have in mind?" he asked, carefully keeping excitement out of his voice.

The boy cocked his head in that curious way he had now. "Only that Bernard was my friend, and there is something very odd about his death. I questioned Sir Hazard about it, but he knew nothing useful." And if Hazard didn't, no one in the Guard did. "But someone sent those shadowmen who killed my friend. That someone ought to pay dearly."

"I agree. I have played hunches all my life, lad. Not always, although when I ignored them I was usually sorry, and once in a while they were wrong and led me into error. Followed or not, hunches should never be ignored, and I had the same hunch you did. There is something extremely odd about this vagrant Grand Duke and his undead pursuers. I can certainly suggest that he add you to his train, for it is pathetically small. Most dukes travel with dozens."

"He may be suspicious, of course."

So Bellman had seen that possibility, too.

Grand Master nodded. "If he has something to hide, he will be very suspicious. He will refuse, in fact. Suppose you discover that the Duke himself summoned the shadowmen for some vile scheming purpose—to win the King's sympathy, perhaps. After all, candles seem to be an adequate defense. The guards were improperly warned, but the Krupinese knew the facts and were safe enough. Suppose the attack turns out to have been a fraud. What will you do then?"

Bellman shrugged. "Nothing. He will have two Blades to guard him, so he cannot be harmed without killing them first, and they are my friends, too. It can never be easy to bring a Grand Duke to justice. I do not even know why his subjects threw him out."

"Nor do I. Did Hazard?"

A flicker of a smile. "No."

"Then let us assume that our King knows what he is about and Rubin of Krupina is worthy of help. If he hires you, I know that you will not betray his trust. But I should like you to do something else, a service for me and the Order, *subject to your loyalty to him.* I will give you money. If the Duke dies, look after his deranged Blades as best you can, will you? And if he fails in his quest and falls into total poverty, as he may, bring him back to Chivial—exiled and friendless, with only his Blades still true. Then Athelgar can keep and feed all three of them."

Bellman nodded, smiling. "Even chance can bring justice?"

"Exactly!" Grand Master said. "But it never hurts to nudge it in the right direction."

◆ 4 ◆

Hammers clinked the beat on anvils, trebles soared over tenors and baritones in the Blades' dedication song, and the rich reverberation of the Forge added palimpsests of harmony. From diminutive sopranos to ancient Sir Bram, who was rarely seen except at mealtimes, all Ironhall had assembled around the octogram. Light from the hearths behind the audience flickered dimly on the roof, making Ringwood worry about shadowmen, but the sky outside was clear and the Duke had assured him that the curse could not come on starry nights.

He hadn't panicked and run away. Dad would be proud of him.

Eight stood within the octogram, of course. Ringwood himself was at earth point, with Ranter on his left, at death. And looking like it. Beyond him was Goodwin, not much happier, for he faced a very long stint as Prime. Then the Brat, grinning wildly down upon the two naked swords at his feet. This was his third binding in three weeks. He had three lines to say each time, and had cheekily informed Ringwood earlier that he would be the fourteenth Blade he had bound and that was a record.

The hymn ended. At fire point Master of Rituals began chanting Invoker. The Duke was at love point, directly across from Ranter, and beside him was Master Armorer, who would be chanting Dispenser—he had a stupendous bass and the lungs of a whale. Apparently elementals were not bothered by his incomprehensible accent. Grand Master was Arbiter, at time point.

Ringwood had witnessed more than a dozen bindings, and the ritual never palled. He was only mildly sensitive to the spirits, but he was very sentimental. His eyes were already brimming over at the thought that he might be gone tomorrow—the day after was more likely, his ward said—and would never witness this again. Dad would surely be proud of him tonight. Oh, spirits! Here they came! Tears cascaded down his cheeks. Try and think of the whole wide world waiting for him out there.

A good man, Duke Rubin, in spite of his shopworn looks. Quiet, courteous, and steely. Guarding him would be a pleasure and much more exciting than being low man in a guard of over a hundred mooning around Athelgar. Ranter as Leader was not a cheering prospect. Ranter had his eyes closed and seemed to be swaying, as if moved by a wind no one else could feel. What happened if he fainted and fell out of the octogram? That might release the assembled elementals! There were horror stories of conjurers who lost control of assemblages going mad or being turned into monsters.

Grand Master stepped forward to the central anvil and

scattered gold coins on it to make sure spirits of chance were not running riot. He peered suspiciously at the results, but then nodded and backed away again.

Why did time rush by so fast when you wanted to savor every second of it?

The elementals were assembled. Now came the Brat, clutching *Invincible*. He was a very small Brat and a long sword was, by definition, long. He laid it on the anvil without mishap, recited his piece in a series of chiropteran squeaks, and went back to his place at chance point.

Ranter was looking anywhere but at that sword. Receiving Grand Master's signal, Goodwin went to help him off with his shirt. Ranter did nothing to make it easier. After that Ringwood had to mark Ranter's chest to show where his heart was, which was not as simple a task as it would be in a good light with dry eyes. He found the bottom rib, counted up, wielded the charcoal. Ranter had a fair crop of chest fuzz already—why couldn't he behave more like a man now? *Just for once don't bollix it!*

Ringwood backed away two paces and realized that nothing was happening. He went back, took his future leader's elbow and urged him forward. Ranter stumbled over to the anvil with Ringwood helping and even guiding Ranter's hand down to grasp *Invincible*'s hilt. He was shivering and slick with sweat.

"Up!"

Ranter nodded, and heaved himself up on the anvil. He raised the sword in salute . . . It shook violently. The only sound was the chattering of Ranter's teeth.

"Upon my soul . . ." Ringwood whispered.

No answer. Grand Master was chewing his lip. Could they stop the ritual at this point? Substitute another man, another sword? Or would it all go awry and kill someone? Ringwood, specifically.

He poked Ranter in the small of his back and prompted again. "Upon my soul, I, Ranter . . ." This time it worked.

"Upon my soul, I, Ranter . . ." He was barely audible.

"Candidate in the Loyal and Ancient Order . . ."

"Candidate in the Loyal and Ancient Order . . . of the King's Blades, er, do irrevocably swear—"

He had it now. Sweating, Ringwood went back to his place, but he twitched nervously at every breath. Ranter finished his oath, remembered what he had to do next, and managed to jump off the anvil without falling flat on his face. He knelt to the Duke to proffer the sword, then backed away until he found the anvil by falling on it. Goodwin and Ringwood were there to grab his arms and steady him for the stroke.

The Grand Duke wasted no time. He strode forward three paces. "Serve or die!" He jabbed the sword into Ranter's chest, but not through it. Ranter jerked against his friends' restraint, but by then the blade was already out and the trickle of blood had stopped. He stared down disbelievingly as the wound closed, then looked up with a big, proud smile.

"Hey!" he said.

Everyone else said, "Shush!"

Ringwood saw him safely over to earth point and put himself at death, thinking his own binding would be a cinch after that. He watched with joy as the Brat brought forward *Bad News* with the bright gleam of her new pommel. He whipped off his shirt without waiting for Ranter to remember his duty. He was relieved that it was Goodwin who marked the target.

Then he jumped up on the anvil, holding that magnificent sword aloft. "Upon my soul," he shouted, "I, Ringwood . . ." This was a dream! For almost four years he had waited for this.

When he rose from his knees before his ward, he even re-

membered to sit on the anvil away from the damp patch
Ranter had left. He spread his arms, felt Goodwin and then
Ranter grip them. Brace for the agony. . . . Here it came. He
watched the sword rush forward.

It didn't hurt as much as everyone had promised it
would. It didn't last long enough to be real pain. He rose to
acknowledge the wild cheers of the audience, accepted his
shirt from someone, and struggled vainly to put it on while
people were thumping him on the shoulder and pumping
his hand. Juniors were "oohing" at his back, where they
had found a scar matching the faint reddish mark on his
chest.

The Duke was peering at the sword. "What does it say?"

"*Bad News,* sire. Bad news to Your Highness's enemies,
that is."

Rubin laughed. "Good! Well done!" He returned her.

Ringwood's heart's blood on the steel looked disappoint-
ingly like any other blood. He wiped it clean with Ironhall's
shirt. Masters and knights came crowding in to shake his
hand. He pushed past them so he could keep his eye on his
ward. He tousled the Brat's hair in passing and said,
"Thanks! Well bound."

The Grand Duke shook Ranter's hand, then turned.

"Sir Ringwood?"

"Sire?"

"I appoint you commander of my Blades."

For a moment Ringwood thought he had misheard, but
the hubbub hushed in widening ripples of silence, like waves
on a pond.

"What?" Ranter roared. "He's three years younger than
I am!"

Two-and-a-half!

"That doesn't show," his ward said.

"Not fair! He's baseborn and I'm not!"

"That doesn't show, either. He is Commander. Grand Master, I think you mentioned food next?"

Ranter's glower at Ringwood promised terrible retribution for this insult.

Candle flames by the score danced on all the tables in the hall and reflected back a hundredfold from the famous sky of swords overhead. Yesterday had brought a Returning, a time for mourning, but now two Blades had been bound, and that was cause for celebration. Ninety young omnivores were free to gorge until they could eat no more and then go away and sleep as long as they wanted. The hall rocked with noise.

Sir Ringwood was at high table, standing behind his ward. No one had told him to do that. No one was going to tell him what to do ever again. Although his appetite was notable even by Ironhall standards, he just knew that all the rumbling in his belly and the oceans of drool in his mouth could not be satisfied yet. He had told Ranter—Sir Ranter, if you please—to go off and stuff himself in the kitchen, then come back and relieve him. So far Ranter seemed to be succeeding better at the former than the latter, but that hardly mattered. Ringwood was not at all sure he could take his eyes off the Grand Duke for any reason whatsoever. The urgency would pass in a few days, they said. At present it was a pleasurable sort of hurt, like the ache of muscles after a workout.

Rubin of Krupina was seated in the place of honor at Grand Master's right. The odious fat Baron was on Grand Master's left, leaning halfway across him to eavesdrop on their conversation, feeding himself with both hands as he did so. The seniors' table was overflowing with sixteen more seniors and five guardsmen. Sir Calvert, whom Deputy had left in charge of the reduced troop, was at high table. So, surprisingly, was Bellman, now officially a guest, no longer a candidate. He was laughing happily with a couple of the yackiest knights and showing no signs of bitterness or regret.

"I am sure he is and he won't," Grand Master said. He poured a glass of wine and passed the decanter on to his left, apparently not noticing that he was putting his elbow in the Baron's eye. Then he failed to let go for a moment, so his arm shut the Baron out of the conversation.

The Grand Duke half turned his head. "Sir Ringwood?"

Ringwood bent closer. "Your Highness?"

"Are you eavesdropping on what Grand Master and I are discussing?"

"Yes, sire."

"Then will you tell me what you think of his proposition?"

"Not here, sire."

His ward chuckled. "You win, Grand Master!"

That felt good. Ringwood was merely following his instincts, and apparently they were correct so far. Then he saw Ranter hurrying back in and decided he could run and eat something after all. A pair of roast boars, say. Dying of starvation would be a poor start to his career.

By the time Grand Duke Rubin returned to Main House with his Blades swaggering along behind him—trying not to bang things with their swords—the Royal Guard was already on duty at the bottom of the big staircase. Ringwood was surprised to see Bellman there, too, talking with Sir Calvert. Grand Master must have pointed him out, because Duke Rubin knew who he was.

"You don't waste time, young man, do you?"

Bellman bowed. His smile was perfect, neither insolent nor buttery. "I am available at Your Royal Highness's convenience."

"Wait upon me tomorrow. Sir Calvert? Have you counted the spiders under the bed yet?"

"No, Your Grace. I was sure Sir Ringwood would just count them all over again." He raised an eyebrow at Ringwood.

Who nodded, meaning, *Yes, I would like a lesson, please.*

"Let's get it over with," Rubin said and went up the stairs at a trot, letting the rest scramble to keep up with him—or get ahead of him in the case of his Blades, who flung open the doors to make sure nothing was lying in wait. Candles were hastily lit, many candles. By the time Baron von Fader arrived, puffing and huffing, there were lights everywhere.

Ringwood had never seen inside the royal suite before. The first room was lofty and large, with big windows out to a balcony. "Presence chamber," Calvert said, and led the way through to another. "Dressing room . . . and lastly the royal bedchamber." The furniture and decor far outclassed anything else in the school—fit for a king, of course.

"Who sleeps in the dressing room?"

"Normally a valet. Now the Baron."

Ringwood regarded the royal four-poster distrustfully. It bothered him, somehow. There had been a cot in a corner of the middle room, not big enough to hold all of the Baron at a sitting. "And we twiddle thumbs in the anteroom?" He frowned at Calvert's smug smile. "I think the dressing room should be the guard room, next door to our ward. The Baron should sleep in the anteroom."

"Then do it. You're the boss now—*Sir Ringwood.*" Calvert grinned more warmly. "I like to go by the book myself, but Tancred didn't make a fuss."

Having been a senior only a week, Ringwood didn't know the book. It just felt right in his bones, the same sort of instinct that was making Ranter stay out in the anteroom with their ward. It was like having a pile of gold bars to guard. Having to make the decisions didn't feel good, it felt worrisome.

Baron Fader came lumbering in, huge and bad-tempered and drunk. "What's going on? His Royal Highness wants to go to bed. So do I."

Ringwood looked at the four-poster again. It *really* bothered him. "My lord, explain to me about these shadowmen. They can go through solid walls?"

The fat man scowled at him. "There are no shadowmen here tonight, boy."

"I still need to know."

"Tomorrow for lessons, boy. Tonight for bed. Now!"

"The sooner you answer my questions, my lord, the sooner you'll get to bed."

The bullfrog swelled with rage. "They can go through walls if there's light, boy. When it's dark, they're solid and dangerous. In light they are only shadows and harmless. Is that so difficult for you, huh?"

"What if there's light on one side of a wall and dark on the other?"

Baron von Fader shook his head as if to clear it of cobwebs; his jowls wobbled. "They can go from the light to the dark, not the other way."

"What're you getting at?" Calvert said, frowning.

"That bed," Ringwood said, "is against the wall. My ward will sleep with candles burning, I expect. I'll *insist* he sleeps with candles lit. So even if the night's hot like this, he'll want the bed curtains closed. Suppose there's light on the far side of that wall? Those undead things could reach through from that room"—it was another guest bedroom, he thought—"right into the bed itself."

Calvert gave him a cold stare. "You trying to tell me my job, shaver?"

"No, Sir Calvert, but—"

"Well, you just did. Never thought of that. The Order hasn't written the book on these shadowmen horrors yet. I'll see that notion gets in it. What will you do about it?"

"Move the bed away from the wall? Make sure there's candles between them?"

"Don't ask me, Ringwood. Don't ask anyone. Command! You have seven men here who will obey your orders and one Baron you can bully."

"What?" the Baron demanded angrily.

"And we'll also be moving your cot out to the anteroom, my lord," Ringwood said cheerfully.

"What!?"

"Sorry, I'm just letting power go to my head." Even so, he mustn't ask von Blubber to help move furniture. "Bring in your oxen, Sir Calvert."

That was not the end of it, of course. He had to look under the bed, and in every chest, wardrobe, and drawer. He peered in the ewer, in the garderobe, behind the drapes, at the casement fastenings, into every fireplace and chimney. Ranter was doing the same in the anteroom. The Baron frothed and gnashed and bugled, but the Grand Duke waited patiently until his Blades were satisfied, making no complaint. A good ward, Calvert whispered.

"Thank you for your patience, Your Highness," Ringwood said at last, returning to the anteroom. He must be covered with dust and cobwebs, and it was almost dawn. "Sorry to take so long."

"It was your duty and I am grateful for your diligence." Rubin headed toward his bedroom, gesturing for Ringwood to follow. "Could you have done all that yesterday?"

"I could, but I wouldn't have felt it was necessary."

Rubin held the door until he was in and then closed it almost in Ranter's face, so the two were alone. "Can you lie to me?"

"Yes, sire."

"You can?" The Grand Duke had not expected that.

"But only if it is necessary for your protection, Your Grace. Only as a last resort. Never otherwise. I need you to trust me." That was soprano-class stuff.

"I see. Grand Master is quite insistent I should hire this half-blind failed student, Bellman. To do what is a little vague."

"He's an excellent man, sire, and I'm not lying to you. I would trust Bellman with my life. Not with yours, of course."

The Grand Duke smothered a yawn. "He will be traveling to Grandon with us. We can decide there. Good night—Commander."

Ringwood bowed low. "Good night, Your Royal Highness. And thank you for the trust you have put in me."

"Thank you for your life," Rubin said.

Out in the dressing room sat Ranter, glowering, fuming, nursing the anger he had been stoking for hours. Both doors were closed, and faint sounds of the Baron's snores were already filtering through the massive oaken door to the anteroom.

Thank you for your life? An odd expression. But apt, in a way. Ringwood's life belonged to his ward now. How old was Rubin? Forty? Sixty? If he died of natural causes and slowly, so his Blades had time to adjust to the idea, then they should survive all right. It was only when a ward died by violence that his Blades went berserk.

Ringwood wasn't sleepy. Bound Blades never slept, or almost never. But he was weary, and a few hours on a bed would be nice. There was no bed here, but there were a couple of half-decent-looking chairs.

Ranter rubbed his knuckles. "We have something to discuss, brother Ringwood."

"Not that I'm aware of." Ringwood sat down and pulled off his boots. The left one was pinching after so many hours.

Ranter grabbed the front of his jerkin and hauled him upright. There was a crazy look in his eyes. "We have to discuss who's leader here, Pimple."

Ringwood had nothing to fear from Ranter now. "I'm Leader. Our ward decided."

"We're going to outvote him, you an' me."

Ringwood shook his head sadly. "No." Poor Ranter. It must be terrible to be wrong so often, wrong about just about everything, every day and all day.

The big lunk balled a fist like a sledgehammer.

"Try it," Ringwood said. "I'm your ward's Blade. You can't hurt me. Your binding won't let you."

For a long minute nothing happened, except that sweat began to sparkle on Ranter's forehead.

"See?" Ringwood said. "Accept it and relax. You got the easy job. I have to do all the thinking. If there are mistakes made, they'll be my mistakes. Then you can ask His Nibs to fire me and I'll back you up, I promise. If he dies, you can stamp me into mush. Now sit down. You didn't bring any dice, did you?"

Then he remembered that Ranter had learned not to play dice.

About half an hour or so later, Ringwood thought he heard something from the bedchamber and came alert. Ranter had seemed to be dozing, but he looked up instantly when his companion moved. Putting a finger to his lips, Ringwood moved to the door and opened it a little way, very slowly, very quietly. The bedroom was bright and if the bed curtains were drawn, his ward should neither see nor hear him.

He listened. After a moment he closed the door again and went back to his chair. Ranter looked puzzled, so Ringwood just shrugged. He didn't bother to explain that what he had heard was the sound of a Grand Duke weeping.

◆ 5 ◆

𝒜 few furlongs east of Ironhall, the Blackwater road dipped into a gully and twisted sharply to get out of it. The top of that bend provided a fine view of the school, with its fake towers and battlements. Bellman knew it would be his last sight of his erstwhile home. He twisted in the saddle to watch it disappear behind the rocks.

"Regrets?" Sir Ansel asked at his side.

"One big regret and many happy memories."

Horseback was a good place for private conversations and Ansel a good confidant, sensible and discreet. He, Bellman, and Bernard had been a threesome until the King's most recent visit. Ansel had been the last man bound on that occasion, narrowly escaping being packed off to Baelmark with Lord Baxterbridge the following week.

"There's a rumor that you're going to work for His Nibs."

"It's only a rumor so far," Bellman said. "Oh, look at that!"

Ringwood had claimed the right to ride alongside his ward. Ranter and the Baron were following close, both trying to move up whenever the trail widened enough to allow a third horse in. The jockeying was fierce, and Ranter had very nearly been thrown off into a patch of thistles. The spectators were laying bets.

The sun had barely cleared the tops of the tors and was already hot. Somewhere aloft a lark was singing, and off to the south a herd of the King's deer fled in panic from the intruders. Starkmoor in summer was breathtakingly beautiful.

After a moment, Ansel said, "His Nibs's visit has not been profitable. Ranter is a social slug and Ringwood's only a boy. They're both untrained. Ironhall can usually do better than that."

"The B Team? He has the option of hiring a blind man as well."

"I did not mean that!"

"I know you didn't. I think they'll do all right. Ringwood has wits."

But did he have enough of them? Bellman was already regretting his promise to Grand Master. He no longer trusted this mysterious Grand Duke and his bullfrog Baron. Yesterday he had knelt to the man and asked to enter his service, but he had been relieved when he was not accepted on the spot. He had a strong hunch that the man was not what he seemed.

"Grand Master speaks highly of you," Rubin had said, leaning back in his chair and frowning. "So do my Blades, whose judgment I must and do trust. But you have no special skills other than swordsmanship, at which I am told you cannot exceed any ordinary man-at-arms now. Sir Ringwood has said you would be helpful to him in Grandon, where he has some tasks he wishes done. He cannot easily leave my side. I understand that. But I do not expect to remain long in Chivial—"

"Language conjuration is expensive!" Baron von Fader interjected. "What can you contribute to offset that expense every time His Highness crosses a border?"

Seeing that he was expected to answer, Bellman said, "Honesty, Your Highness, and an eagerness to serve. Although I am master of no trade, Ironhall has made me jack of several. I write a fair hand. I know horses." Also dancing, basic conjuration, court protocol, Chivian history and law—nothing relevant, in short.

"I have a hostler and a secretary already." The Grand Duke shrugged. "Grand Master says you can have the charges against you dismissed?"

"There were no formal charges, sire, but I am confident I can clear my name as soon as we reach Grandon."

"Do that. Assist Sir Ringwood as he requires, and then we shall see. I will pay you for your time. You have our leave . . ."

Ansel broke into his reverie. "What did you name your sword?"

Instinctively, Bellman's hand sought the comfort of that hilt at his belt. The stone of the pommel was black, for cat's-eyes were reserved by law to the Blades. Even an anonymous sword from the Ironhall armory was an illegal gift, but Master Armorer had insisted with a straight face that this was just one he'd found lying around. Obviously Grand Master had approved that happy discovery.

"No name so far," Bellman said. "I was tempted to call her *Bluff,* or *Fraud,* but I could not insult her so." Being honest with himself, as was his custom, he knew a flippant inscription would reduce her value. He might have to sell her just to buy food, and only gentlemen were allowed to wear swords anyway. "Can you spare me a couple of hours when we get to Nocare? I'll need a guide."

Ranter had lost out in the jostling stakes again and was riding alongside the Baron. Pity that one's horse!

"Can probably arrange it." Ansel smirked. "There are better bordellos in Grandon itself. That *is* what you have in mind?"

"No. Ranter has, though. He talks of nothing else."

"How about Ringwood?" Ansel said thoughtfully.

"Let him wait. The kid has enough on his mind without starting that."

*   *   *

With dry roads and days still long, aided by the new bridge over the Flaskwater, they pushed on into the night, reaching Nocare before the moon set. The Grand Duke's party moved back into Quamast House. Yeomen and Blades were dragged out of bed to guard it. Nothing molested them.

Next morning Ansel appeared at the door, come to collect his friend. Although Bellman was wearing the best hose, jerkin, and cloak that Ironhall could provide, he was not dressed for a palace. Moreover, the dispatch folder he carried marked him as a clerk, so he'd left his sword behind.

"The Dark Chamber," he said as they set off through the grounds. How huge they were! Far bigger and grander than he had imagined, a parkland of trees and flowers and lawn. The palace itself was a small city of marble and glass, of red tile and tall chimney stacks. He had long dreamed of living there, guarding his king. And yet . . . Being older than his peers, he had mostly befriended boys ahead of him in the school, and in the last year they had all flown the nest. Those who had visited since had raved about their wonderful life in Grandon, and the girls; the King's fine palaces, and the girls; balls and masques, and girls. But when cornered they had also admitted that their life was mostly very boring—except for the girls, of course. Ansel was a Blade, in fine blue livery, with a cat's-eye sword. He could go almost anywhere in the land unquestioned. But what good did he do, really?

Bellman reproached himself for belittling what he could not have. That was mean-spirited. "You should have brought a couple of horses."

"For an extra fee I will carry you," Ansel said cheerily.

"I'll double your fee and it still won't buy a beer."

"I'll buy the beer. Where else do you need to go, so I can plan our route?"

"I need to see the Yeomen, the White Sisters, and Griffin King of Arms."

"They're all close together," Ansel said, scowling, "but you'll be kept waiting an hour at each, just on principle. Three hours at the Sisters'."

"No need for you to wait. Just show me where they are. I'll find them again."

"You may get challenged. Oh, look at those roses!"

"Gorgeous." Bellman took his pass from his folder. "How's that?"

The paper identified the bearer as Jack Bellman, Esq.— legally so, since he was now on His Majesty's service. It was signed, "Ringwood, Companion in the Loyal and Ancient Order of the King's Blades." That, Ansel agreed, ought to admit him to anywhere short of the royal apartments.

"I bet the kid enjoyed doing that," he said enviously. As the most junior man in the Guard, he would not be signing anything meaningful for years yet. "That's the Blade barracks. Head there if you need more help."

At the palace headquarters of His Majesty's Office of General Inquiry, a solitary black-robed inquisitor sat reading at a desk heaped high with papers, a window at his back. A door ajar on his right admitted faint sounds of voices from inner rooms. He looked up at Bellman with the fixated stare of a strangled fish. Young though he seemed, his pasty, bookish appearance cried out for fresh air and exercise, as if he spent his entire existence in this dim and stuffy chamber, working his way through these reams of paper. No doubt there would be new stacks waiting when he returned tomorrow.

"Good chance!" Bellman said cheerily, thinking that few people would be pleasant to a Dark Chamber snoop. "I need to have an affidavit certified as true testimony."

"We don't do that." The inquisitor's voice was as thin and dusty as his appearance. He went back to his papers.

Bellman reached in his folder. "I have here a letter from Earl Roland of Waterby."

The inquisitor laid down his reading and took the letter. He glanced at the inscription, broke the seal, and dismissed the contents with a glance. Admittedly, most of that long text was a list of Grand Master's titles, honors, and offices, and only one of them mattered in this case—the two letters, "P.C.," denoting that he was a member of the Privy Council.

The snoop held out his hand again. "The affidavit!"

That, also, he gave the merest glance before handing it back. "You wrote this?"

"I did."

"You are the person named, known formerly as Jack, son of John Eastswine of Camford, known later as Candidate Bellman of the Loyal and Ancient Order of the King's Blades, currently calling himself Jack Bellman?"

"I am."

"Read it to me." It was by listening to voices that inquisitors detected falsehood. "Faster."

That was easier said than done, with half an eye missing and the light in his face. Apparently the snoop had memorized the entire text, because twice he corrected Bellman's reading. When it was finished, he took back the document, dipped a quill, and began to write on it.

"He should have stayed in bed," he remarked without looking up.

"What? Who?" Bellman was feeling rattled and angry at knowing he was meant to feel rattled.

"Sheriff Glover. He suffered an apoplectic fit the day before, his second that month." The snoop sifted sand over his writing. "He refused to be bled and the doctors did not consider him well enough to be transported to an elementary."

"How do you know all that?"

"He was a keeper of the King's peace. A report on his death came through here that year . . . the fourth of Eighth-moon, I think it was." The clerk held wax and candle over the paper, pressed a seal on the puddle. He handed the affidavit back. "I added a note that the coroner attributed his death to natural causes."

"Thank you!" Bellman said, amazed. "That was kind of you."

The inquisitor did not reply. He was back reading already. His world existed only on paper.

Bellman did not covet his job.

The Household Yeomen's guard room was a sunnier place and less menacing, despite the two rigid sentries outside it, all shiny and plumed. The man-at-arms behind the desk greeted Bellman with a cheerful, "Good chance!" and seemed well disposed toward him—until he read his pass, for it was signed by a Blade. That old rivalry soured milk faster than thunder.

No, Sergeant Bates was not available. He had no idea when Sergeant Bates would be available. It took a lot of wheedling and all the humble charm Bellman could muster to win a reluctant agreement that the deaths of three Yeomen on duty might possibly—but certainly not necessarily and this concession was purely theoretical and without reference to the particular case that had been discussed earlier—result in their immediate superior being subject to court-martial.

In other words, the unfortunate Bates was in a dungeon somewhere. Bellman decided he did not want to be a man-at-arms, either.

The offices of Griffin King of Arms were tiny and hidden away in a neglected corner of the palace that had not been dusted since King Ambrose built the place, more than forty years ago. It contained one bored young herald, with freckled nose, thinning sandy hair, and ink-stained fingers. He became quite excited when he realized he had a visitor who was genuinely interested in what he might have to say. Ringwood's signature was all the authorization he needed to spill information. Out came the great dusty tomes. Their contents were not enough to prove anything, but they certainly did not dispose of Bellman's suspicions.

"Let me see if I have this right," he said. "The Everard who was made first Duke of Brinton was the younger son of King Ambrose the Third? Ambrose the Third also begat Taisson the Second, who begat Ambrose the Fourth, who begat Malinda the First, who begat Athelgar the First, who so far has begotten Prince Everard?"

"May the spirits guard His Royal Highness. And we don't usually start numbering a name until we have two of it," the herald murmured diffidently.

"I stand corrected. And on the other line, Ambrose the Third begat Everard the first duke, who begat Lady Estrith, who married the Maréchal Louis de Montmarle, who begat Lady Yvette, who married Grand Duke Hans of Krupina, who begat Rubin, also Grand Duke."

"I believe he's the seventeenth grand duke."

"Good for him. And does he have any children?"

The herald opened a drawer and rummaged through a chaos of papers that would have horrified the inquisitor. "Yes. I have this to add . . . a son, Frederik, Marquis of Krupa. A courtesy title, I imagine."

"That's recent news? Any idea when he was born?"

"Four hundred and two by our reckoning. I'm not sure what month."

"Same age as our own beloved prince," Bellman said, sensing his quarry drawing closer. "And the same number of generations since Ambrose the Third. Remarkably tidy! But on one line we have three men and one woman, and on the other two of each. The ladies usually marry younger. Isn't Grand Duke Rubin a little *old* to have a three-year-old son? How old is he?"

The herald was aghast at not knowing. Soon he brightened. "If you would allow me a few minutes down in the archives, Master Bellman, I would be able to answer that."

Bellman went with him and spent two hours standing in a cellar. He decided he didn't want to be a herald, either.

He certainly couldn't be a White Sister.

Ansel had warned him about the White Sisters, after conceding that he was biased. Most White Sisters found Blades' bindings as attractive as warm carrion. Not all did, certainly, but Ansel had tried to date one of the unlucky ones and had scars to prove it.

Being unbound, Bellman was hoping for a better reception when he knocked at the Fellowship's door, which looked out on a quiet courtyard behind the Treasury wing. The woman who answered it was tall, thin, and colorless in her white draperies and steeple headdress. She recoiled ominously from him. He explained his purpose and offered his pass, which she held with her fingertips as if it were rotten.

She returned it quickly. "Please wait." She closed the door.

He cooled his heels out in the courtyard, happy enough to watch courtiers and their minions stroll by. His day had been a personal success, in that he was no longer a fugitive on the run. Both his record and his conscience were clear at last, thanks to the worker-ant snoop. If he wished, he could even go home again to Camford, that bucolic backwater, where he must still have family. The prospect appalled. His mother had called him a murderer, his sisters had fainted, his father had ordered him out of the house. Besides, since then he had caught the scent of a wider, infinitely more appealing world, where the status of the hay crop was not the most gripping topic of conversation in town.

On his other quest he had failed. Ringwood had asked him to investigate several things without actually mentioning his ward's background, but the kid had dropped hints. He was hurt that his ward had not yet confided in him and smart enough to see that he might have been bound to an imposter. Sadly, Bellman had failed to gather any real evidence either for or against Grand Duke Rubin. His suspicions were stronger than ever, but he had nothing he could take back to justify his day.

Eventually the door opened to reveal an older woman, taller, thinner, paler, and even more refined, under a hennin even higher. He assumed she was a Mother, although he couldn't read the signals displayed by the lace on her headdress.

"Mother Celandine is unavailable," she announced and tried to close the door.

Bellman put a boot in it and began to talk. "I am here on behalf of Sir Ringwood, newly appointed Commander of the Grand Duke's Blades. He needs information on the attack that almost killed his ward five days ago."

That was incontestable, and she pouted. "The Fellowship has already cooperated fully with the Blades, the Yeomen, the Dark Chamber, Chancery, the Lord Chamberlain, and the College of Conjury. He should consult the Guard."

No doubt that was incontestable, too.

"But if the shadowmen attack again," Bellman protested, "Sir Ringwood and Sir Ranter are likely to *die,* Mother."

With poor grace, she said, "Mother Celandine has been granted leave to return to Oakendown to recuperate. In point of fact," she conceded, "the reverend lady suffered a nervous breakdown."

"Very understandable. I offer my deepest sympathy. How about Sister Gertrude?"

The Mother drew herself up so sharply that her hat almost skewered the lintel. "Sisters of her rank are not authorized to speak to outsiders."

Bellman continued to plead. Eventually the door was closed again.

The wait this time was even longer. Despite his promise to Grand Master, he could not in good conscience enter the Grand Duke's service if he suspected the man of being a fraud. Obtaining two Blades under false pretenses was at least grand larceny and would mean disaster for Ringwood and Ranter. The law did not hold Blades responsible for their ward's actions, but that was no help, because neither did it recognize their compulsion to defend him from arrest. Spirits! If Athelgar had fallen for some confidence trickster's spiel, then the mess was well beyond Bellman's powers to unravel. Even to disclose it would be lese majesty.

But if Rubin was not who he said he was and Athelgar knew the true story, then Bellman was trespassing in state affairs, a dangerous labyrinth.

The door opened. The ancient Mother who appeared was emaciated, elongated, and so ethereal it was hard to believe she continued to exist at all. In ghostly tones she announced that Sister Gertrude would have no statement to make and Master Whatever-his-name should consult with the Blades or Grand Wizard. The door was then closed and noisily bolted.

Baffled and furious, Bellman walked around the corner, heading back to Quamast House.

A laurel bush said, "Hey! You!"

The rightful owner of the voice stood up. She wore the

white robes of a Sister and a hennin with almost no lace
on it at all. She was probably no older than Ringwood, and
completely unlike the women Bellman had just been fighting with. Her face was plump and wide, unfashionably
tanned, with a nose indubitably snub, eyes dark as coal
and shiny as gems. Ethereal she was not. Sturdy, more
likely. He thought of dairy maids or farm girls plucking
chickens. He tried desperately not to stare at the fascinating curve of her robe over her breasts.

She put her fists on her hips and regarded him with suspicion. "I'm Sister Gertrude. What do you want to know?"

Many things, like where can I find you this evening . . .
"My name is Bellman, Sister. Until yesterday I was a candidate for—"

"You were at Ironhall. I can see a faint shimmer on you,
but you're not bound."

"No, and never will be. I injured my eye," he explained
quickly, seeing her frown. "But my best friend at Ironhall
was a man called Bernard, who—" Her expression
stopped him.

"What about Sir Bernard?" she snapped.

"Just what I said, Sister. He and I were close friends. The
King bound him about three weeks ago. He came to Grandon,
I stayed behind. I just got here. Last night, very late."

She gnawed her lip for a moment, although it was already
a gorgeous ruby shade. Plump, soft, moist lips . . . "Did you
hear from Bernard at all after he came to Court? Did he ever
mention me?"

Ah! "I heard not a word from him, Sister Gertrude, I
swear. Blades don't write letters much. Were you also his
friend?"

She turned her back on him. "I was," she told a holly tree.

"Then we have both suffered a very great loss."

She continued to stare into the shrubbery. He waited.

At last she said, "What do you want?"

"Justice for his murder."

"So do I." Sister Gertrude glanced up at the windows of the building. "I mustn't be seen talking with you. Follow me."

She pulled off her hat, spilling out a flood of raven-black hair, then plunged into the bushes. Bellman followed, hard put to keep up with her, even when they reached a cleared path. She barely came up to his shoulder, but she could move like a racehorse. She stopped abruptly on the edge of a pool overhung by willows. Golden fish moved between the cold underwater stones.

There she turned to look at him. "Tell me about yourself. Tell me all about yourself!"

He told her.

"And who did send those monsters?"

"I was hoping you could tell me, Sister. The shadowmen multiplied, turning their victims into horrors like themselves. But who or what started it? Where did it come from, and where did it go to after it killed the first Yeoman?"

She walked over to a stone bench almost hidden in the foliage, sat down, and started brushing leaves and twigs off her robe. She had left room beside her, which he took as an invitation. He had understood that women did not normally choose such secluded places for meetings with men they did not know. Sister Gertrude seemed quite oblivious to such concerns. She also looked capable of breaking his arm if he misbehaved.

"I don't know," she said, pouting. "And I cannot find out what the Mothers or the College are thinking."

"I was told that one of the Yeomen was slain with his own halberd and his dagger killed another. I was also told that you detected conjuration on one of the sentries as you were leaving."

"I have done nothing but answer questions about that

since it happened," she said grimly, staring at the pool. "It was a fluke that I happened to pass very close to him and happened to be sensitive to that particular combination of elements. Mother Celandine misinterpreted it, but that's not why she's . . ."

"She's what? Don't stop there!"

Trudy pouted. "Prostrate with guilt, poor old bat. No, where she went wrong was inside Quamast. I wanted to inspect something suspicious, and she wouldn't let me, because the reverend ancients had let it pass earlier in the day." She shrugged. "Of course she may have been less than usually sensitive to whatever I detected, but she should have given me the benefit of the doubt. That's what the Sisters are trying to cover up, Master Bellman—incompetence! What followed was a monstrous, horrible crime."

Did she mean the danger might still be there? Ringwood must hear this.

"Vile," Bellman said. "I cannot even think of a motive."

"But you have a theory! Tell me."

Surprised by her insight and a little amused at her vehemence, he said, "It is bizarre. I keep wondering if the attack was a fake to enlist His Majesty's sympathy for the apparent victim. If so, it succeeded, because Grand Duke Rubin now has two Blades."

"Have you met this Grand Duke?"

"A few times. Briefly."

"Describe him. What sort of person is he?"

"Middle aged, not plump, exactly, but he has a sedentary look to him. Not quite debauched . . . well used? But he's also courteous and patient. Ringwood's very happy with him. A bad-tempered, unreasonable ward can make a Blade's entire life a hell."

"Except what?" she demanded, looking around.

"Except nothing."

"No, you meant to say more. What?"

She might look like a buxom farm girl, but she had the mind of an inquisitor.

"Blades never gossip about their ward's affairs, even to their friends. But Ringwood asked me to find the witnesses—you or Mother Celandine, and also Sergeant Bates. The Blades of the Guard have told him all they can, but it's reasonable that he should want to talk to the other people who know something about his mortal enemies, for that is what they are, whoever did this."

"And?" she said.

"You will not repeat what I say?"

"I promise."

Bellman had already decided that Trudy would start a riot long before she would ever stoop to lying. "He also hinted that he wanted me to see what I could learn about the Grand Duke's background."

"You're joking! You mean Rubin is keeping secrets from his *Blades*?"

"Seems so. That makes no sense at all. They've had plenty of time to speak in private. Even the Guard doesn't seem to know how or why he lost his throne, or what he plans to do about it. Nothing. It's unusual for the Guard not to know what's going on." He felt disloyal saying that, although the Order was nothing to him now.

"The Sisters don't seem to, either, which is even stranger. We usually have sources the Blades don't. And Baron von Fader?"

"You are taking more information that you are giving, Sister. Let's hear your opinion of the Duke."

She flashed a smile. It was gone in an instant, for this was not a happy discussion, but it had made her look like an apple-cheeked child. "Fair enough! He wears a seeming."

"Spit!" Bellman said. "Fire and death! You mean he isn't

what he seems to be? But surely he would not be allowed near the King if he has been conjured?"

"I gathered he is not enchanted personally, it is something he wears."

"Even more, then. He should have been made to take it off." What had the Guard been thinking of?

"He may remove it when he is granted a private audience. In other words, Mother Superior and Commander Florian may know the truth."

"But they don't talk?"

"Correct. We were told it was a translating device, but it isn't. I don't know what it does exactly, but I think it probably changes his appearance."

"So do I!" Bellman's suspicions were confirmed.

"Why?" Sister Gertrude twisted her hair into a pile and slid her hat on top of it. "No, not now. I must go." She surged to her feet. "Are you staying at Quamast House, Master Bellman?"

"Yes." He stood up. He didn't want her to go. "I wish you'd just call me Bellman. I've gotten used to that name."

"Call me Trudy, then. I'll see you at midnight. I'm back on duty there. They took me off it, but I really want to have a close look at that medicine chest, so I told them it's like a horse."

"The medicine chest is like a horse?"

"Naw!" She grinned mischievously, displaying a fine set of teeth with one missing. She pointed to the gap. "See? You have to get right back in the saddle after being thrown." Her eyes twinkled. "I'm an expert at putting a horse over ninety percent of a hedge."

"My speciality is three-quarters of a ditch. Did they argue?" This story of incompetence—or even treachery?—in the Fellowship was worrying. Although the Guard rarely had good words to say about the Dark Chamber or the Yeomen, Bellman had never heard them speak ill of the White Sisters. He liked puzzles, but there were too many clues missing in this one.

"I can be loud when I want to be."

Very likely. Sister Gertrude's starched superiors must find her quite a handful and would not tolerate her unless she had real ability to back up her freewheeling ways. Hiding in bushes!

"The Duke is supping with the King," he said, "but they'll probably be back by then or soon after. I know Ringwood will want to talk with you."

"I'll bare my soul." With a grin and a slap on his shoulder as if he were a horse, she strode off along the path, swinging her arms.

Bellman headed the other way. Now he had to go back to Quamast and tell a pair of Blades that their ward was a fraud. That was not the safest procedure imaginable.

Yeomen were thick around Quamast House. They insisted on seeing his pass and then called for a Blade to vouch for him. Out came Sir Clovis, one of the senior members of the guard, wearing a gold sash, no less, which meant at least ten men. He regarded Bellman suspiciously.

"What's above the royal door?"

"Grand Master's bedroom."

Only then did he smile. "Pass, friend." He was showing off for the Yeomen. He knew Bellman perfectly well; they had fenced dozens of times.

The big hall held at least two dice games and several arguments. Even the King was not guarded so ostentatiously. Ringwood stood at the top of the stairs, so he must have been looking out the windows. He beckoned impatiently. Bellman ran up.

"Well?"

"It's not good news," Bellman said cautiously. Although Ringwood had been ahead of him in the school, he had always been too young for friendship, a boy to Bellman's youth, a youth when Bellman reached manhood. Recent changes had brought them closer together, and responsibility had already aged him. It had also made him dangerous.

He grinned. "I can see that. Go on, I won't kill you."

"Your ward wears a conjurement, a seeming. He is not what he seems."

Ringwood's eyes narrowed. He thought for a moment. "Do you know who he is or what he is?"

"No, but I think he's much younger than he pretends. I got suspicious the other night when he ran up the stair to the royal suite. It was the small hours of the morning and he'd had a grueling couple of days. The real Grand Duke is fifty years old! Men of that age don't behave like that. And he put his hands down to his thighs before he did it."

"Any more?"

"Yes. Next morning I snooped a little. After you all came down, I asked the Blades watching the stair if anyone had gone up, anyone at all. They said no. The Baron wears a full beard. Ranter was stubbly, but he's fair and doesn't bother to shave every day. Nor do you. Your ward looked fine. Did he shave in cold water, when all he had to do was pull a bell rope and ask for hot? If he's a fraud, then who is he? He can't be the *next* Grand Duke, he's an infant." Bellman realized how weak it all sounded. "None of it's proof, but it worried me. Then I learned about the seeming from Sister Gertrude."

The Blade brightened. "I must speak with her!"

"She's forbidden to speak with you. Fortunately she was so charmed by my profile that she promised to come here at midnight. Sergeant Bates is being kept under wraps, unavailable."

"You've done very, very well. Follow me!" Ringwood headed to one of the doors, knocked, and went in.

The knock might have been intended to avoid startling Ranter, who was standing by the window, being fussed over by an elderly man with pins in his mouth. The Grand Duke sat patiently on a stool. The Baron was perched on the edge of the bed, half-enveloped in the feather mattress, barrel legs dangling, flaccid face working in anger.

Bellman bowed to the Duke.

"He passed," Ringwood said. "Brilliantly. He worked it out and even discovered how you do it."

"Silence, fool!" the Baron shouted, pointing at the tailor.

The Duke ignored him, as he often did. "Congratulations, Master Bellman. You must give me lessons in where I went wrong."

"I . . . I had not realized I was being tested!" Bellman said coldly.

"Testing was not the original purpose. Sir Ringwood and I had a chat this morning. I asked him what you were doing for him and he confessed. We agreed this might be a fair judge of your abilities. Tailor, measure this man, also."

The tailor dropped a length of tape and took the pins out of his mouth to say, "I am most grateful to Your Royal Highness."

"Sire!" the Baron growled. "I have asked you what use is a blind swordsman, but you do not tell me. Your finances are already strained."

Rubin snapped out a sharp retort in a foreign tongue, then smiled again at Bellman. "But I am presuming you still want to enter my service. I promise you that King Athelgar is aware of what you discovered today and knew it when he so generously deeded me Blades."

Ringwood was grinning. Ranter was not, but Ranter often

scowled like that. Ringwood knew the truth, whatever it was, and he thought it was something to laugh at.

"In that case," Bellman said, much relieved, "I am indeed eager to serve Your Royal Highness."

• 6 •

𝓛ater, after Bellman had sworn to be true and been appointed the Grand Duke's equerry, a suitably vague title, he met the two servants who had accompanied their master into exile. Manfred was coachman and hostler. Harald served as secretary, valet, or footman as required, and sometimes man-at-arms before Ringwood and Ranter joined the team. Ringwood referred to them as Indoors and Outdoors, and made jokes about how miscast they seemed. They looked like a woodcutter and a clerk, but Harald Indoors was the amiable young giant, even beefier and blonder than Ranter. Manfred Outdoors was older and smaller, with a bookish stoop and a face like dried clay, cracked in worried wrinkles. Neither understood Chivian, so conversation was limited to smiles and handshakes.

At sunset Duke, Baron, and Blades went off to the royal supper and the guard was changed. The new Blade contingent was led by Sir Cedric, who had now won the King's Cup for fencing three years in a row and seemed to be the only Chivian capable of holding off challengers from Isilond. He had probably asked for this assignment just so he could check on Bellman. However fine his intentions, the world's best swordsman was a little too aware of his abilities, and Bellman was tired of being a medical curiosity.

"Go and get your sword, lad."

"I have abandoned swordsmanship and taken up embroidery."

"Then go and get your bodkin."

Seeing he could not escape the ordeal, Bellman fetched his sword and proceeded to let Cedric show him again how very bad he was as they danced back and forth in the big hall—Cedric forth and Bellman back. The moon was up to keep away shadowmen and the guest the Blades had come to guard was absent, so all the rest of the squad used the big staircase as a grandstand and watched in disgust and worry. They did not enjoy being reminded how easily their own skills might be destroyed.

"You're no worse," Cedric declared at last. "But you're certainly no better. Let's try it over there where there's less light."

Bellman said, "No! This is ridiculous. It would be suicide for me to wear this. Somebody see that it goes back to Ironhall."

He was answered with a chorus of protest.

"*Nonsense!*" Ansel's voice prevailed. "Bluff it, man, bluff it! You *look* like a swordsman. You *move* like a swordsman. Your stance, your wrist . . . The moment you draw, your opponent is going to change his mind and back down. Even if he doesn't, you are still a better-than-average fencer. Stay away from Blades and Sabreurs and you should have no trouble."

Bellman looked longingly at the superb weapon he held. "What do I name her? *Crutch? White Cane?*"

"*Bravado!*" Ansel shouted.

Everyone joined in the laughter and Bellman let himself be talked into hanging *Bravado* on his belt. He was only humoring his friends, after all. Soon he would be gone from their world and likely would never see any of them again.

*   *   *

Midnight sent Cedric's squad home and brought in others and a new flood of painful commiserations. The sash was around Sir Valiant, who evidently believed in Sister Gertrude's theory about getting back on the horse that threw you. He was faring better than Sergeant Bates of the Yeomen, but then Valiant had taken part in the battle and required a healing after it; that made a difference.

The newcomers had not even brought out their dice before a platoon of Yeomen delivered Trudy herself, who came marching in like a drill instructor. The resemblance did not end with her walk. Her dark-eyed appraisal made every man there wonder if his hose were wrinkled or his codpiece laces untied.

She spotted Bellman at once and flashed him a triumphant wink. He soon saw that her friendship with Bernard was widely known, for the ribaldry was subdued and a couple of remarks that went too far resulted in the speakers being savagely elbowed. But Trudy herself seemed determined to avoid sympathy or maudlin regrets, for she flirted with four men in rapid succession and cracked a couple of off-color jokes that made Bellman blink. He had not known young ladies behaved like that. He suspected from the Blades' delight that few did. Obviously Trudy was bluffing, for any man in her life other than Bernard would have been mentioned right away. Had she been warned that flirting with bound Blades was wrestling lightning? Most of them regarded their enhanced power over women as the best part of their wages. It was not the part they saved for their old age, either.

Watched by admiring eyes, she made a circuit of the hall, ending at the base of the great staircase, where Bellman was playing watchdog, determined to challenge anyone who tried to go up. He did not suspect Blades of stealing, but he

knew some of them were nosey. She grinned at him, showing her missing tooth.

"His Grace is not back yet." That was not a question.

"What makes you think so?" Bellman countered.

"I could sense him if he were. But there is something upstairs that I need to inspect." That was her duty.

"I shall be happy to escort you, Sister." As the group of
Blades surged forward, he added, "She must not be
crowded, Sir Valiant."

"The rest of you stay here."

"Race you!" Trudy said. She gathered up the front of her
robe and sprinted.

Bellman and Valiant let her win, but would have had trouble doing otherwise. She marched confidently around the
balcony to the door she wanted.

"In here."

Valiant looked to Bellman.

"The Baron's room," Bellman said.

Valiant was unhappy. "Sister Gertrude's testimony should
be adequate excuse to search it."

Bellman chuckled. "You expect me to fight you over it?"
He had no desire to see his friends or himself turned into
killer corpses. His duties for the Grand Duke did not include
sheltering a murderer, if that was what the Baron was.

"Extraterritoriality!" Valiant looked even more miserable.
"A visiting head of state? This building may legally be
Krupinese territory at the moment. There has been nothing
official from the Council, but I was warned to be careful."

Bellman weighed loyalties—to his new employer, his
king, his friends . . . "His Majesty has not awarded the
Grand Duke royal honors so far. His Highness did not instruct me to claim immunity from the laws of Chivial. I
might draw the line at letting you search his own room, but
the fact that he has accepted you as guards means that he ex-

pects you to perform your duties. If I get fired for this, I will be sorry, but I'm doing what I see as right."

"Thanks. Master Bellman," Valiant said formally, "the Royal Guard has reason to believe that there are illicit conjurements on these premises and will now exercise its right to inspect them."

Bellman grinned. "As the Grand Duke's representative, I reserve his right to lodge a complaint about this harassment."

"Oh, a pox on yours! No, let me open it, in case it's booby-trapped."

"You think I wouldn't *tell* you if it was booby-trapped?" Trudy said indignantly.

It was locked.

Valiant shouted down to his men and East came running up with a huge ring of keys. On the third try, Valiant found one that worked and threw the door open. The room was vast enough to hold a four-poster as large as a haystack, two palatial sofas, four chairs, a couple of tables, a washstand, a desk, and a bookcase, and still seem spacious. The carpets were thick, window drapes sumptuous, tapestries intricately patterned. Without hesitation, Trudy strode across to a pair of studded cowhide traveling boxes, shabby and well-used, seeming strangely out of place amid such luxury.

"This one. Don't touch it!" she added quickly as the men arrived beside her.

"Warding cord?" An innocent-looking rope had been tied around the box that interested her, secured with a very simple knot.

"Definitely. It's not the same conjuration the inquisitors use, but there's enough death in it to hurt you."

"I do believe this trunk was inspected when His Grace arrived," Valiant said, uncomfortable again.

Trudy flashed her big grin at him. "But not opened. And now we have five deaths to explain. I'm surprised the coroner hasn't impounded this box as evidence. Move that one out of the way, please, Bellman. And lift this one away from the wall, but *don't* touch the rope." Then she dropped on her hands and knees to peer along the top and sides of the box, moved around it to try the same thing from other angles. No wonder the Sisters were known as sniffers.

"There's a lot of odd stuff in here," she muttered. "All mixed up together. That is a way of hiding death elementals, of course. Can't make anything dangerous *without* a death component. Hard to make almost anything without at least a trace of it."

Now Valiant was even more uneasy. "I thought you said last time that you could detect anything really deadly from downstairs?"

Trudy sat back on her heels, looking frustrated. "Mother Celandine said that, and now she's catatonic. But I sensed this box from downstairs far more readily tonight than I did a week ago—I don't think even she would ignore it now. And it's not as simple as she said, anyway. What I'm detecting in there is several small conjurations. Yes, those may be jars of pills or ointments. Or purges," she added with an unladylike leer. "But there's at least two that feel scary, *really* scary. They're also very localized, very small. That makes them hard to analyze at a distance, of course. It is not impossible to make something very small and very deadly! A poison pill conjured with fire to speed up its action is difficult to sense. I know, because they tried to trick us with that one on a test at Oakendown and I was the only one in the class to get it. We're taught exceptions like that and then tend to forget them when we don't meet them in real life."

She couldn't have more than a month's real-life experience if she had arrived at the palace about the time Bernard did. Trudy certainly did not lack confidence in her own abilities.

Bellman said, "Were you told to examine this box closely tonight?"

She looked up with a conspiratorial grin. "I was told to be thorough."

"How tactful of them!" Valiant said furiously. "Are they having cold feet or second thoughts? Or both? Have you any idea what the next session of Parliament is going to say about spiritual murders inside the King's palace?"

"That's why the old dears are flapping like chickens," Trudy said, grinning.

"What do you want me to do, Sister? Is this box dangerous enough for me to order it removed at once, or will it wait until the Baron returns to open it? Or," he added hopefully, "will it wait until tomorrow?"

She shrugged. "I think it will wait until the Duke returns. And so will I. Why don't you put a guard on it for now and inform my escort that they needn't wait for me?"

Valiant's eye settled on Sir East lurking in the background. After delivering the keys, he had remained to snoop with a nosiness worthy of Hazard himself.

His commander smiled. "Good of you to have volunteered, brother! Stay in this room and let nobody touch that box."

East pouted. "All by myself?"

"Read a book. Exercise that mess you call a mind."

"You'll soon have the Baron to keep you company," Bellman said helpfully. "You can read him a bedtime story."

East glared at him.

"What's in here?" Valiant crossed to a second door and threw it open.

Voices yelled in outrage. Little Manfred came storming into the room. Harald, the pale ox, loomed in behind him without his normal smile.

Valiant tried to explain—in Chivian. Shouting and gesticulating, the two servants were obviously ordering the intruders out. Harald looked ready to start picking them up and throwing. Bellman tried to mediate, pointing to the royal insignia on the Blades' livery. Everyone got louder and louder.

* 7 *

Sister Gertrude, however, was enjoying the confusion. Her new supervisor, Mother Evangeline, had approved Trudy's request to be returned to the Quamast night patrol with almost no argument at all. When her friend Sister Seamist had heard this news, she had been instantly suspicious.

"They're setting you up!" she said. Seamist had been Trudy's best friend all through Oakendown and was still her best friend here in the palace—very supportive and great company, even if she couldn't tell a love potion from a vomitive at arm's length.

Trudy was suspicious, too, but didn't care much. "Possibly. Not bothering to open the medicine chest? Calling a seeming a 'translation device'? I ask you! Pull the other one."

Seamist's eyes opened very wide. "Sister Gertrude! Surely you are not suggesting that the Reverend Mothers are covering their ethereal asses?"

"Do Reverend Mothers even have asses, Sister Seamist?"

They sniggered in unison.

"Just what are you trying to achieve?" Seamist asked.

"I want justice for Bernie! But at least I'll get to meet a Grand Duke. And a lot of slinky Blades."

Seamist shuddered. To her Blades stank worse than rotten eggs.

"Besides," Trudy added, "it's the only bear-baiting in town. All I ever do is stand around watching other people have fun. I never thought palace life would be so *boring*!"

Now it wasn't. That traveling box was definitely unboring. It made her skin crawl.

Adventure loomed. And so did young men. Although he lacked the shine of a bound Blade, Master Bellman had a quiet, nonspiritual sparkle of his own. Seamist would say he was obviously dependable and dependable just meant dull, but he was good company. As for Sir Valiant's current gaggle of Blades, they were entertaining, although none could compare with Bernard. Trudy had just reached that melancholy conclusion when she detected the glow of two more Blades beyond the outside door, and then the Grand Duke's seeming. She could sense a Blade binding at thirty-three paces. She'd measured it.

The moment the Duke and his train entered the hall, tumult broke out. The big servant, Harald, began shouting from the balcony in whatever language he used. The Baron roared back. Then the smaller servant, who had been keeping watch on the Blade keeping watch on the box, appeared and joined in the shouting. The Duke looked to Bellman, who explained.

"We must discuss this, Sir Valiant," His Highness said, and led the way upstairs to the audience room.

Trudy was not impressed by the Grand Duke so far. If his seeming could manage nothing better than that worn-out, decayed look, then his real appearance must be gruesome indeed.

Nor did she think much of the audience room, which was smaller than the Baron's bedchamber, and unpleasantly stuffy, with crazy insects hurling themselves around the candles. The tapestries were heavy and faded, moth-eaten in

places, and the ceiling frescoes had suffered water damage.
The Duke settled on a raised chair of estate on a low dais at
one end, which gave him a royal heft he had lacked before.
A dozen or so ordinary chairs were set around the walls, but
he did not invite anyone else to sit, so they stood around in
a half-circle facing him: Bellman, Sir Valiant, the gross
Baron, one servant—the big blond one—and Trudy. The little wrinkled man had gone back to guarding the guard
guarding the box. The Duke's new Blades were also there,
one on either side of his chair. They were an odd couple, one
short, dark, and surprisingly young, the other fair and husky.
He winked at her. Before she could decide whether his
blondness and beefy calves justified such brashness, she was
pulled into the discussion.

"Sister, er, Gertrude," the Grand Duke said. "That atrocity last week was only the latest in a series of attacks directed at me. I have been hounded across Eurania by them,
and I have no doubt that they originate back in Krupina. I
even know who is behind them, although I cannot prove it.
Now you are suggesting that they are local in origin. You are
accusing some member of my entourage of five attempts to
kill me and the deaths of more than a dozen people! These
are serious charges."

Oh no! It would make an interesting start and even more
interesting sudden end to her career, but Trudy was not going
to be trapped that easily. "Your, er, Grace. With respect, I did
not say any such thing! I merely report that there are many
conjurations inside that box and some are dangerous. Even
deadly. They should be properly inspected. That's all I say."

"The box was approved by the White Sisters when we arrived. It was inspected on the very night of the attack."

"That was me that night, Your Grace. Five men died soon
after. Nobody opened it, either time. Nobody even went
close to it. And it has changed since then."

The Duke frowned. "And were you told to reexamine it tonight?"

"No, Your Grace. I was merely told to do my duty."

"Did you not do your duty the first time?"

"I was not in charge that night. I wanted to inspect the box more closely and was overruled. Sir Valiant can support my testimony."

Sir Valiant nodded, but the Duke kept his frown aimed at her.

"You are certainly implying, even if you are being careful not to say so, that something in that box can be used to summon shadowmen. But the only people who have access to the box were all in this building that night. The perpetrator would have drawn danger upon himself."

She had never crossed swords with a head of state before, but nor did she let Mother Superior browbeat her, and she was not about to kowtow to old Baggy-eyes.

"I am not a conjurer. I don't know how to summon shadowmen, although I suspect you'd start by using some special sort of contagious poison to kill the first one. That would be easier than shooting a conjured arrow all the way from Krupina, wouldn't it? All I am saying—"

"*She says too much!*" the Baron roared. "Sire, this is intolerable insolence!"

Grand Duke Rubin nodded as if agreeing, but what he said was, "I may have been listening too much and thinking too little. Continue, Sister."

That was flattering. "It's late, Your Grace. If I'm wrong and everything in that box is harmless, then the Fellowship will certainly discipline me and apologize to his lordship. Why don't you let the Blades guard it until tomorrow, and then we can bring in more Sisters and take a look? I am very good, but having more opinions is always a smart idea in sniffing."

"Your Majesty knows very well that everything in that box is harmless!" the Baron shouted.

"You're lying," said Trudy.

Hm. Not diplomatic. Everyone was staring at her in shock. The Baron was turning purple, about to set his whiskers on fire. Even the Grand Duke was frowning again, and he'd almost been on her side.

"I shouldn't have said that, Your Grace."

"No, you certainly should not!"

"But not because it isn't true! It's just that we're not supposed to claim truth-sounding powers. The inquisitors do that. Most White Sisters can do it, too, because words are made of air, obviously, plus wisdom, which means light, which is largely fire. So words are air and fire plus a little earth for solidity. But lies also contain death and water. Water for shapelessness. So a lot of Sisters can truth-sound as well as the snoops do, but it's not part of our claim, so I'm not supposed to mention it." She pouted at the fat old Baron. "He *was* lying."

"Your Highness!" the old man screamed.

The Duke raised a hand for quiet, smiling gently. "Remember, Baron, you said I knew very well that everything in the box is harmless. Obviously I do not, because I did not pack it and have very little idea of what's in it. I know only what you have told me. Had you asserted that you knew the box contained nothing harmful, then your statement would have been strictly true."

Everyone waited for the fat man to accept that invitation, but he didn't. He fumed, "It is still intolerable! My honor has never been questioned before. For full ten generations my forebears have born arms for Krupina. All my life I have served. And now you submit me to this! The wench should be whipped. King Athelgar must apologize in person!"

The Duke sighed. "It is late. Sir Valiant, please guard the

box until morning. His Majesty waived inspection of my baggage, but to clear all suspicion in this matter, we shall do as Sister Gertrude suggested."

"Intolerable!" the Baron roared. He spun around with remarkable agility for a sack of custard and waddled rapidly to the door. The big fair-haired servant ran to open it for him and followed him out.

After a moment, the Grand Duke said, "What you're all thinking is impossible. Ernst von Fader is no conjurer. He cannot have been behind those murders, never! I have known him for years and no one has been more faithful to me. He has lost everything in my cause. Am I lying, Sister Gertrude?"

"No, Your Grace."

He smiled at her. There was something lacking in his smiles. He did not smile at her the way most men did. Not like that lecherous leer coming from the taller Blade, or even the boy's shy yearning. Bellman wasn't smiling at all. Nor was Sir Valiant.

It was to him that the Grand Duke spoke next. "We thank you for your service. I assume you can provide the Sister with an escort when she leaves? We do need a final word with her first, though."

Sir Valiant took the hint. Saluting, he withdrew, and when the door closed the company was down to Trudy and four men. Interesting odds, Seamist would say.

The Grand Duke took a moment to study his signet ring. Then he said, "Do you sense conjuration upon me, Sister?"

"Yes, Your Grace."

"What is it?"

"A seeming of some sort. It probably changes your appearance in some way."

He nodded. "I will be leaving Chivial soon, to continue my quest for justice, my mission to overthrow the

usurper. It may be a long and painful campaign. When
King Athelgar offered me Blades, he said that I needed
some White Sisters to go with them. Without Sisters I
would have only half a team, he said, but he could not
command the Sisters, he could only ask. Tonight he told
me that Mother Superior had canvassed the entire Fellowship and no Sister wished to volunteer."

What!?

He smiled at her expression. "You were not asked?"

"No, Your Grace! I didn't hear of anyone else being
asked, either." The more she saw of the workings of the Fellowship, the more it seemed like a toothless gaggle of incompetent old women.

"Well, keep it in mind." Rubin rose and stepped down
from the dais. Everyone else shifted, sensing an end to the
meeting. "I have been promising my Blades and Master
Bellman that I would tell them the whole story. I have de-
layed too long. If you will give me your word not to repeat
what you hear, then I invite you to stay and listen."

She hesitated, wondering if her oath allowed her to keep
secrets from her superiors. Mother Evangeline was a terrible
gossip. She thought, too, of that veiled invitation to enter the
Grand Duke's service. Palace life was *dull,* just endless
standing beside doorways as visitors trooped in and out, or
against the walls at parties, watching other people enjoy
themselves.

"I swear, Your Highness."

He noticed the honorific and nodded acknowledgment.
"Then let us make ourselves comfortable, and I will tell all
four of you. Lock the door, Sir Ranter. Mine is a sad tale, but
you can testify to the others later, Sister, that it is a true one.
Now sit, all of you."

He pulled a chair around to face two others, and Bellman
quickly dragged in two more to make a circle.

*   *   *

Bellman had watched the Trudy-Baron match with amusement and no little admiration. From all he had been told about the White Sisters' prim and stuffy ways, she must be a mammoth-sized gadfly for them, and the fact that she was tolerated at all suggested that she must have considerable ability.

"Master Bellman?"

"Sire?"

"Sir Ringwood said that you had penetrated my disguise. I want to hear where I slipped up. I have been living my role for months and thought I was close to perfect."

"I suspected nothing, sire, until you ran upstairs in Main House. Under the circumstances, that surprised me in a man of your apparent years. This evening I watched Trudy do that, and she first lifted the front of her robe so she would not trip over the hem. You made the same gesture, although you were wearing hose. I snooped and learned that you either did not shave or were content to do so in cold water."

The duke laughed. "Well done! Sir Ringwood inspected my baggage that night and discovered some garments not normally worn by dukes, grand or otherwise. As my Blade, he told no one except Sir Ranter."

Ringwood grinned. Ranter pouted.

"I told them today . . . that's yesterday now. Now I will show them, and you. Everything I said was true, except I switched identities." He reached both hands to the back of his neck and fumbled. "I wear a locket containing a miniature of Grand Duke Rubin of Krupina. It is a conjurement to make the wearer look like him." He lifted the ends of the chain and pulled the locket free of his collar. "In fact I am his wife, Grand Duchess Johanna."

His image shimmered and blurred, startling Bellman, who blinked until he decided his eyes were not at fault this time.

The Grand Duke had gone and in his place sat a girl. She was slender and radiantly beautiful, despite her unflattering male garb, and the way her golden hair had been crudely coiled up and pinned on top of her head.

Trudy let out a yelp. The others just stared. The Grand Duchess smiled as she surveyed their reaction, yet her pleasure failed to cover a deep sadness in her sapphire-pale eyes.

"Sir Ringwood, Sir Ranter, now you see your ward. The conjuration is very effective, but it has its limits. It changes my face very well, my upper body fairly well, but it cannot make my feminine calves look as manly as my husband's and I dared not trust it to deal with communal bathing. Did my modesty in the Forge start the juices of suspicion flowing, Sir Ringwood?"

Ringwood was glowing with joy at the transformation. "Not at all, Your Highness."

"No regrets, I hope?"

Ranter muttered a surly, "No." A lifelong binding was less attractive when his ward was his own age, instead of thirty years older.

Ringwood said, "Oh, no, Your Highness! I mean, I thought His Highness was . . . I am sure His Highness is a very fine Grand Duke, but you're . . ." He blushed scarlet and his voice trailed away. Ringwood was smitten already.

So was Bellman. Oh, spirits! She was gorgeous. Trudy disappeared in her presence. He felt like a boy compared to her. Now he understood the "Grand Duke's" curiously gentle manners. She should learn to use more bad language.

"I thank you both." She sighed. "Master Bellman, your oath is revocable, as theirs is not. Do you wish to leave my service now?"

"Never, Your Highness!" He was tempted to say that he would serve without pay forever if he could just have one of those smiles each day. The pain that lurked behind them tore at his heart. "I trusted you when I knew you were not what you seemed and I certainly trust you now."

But she could never trust him as she trusted her bound Blades. He could swear absolute loyalty and mean it, but without the conjuration it could never be the same. Human fidelity could fail.

"Sister Trudy?"

"Just what Bellman just said, Your Highness! This is wonderful!"

"Is it? Is it truly? Nay, it is worse than before, for I am still an exile and now you see I am of common stock. I lack rank and breeding. My husband is dead or a prisoner, I know not which. My infant son is dispossessed and in mortal danger, for he will certainly be murdered if his uncle finds him. My efforts to enlist support from the rulers of Eurania have met with no support, at least until now, here in faraway Chivial, where your King and Queen have been wonderfully kind. But even they will be glad to see me go."

"Why?" Ranter snapped.

"Because death follows me everywhere. Also—although less in their case than elsewhere—because I am not of noble birth. That was why your King refused to grant me the royal honors he would have shown the real Grand Duke. My father was a mere knight, Erich von Schale. He owed knight's service to the lord of Fadrenschloss, Baron von Fader, as his forebears had for generations. He followed the Baron's banner in his youth, but when I knew him his fighting days were long over; he was a farmer who shoed his own horses and helped bring in his own hay. I barely remember my mother, for she died trying to give me a brother. Sir Ringwood?"

"Your Highness?"

"I was much moved by your story. How old were you when your father brought you to Ironhall?"

"Almost thirteen, Your Grace."

"I, too, lost my father when I was twelve. He cut his foot and the wound festered. Had he asked the Baron for help, the Baron would have sent him to Vamky with gold for a healing, but he was too proud to beg. When the Baron heard the news and rode to our cottage, my father was on his deathbed. Ernst swore he would take care of me. That was his duty as liege, but he meant it, which matters infinitely more. I moved into his house and he was wonderfully kind to me. Fadrenschloss was a rambling old place, part ancient castle and part modern timber house, comfortable but still defensible. He had no family left, so it would revert to the Grand Duke when he died. I lived there for two years. Of course I mourned my father, but they were two wonderful years.

"But I must tell you also of the villain in the story, Lord Volpe. He is Rubin's uncle, but only a year older. They grew up together in the palace in Krupa and I have heard hints that they disliked each other in those days. Volpe may have resented that he was not Grand Duke Hans's heir although he was the elder. Rubin may have been frightened of Volpe, for he is prone to wild rages and Rubin is . . . peaceable. My husband would rather outfox a foe than fight him. I do know he would sometimes accuse his uncle of being illegitimate, for Volpe was born eight months after his father's death and thirty years after his only brother. By the time I came on the scene, they had long been reconciled. Rubin obviously trusted his uncle, for he had appointed him Provost of Vamky, which made him the most powerful man in the realm, more dangerous than the Grand Duke himself.

"You know that highborn families everywhere have trouble dealing with younger sons. Dividing an inheritance weakens it, so in most of Eurania the firstborn takes all. Rulers have this problem more than any, and none more than the Grand Dukes of Krupina, for their realm is too small to support numerous royal offspring. Letting them die nobly in battle is usually the preferred solution, but Krupina has historically avoided war as much as possible. Krupina's solution is to enroll surplus sons in the Vamky Brotherhood and send them off as mercenaries to die in other people's wars.

"The brethren are sworn to poverty, celibacy, and complete obedience to their abbot. Their fortified monastery at Vamky controls the Pilgrim Pass, the northern gateway to the realm. Contingents of its knights are always in demand as warriors, usually supported by conjurers, for the brethren know more than anyone else about the use of elementals in warfare. All the money from these contracts flows into the coffers of the Brotherhood, so it is very rich. It has the only standing army in the realm, so obviously whoever controls the brethren can control Krupina, and the Abbot is a man of enormous power. Successive Grand Dukes have sought to control him by appointing a provost as a sort of co-ruler. In theory the Provost controls the military side and foreign contracts, while training and discipline are the domain of the Abbot. The division of power is complicated and does not always work, but by appointing his heir to be Provost, Rubin was only following tradition."

"Celibacy?" Ranter said. "That means they don't do it with women?"

"It means they are forbidden to marry. They are supposed to have no dealings at all with women, but of course no one is perfect. Their discipline is strict and the punishments dire." His ward looked around the meeting with another of her wistful smiles. "It is almost morning. Do you want me to stop?"

"Certainly not, Your Grace," Ringwood said. "We must know these things if we are to help you."

"Very well, I will be as brief as I can. The Baron's Fadrenschloss is close to Vamky, in the north of Krupina, where the land narrows between the ranges. You could see the monastery from the top of the tower. Most of the hills are wooded, home to deer and wild boar, even bears. Eagles ride the winds there and the mountains keep their winter plumage until high summer. One shining fall day when the hills were golden, Grand Duke Rubin rode through the area. He was hunting.

"What he found was me."

II

from a find to a Check

◆ 1 ◆

Ah, what have we here? A forest primrose?"

Johanna wheeled in surprise to locate the speaker. Having spent the day helping the hands with the harvest, she had come home to find the bailey full of horses and unfamiliar men, some of them liveried swordsmen, others in the green garb of foresters. The Baron's grooms were rushing around, trying to cope with this sudden invasion of loud, impatient strangers. The Fadrenschloss hounds had scented the visiting pack, and both were baying furiously.

The man who had addressed her was portly, of middle years, and must be the noble whose train this was, for his riding garb of lovat leather outclassed anything else in the courtyard, from his spurs to the feather in his cap. He carried a falconer's glove tucked in his belt and a silver hunting horn hung on a jeweled baldric. She ought to curtsy to a visiting lord, but something about the way he was looking at her froze her to the spot.

The evening sun blazed in a sky as vast and blue as summer. She was weary and happily sweaty, for harvesting was joyful work involving every able-bodied soul living in or near Fadrenschloss, from toddlers to elders. The boys all worked bare-chested, leading to much chaffing and hinting, flirting and promises that might or might not be kept when the day was done. Girls no older than herself were being seriously courted.

"Well?" asked the nobleman. "What is your name, little primrose?"

Her green linen shift was a better-quality garment than the peasant girls wore, but very far from being ladies' wear. Her hair, tied back with a ribbon, had been bleached by summer to flax, so the thought flashed through her mind that she was more fittingly a daisy than a primrose. She found her manners and bobbed a curtsy.

"Johanna Schale, my lord." At once she guessed that she had given him the wrong title.

"A pretty name for a very pretty girl. Such lovely brown arms!" He must be joking, for only peasants were brown. Fashionable ladies had very pale skin, the paler the better. His finger snaked out to lift the edge of a shoulder strap and he added, "and pale shoulders."

"My lord!" She recoiled, knowing he was thinking of more than shoulders.

He frowned reprovingly at her reaction. "Who is your father, Johanna?"

"My father died two years ago. I am the Baron's ward . . . my lord." Horses and men were moving around, but none of them looked in her direction, as if she were invisible, or hidden in some dungeon far away, locked up with this man. They could not, would not, see her.

"How old are you?"

"Fourteen, my lord."

"You live here, in the castle?"

She nodded, seriously frightened now.

"Then we shall get to know each other during my stay." His heavy lips shaped a smile. "You don't know who I am, do you? Let me show you a picture. There! You know me now?"

Finger and thumb, he held up a coin, a glittering golden kru. She had seen krus before, although even the Baron rarely had need to use them. This one looked fresh-minted, but bore an old image, a much younger Grand Duke.

"I beg Your Highness's pardon!" She attempted a ball-room curtsy in a peasant smock.

He bent to raise her, soft hand closing about her upper arm. "You are forgiven already, Johanna. I do hope we can be friends while I am here, enjoying your guardian's cele-brated hospitality. Perhaps I will leave you that picture of me when I go, mm? As a memento of our happy hours to-gether?" He did not release her, holding her close, smiling.

What sort of happy hours had he in mind that he was of-fering her gold for them? Was she some gutter trollop to be so insulted?

Before she could think of a suitable but polite response— and maybe there was none—the Baron himself came wad-dling at high speed across the bailey, obviously hastily garbed in his best, for the laces on his jerkin were undone and his hose wrinkled. "Your Royal Highness!" He doffed his cap to make a courtly bow and display scanty white hair all awry. "This indeed is an honor! Had Your Grace only warned us, Fadrenschloss would have prepared a fabled feast to celebrate—*make yourself presentable, girl*—such a historic occasion. But if Your Highness will doubly honor us by extending his visit for a few days . . ."

Johanna jerked her arm free and fled.

*   *   *

A ducal visit required only the best, but Johanna's best was very ordinary. In two years, maybe three, she would be launched onto the social stage. The Baron had promised her that, and a rich dowry to win a fine husband, too. When the time came, she would have gowns and jewels and perfumes. But not yet. At the moment her best was a simple brown linen with puffed shoulders and hand-me-down lace over a square décolletage. Heidi, who was her lady's maid when she wasn't being chambermaid, plaited her hair in a tail for her. Johanna pinned a discreetly feathered toque on top of her head, and set off in search of her guardian. She needed guidance in how to handle a rutting ruler.

The living quarters at Fadrenschloss were known as the New Wing, but were themselves ancient and much muddled by repeated attempts to improve them. The Baron would certainly have conducted his visitor to the guest suite so His Royal Highness could refresh himself after his journey. When Rubin had completed his toilet, he would likely monopolize the Baron for the rest of the day, and perhaps several days to come, so Johanna must consult him before he was caught up in the duties of being a host.

She hurried first to the solar, up a narrow stair from the banqueting hall. Finding the door ajar, she peered in and saw it was empty, only a dusty bottle and two crystal goblets on a silver tray giving lonely warning that the visitor would be entertained here shortly.

The only other door at the stair head led to the Baron's own chamber, and that was closed. Since he had already changed, he was unlikely to be in there, but she knocked anyway. A voice already familiar bade her enter, just as she saw von Fader plodding up after her, filling the stairway from wall to wall. Oh, horrors! He had given up his own chamber to his royal guest and she was knocking on the Duke's door.

Again he called for her to enter, perhaps expecting his valet or baggage or shaving water or something. What a delightful surprise he would find if he came to investigate! The Baron made heavy work of stairs and had not noticed her. She plunged into the solar to hide. It was a small room, full of large, shabby chairs, one desk, and a couple of muniment chests. Those were kept locked, because this room also served the Baron as a countinghouse, so the only possible refuge was the fireplace, whose blackened stonework was concealed in summer by a tapestry screen. There was just room for Johanna to crouch in behind it, among the soot and cold ashes, well aware that she had already ruined her best dress.

Voices outside the door . . .

Then inside it. Oh, spirits! Could they hear the thunder of her heart?

". . . partridge galore up there," the Baron said. "Early in the season for boar, but if Your Grace fancies that excitement—"

The Duke laughed. "No! I leave such nonsense to the young and foolish. These roe deer you mentioned . . ." A chair creaked under someone's weight.

For a while the two men talked game. It sounded as if the Duke planned to use Fadrenschloss as his hunting lodge for several days. As the Baron's liege, he could claim such privilege. Glasses clinked. Johanna was convinced that she was about to vomit from sheer terror. She should not be eavesdropping on the Grand Duke and her guardian! If they discovered her, the Baron would have no option but to order her whipped, or even just handed over to serve Rubin's pleasure.

"That girl I was talking with, Ernst? A pretty thing."

"When she grows up she will be a great beauty."

"She's one already. Skin like porcelain! Lowborn, though?"

"Her father was the best of my knights, a most fine man. I swore to him on his deathbed that I would see his daughter well and honorably married." The Baron's voice had taken on its stubbornest tone. "Of course she is too young to be thinking of marriage for years yet."

The Duke's laugh was metallic, unpleasant. "I'd wager you would find girls her age suckling babes in your own kitchens, my lord baron." Pause. "Of course I would make a generous donation toward her dowry. I know of several young men of promise in need of a wife."

"Your Grace is most generous, but shortage of suitors will not be a problem, and I have already made provision for Johanna's dowry.·I confess that I have grown attached to her over the last couple of years. She is a great comfort to me in my old age. There is no need for Your Highness to worry on her account."

A longer pause, while Johanna frantically wondered what signals were being exchanged by eyes and eyebrows and silent lips.

The Duke broke the silence. "She must be a remarkable comfort?"

"Sire!" Von Fader's roar might be audible down in the bailey. "That is an unworthy slight upon my honor."

"Oh, Ernst!" The Duke yawned. "We are both men of the world. You know what I want. If she is not yours, she can be mine to cuddle for a few days. A little experience will help prepare her for marriage and do her no harm. No one need know. Name a price."

"My life!"

Pause again. Johanna heard a goblet being set down.

"You are being foolishly dramatic. I claim your allegiance!"

"I am Your Highness's man in the ways of chivalry and always have been. I have risked my carcass many times for you and your father. I am loyal to you in all things, except this: I will *not* pimp my ward to any man's lusts! An honorable liege would not ask this."

The chair creaked again. When the Duke spoke, his voice came from farther away.

"Do not provoke me, von Fader! I have ways of getting what I want."

"I will go to the scaffold before I surrender."

A harsh laugh . . . the door closing . . . the Baron's heavy tread across the floor . . . a bolt being shot . . .

"You can come out now," he said.

He lifted the screen away, and Johanna crawled out in a shower of ash. Still on hands and knees, she peered warily up at him. From that angle he looked like a gigantic storm cloud, and his face was purple with fury.

"Disgusting! I should have you sweep the chimney while you look like that. Stand up and don't come near me!"

"Thank you, my lord," she whispered, rising. "I don't want to cause you trouble." She had never seen Ernst von Fader so enraged.

"*You* are no trouble!" He spun around and marched to the far side of the room. "You will swear me an oath now, Johanna Schale! You will swear me the most solemn oath of your life. You shall not give in to that disgusting lecher. No matter what he offers you or what he threatens, you shall refuse and keep on refusing." Back he came, still blazing, glaring down at her. "You will be polite and respectful at all times, but you *shall* refuse him." He loomed over her. "Swear!"

She swore as he dictated.

He turned to fill a wineglass, leaving her still shedding ash by the fireplace. His tone became flatter, duller, more guarded. "He is not a bad ruler, Rubin. Better than his father or grandfather. But he does have a weakness for young girls.

Everyone knows about it, and it probably does little harm if both the girl and her parents are agreeable. He cannot marry." The Baron handed her the goblet without meeting her eye. This conversation must be intensely painful for him, for he would never normally criticize his liege lord or discuss carnal matters with a young woman. Johanna knew much more about those than he realized, just from listening to the palace staff.

"Normally," the Baron growled, "he confines his attentions to the lower classes, and he is reputedly generous. In Krupa they use girls as bribes to win contracts, promotions, preferments, or high office. But a nobleman's ward is not for sale!"

"Why? I mean why did you say His Highness cannot marry?" The wine trembled unheeded in the goblet she held.

Ernst wheeled his bulk around and stomped back to the window. "Because Grand Dukes of Krupina have always married royalty—usually minor royalty, to be sure, but royalty. Rubin was married twice, when he was very young, and both wives died in curious circumstances. That is enough to shut the ruler of a wren-sized dukedom out of the market for princesses. His debauchery doesn't help, for it is well known. He has an adequate heir in his uncle and seems content to leave matters so." The old man turned to scowl at Johanna. "I can't send him packing, as I would any other man who spoke to you as he did. I can't send you off to some neighbor's—that would be insult now he has met you. We'll just have to put up with him until his eye lights on someone else. I'll pass the word among the servants, and hope some lass gets ambitious. Meanwhile you will sleep in the foxhole, and by day you must never go around without companions."

For two weeks Johanna was never alone, except at night, when she slipped away to sleep in the foxhole.

No one knew who had made the foxhole or when. Had it been able to speak, it would doubtless have told many hair-raising tales of fugitives, escapes, and betrayals, some of them centuries old, others not. Even searchers who had reason to believe such a place existed would need weeks to find it, for it was cunningly concealed within the thickness of the tower wall. Ernst himself had never had need to use it, but he kept it in good order—the secret door, the warning bell, the cunningly placed spyholes that let occupants keep watch on events outside. Cramped though it was, it was set high in the tower and did not trigger Johanna's lifelong dread of being underground.

Mealtimes were bad, when she had to sit beside the Duke and endure his wiles, but most days he went hunting. Evenings were the worst, because then she had to attend him in the solar, and his propositioning became much more blatant, provoking outraged protests from the Baron. For a notorious seducer, Rubin was curiously inept. Spotty-faced farm boys could spin a far better line than he could, as she knew from experience. He offered her wealth and jewels, dropped hints of land and a baronetcy that she could pass on to a son when she had one. She should be flattered, but she felt soiled instead. He never thought of taking her hunting, or inviting her to Court, or trying anything other than straight bribery. He ignored the pretty servant girls who flitted and flirted around him.

He could hardly hope to bribe the Baron, who was rich and very old, but he could threaten him, and did so. Another fifty retainers swarmed in from Krupa and ate like locusts, emptying the castle larders and forcing Seneschal Priboi to buy supplies from far and wide, at great expense. Ancient land claims and lawsuits were mined from the state archives and brandished over von Fader's wealth and even his title. These tactics terrified Johanna, so that she privately begged to be allowed to submit and get it over with, but they merely made the old man more furious, more stubborn. He swore he would never surrender.

Then the Duke did.

Rumor said the chase had gone badly that day, which meant he would be more persistent than ever—after a good hunt he was usually more ready to settle for a couple of bottles of wine and an early night. As soon as his train had been observed riding up the road, Johanna had headed for the safety of the kitchen, where she tried not to get in the way of the frantic dinner preparations. Soon the tattlers reported that Duke and Baron were closeted in the solar. She waited for the usual summons. And waited. The food was ready. Then the food was spoiling. Whatever was going on?

At last a page came for her, but when she reached the solar she was surprised to find the Baron alone, staring out the window. He did not turn when she shut the door.

"You sent for me, my lord?"

"Yes," he told the little diamond panes. "I did. I have news. We have lost, my dear. Or won, I do not know. Or his lust has won." His voice was slurred and two wine bottles lay empty on the floor. "My liege lord has asked for my ward's hand in marriage, and I can see no honorable way to refuse him." Then he did turn, to see what she thought.

She was so startled that the words made no sense to her. *"Marriage?"*

The fat man nodded gloomily. "Full legal marriage, no morganatic nonsense. Grand Duchess Johanna. He has decided the succession matters after all. He *says* he wants an heir. Your son will inherit the dukedom, my dear."

If the sun had reversed course and come storming up over the hills again, she could not have been more surprised. "But is that not wonderful news, marvelous news, my lord?"

He grunted. "Rubin is forty-six years old and not a very glamorous lover. I suppose women can put up with that, or there wouldn't be so many of us around. He will not give up his philandering, I am certain. You do know what happened to his first two wives?"

The sun quickly ducked out of sight. "Not really, my lord." There had been hints.

"The first died of a fever. So did many others that year, although the rich were mostly able to afford the necessary healings. Unfortunately the Grand Duchess was sensitive to spirituality and put off summoning the conjurers until too late. So it was reported. His second was even younger. A month after the wedding, she had a dizzy spell and fell out a window."

"Oh, no! That's horrible!"

"Of course it is. You can understand," the Baron said, "that evil-minded persons said she was pushed or jumped. Even if she did kill herself, a woman may do that either because her husband abuses her or for reasons that have nothing whatever to do with him. Believe me, my dear, if I had the faintest trace of suspicion that Rubin bore any blame at all in those two tragedies, I would not entertain his suit for one instant. If you have doubts, then say so now, and I will inform His Highness that you decline his proposal."

Johanna knew that the Baron's code would force him to give his sovereign the benefit of the doubt. "He was already Grand Duke when this happened?"

"He was. If there had been any evidence of foul play, there would certainly have been talk of deposing him and putting Lord Volpe on the throne. There wasn't. None at all."

Johanna tried to imagine Duke Rubin hurling a wife out the window, or deliberately keeping treatment from another when she was deathly ill. She couldn't. He was a foolish, besotted lover, not a monster.

"I can see why he was offered no more princesses," she

said. "But even if he did kill two wives, he won't ever risk killing a third, would he? That would be too much for anyone to swallow!"

"The choice is yours, my dear."

She laughed aloud. "But this is a fairy tale! Me—Grand Duchess?" Her ambitions had never gone beyond some husky young farmer, perhaps a forester or a prosperous merchant. Suddenly she was being offered jewels, gorgeous gowns, people groveling to her? Crowds would cheer her as she drove by in her gilded coach! "How can I possibly refuse? Oh, thank you, thank you, my lord!" She threw herself into the old man's arms.

Relief like sunlight drove the last shadows of doubt from his face. "I am so happy for you, my . . . But you aren't 'my dear' anymore, are you?" He released her so he could bow. "From now on I must address you as 'Your Royal Highness.' "

Johanna squealed with excitement and embraced him again.

◆ 2 ◆

Yet she did not really believe what was happening until a few minutes later, when her sovereign lord was kneeling at her feet and offering her a gold ring bearing a sapphire the size of an acorn.

"I wanted it to match your eyes," he said, "but they make it look so dull! Oh, my dearest, most wonderful Johanna, if I have frightened or offended you these last two weeks, then I am deeply sorry. My earlier experiences with marriage were so painful for me that I swore I would never remarry unless I could find a woman who was beautiful, courageous, chaste, and honorable. In more than twenty years, you are the first who has qualified. Will you grant me your forgiveness and do me the honor of becoming my wife and consort, to rule at my side?"

She was so tongue-tied that all she could do was nod. It was enough. Rubin smiled, put the ring on her finger, and rose to kiss her. His kiss tasted of wine, but it was surprisingly gentle.

The engagement was announced in the hall soon after, and won a tremendous ovation. The display of affection went on and on until the Grand Duchess Elect made a fool of herself by starting to weep.

Rubin the fiancé was as charming as Rubin the suitor had been repellent. He had won the race and all that remained was to claim the prize, so there was no more urgency. Except that he did have important affairs of state to see to. Johanna was free to make any wedding arrangements she pleased, he said, regardless of cost. Brass bands, a parade of cavalry, fireworks—anything she wanted. She could invite the entire duchy if she wished. Certainly the ceremony could be held there at Fadrenschloss. His only stipulation was that it be held the day after tomorrow, heedless of the scandal and inconvenience such haste must cause.

The Baron summoned Seneschal Priboi and told him to organize a state wedding and banquet for five hundred two days hence. The stooped old man barely flinched.

The following morning Rubin was off early to Krupa to collect his finery and attend to the formalities of a sovereign taking a wife. He promised that seamstresses would arrive at Fadrenschloss before dark and complete Johanna's wedding gown before dawn. He was ruler, and his wishes were not subject to argument. He kissed his bride again and promised to hasten back.

Johanna found herself at a loss. Everyone else was in a frenzy, but she had no duties to perform.

"This is really your last day here," the Baron said. "How will you spend it?"

"I'd like to go riding with you, my lord, and store up some last memories of Fadrenschloss."

She ran off to change. When she came down to the bailey, she found him standing with the mounts saddled and a groom in attendance, but no one else in sight. His face was grim.

"We are about to have visitors," he said. *"Argent, a pile azure from the chief."*

A knight's daughter must know something of heraldry. A blue V on white was the blazon of the Vamky Brotherhood, symbolizing the Pilgrim Pass.

No one could approach Fadrenschloss up the long roadway without the lookouts seeing. With the land at peace, to close the gates would have been grave insult, and already hooves thundered in the barbican. Into the yard poured a troop of knights wearing full panoply of helms, plate mail, lances, and shields. The Brotherhood still trained in such archaic armor and used it for show, but even they rarely fought in it anymore. While his followers formed up in a line across the whole width of the bailey, the leader rode close and reined in, peering down at Johanna from his great warhorse as if he were looking between the slats of a second-story shutter.

The Baron bowed. "My home is honored by your presence, Lord Provost."

"This is the slut?" Volpe glared at her as a tethered hawk eyes a mouse.

The Baron bristled. "My dear, may I present—"

"Trash!" he roared. "Peasant strumpet. What sty did you find her in? From what lineage does she spring?"

"Her father was a knight in my—"

"Baseborn! Spirits of death! What is a lord of your rank

doing pimping gutter wenches to his sovereign? Where is
your honor, if you won't respect his? Don't try and tell me
that marriage was my nephew's idea. I know him much too
well. He loses interest in a woman the moment he rolls off
her. A coin and a pat on the rump and on to the next one,
that's his style."

Von Fader was steaming. These insults came on top of
two weeks of torment. If the two of them had been on equal
terms, he would likely have struck the Provost. As it was, he
tried to issue a challenge.

"My honor required me to see my ward honorably married, my lord, just as it now requires satisfaction of you."

"Old fool! I don't fight with geriatric pimps. You have political ambitions, I suppose, selling bedstuff to your betters?
Good luck with them. For centuries the rulers of this land
have sprung from royal loins and you want to put a strumpet's get on the throne of Krupina!"

Johanna intervened then, for it was her character that was
being blackened and she feared the old man would suffer an
apoplexy. "If I were what you call me, my lord, I would not
have been chosen as your future Grand Duchess." She was
pleased to hear her voice sounding so steady. "By insulting
me you insult your sovereign lord."

The tercel eyes returned to her. "Half a day's notice of a
state wedding? I have known stallions take longer to cover a
mare. You know what happened to your betrothed's previous
wives, don't you? Or didn't this sleazy old fleshmonger
think to warn you?"

That jibe struck at her secret fears, and her own temper
flamed. "And who gained by those women's deaths? You
will not dispose of me as easily as you did them, Lord Volpe.
I intend to live long enough to give Krupina an heir who
does not have blood on his hands."

There was a momentary pause before he responded to that

accusation. "You are more of a fool than I thought. I won't wish you long life and happiness, because you won't get either. Don't boil up too many cabbages for the wedding feast, old man. There won't be any guests. Just the local scum."

One of the knights behind him shouted a warning. The Baron's men were coming into view along the battlements, carrying crossbows. It was certainly a bluff, but there were a lot of them and the seneschal had mustered them with impressive speed.

The Baron returned to the fray. "Better a ruler of honest peasant stock than a gutter-mouthed hireling." No matter that the Provost truly was a mercenary, to use that word to his face was insult. "It is clear this land will be better off without you wearing the coronet, my lord—a professed soldier who will not even fight a man nigh twice his age. Leave my house. Go drop your vomit in your own kennel."

Volpe turned his horse and led his men out through the barbican.

His prophecy about the wedding guests was fulfilled. No grandiose coaches rolled into the bailey. Johanna's sister, Voica, arrived on a lathered donkey with minutes to spare; the Baron's vassals and bondsmen from far and near brought their families to cheer the happy couple; but no one came from Krupa.

The Baron conducted the ceremony and declared his liege and his ward to be man and wife.

Trestle tables had been set up outdoors in the fall sunshine, with a backdrop of the ivy-garbed tower and gold-tinted hills. The humble who had come to stare were invited forward to help consume the feast prepared for their betters, delicacies they had never even heard of. While the servants were carrying out the scores of dishes and others were carving the ox, the bride and groom—a lividly furious groom—

stood under a massive beech tree, accepting the respects of the guests as they trooped by. Had Johanna been marrying a man of her own rank, they would have been heaping gifts at her feet—knitwear, pots, pewter, furs, spices—but they all knew that she would have no need of those in the Agathon Palace, so they had nothing to offer except shy good wishes.

Then a youth of about sixteen summers sauntered up to the head of the line, obviously a young gentleman, because his red, green, and gold riding costume must have cost a fortune, and a jeweled sword hung at his side. No one contested his claim of precedence. His confidence and arrogance sprang from both rank and awareness of remarkable personal beauty—straight nose, clear dark eyes, clean-shaven face marred only by a few acne zits and the dust of the road. He bowed low to the Duke and then appraised the bride, raising both hands in amazement.

"Exquisite! Perfection! The face of a child and the body of a woman. Krupa will swoon at your feet, Cousin."

Annoyed at this crudity and even more annoyed to feel herself blushing at it, Johanna looked to her husband for an explanation.

Rubin seemed, were it possible, even more angry than before. "The black sheep, my dear. I am embarrassed to present my cousin, Lord Karl. Undoubtedly the only reason he has come here today is because I did not invite him."

"Not so!" Lord Karl said with a pout. "It was mostly because my father forbade it." He flashed a smile at Johanna as if she would understand. "I could not pass up a chance to annoy both of them. Sorry I'm late. My dear father has set up pickets on every road. I had to ride all around the dukedom to get here. But I look forward to the rest of the party. May I have the second dance?"

Father? He could only mean Lord Volpe, but Johanna had

always understood that the Vamky knights were sworn to celibacy. Karl must be illegitimate.

"No," Rubin said, speaking quietly because of all the on-lookers, but looking as if he meant it. "No dances! Stay away from this libertine, my dear. He is a wastrel and a sponger."

"Ah, *that* reminds me!" Karl declared, fishing in a pocket. "A wedding gift for you, Cousin." He pulled out a string of pearls and moved as if to hang it around her neck.

Rubin snatched it away and glared at it. "Stolen, I suppose?"

Karl feigned hurt. "Of course! Where would I get the money to buy something like that? But I took it off the lady's dressing table and she'll never admit I was in her bedroom, so it will be quite all right for you to wear it, Johanna dear."

"It will not!" Rubin was seething. "And you address our wife as 'Your Royal Highness'!"

"Verily!" Karl shrugged, flashing Johanna a look that plainly commented on the impossibility of dealing with old folk.

Now Johanna was having trouble not smiling, which would be an unwise act. She wondered if this Karl might be an asset to life in a stuffy old palace. On the other hand he must have a claim to the throne, and his eyes were missing nothing. His cloak of antics might hide a dagger of mean-ness.

He did not get the second dance that night. There was no dancing. Right after the banquet the Grand Duke declared the party over and took his wife upstairs to teach her some of the realities of life.

Nine months and one day later, she was delivered of a son.

✦ 3 ✦

$\mathcal{A}$ Grand Duchess was never alone. Even taking her son out for some fresh air one fine morning, dawdling along a corridor at Frederik's erratic pace, Johanna was attended by three bored ladies-in-waiting and, farther back, his nurse Ruxandra with a bag of necessary supplies. Frederik, being two-going-on-three, insisted on exploring everything and threw tantrums if his mother tried to carry him or hold his hand. Progress was achieved only by negotiation, supplication, and distraction. He slowed the business of the palace, because servants must bow or curtsy and then stand aside until the Heir Apparent had passed. Few members of the nobility were around at that hour, but those who were swept by without a glance, as always. Johanna was used to that. As far as the aristocracy of Krupina was concerned, she still did not exist.

The fairy tale had not worked out as planned.

The Marquis of Krupa, busily banging his little fist against a suit of ornamental armor, paid no heed to sounds of marching boots and jingling spurs as a troop of a dozen or so Vamky knights came around the corner ahead. The man in the lead had a slight limp, identifying him instantly as Volpe. At that moment Frederik noticed his favorite stuffed horse on the other side of the corridor and went trotting across to inspect it. Johanna did not believe even Volpe capable of trampling a child to death, but she swooped anyway, snatching Frederik up and moving them both to safety against the wall.

"Oh, look!" she exclaimed to forestall his inevitable scream of fury. "See the soldiers!"

"Soldiers!" Frederik agreed. He liked soldiers.

Vamky brethren were a common enough sight in the Agathon Palace. They usually went about in twos or fours, gliding along in their white robes with the blue Vamky V over the heart, going about spirits-knew-what business, hands tucked in sleeves, faces hidden in hoods. Less often they would appear in military mode, clad in anything from antique plate mail to leather riding gear, but even then they usually managed to conceal their faces to some degree, and invariably they bore swords. Today's fashion comprised brimmed helmet, cuirass with tassets, and leather breeches tucked into long boots. They were well spattered with spring mud, as if they had just ridden in. Their helmets lacked the usual cheek pieces and nose guards, leaving their dusty, wind-burned faces exposed.

To Johanna's amazement they did not go matching straight past her. Volpe barked, "Squad . . . halt! Left . . . face! Pre . . . sent arms!" Steel *swooshed* against scabbard and she found herself staring at thirteen swords held in vertical salute.

She was so astonished she almost dropped Frederik. The brethren were forbidden to speak to, or even look at, women unless absolutely necessary. Although that rule did not apply to Provost Volpe, for his own reasons he had never acknowledged her existence since their first meeting. It was his lead that the lesser nobility followed in snubbing her, his authority that gave them courage to defy their sovereign.

The Provost had the same heavy, solid build as Rubin, but in his case it seemed all bone and muscle. His face had been hewn from oak—jaw, cheekbones, heavy brow ridges—and the weatherbeaten skin glued on without any intervening flesh. He was clean-shaven, which was unusual in Krupina, and no hair showed under his helmet, as if he shaved his scalp also. His eyes were extraordinary, jet black and very round, frozen in an intense stare.

He regarded her in silence with a faint sneer, pretending to be amused at her surprise.

"Good chance to you, Uncle," she said. "I presume you honor the Marquis, not myself?"

"A reasonable assumption but not necessarily correct. He is a big, strong boy."

Little thanks to Rubin, she thought. "My father could hold his halberd extended at arm's length with one hand."

"I saw him do it more than once. And so can I. Still." The predatory glare did not soften, but Volpe clearly thought he had won that round.

"I did not know you ever met my father!"

"Why should you?" Point two.

Frederik was staring with interest at the warriors, yet content to remain safe in his mother's arms.

"Greet Lord Volpe, Frederik." She expected him to bury his face in her collar, but he could surprise her as well as Volpe could.

"Good chance, my lord!" he recited in his sweetest best-behavior voice.

"And may chance always favor you, Your Highness," Volpe responded solemnly. "I hope that soon I may wait upon you at leisure, but now, by your leave, I must be about your father's business." He snapped orders, the men shot swords back in scabbards, turned ninety degrees, and resumed their progress along the corridor.

Several servants had witnessed the incident, as well as the three harpies-in-waiting. All mouths hung open, and the story would be everywhere very shortly. On the face of it, Volpe had granted Johanna a vital concession by acknowledging the heir apparent. Having survived the most dangerous years of childhood, Frederik could no longer be ignored, and Volpe could hardly give him due respect while snubbing his mother as a parvenu commoner. Yet somehow she did not feel as if she had won a victory. A man as devious as the Provost could easily throw a battle to win a war. What was he up to?

*   *   *

The Agathon Palace was a maze, a mad assemblage of additions, restorations, and renovations whose original nucleus had been lost centuries ago. Successive Grand Dukes had improved it beyond all reason, elaborating it into an architectural nightmare, the sort of nightmare that involves endless running going nowhere. Staircases plunged through halls, corridors doubled back on themselves, stable yards divided dining rooms from kitchens. It was Johanna's prison. Right from the start, Rubin had forbidden her to leave it, lest she be hissed or pelted by the crowd. She had never walked the streets of Krupa.

She knew the labyrinth as well as anyone, for exploring it had been her main occupation during the first months of her marriage, before Frederik was born. She knew the windows that offered views over the roofs of the city to the distant hills she missed so much, and others where she could see down into busy streets and watch real people living ordinary lives. She cherished its two private little gardens and hated the gloomy, musty rooms, the twisted stairs; above all she hated the throne room where she was sometimes required to sit beside Rubin and suffer the resentful glares of an assembly. Yes, she occupied the consort's throne beside the grander ducal throne, but she had never been formally installed on it, never crowned with the silver coronet, never hailed by the people. *Fraud!* their eyes said. *Intruder! Upstart! Peasant!*

Disturbed by the encounter with Volpe, she changed her mind about taking Frederik to play on the grass and went instead to her favorite place, a gallery overlooking the main courtyard. It was narrow and went nowhere, so only she and the pigeons used it. On sunny days she could sit there and watch the business of the palace ebb and flow below her in a vast gavotte—horses, wagons, carts, men-at-arms, bakers' helpers, footmen, chambermaids, minstrels, buskers, couriers, and dozens more whose purpose and occupations she could try to guess. Frederik could safely play there, for the iron balustrade was tightly woven. Furthermore, she was in plain view and that mattered. Never let them forget they had a Grand Duchess!

She arrived to see Lord Volpe and his troop making ready to depart, causing much shouting and hoof-stamping down in the courtyard. Bystanders bolted out of the way as the brethren took off. The timing surprised her, because it meant they must have already completed their business before she met them, yet they had been seriously mud-splattered, so she had assumed that they had just arrived and had not had time to clean up. If their visit had been so brief and their business so urgent, why had Volpe taken time to stop and greet Frederik? Most curious!

As usual, she ordered a chair placed at the far end of the gallery for herself and took her son and a bag of toys with her, leaving the hags-in-waiting to attend to their crochet work and character assassination beside the door. Smaranda, Eupraxia, and Cneajna were all older than she, sullen burghers' daughters with ambitious mothers, all ugly enough to need promoting as matches and willing in the cause of husband acquisition to attend the fraud duchess, which the noble ladies of the realm flatly refused to do. Johanna wished she could help their efforts, dreaming private fantasies of hanging price labels on them. The faster she could move her stock, the more choice she would have for their replacements. She might even find some congenial companions. Alas, only too often her ladies succumbed to the temptations of the palace and had to be sent home in disgrace. That did not encourage other mothers to put their daughters forward.

Speaking of debauchery . . . Johanna had just made herself

comfortable and Frederik was still contentedly peering through the ironwork at the activity below when Cneajna, Eupraxia, and Smaranda dropped their handiwork and jumped up so they could curtsy to the most eligible bachelor in the dukedom as he strolled out onto the balcony.

Maturity had not improved Karl. He had just turned twenty, yet those startling good looks were already sagging and the most expensive raiment in the country could not quite mask the start of a potbelly. His tailors' bills would be crippling if he ever paid them. Even that day, when there was no special reason to shine, he was a startling vision of rainbow impracticality in brocade and taffeta, puffed, padded, and slashed. Spurs jingled on knee-length, tight-fitting kidskin boots; his gloves had cuttes on the fingers to show off his rings; fur trim edged his cape; his beard was carefully curled; and the apparition was topped off by a tall, crowned soft bonnet. None of the three ladies was attractive enough to delay him long. He strolled on toward Johanna.

His morals had not improved, either. That pose of indolent sensuality concealed at least some of his father's ferocity, for he had fought two duels and killed his opponent each time. Outraged husbands no longer challenged him. Women who valued their reputations kept well away from him.

Frederik, too young to know better, doted on him. Now he went happily trotting to meet him, chirruping, "My lord, my lord, my lord!"

Karl scooped him up and tickled him as he continued to advance. Admittedly there had been times when Karl had been amusing company for a lonely duchess, but Johanna had always been careful to give no grist to the scandalmongers' mills. Lately his efforts to flirt with her had taken on a more intense tone that infuriated her. He had started pestering her with notes and flowers, even sending her gifts, although he knew as well as anyone that there were no secrets in a palace. He had never intruded on her privacy out here before.

"What are you doing here?" She tried to keep her tone threatening and her face noncommittal. Even to raise her voice to him would start gossip.

"I sorrow!" Karl somehow contrived to strike a dramatic pose while balancing Frederik on one hip. "Ask first the bee why it haunts the blossom. Ask the ocean why it seeks the moon." He put his mouth to Frederik's neck and created a noise that no one else in the palace would dare make: *Phwurp!* "Ask the lark why he sings so melancholy. You know I cannot stay away from you."

Frederik squealed with glee. "More!"

"Your attentions are neither welcome nor credible, my lord!" Johanna knew what a lustful look was and Karl's did not convince. He did this just to frighten her. It was a pulling-wings-off-flies thing. "Did your father put you up to this?"

Phwuurp! "My father is insane. Too much sun on his helmet, you know? He considers you a despicable gold-digging slut and me unworthy to kiss your shadow."

"In that last opinion he is correct, but he would love to see you expose me as a wanton."

"Oh, so would I!" Karl sighed. "I could play your body like a harp, woman. Drown you in floods of ecstasy. I long to caress your breasts with my lips. Like this." *Phwuuurp!*

Frederik screamed with glee.

Johanna remembered a hysterically weeping Helga, one of her first ladies-in-waiting and even younger than she, who had fallen prey to Karl within a week of arriving at Court: *I thought he was just joking, Your Highness! Then suddenly it was too late.*

"You are not welcome here. Release my son and go away."

Phwuuurp! "You know I am drawn by your fatal beauty."

"Go away! I shall complain to my husband." But Johanna had seen Rubin order his errant cousin to leave the palace and never return. Karl had gone out into the streets, admittedly, but he had returned in a few minutes with a trollop on each arm. Volpe was known to rage at him, too, but Karl went on being Karl.

"Rubin? Why should he care? He never spares you a thought, my beloved. You really think he would mind if you were to drop your futile resistance and stop torturing both of us? Admit your passion for me, my honeycake, and find surcease in my arms. The old porker will be happy to see you happy again, instead of mooning around unrequited."

"My lord!" Frederik squealed. "Again!"

"You are an incorrigible pest!" Karl said cheerfully. *Phwuuuurp!*

"Again!"

Karl blew a strident fanfare on Frederik's neck as he sank to his knees and set the boy down. "That's all! Johanna, my beloved, don't you see we were made for each other? Two lonely orphans in an oversized cattle barn? I have mooned around this awful slum of a palace all my life and never known—"

His levity annoyed her. "You are not an orphan!"

"You think not?" Suddenly he was looking up at her with an intense stare almost comparable to Volpe's. "You call my father a father? After what he did to my mother?"

He had a point. Karl was, as Johanna had long since discovered, a legitimate son, eligible to inherit. Although Vamky brethren were sworn to celibacy, affairs of state took precedence, and Volpe had been heir presumptive. He had been given a special dispensation to marry, but after Karl's birth he had abandoned his wife and kept the baby.

"Perhaps he was just obeying orders when he sent your mother away?"

"No," Karl said confidently. "My mother never existed and my father is sworn to chastity. I am a mirage, an illusion. I was created out of nothing!" His bitterness soured into mockery again. "Let me describe how I will make love to you. First, I caress your nipples with my tongue. Then as they flush and rise, I start gently nibbling . . ."

Johanna gasped, partly at his vulgarity, partly from relief as she saw rescue in sight. Gripping the railing hard enough to hurt her hands, she said, "Speak louder."

Karl was too wily to be trapped so easily. He rose and turned and bowed in one smooth flow.

Rubin himself was parading along the balcony. Johanna had never known him to come out here, either. Where had her precious privacy gone? And was he about to reprimand her for Karl's public flirting? Frederik fled to safety behind his mother. Compared to Karl, Rubin looked old and dissipated, which he was, and even shabbily dressed, which he was not.

Johanna curtseyed. "Your Grace does me honor."

"I find you in bad company, my sweet. You have our leave, Cousin."

Karl remained unabashed. "Then I wish Your Highnesses good chance. I shall see you in Trenko, if not before." He withdrew without explaining that last remark, pausing for a final word with the three watchdogs, who were agog at this parade of royal visitors.

"I assure Your Grace," Johanna said, "that he was not here by my invitation." She staggered as Frederik tried to climb up her skirts. She stroked his hair to let him know she had not forgotten him. As always, Rubin ignored his son. She often wondered if he would be able to pick Frederik out in a random pack of two-year-olds.

"Even if I doubted you, my dear, which I do not, I would expect you to have better taste in men." Rubin's smile was transient and mechanical. He had other matters on his mind. "Ion has died, Ladislas's son."

Ion she had never heard of, but Margrave Ladislas ruled the March of Trenko, the land beyond the Pilgrim Pass. Now Volpe's hurried mission was explained, but what in all the world did it have to do with her?

"I am unhappy to hear it," she said hesitantly.

Rubin shook his head sadly. "We must all be. He was very young. I propose to attend the funeral and hope that you will consent to accompany me and brighten my journey." He raised well-trimmed eyebrows inquiringly.

Had she fallen off the balcony and suffered concussion? Release from jail at last? Probation, anyway. "I regret only that an occasion so sad should bring me such happiness, Your Grace." He appreciated well-turned phrases.

"You can ride, I believe?" Three and a half years they had been married and he had to ask!

"I ride well, sire." But she was certain that none of her burgher maidens did. Would that ill chance snatch away her unexpected joy? If Rubin did not mention the problem of providing proper companions for her, she would not.

"Tomorrow, then," he said airily. "Leaving at dawn, we shall ride to Vamky and spend the night there before attempting the pass. We may not be able to risk a crossing if the weather sours, but the courier had no trouble."

"I look forward to it greatly. Will Lord Volpe be accompanying us?"

Rubin smirked wet, painted lips. "If he behaves himself. Till then, my love." And off he went.

Frederik peered around her to see if it was safe to appear. *Well!* This was the most interesting day his mother had known since he was born. She left him with Ruxandra. She solved the attendants problem by ignoring it and taking only her senior maid, Arghira, who was a country girl like herself

and knew horses outside and in. The rest of the day and half
the night flew by in frantic preparations. Johanna felt she
had hardly slept before she found herself riding out the
palace gate at her husband's side.

◆ 4 ◆

The day was blustery and sunny. City folk cleared the
streets ahead of them, men uncovering and bowing, women
curtsying. Rubin chose to cross the river and go by the west
road, setting an easy pace. There were two women and thirty
men in the procession, for no grand duke ever traveled without heralds, servants, and troopers of the Palace Guard.
Most of the time he rode in silence, thinking unknown
thoughts, but from time to time he would rouse himself to
make conversation, and then he could be charming company. They discussed the countryside, lambs frolicking,
peasants ploughing and sowing. He was knowledgeable
about agriculture, his main tax base.

Rubin was never deliberately cruel to his wife, he just
could not relate to someone so much younger and lower on
the social ladder. They shared no friends, no background, no
interests. He was usually generous when she asked for
something, but the aristocracy's rejection of a commoner
duchess meant that he never took her to balls or banquets,
and she suspected he was glad of an excuse to stay away
from them. His only real interest was his obsessive pursuit
of young girls, and that wooing was done by bribing or bullying their parents. Johanna had always been careful not to
protest his infidelities, because they obviously mattered to
him more than anything else did.

Now he had found something he could share with her, a

state visit to Trenko. He had no qualms that she might be rejected there also, he said. That would cause a serious diplomatic incident. She did not ask what sort of incident he might create by taking a lowborn wife to a state funeral.

"Will you instruct me about Trenko, Your Grace?" she asked.

He shrugged. "About the same size as Krupina, but a recent creation compared to our long history. We have little in common—different language, different crops, different climate. The two states have been united under one ruler a few times, but never for long. We do better going our separate ways, cooperating to keep the pass open for trade and closed to armies."

Gradually the hills crept in on either hand, bringing vineyards, then pasture, and eventually forest. Late in the day they passed by Fadrenschloss. Johanna did not comment, but she knew its tower was visible from a few places on the highway, and she was waiting to blow it a mental kiss. Happy memories!

Her husband noticed it also. "Do you correspond with von Fader?"

"We exchange letters once in a while, sire."

"You haven't seen him since your wedding day?"

"The morning of the day after."

"Of course." The Duke smiled as if he, too, enjoyed happy memories. "We cannot delay now, but if you would care to visit him on our way back, I would have no objection."

Do mares eat oats?

They crossed the Asch on Olden Bridge, built by the Empire long ago, and from it saw the looming mass of Vamky to the north, set against a backdrop of snowy peaks. Pilgrim Pass was one of the great trade routes of eastern Eurania, and nobody crossed it without passing under those sinister towers.

Very soon the west road joined the east road and began climbing steadily through forest, parting company with the Asch, which grumbled to itself in a deep canyon. After an hour or so, the road emerged from the trees and angled steeply up a treeless slope. The monastery beetled on cliffs above. Johanna had never realized how colossal it was—dark stone walls, minatory battlements, and towers with pointed roofs clad in lead, a gloomy complex outstretched along the crest of a ridge that almost blocked the valley.

"You do know," Rubin said abruptly, "that the brothers are forbidden to speak to women?"

"I do, sire."

"You and your maid will be welcome guests, and you may ask for any comfort you require that is not already provided, but you will be answered only with gestures or, in extreme cases, with a written note."

"I understand."

"Abbot Minhea will make you welcome, of course." The Grand Duke smirked. "And so will the Provost, we shall see."

Emboldened by her newfound freedom, Johanna said, "Lord Volpe did stop and speak a few words to me yesterday, sire."

"Ah, good. When word of Ion's death arrived at Vamky, my uncle rode posthaste to Krupa to tell me and offer to represent me at the funeral. He seemed curiously eager to visit Trenko, suspiciously eager, in fact. I told him I would go myself, but he could accompany us provided he treated you with the respect your rank requires."

"I am grateful, sire!"

"You have been very patient, my dear," Rubin murmured. "But I must move to secure recognition of my heir, and that means that his mother must be recognized as my consort. Once I bring Volpe to heel, the rest of the fools will knuckle under."

She wondered if she had passed some sort of test, perhaps an endurance test. She had not jumped out a window, so he was going to make the best of the situation. No doubt she ought to feel ungrateful for thinking so, but she didn't. All she felt was resentment that she had not been given her due long since.

Weary horses brought them to the crest of the ridge, a stony plain with breathtaking views of mountains ahead and Krupina behind. North, south, and west, the ground plunged steeply. To the east stood a great barbican, with the rest of the monastery behind it, rising gently to where the ridge merged with a spur of mountain. An honor guard of mounted knights in plate mail flanked the road to the gate, their lances grounded and vertical, as regular as the teeth of a comb. Johanna could not imagine how they endured the shrieking, freezing wind. To keep horses facing into that must require incredible training and skill, but neither man nor beast moved a muscle as the visitors rode slowly along between the two lines. Why didn't their armor rattle?

She was stiff and sore from unaccustomed hours in the saddle. In the great and gloomy bailey she slid with relief onto a mounting block, and Rubin himself handed her down. They proceeded together over to the welcome party, where eight sword-bearing brethren waited, all wearing white robes with cowls and the blue Vamky V. The wind whipped their skirts around so hard that once in a while a man would stagger slightly; otherwise she might have thought them scarecrows stuffed with straw. Six stood with their heads bent and faces hidden, hands in sleeves. Two had their hoods back and dared to look the guests in the eye. One, of course, was granite-faced Volpe. Yes, he did shave his entire head. It was smooth as a building stone except for two patches of black moss, the bushy brows above the staring eyes.

The other man was Abbot Minhea, older and shorter. The stubbly white fringe around his tonsure was white, the face below it smooth, unweathered, and utterly bland. His bows were slight, his smiles barely skin deep, his words almost inaudible in the gale. "Your Highness does us honor. Vamky is yours to command. And your dear lady is also most welcome."

"We thank you, my lord Abbot," Rubin retorted.

Then it was Volpe's turn. "Welcome, dear Nephew." His bow was respectful and respectable. "And Your Royal Highness, also." He bowed low to Johanna, and when he straightened up he even gave her a small, ironic smile, as if conceding defeat.

Triumph! She curtsied, slightly.

The rest of the welcoming committee were not introduced. By that time scores of white-robed brethren had appeared to assist both visitors and honor guard dismount—and Johanna realized that helping an armored knight safely down off an armored horse must be no mean task. Rubin's heralds cut the valets and servants out of the confusion and shepherded them over to him, Arghira included. The guests were led off to their quarters by anonymous, white-robed guides.

The way was long, climbing by gentle ramps up the slope of the ridge, rarely going straight for long. The arched corridors were cold and dim, and the curve of the ceilings was reflected in the tops of all the windows and doorways, giving an odd effect of tunnels. High as the monastery itself was, and high as they seemed to have climbed within it, Johanna could neither stop the tremble of her hands nor relax the knot of terror in her belly. This was like being underground, and all her life she had been terrified of that.

Her guide brought her eventually to a large room with a barrel ceiling and shuttered windows. The plaster on the stonework was whitewashed, the plank floor covered with straw, the furniture starkly plain. Although the bed was large enough for two, its mattress was thin and lumpy. To offset those discomforts, a huge log fire blazed in a massive fireplace, making even that sparse chamber warm and cosy, and a big copper jug on the hob offered copious hot water. She hurried across to open a shutter, just to convince herself that she was high on a mountain, not down in a crypt. The air struck at her like an ax of ice, but she filled her lungs with the cold, sweet stuff.

Arghira was impressed, but worried by the solitary bed. "Do I share with you, my lady?"

"I doubt it," Johanna said. Rubin might have had more than one reason for bringing her along, but she could guess the main one. Besides, her two hooded guides were waiting just outside the open door, gazing patiently at the floor. "Where will my attendant sleep?" she asked.

The taller brother stepped across the corridor to a smaller chamber, with a smaller fire. It would do. He opened another door to reveal a garderobe. More brethren arrived with luggage, which they set down and stared at, waiting to be told which were Johanna's. These faceless puppets were starting to make her skin crawl.

Once she had freshened up and changed and sent Arghira off to do the same, she found herself at a loss. She missed Frederik, for she had never been apart from him before. Deciding to test the system, she opened the door. A hooded swordsman stood on either side of it—guardians or jailers?

"I wish to write a letter," she announced. "I need paper, ink, pens."

The shorter one bowed to the opposite wall and made a gesture. The other bowed also, then strode off along the corridor. Ten or fifteen minutes later, something thumped hard against the door. Johanna, opening it, was handed a tray bearing paper, quills, knife, inkwell, sand shaker, and even a stick of wax. She penned a note to the Baron, telling him where she was and that she hoped to visit Fadrenschloss in a few days, on her return from Trenko. No light was showing through the shutters when she finished, so the message could not go until morning. Nevertheless, she sealed it, addressed it, and went back out to the corridor to ask that it be delivered as soon as that was possible. The brother who took it had age-spotted hands. The one who had brought her the paper had had the hands of a boy.

Soon after that who should walk in but the Grand Duke himself, shaved, changed, and beaming happily.

"Everything satisfactory, my dove?" He peered around.

"The brethren have made me feel most welcome, sire."

He nodded, looking around. "Good, good! I will dine in the hall. It would be more seemly if you ate here."

"I shall be happy to do so."

He nodded. "Till later, then?" And off he went. He always warned her when he planned to come visiting. It happened rarely, only when he was between mistresses or his current favorite was indisposed, but clearly tonight was one of the times his wife would have to do, old though she was. She was sore after the long ride, but would make him welcome. He was always tender—spirits knew he was well practiced!—and tonight she thought he had earned his reward.

The following morning Johanna's breakfast was handed in on a tray, along with a reply from the Baron, promising she would be welcome. There was no moon so early in the month, so someone had ridden all the way to Fadrenschloss and back in pitch darkness.

The travelers departed soon after dawn, fighting an icy wind. The Palace Guard was left behind at Vamky, replaced by Provost Volpe and a score of the brethren, wearing sensible leather and fur garments, armed only with swords. The path descended almost as steeply on the north side of the ridge as it had risen on the south, rejoining the Asch as a much smaller stream of milky water babbling through forest. Gradually the land rose again. Trees dwindled and disappeared. At the crest of the long climb the way ahead was a V of blue sky between great peaks draped with glaciers, the Pilgrim Pass.

The stony plain still bore winter snows, and in places the road narrowed to a single file through a maze of boulders. When the riders doubled up again, they often exchanged partners, and eventually Johanna found herself alongside Karl.

"How brightly the glaciers reflect your glory, Oh Pearl of the Mountains."

"I didn't know you were with us, my lord."

He was so wrapped up against the wind that his customary sneer was barely visible. "Now is your joy transcendent."

"Now is my trip ruined." His father had acknowledged her. Her husband was including her in a state visit. She was a real Grand Duchess at last and need not endure this wastrel's mockery.

"Nay, you should savor every moment, Fairest One. When you return to Krupina you will be back to wiping dishes and scrubbing floors!"

Was he hinting that Volpe would revert to form once he had achieved his purpose in Trenko, whatever it was? She did not reply.

"Let me take you away from your scullery duties, Beloved! Fly with me to farthest Skyrria and let your beauty outshine the fabled jewels of Orient."

"If you won't talk sense, go and bore somebody else."

"Ow, it scratches! You expect me to be *serious*?"

"Yes. Tell me about your mother. All I know is that her name was Tatjana. She died when you were young?"

"If she ever existed."

Johanna rode on in silence. He tried a few more stupid remarks and she did not respond.

"Oh, very well! But it is a waste of a fine morning. My father wasn't provost then. He was heir presumptive, but unmarried and sworn to remain so, and Rubin wasn't capable of staying married long enough to breed a legitimate son. But Krupina needed another heir. So it got me."

"How?"

"The usual way, I expect."

She rode on in silence and when he spoke again his voice held a snappishness so unlike his usual flippancy that what he said was probably genuine. "Vamky knights do as they are told. There was a nice war brewing and the King of Drasia needed help badly. He had a widowed sister, Princess Tatjana, who was too old to make a decent royal match but not too old to pop one royal brat with the proper assistance. Volpe was ordered to marry her, breed me, and win the war. He did all those things with dispatch. Then he came home and brought me with him. Aren't you sorry you asked?"

"Ordered by whom?"

"I don't know. Ask him." Karl put his horse into a narrow gap between toothy boulders.

Johanna followed, deciding that for once she believed her scoundrelly cousin-in-law, mostly because the horror of the story explained why she had never heard the details before. If he had been reared by servants in the inhuman warren of the Agathon Palace, his bitterness was understandable.

He was waiting for her where the trail widened.

"I can understand the first part," she said. "A country needs a ruler. But taking you from your mother—didn't your father have any say at all?"

Karl shrugged. "I expect it was his idea. She was a lot

older than he was. Anyway, she's dead now, so it doesn't matter, does it?"

"It would matter a lot to me if she had been my mother."

He did not comment. They parted to go either side of a large rock.

"What causes this sudden attraction to Trenko?" she asked when they met again. "Why are you and Lord Volpe so eager to attend a funeral?" Rubin, too, for that matter.

Karl looked at her in surprise. "Didn't your husband tell you?"

"No."

"Then you think my father would tell me?" Smirk. "There must be something more. He never travels just for pleasure."

He was back in his sarcastic mode again, but she was seeing him in a different light and willing to make a few allowances. "Don't you have any ideas?"

"Lots of them, but you keep refusing me, my rosebud, my honeycake. I suspect the succession troubles them. The Margrave has no more sons and his health is poor. Who will hold the north end of Pilgrim Pass after he has rejoined the elements?"

"And your purpose, my lord?"

"Business, also." He sighed. "As thou spurnest my troth, I go to woo the sweet Margarita!"

"Who?"

"Ah! You were not warned? How unfair!" Karl's sneer was barely visible but clearly audible. "Ladislas's only surviving child is his daughter, Margarita. Her brother is barely cold, but I imagine offers for her hand will be flooding in. I thought I would enter the lists."

"I wish you good chance, my lord." And bad chance to the heiress. May she sweep him off his feet and keep him there! He would be a logical choice, though. Matchmaking might explain Lord Volpe's eagerness to make the journey.

"And what can your dear sovereign lord and husband's

purpose be, do you suppose?" Karl mused. "We cannot recall him ever going to a funeral before. He is usually too
busy to attend his wives'. Business or pleasure?"

"Being neighborly is good business for a ruler," she said
brightly, but she had guessed what was coming. She could
feel the pain already.

"No, I think it must be pleasure," Karl said judiciously.
"Margarita is said to have tresses whiter than flax and
breasts like sweet cherries. Thirteen she is, and a right dainty
royal morsel."

Where the long descending trail curved around a spring-fed
pool and a bank gave shelter from the wind, Lord Volpe
called a halt to rest and water the horses. The mounts all
had to be inspected, of course, especially their hooves. Johanna was quite capable of doing that, but it was not a task
for a grand duchess, so she waited to see who would assist
her. Her husband was already inspecting the refreshments,
leaving his horse to the junior knight who had been appointed his custrel for this journey.

For a while she was ignored, but when that same knight had
finished with the duke's horse, he strode over and set to work
on hers without a word or a glance in her direction. She found
being invisible to young men a disconcerting experience.

"Knight-brother Nickolaus, isn't it?" she asked sweetly.

He ignored her. He had an admirable profile and no doubt
its sudden flush was caused by the cool wind. As he released
the first hoof, a voice spoke behind her.

"I will attend Her Highness, Nickolaus."

"Sir!" The youngster saluted and walked away.

Lord Volpe patted the mare's neck and bent to lift its right
forefoot.

"Again I am honored," Johanna said. "Good chance to
you, my lord."

"And to you, Highness." He gripped the hoof between his knees.

"Your newfound courtesy is very welcome. Complete abasement is not required."

Volpe scratched snow from the horseshoe with the quillon of his dagger. "It is no abasement for a knight to tend a horse."

"My husband will be pleased to see what you are doing."

"You do not appreciate the military mind, girl," he told the shoe. "I am the greatest, most renowned warrior in Eurania. States have retracted declarations of war when I signed with their foes." He ducked under the reins to inspect the left foot. "I have never surrendered and never will. Tactical withdrawals I have made many times."

"I see. So after you have negotiated your son's betrothal, it will be back to studied rudeness, will it?"

Volpe released the hoof he had been about to lift and straightened up to stare at her. "After I have done *what*?"

Evidently Johanna had revealed a secret. With anyone else she would have backtracked, but a flash of wicked joy drove her on.

"Lord Karl informs me that his purpose in coming is to woo the Lady Margarita. Are you not backing his suit?"

Volpe snorted, a sound perilously close to a laugh. He bent to his work again. "He has not mentioned it to me. I was even considering courting her myself. No, my main objective in coming along was to prevent my nephew from making a total idiot of himself."

Was he mocking her, or did that remark hint at his real purpose in staging this conversation? She did not know him well enough to guess his motives. She would never outwit a warrior of his stature.

"Then we are allies on this mission," she said. "What can I do to help?"

"Keep him well exercised, although I truly believe he is insatiable, even now. At seventeen, he . . . Never mind. Was Karl serious, for once?"

"I do not know, my lord."

Volpe straightened and tucked his dagger back in its sheath. His raptor eyes stared at her over the mare's neck, making her feel like a mouse about to die.

"I hear he has been pestering you, back in Krupa."

"Yes he has." Had Rubin complained, or did the Provost have spies at his nephew's Court? Of course he did. Did they spy on his son? Why wouldn't they?

"Is he just amusing himself tormenting you, or does he plan real trouble for you?"

"Explain 'real trouble.' "

"Getting you with child to disgrace you."

"If he tries that he will not succeed, I assure you!"

Instead of starting on the mare's saddle and girths, Volpe scanned the hollow, studying the travelers. "Our family is the oldest in Eurania, did you know?"

"I know it is very distinguished," she said, puzzled.

"It is also well documented. Over the centuries it has produced many odd characters and several crazies. Even a few warriors as renowned as I. Rubin's predatory ways recur every few generations. One grand duke acquired a retinue of over two hundred dwarfs. Another set out to father a thousand children. Our ancestors have all shared one trait, a mark as distinctive as a malformed lip or a white forelock." The midnight eyes fixed on her again. "Lazy and cowardly as your husband is, his success with women is extraordinary, would you not agree?"

She wondered where this harangue was leading. Volpe trying to be pleasant was almost worse than Volpe spurning.

" 'Disgusting' would be a better term."

He shook his head, sneering. "Not as long as he confines

his attentions to people who cannot cause trouble. My purpose in going to Trenko is to ensure he makes no obscene advances to Margarita. When he got trapped in marriage with a baseborn floozy, *that* was disgusting. We are descended from fourteen generations of rulers. Your son is a peasant's child. Nobody worthwhile will ever marry that one. Our web of royal alliances will wither and Krupina will be put at risk."

"An outcross strengthens the breed," she said furiously. "It may reduce the number of crazies in future."

He ignored her comment. "A Krupina always succeeds, you see. Whatever it is he sets as his life's goal, he will achieve it, without exception."

"Even the one with the thousand children?"

"He made a good start, but died young. That is why Karl annoys me so. At his age I had fought in three major battles. His only aim seems to be to have no aim and I find that intolerable. If he has set out to seduce you just to annoy Rubin, he will have to be spanked. And he should not be babbling of marriage without my permission. Inspect this saddle yourself." Lord Volpe limped away.

Frederik was the only sane one in the whole family.

◆ 5 ◆

Trenko was a jewel in a mountain setting, a pearl of many-colored buildings where forested slopes swept down to the shores of a jade green lake. With city and state in mourning for their young prince, there were no festivities during Johanna's brief stay, but it was a happy time for her. The palace was so crowded that she and Rubin had to share a room. Rubin made the best of it, giving her hope that Frederik would gain a brother or sister from this rare opportunity.

Representatives of many neighboring states had come to the funeral, most bringing their wives. The men tended to collect in corners, like cobwebs, spinning alliances and plotting the dismemberment of rivals. The women, likewise, exercised their claws in small groups, rending reputations and plotting the future matrimonial geography of Eurania. Johanna found herself accepted into genteel company for the first time. The gossip would soon have palled on her, but for a short while it was an interesting change. The wine and cakes were delicious.

Lovely Margarita stood at the head of the agenda, of course, but was not on display. She was incommunicado, distraught at her brother's death and the importance thus thrust upon her. Competition for the damsel's hand was going to be ferocious. So the good dames said, frequently.

Detecting glances in every direction but hers, Johanna learned to go on the offensive at this point in the masque. "Very wise! The child is far too young for public duties yet."

More glances. Just thirteen, the harpies would agree. And promising to be a great beauty!

"My husband was interested," Johanna would announce then, pretending not to notice the reaction, although obviously Rubin's reputation had preceded him. Then, "But we agreed that the age difference is far too great." More shock. "Frederik is not yet three." Ah!

"But there is Lord Karl, isn't there?" a henna-haired hag inquired once. "Your husband brought him along?"

"No, he followed us here," Johanna said cheerfully. "We forgot to tie him up."

"I heard he had an accident on the journey?"

"Nothing serious. He took a tumble off his horse." Johanna had not witnessed that accident, but she had seen Karl arriving at Trenko with a very muddy cloak and his face so badly bruised that he had gone straight to the town elementary for a healing. No one had been crass enough to ask how he had managed to muddy the back of his cloak while landing on his face. Life was full of little mysteries like that. The same first evening, during the formalities of welcome, she had been standing beside Lord Volpe and wondering how he had grazed his knuckles so badly. Perhaps he had fallen off his horse also. She did not discuss those family matters with the harpies.

Their next gambit usually went: "Her father dotes on her. The Margrave is insistent that Margarita choose for love."

To which Johanna would respond that she thought that was an excellent procedure. She was sure it would rule out Rubin and Volpe, and probably Karl also. Karl did have looks and birth, of course, and might stand a chance if he could mend his manners. Unless he was being favored above the other suitors, he had no opportunity to try his wiles on the young lady during that visit, because the fair Margarita had still not made an appearance when the time came for Grand Duke Rubin and his retinue to return to Krupina.

◆ 6 ◆

Good news and bad news flew together, so they said.

The good news had arrived nine days earlier, setting Fadrenschloss agog and atwitter—the Grand Duchess coming to visit, their own fledgling returning at last. The cooks planned a great feast, the minstrels and musicians rehearsed interminably, and Seneschal Priboi organized the greatest clean-out and pretty-up the old castle had known in centuries. Ernst himself stumped around, inspecting, interfering, approving, and generally having a wonderful time. Life had been boring for too long, and he could not expect to see many more happy occasions in whatever years he had left.

The bad news followed Priboi home. With preparations

all complete, Ernst had been happy to grant the old seneschal a few hours' leave. It wasn't as if he asked for it every decade, Ernst told him, but he mustn't make a habit of it. When he returned and reported what he had learned at Vamky, joy gave way to terror. There was nothing Ernst could do before Johanna arrived, except swear Priboi to secrecy and order him to make sure the foxhole was clean and well stocked.

The following morning the lookout saw her procession approaching, two women and a contingent of the Palace Guard. The entire staff assembled in the bailey to greet her, their cheers almost drowning out the fanfare from the battlements. Ernst himself lifted her down from her mount, and then tried to kneel to her, but she caught him in a hug and would not permit it. She was both laughing and crying as she greeted all the old familiar faces.

The terrified child who had disappeared into the ducal coach three and a half years ago was a woman now, a poised royal beauty. She told him he had not changed at all. Just fatter and uglier, he said, priding himself on being as spry as ever. It was wonderful to be home, she said, but the look she gave Ernst after that first happy moment told him she had already guessed that something dire weighed on his mind.

It was an hour before all the reminiscences and pleasantries were over and he could get her to himself. The two of them settled comfortably in the solar and the talk turned to serious matters. He confessed how much he still missed her. He complimented her on growing up so beautiful. She admitted that she was no longer as homesick for Fadrenschloss as she had once been. She did not tell him how far her married life had fallen short of what it should have been, but she did not have to. Although he was no longer *persona grata* at Court, he still had friends in Krupa, mostly sons or grandsons of men he had fought beside in his military days.

He knew how she had been humiliated and shunned. She had never complained in her letters, but her face glowed with happiness as she spoke of Trenko—the people, the houses, the land itself, all new to her—and especially how she had shared in the royal honors paid to Rubin.

The timing began to make sense. "So Lord Volpe deferred to you at last?"

"He was cool and correct the whole time." The wry little smile he remembered flickered momentarily. "He hinted that this state of affairs might be temporary, though."

"He is a strange man." Ernst remembered Volpe as a child, a bitter, tight-wound, melancholy child. Even then, it had been obvious that he would make a much better Grand Duke than Rubin, his nephew and playmate, ever could. By the time the boy had gone riding to war with the Brotherhood, Ernst had been ready to hang up his lance, so their military paths had crossed only briefly. Even as a stripling, Volpe had gained a reputation for courage and ruthlessness.

"The greatest warrior in Eurania, he told me." Johanna's tone asked confirmation.

"The most sought-after mercenary, certainly. Most hirelings take their pay and never earn it. They march and maneuver and dance gavottes with their opponents; do anything rather than risk their skins. Volpe was never like that. With him it was a point of honor to go on the offensive as soon as possible. With the might of the Vamky conjurers behind him, he never lost a battle, never failed to take a stronghold. Few rulers could afford his prices, but he did give good value."

" 'Did'? He has retired?"

"It seems so. He did not campaign last year or the year before." The man must be fifty! Incredible! Where had all the years hidden themselves?

"Why does he limp? An old injury?"

"Deformed foot," Ernst said. "It was more obvious when he was a child." And that flaw had mattered infinitely more to the sensitive orphaned boy than it did now to a veteran of many battles. "It shows less when he is wearing a sword."

"Now, my lord!" Bright azure eyes were missing nothing. "I have talked enough. Tell me what is wrong."

"Ah, women! We poor simpleton men can never keep secrets." And must not keep this one. "Yes, my dear. But please remember that this is third- or fourth-hand information and may have no truth in it."

"Go on!" She had learned the tone of command.

"You remember Harald?"

"Which Harald?"

"Priboi's."

She nodded. " 'Teensy,' we called him. How is he?" They were of an age.

"Turned out the biggest of the litter. He is a novice in the monastery. He is allowed one visitor every six months. His father went to see him just yesterday and found him quite upset."

"So would anyone be who had to live there. What of it?"

"This may be a test," Ernst warned. "They test the novices in strange ways, and it would be easy to pass along a rumor just to see if the boy told his father. Harald did tell, so he may turn up here at any time with sore feet—rejected, expelled."

"What rumor?" she snapped.

"A coup being plotted."

Color drained from her face. "Volpe? How? When?"

"I don't know," Ernst said. "No details. It would be easy! He can muster four hundred knights without even calling in troops from foreign service. He could just ride down to Krupa and take over. A few hours would do it."

"The Palace Guard would fall flat on its face," she agreed. "What was it you used to say—'Throw down their arms and put up their hands'?"

She knew it was no laughing matter. She was playing for time to think. Although Rubin ruled competently enough, a man with his moral shortcomings could never be popular. The people would not rise if the military hero took the coronet from the libertine.

"Rubin will abdicate if Volpe holds a sword to his throat?" Ernst asked.

"He would pass out cold." She shivered, hugging herself, staring at the floor. "The wonder, I suppose, is that Volpe has not tried this long ago."

"Mercenary's honor again, I think. Oaths are sacred to him, and he is Rubin's sworn vassal."

Johanna looked up—two sapphires set in white marble. "So what was negotiated at Trenko, I wonder? My lord, I hardly mind what happens to my husband. I care nothing at all for my own place and title. But I will *not* let my son be cheated out of his birthright!"

Had she thought of murder yet? An unwanted widow might be tossed in the gutter, but legitimate heirs were prone to nasty accidents. Again and again in his career Volpe had proved that he was ruthless. If he now chose to set aside his fealty, Frederik would have to die.

"When will it happen?" she asked.

Ernst spread his hands. Fat, soft, useless old man's hands. "Soon, I imagine, if even a novice has heard of it. Remember, this may not be true!"

"Nevertheless, my husband must be warned."

"I would have sent word to Court if he had been . . . He has gone back to Krupa?"

"I think so. He left the monastery before I did this morning." She bit her lip in sudden doubt. "So I was told."

"That does not sound like him." At Fadrenschloss he had regularly slept till noon.

Johanna sprang up. "I must go to my son!"

This was not the hesitant, uncertain child the Duke had married.

Von Fader heaved himself to his feet. "Volpe may be there before you." And the babe dead?

"I must know he is all right!"

"Or the story may be false. Rubin may be there, carrying on as usual."

"And if he isn't? Suppose Rubin has heard the news and fled? Advise me, my lord!" Fury shone in her eyes like sunlight. Why did the spirits of chance persecute some people?

Ernst had thought about this all night. "Your son's safety must come first. Can you smuggle him out of the palace?"

"I can try. It will be dark by the time I get there. The gates close at sunset."

"And the guards are more alert at night. If Rubin is there, warn him. If he is not, wait until morning. Dress in servant clothes, put a basket on your arm and Frederik in a sling on your back. Walk out chattering to someone and the guards won't look twice at you."

She nodded.

"I can drive you down there now in my—"

"No! A horse is faster."

He sighed. "Then all I can offer is refuge. You remember Hunyadi, who used to work here? He runs a hostelry on Coppersmiths Street, just before it bends. You can trust him, and probably his men also, if he is not there. He can get you to Fadrenschloss. Here you will be safe."

Aldea had first come to Fadrenschloss at the time of Johanna's betrothal, a trooper in the Palace Guard. Now he was a captain but had not learned much. A large, dull man, he turned surly when the Grand Duchess announced her change of plan; he started arguing that his orders said she was to stay for three days. Ernst watched with amusement as she brought him to heel. Even lacking the status and authority Rubin should have granted her, she knew how to get her own way now—

"Must I complain to my husband that you defied my express orders? . . . By what right do you question my decisions? . . . I'm sorry you are not eager to get back to your family, Captain. Don't your men want to return to theirs? If we do not leave at once we shall still be on the road at nightfall." And so on.

The bailey was full of dismayed people. The feast, the music, the decorations . . . Her Royal Highness was *leaving*?

Aldea argued again when Johanna told her maid to remain behind to look after the baggage and that Ernst would arrange for her to be escorted home the next day. Ernst had agreed to no such thing. He would be happy to do so, of course.

Johanna fussed and fretted while the horses were brought out and saddled. When all was ready at last she gave him a farewell hug and protested when he cupped hands to help her mount. He insisted.

Her mount skittered and she brought it under control.

"Can we be there by sunset?" she demanded.

Aldea glanced at the sky. "*We* could, Your Highness."

"Then I can. Ride!"

Even with less imagination than a walnut, Aldea was starting to wonder at this urgency. "Something wrong?"

"I am anxious to see my child, is all. I just meant you needn't hold back for me. I can ride you all into the ground."

An outburst of coughing all around her conveyed widespread skepticism. She glared at them defiantly.

"Watch me!" she said, and went out the gate at a gallop.

They were big men all and wore half armor. She was much lighter and had a superb horse. Just after sunset they turned onto the Krupa bridge and she knew where she was. Her impatience drove her to kick in her heels for a final spurt; outstripping the men, she thundered up to the gates alone. They were closed. No one answered her hail. She had to dismount to haul on the bell rope and then the stupid, hairy face that peered out the wicket refused to understand who she was. Grand Duchess? He called her a drunkard and spat at her. Only when a furious Aldea rode up would the guards open the postern.

If she had been in any doubt, that incident proved that she could never smuggle Frederik out of the palace by night. In daylight it should be easy. She had watched all sorts of shady-looking people wander in and out unchallenged.

His Royal Highness had yet not returned from Trenko, but even to establish that took much effort and self-control. By itself, Rubin's absence meant nothing. He often vanished for days at a time when he had cornered some dainty nymphet. This time, combined with what she had been told at the monastery that morning and what von Fader had told her, the news knotted her with terror.

She fled in search of Frederik and found him in the capable hands of Ruxandra, being made ready for bed. Frederik took one look at her and flew into a screaming tantrum.

"He's just punishing you for going away," Ruxandra said reassuringly, and cuddled him. "Where's a good boy, then?" She was a dumpy, grandmotherly woman, as respectable as a snowy owl. Having spent her life rearing other people's children, she knew a lot more about babies than Frederik did. If she had a fault it was that she thought the Grand Duchess spent far too much time with her own child than was good for either of them. At the moment, Frederik seemed to agree.

In the end he lost the battle, though. His crib was moved back into Johanna's room, he grudgingly allowed his mother to hug him, and eventually he lost his nightly battle against sleep. So did his mother. Worried as she was, haunted by fears that Volpe and his killers might already be on their way, she had spent two hard days in the saddle. She fell into bed and followed her son's example.

She was awakened by a voice calling her name from what seemed a very long way away. Light on her face . . . bed curtains open . . . moonlight pouring in through opened shutters . . . a man standing beside her, holding a lantern . . . Illuminated from below, his face seemed bizarre and weird until she identified the goatee and the heavily pouched features of her husband.

"Johanna, awake! My violet, my faun! Waken!"

Bewilderment. "My lord! You're back!"

"I should say the same to you. You were supposed to be safely out of the way at Fadrenschloss."

"Safely? Oh, yes, yes! There's a plot! Von Fader warned me. Lord Volpe—"

Rubin chuckled. "I know all about my foolish uncle's mischief, my rosebud. It will not prosper, I promise you, but we must leave the palace for a while. I came back to rescue Freddie. I did not expect to find you here as well. Come, my turtledove. We must hurry. There is some danger." He sounded extraordinarily cheerful. Those foolish endearments were what he called her while making love.

Sleep fell away. She sat up, clutching the covers to her. Rubin was wearing a traveling cloak with a hood, and surely a sword under it. She had never seen him armed before.

"My evil uncle is on his way, turtledove. Dress and bring our precious. We must fly."

She slid from the bed and stumbled across the room. She had never dressed in front of him before and was absurdly conscious of his eyes upon her, but modesty would be an insane luxury when their very lives might be at risk.

In his cot in the corner, Frederik whimpered at the disturbance and then fell silent.

"Ruxandra!" Johanna said, fighting with stockings. "No, better let me get her." Laces streaming, she sped to the anteroom and then the nurse's bedroom.

Ruxandra gaped and gasped as her mistress shook her awake and shouted at her, but even ravings about revolution did not ruffle her. "Don't move him yet, Your Highness," she said, as calmly as if discussing colic. "I'll pack a bag for him first." She started stuffing clothes in a pillowcase. Johanna ran to fetch her jewelry.

They rushed along dark corridors, their lantern making monstrous shadows dance around them. Rubin went first, with his hood raised—because, he said, the sight of him flying by night might start a panic. Johanna clutched her son bundled in blankets, trying to soothe his sleepy grumbles, terrified he would erupt in screams of rage. Ruxandra followed, carrying the bag and spare blankets. Down back stairs, across a deserted kitchen . . . when they emerged into the chill of the stable yard, they found men harnessing horses to two carriages. Breath smoked in the torchlight. A fat moon sailed among silver-trimmed clouds.

Johanna headed for the great eight-horse ducal coach.

Rubin caught her arm. "No! We will take the other." He guided her over to the smaller coach and climbed in first, so he could take Frederik. The Marquis of Krupa took fright and screamed. Johanna scrambled up to take him and comfort him. He screamed louder. Ruxandra was helped, almost heaved, in by a groom, and the door was slammed. A voice shouted, a whip cracked, and the state coach began to move with much clattering of horseshoes and creaking of cold axles. Iron-rimmed wheels rumbled like thunder on cobbles, fit to waken the whole city. Then the second coach followed.

Frederik continued to howl. Johanna handed him to Ruxandra to let her try.

Her husband put his arm around her. Startled, she drew away until he removed it. Not much light entered through the horn-paneled windows, but the interior was not totally dark. Intimacy in front of a servant was unseemly.

"Now, Your Grace," she said. "Pray tell me what is happening."

"Volpe has turned traitor, my lovebird. He has been planning this for some time. Fortunately Abbot Minhea is loyal, so I have been kept informed. Now Volpe and several hundred knights are on their way from Vamky, intent on deposing me. We should be clear of the city before he arrives, but we shall be back, never fear." The coach rumbled and clattered along narrow lanes where moonlight could hardly penetrate.

"And where are we headed now?"

"Wait and see. I have plans." His voice was smug in the darkness.

The carriage rocked and bounced sickeningly on the rough roads. Johanna wished fervently that they had gone on horseback, although Frederik was too big now to carry easily in a sling. He did not like the coach. No sooner had he howled himself to sleep than it would lurch and jostle him awake again, so even Ruxandra could do nothing with him. The roads grew rougher and steeper, up and down. At times rain pelted on the roof and trickled in around the windows.

Eventually Rubin took his son to hold, which he had never done before. Frederik perversely stopped yelling. Either he appreciated the honor or he was just too astonished to object. He whimpered a few times and slid into a sound sleep at last. Moments later, Johanna realized she was doing the same.

*   *   *

She wakened with a start, uncertain where she was. Rubin was still holding his son. Ruxandra was snoring. The carriage was climbing a steep hill.

"We are going north?" she said.

"We are. The other coach went south, to Zolensa, and I hope my wicked uncle chases it in person until he falls off the edge of the world."

"But where? Not back to Trenko?" Even much later in the year, crossing the pass in this contraption would be a feat. They would certainly need fresh horses. And they would have to go by Vamky, the traitor's lair.

Rubin uttered his strange chuckle again. "I hope not that far, but the Margrave did promise me support if this happened. No, I told you that Minhea is loyal. We shall turn the tables on the turncoat. Volpe can have the palace. We shall reign secure in the monastery!"

"Wonderful!" she said, amazed at his confidence. This calm courage was a side of him she had never suspected. "Didn't something like this happen in your grandfather's time?"

"Everything imaginable happened in his time. Don't worry, my honeycake. All will be well."

Ruxandra had wakened. "Here, woman," the Duke said. "The boy needs attention. Take him . . . What?—"

The carriage had picked up some speed again, but suddenly horses screamed, the coachman hauled on the brake, gravel scrabbled under locked wheels, the whole world tilted. Johanna cried out, reaching for her child just as Rubin fell on top of her, and then baby and nurse on top of them both. The carriage rolled upside down, fell, crashed into trees, rolled again, bounced, and burst apart, spilling its contents down the cliff face.

✦ 7 ✦

After a long age the sky began brightening over the ranges to the east. The world was dark and wet and very cold. Johanna had no memory of being thrown clear of the wreck. Either she had caught hold of Frederik before it happened or she had found him later in the darkness, but she remembered doing neither. She was huddled against a spindly pine tree, which was all that kept her from rolling down a very steep slope and vanishing over the lip of the cliff. Frederik was asleep in her arms, wrapped in a filthy, grass-covered blanket. He had mud and blood on his face, but he was breathing. She had too many aches to think of trying to catalogue them. A trail of snapped trees and wreckage and dead horses above her showed where the carriage had rolled down the hill. Its remains were jammed against a tree some distance below her, with one wheel and a dead horse suspended over the final drop to the Asch, rumbling in its canyon.

She must find help. It took her a while to work that out. She had lost her shoes. She was shivering uncontrollably. The familiar skyline told her that she was not far from Vamky monastery, on the west side of the river, downstream from Olden Bridge. She must be close to Fadrenschloss, but she would have to walk there in bare feet, carrying Frederik.

Before she reached the road, she heard voices shouting. She did not bother to reply, because her son was already making all the noise necessary. Two men came clambering down through the scrub and trees. One young, one older. Father and son. Woodcutters. Help. The old one took Frederik, the younger lifted her into his arms as easily.

Later she was in a cottage, women tending her, more people, and eventually even the Baron, huge and haggard, his face pale as his beard. Just a few bruises, she insisted. They told her she had several cuts, the worst being on her leg, but she would not scar anywhere visible. They had both been very lucky. Frederik had escaped almost completely. Infants' bones bend like green twigs. She gathered others had not been so lucky. There was something important she ought to be telling the Baron. It escaped her.

Ernst sent for his coach and packed her in it. Frederik expressed his feelings about coaches very forcefully, but was overruled.

By the time they reached Fadrenschloss she was starting to come out of her daze and the horror was rising in her throat like vomit. The Baron fancied himself as an herbalist. He brought out his mother's old box of simples and concocted a draft with the impact of a woodsman's ax.

They put her to sleep in her old bed.

At first light Frederik's wails triggered her maternal instincts and wakened her. She found him in the next room before the woman sleeping with him had opened her eyes. The Baron had left orders that he was to be called as soon as Johanna awoke.

When she had soothed the boy back to sleep, she joined the old man beside a pinewood fire in the solar. There she sipped mulled ale from a silver goblet and gobbled bread, cheese, and sausage as if she had not eaten for a month. She had a wonderfully swollen face, several bandages, and enough aches to torture an army, but no time to care about any of them. The old man looked as if he had not slept at all.

"It is good to have you back, Johanna," he said. "I wish the circumstances were happier."

"Me too."

So much for pleasantries. Ernst seemed at a loss for words, and she did not want to speak at all.

He sighed. "Are you well enough to talk, Your Highness? I don't want to bully you, but there are . . . there are important things we must discuss."

She nodded. "I'm still shaky, but please go ahead."

He clawed at his beard as he did when he was worried. "Tell me if it becomes too much of a strain!"

"I will. I don't remember much about the accident."

"Yesterday you were babbling, not making sense. Petre and his son found you climbing back up the slope, carrying the Marquis. The body of the driver was near the road. He had been thrown clear and crushed when the coach was dragged over him. We also found an elderly woman in servant garb. Dead too, I'm afraid. Who else was in the coach?"

"Only my husband. Lord Volpe launched his coup, just as you predicted. Rubin woke me and told me we must fly at once. And we did."

The Baron grunted and tore his whiskers again.

"Where is Rubin?" she demanded. Why had she not asked that before?

"We found no other bodies, my dear."

The cliff! Her husband. The duke. Frederik's father and protector.

Von Fader's flabby face had taken on the stern expression she remembered from watching him sit in judgment here in Fadrenschloss. Having right of justice over his tenants and vassals, he took pride in being an honest and impartial judge, punctilious in collecting all the facts before rendering a verdict, even ruling against his own best interests when law or custom required it—something most lords never did.

"Johanna, my dear, are you certain that the man in the coach was your husband?"

Such a question must be a joke. She resisted laughter because laughter would be easier to start than end. "Of course I am certain, my lord! How could I not be? He had known about the plot for weeks, he said, and had made plans. Alas, it seems chance favored Volpe. He has won and I must flee into exile with Frederik. This is what you are saying?"

Von Fader shook his head. "It is more complicated than that. First of all, chance was not involved. The crash was no accident, but deliberate murder."

"No!"

"I beg Your Highness to hear the evidence before you say that!" Sometimes she was the Grand Duchess and sometimes just the child he had fostered, the years between forgotten. He leaned sideways to haul on a bell rope. "That is a very dangerous corner for anyone who does not know it. The bend is unexpected and the surface slopes outward. Mud washes across it and makes it slick. That can be turned to our advantage. Enter!"

The heavily wrinkled monkey face that peered in around the door belonged to Manfred, the Baron's forester, of whom it was said that he could follow a crow's tracks across a lake. He must have been awaiting the call. Johanna knew him of old and tried to smile at him, but smiling hurt.

"Close the door," the Baron growled. "Tell Her Highness what you saw."

Clutching his hat with both hands, the forester said nervously, "It had been raining, Your Royal Highness, and then stopped. Marks were very clear. Someone had put a wagon there, blocking the road. Driver didn't have a chance."

Wagon? She said nothing, refusing to accept the implications.

He squirmed under her stare. "A wagon and a man on a horse, Your Royal Highness. They came from the north. The horseman led the way coming, and when they left, he led the way again."

"They left after the crash?" the Baron said.

"Yes, my lord. His marks were both under and over the coach tracks. The wagon stood there quite a while, waiting. Lot of drip marks."

"And his horse?" the Baron prompted.

"Very big horse. A warhorse, likely, a destrier. It still wore winter shoes, with cleats."

Von Fader studied his former ward, waiting to see if she were taking this in.

"The Brotherhood?"

He nodded approvingly. "That's a very reasonable guess. We can't be certain he came from Vamky, but it's very likely. There are few destriers in Krupina, and only the brethren's would be shod with cleats. They patrol the pass. Tell her what happened, Manfred."

"Wagon and horseman, Your Highness . . . horseman rode around a bit, driver turned and backed the wagon to where he wanted, about halfway across the road, so there was a gap, but not wide enough for a team to pass. And the horseman dropped some caltrops." Manfred produced a caltrop, which he must have been holding in his hat, because anyone who put a caltrop in a pocket would be stabbed by its spikes. Nasty, evil little thing! "Not many. Just enough to panic the team, make sure it wouldn't stop in time. I took this one out of one of the horses' hooves."

"All the horses died?" Four beautiful horses!

Manfred nodded. "Horseman went around after the crash to pick up caltrops left over—his prints were on top. He wore riding boots, not sabotons."

"Armor," the Baron explained.

She shuddered, trying to comprehend such cold-blooded evil being directed at her and her child. She was a widow. That idea was too big to fit anywhere . . .

"Someone knew you were coming," the Baron said. "A fast horse will outrun a coach. Could have gone from Krupa to Vamky by the east road, come around by the bridge. Might have been time to set up the ambush. Tight, though."

"Rubin sent his state coach south to draw off pursuit. He was betrayed!"

"Not necessarily." Von Fader sighed wheezily. "I'm afraid there is more, my . . . Your Highness."

"No!" she said sharply, and stood up. There must not be more! She had not caught up with murder yet. She limped over to the window, seeking escape, wringing her hands. The sky was bright, not much short of dawn, with early foliage outlined like black feathers on the trees. This room was familiar, unchanged, home. But she couldn't stay. Someone had tried to kill Frederik. They might try again. The future was a blank wall across her path. Where could she go? Who would give her refuge? Nothing in her life or upbringing had prepared her for such a dilemma.

She turned to see the Baron's eyes on her, full of concern, but was that *pity* on the wizened forester? She would not concede pity. She went back to her seat.

"Very well, my lord. What more horrible news have you for me?"

"Manfred found this locket. Tell her where."

She had taken her jewel box with her. Not the state jewels, just a few trinkets Rubin and the Baron had given her and beads that had belonged to her mother. The Asch could play with the pretty things down in its canyon.

The forester was talking. ". . . a bush on the edge of the big drop, Your Royal Highness. Lot of branches broken, some blood, bits of damask and silk, some hair." He produced a couple of wisps from his hat. She did not take them. She could not remember what Rubin had been wearing. Nothing special, nothing she would recognize.

"So a body was thrown into the bush and then fell through, into the river?" the Baron prompted.

"Looked that way, my lord."

"Could it have been faked?"

The little man hesitated, but only to choose his words. There was no doubt in his voice when he spoke. "I do not believe so, my lord. No footsteps on the mud there after the bush was crushed. Don't see how it could have been faked."

Johanna knew his reputation, and obviously the Baron accepted Manfred's opinions as infallible. He flickered her a reassuring smile, which did not work.

"So the question before the court, my dear, is who went into the Asch leaving this locket behind? His Highness? Gold locket, heart-shaped, on a golden chain. Expensive. Was it his? Is it yours?" He passed it to Johanna.

"I've never seen it before," she said. The portrait inside was a flattering one of Rubin, head and shoulders. "No, it's not mine." Rubin had probably given it to some lady friend in the past, but to say so in front of Manfred would be disloyal. One should not speak ill of the dead. Why was the Baron pulling faces?

"I doubted it belonged to either of you. You see, Your Highness, it is a conjuration, the sort they call a seeming. Brace yourself for a shock, my dear. Manfred, put it on. Show the Grand Duchess what it does."

It turned Manfred into Rubin. When Johanna tried it and peered at her image in her goblet, now she was Rubin.

She must have cracked her head in the fall and gone crazy.

Someone else had died? Rubin was still alive?

Von Fader's doughy face was congealed in misery. "Thank you, Manfred. In thirty years you have done me no greater service."

When the forester had gone, Johanna said bitterly, "You think I was trying to elope with someone." That was what the world would think. She was ruined.

"I know you better, my dear. I had seen you earlier that

day and you were not plotting any such nonsense then. You would not cheat your son out of his birthright." He scratched his beard again. "But that may be how others will interpret it. Oh, death! I cannot make sense of all this evil! Surely only Vamky is capable of conjuring that trinket, and the ambush was set up by men from Vamky. If that had been your husband in the carriage, then the murderer had a good chance of killing both him and his son, leaving Volpe as unquestioned Grand Duke and Karl his heir. Men have been hanged on weaker evidence.

"But the locket changes everything! Someone was masquerading as your husband. What was the imposter trying to achieve? Abduction, most likely. But was he abducting your son, or you, or both of you? Did two conspiracies defeat each other? Did he say where he was taking you?"

"He said Vamky." Would she ever have emerged from that gloomy keep? "Or was he just planning to compromise me? If I ran away with another man Rubin could divorce me." And be free to marry sweet Margarita of Trenko.

"He could have found easier ways of arranging that!" the Baron protested.

Johanna avoided his eye. "The imposter knew certain intimate endearments my husband bestows on me sometimes. Only he could know what they were!"

The Baron harrumphed. "Pardon my crudity, Johanna dear, but you may not be the only woman he has so addressed."

"Of course!" Hundreds of them. She should have seen that. With the locket, the imposter might have been anyone, even a woman. Margarita of Trenko, perhaps? One of her own ladies-in-waiting. "He held Frederik!"

"Does Rubin not do so?"

"I have never known him to touch his son since Frederik's naming ceremony." And his laugh. That had not been

Rubin's laugh. People's laughs were often distinctive. Had she met that laugh before?

"Your husband would not put his own son in danger."

"Oh, never. He told me just a few days ago he wanted to see Frederik acknowledged as his heir."

After a moment's silence, she realized that the Baron had really been asking her a question. Because she was now the expert in Rubin's marital behavior. Rubin would not harm his son *unless*? Unless he had already murdered two wives and wanted to dispose of a third so he could bed the fair Margarita, who was of noble blood and thus available only in legal matrimony . . . ? Staring at the old man, Johanna saw in his eyes the horror that must not be spoken. No one would suspect a man of killing his own son just to dispose of an unwanted wife. Not to mention three innocent companions. But if the Grand Duke had not been in the carriage, could he have been the man on horseback?

"You are saying," she said, although Ernst was deliberately *not* saying, "that the purpose was to kill me and Frederik?" No, that wasn't right . . . Ernst had had a whole day to work on this. "Just to kill Frederik? That I was supposed to be here in Fadrenschloss and not in the coach at all? That it was a plot by Volpe to kill Frederik so that Karl could be second in line again?"

Surely that was nonsense. If Volpe's code forbade him to depose his nephew, how could he murder an innocent child to promote a dissolute son he despised?

Then was *Karl* behind it? He had the most to gain if Frederik died. He would be second in line again. Ridiculous! Karl wasn't capable of organizing anything beyond a shoddy seduction.

So?

So it came back to the fact that Johanna had been present only by accident, when she was not supposed to be, so the fake Duke had been forced to take her also. It was Frederik who had brought the threat of revolution. Restore Volpe to his former place as heir presumptive and the coup danger would fade away. Rubin was not the bravest of men. He hated anything that interrupted his quiet life of studied promiscuity, and what happened to Krupina after his death interested him not at all. From that point of view, Frederik had been a mistake, perhaps a mistake that could be corrected. The fake duke had not known of the ambush, of course.

She shook herself to banish the nightmares. The Baron was studying her. He looked ten years older than he had two days ago.

"Advise me, my lord," she said.

"I cannot," he said angrily. "I am too old to straighten such a tangle. There are so many possible explanations! Were there two conspiracies? Or was it a double bluff? Who was the intended victim? Perhaps Rubin did know of a plot to overthrow him. So he sent you and your son off to safety, not realizing that Volpe would go so far as to ambush the carriage. Then where is your husband now? Who rules in Krupa?"

And dare she go back there?

"I am not fit to travel yet," she said.

"Of course not." The Baron heaved his mass off his chair and waddled over to stare out the window. "Daylight!" He sighed. "Neither the coachman nor the woman could be identified. The coach was firewood. But the horses carried the Grand Duke's mark. By the time we had collected the bodies yesterday it was too late to send word to Krupa, you understand? So I can claim, anyway. But I dare not delay longer. I must send word to the palace today. Now! Someone will be here before dark. If your disappearance is already known, another someone may be here even sooner. This is the first place they will look for you."

She saw that she was not merely in danger herself. She brought danger with her like a plague. "You must not take risks for my sake, my lord."

The Baron remained at the window, a monolith staring out at the mountains. "No risk. Very few people know you have come back, and I swore all of them to secrecy. You could be wandering in the woods or sheltering in some charcoal burner's cottage."

"No!" She rose, and was at once reminded of her aches and bruises. "You must not take the risk!"

He turned to frown at her. "Do not be foolish, Johanna. It is no risk for a few days. Your husband told you that rebels were about to seize the palace. You were abducted by someone unknown. Your husband is dead. He tried to kill you. His uncle tried to kill you. Not all of those statements can be true, but any one of them is enough excuse for you to remain in hiding until you know it is safe to emerge. I ordered the foxhole made ready."

"But hiding the Grand Duke's wife from him must be treason at the least!"

"Nonsense. Hiding her from rebels is true fealty. Fadrenschloss will give you sanctuary, and I will hear no argument."

She was back to being a child again. She went to him and hugged him.

◆ 8 ◆

The foxhole had not changed. It had been her refuge before her marriage and now was to perform the same service again. Frederik found the strange, curved, dim little room very interesting to visit—but only for long enough to walk to the cot at the far end and back again.

"We are going to stay here for a while, darling," his mother told him. "See how nicely it has been cleaned and prepared for us! Are you hungry? Thirsty? There's food here. And I think there are toys in this box. There is everything we can possibly need here."

"Need go potty," the Marquis said firmly.

Johanna stared around in panic. *Almost* everything.

Once that emergency had been dealt with—it was under the bed—he was reasonably content to have his mother all to himself and not be in a coach. His bruises and scrapes bothered him, but he found her swollen eye very amusing. He kept trying to punch it. Small boys are like that.

"I do hope you grow out of this," she told him, fending him off.

About the only thing that might betray the foxhole to its enemies would be a two-year-old's temper tantrum, which no stone wall in the world could muffle completely. However, after an hour or two of throwing the toys around, Frederik settled down on his mother's lap to hear a story and went to sleep before it was finished. This was good fortune. Johanna had barely laid him on the bed and covered him with a blanket when the bell tinkled and she rushed to the nearest squint. There were three such spyholes, one overlooking the roadway up to the barbican, one the bailey, and another the Great Hall. Since none of them currently showed any activity at all, she returned to the driveway view and stayed with that, waiting.

There had not been time for the morning's courier to reach Krupa, let alone for a response to arrive at Fadrenschloss, but Vamky was only a couple of hours away. Whoever was coming now must be specifically hunting for the missing Grand Duchess, as von Fader had said, and this was the most likely place. Soon a cavalcade appeared in her field of vision: heralds, standard bearer, a troop of the Palace

Guard escorting a man in civilian dress. No armor, no blue on white. Soon she recognized the ducal banner in front. So it was Rubin. She felt a great surge of relief. Her married life had been far from perfect, but had the newcomer been Volpe, her lot would have been exile and penury.

The procession disappeared out of her field of view, and she shifted over to watch the bailey. The Grand Duke rode forward to the steps. The Baron was waiting to hold his reins. In a moment the two men went indoors together.

No doubt Ernst would lie his head off to start with. He would not admit that Johanna was there until he was certain that her husband's intentions were honorable. That would be tricky. He could not ask about coups or imposters or conjured lockets without revealing that he knew more than he should. Johanna must wait for his signal. The guards were dismounting, handing over their horses to the Baron's men, and there were a lot of them, a big escort.

No doubt host and guest had gone to the solar for a private chat and she would learn nothing more until after Rubin had left. If he was really suspicious, he might stay a week or two. Or have his men search Fadrenschloss. That would be a deathly insult to the Baron, of course, equivalent to calling him a traitor to his face, but Rubin was capable of that. With little hope, she crept halfway down the narrow stair to the spyhole overlooking the Great Hall. Her view was again restricted, covering little more than the throne on the dais at the far end and the approaches to it. Shafts of sunlight angled down, turned to silver by dust motes. Ancient banners hung motionless from the rafters.

Then the two men came into view below her, heading toward the throne. The Baron thumped along on his cane, grotesquely foreshortened. *Rubin was limping slightly on his right foot!* Oh, spirits! She stared in horror, trying to will that limp away, but it just became more evident as her angle of view improved. Where there was one enchanted locket, there could be more. Had the Baron noticed? If he hadn't, would he notice in time? Frederik moaned and Johanna raced up the stair to comfort him before he discovered her absence and erupted.

But now she knew how the Grand Duke had managed to ride from Krupa to Fadrenschloss so quickly this morning—he hadn't. He had come from Vamky. And he wasn't the Grand Duke.

It took some time for the entire staff of Fadrenschloss to answer the summons and assemble in the Great Hall. When they had done so, Johanna could only watch what happened. She could not hear. The Baron introduced the Grand Duke, although just about everyone in the castle had been employed there long enough to remember him only too well. They cheered politely, no more.

The disguised Lord Volpe then made a brief speech. Johanna could supply the words for herself, except that she did not know how much she was worth and had to guess at the numbers. Soon the two nobles departed and the audience dispersed to go back to work. How many people knew of the foxhole? How many would sell out? One would be enough.

By then Frederik was awake again, wanting to be fed.

"You should be proud of yourself," she told him as she buttered his bread. "Here you are, not yet three years old, and already you have a price on your head."

Grinning, he patted his curls with both hands, trying to find the price, whatever that was.

It would not be called a price, of course. "Reward" would be the word used, but blood money was what it was. Find the poor little heir lost in the woods and win a fortune. Whether you ever collected would be another gamble altogether. A fake Grand Duke need not worry about his reputation for honesty, because he would not be using that reputation for long. Once the loose ends in the succession had been tidied up, he could arrange for his predecessor's official death and start to rule in his own name, his own face.

She wondered if Rubin were dead already. More likely, she decided, he would be kept locked up somewhere safe until his son could join him. The strength of monarchial government was that you solved nothing by striking off a crowned head: *The Grand Duke is dead, long live the Grand Duke!* Frederik must die before or right after his father. Also, since there was a slight chance his mother might be carrying a brother or sister, she had better be sent off too. Tidier that way.

About noon the imposter rode off down the road with his guards, but the alarm bell gave no all-clear signal. Johanna had expected that. If Volpe had posted a reward for her capture, as she surmised, then he would have left some men behind to wait for snitches to take the bait. Then they could secure the prisoners. Wishing she had counted his entourage when it arrived, she reconciled herself to a day alone with a screamingly bored Frederik, perhaps several days.

The tantrums would stop when he turned three, Ruxandra had promised, but he had still had a few months in hand and tantrums were his only way to express dissatisfaction. He could not understand that bad men might be prowling the castle listening for a baby yelling. He did sense that temper fits were attracting more attention than usual that day, so he used them more often. There were times when Johanna thought her son would drive her crazy. She also knew she would have gone crazy already if he were not with her.

When darkness came at last, she closed the shutters on the squints so it would be safe to light a candle. Frederik went to sleep to dream of another day of mayhem ahead. She tried to read a book, gave up, and lay down fully dressed with a lantern still lit, knowing that the summons might come at any hour of the night. To her surprise, she was asleep when it did. She came awake instantly, caught up the lantern, and hobbled down the narrow stairs, wincing at the aches in her stiffened muscles.

The entrance to the foxhole was through the top of a closet. She knelt to slide the bolts and lift the trap, which was so narrow that the Baron could not have climbed up there at any time in the last forty years. He could still stand on a stool, precariously. His head appeared at her knees.

"All right, my dear?" He spoke in a whisper.

"We're very well. It was Volpe! You noticed his limp?"

"I did. He offered a reward of a thousand Hyrian ducats for each of you."

"Is that all?" Johanna said indignantly. "A dukedom cheap at the price!"

"But it is a great fortune to a drudge or a turnspit."

"Of course," she said sadly. It would have seemed a great fortune to her not long since.

"He left six men here," said the disembodied head. "We have girls distracting them, but I mustn't stay. Anything you need?"

"Tomorrow, if we're still here—more toys, fresh water, and a fresh slop bucket." She did not suggest throwing in a gag for her son; this was no time for humor.

Frederik wakened her. He was whimpering, not howling, and with luck would go back to sleep. Grunting at her aches and bruises, she rolled over and was about to stuff her head under the pillow when she realized that the bell was jangling. It was a very small bell, emitting a very quiet tinkle. On and on. One ring for alarm, three for all clear—that was the agreed-upon code, but now someone was jiggling the cord continuously. She sat up.

From far away came a sound of hammering. She surged out of bed, uncovered the lantern, and ran down to investigate. Someone was banging on the trapdoor, trying to waken her.

Then she smelled smoke.

Fadrenschloss was ancient; it would burn like tinder. Bruises forgotten, she hurtled back up to the room . . . gathered cloak, shoes, and her son in his blanket . . . back down the stairs in the dark . . . Frederik began wailing at yet another rude awakening. The noise was louder now, jarring strokes of a sledge that she could feel through her feet on the stonework. Before she could even start to struggle with the bolts, they tore loose and the trap flew up with a blaze of light and a gush of acrid, eye-biting smoke. The amount of coughing going on down there suggested a sizable reception committee waiting.

"Take him!" she cried, thrusting her son into the arms that appeared. Even if those belonged to Volpe himself, being burned alive was not an option. Heedless of the indignity, she slid her feet out through the gap and felt many strong hands grab her and lift her down. She wore only a nightgown and a cloak and her shoes; the hands lingered a little longer than necessary.

"Captain Aldea, Your Royal Highness," said a satisfied voice.

Tall, solid, stolid, with the imagination of a gnat. Useless to explain to Aldea that the man he thought was his sovereign was a usurper wearing an enchanted locket. She had a matching locket with her, but she would solve nothing by suddenly turning into Rubin now. She coughed as the smoke bit her lungs.

"Come!" Aldea said. "We should get out of here. This is getting dangerous." He grabbed her arm and hustled her out into the corridor.

She resisted. "Let go of me!"

"No." Aldea did have enough imagination to see that she might try to escape in the resulting confusion. He forced her to keep moving. "Baron says the whole castle will go up very shortly."

She hurried along with his fingers around her arm like steel bands. She could hear Frederik's howls amid the coughing ahead of her. She could also hear a terrible roar, a waterfall noise, which she feared might be the fire itself.

"Did the Duke give you authority to put Fadrenschloss to the torch?" she raged.

"Not our doing, Highness. Baron thinks there's a firefly loose. Oh . . . *death*!"

They had reached the door to the Great Hall. All one side of it was a wall of fire, glowing through dense smoke.

"Can't go in there!" another man cried.

"You know another way out, Highness?" Aldea asked.

"Yes. Let go of my arm." She waited until he did. "Now follow me!" She squirmed through the crowd, grabbed a lantern, and led the way, listening for Frederik's howls to be sure he was coming. At the door to the cellar she hesitated just for an instant, dreading the thought of going down there, of the whole weight of the castle above her, but she could not leave her son to be burned alive. She stumbled down the stair with a tattoo of drumming boots following her, into cool, breathable air. When she struggled with a door, male hands reached past her and almost tore it off its hinges. Back up again. She emerged into the bailey and cried out in dismay.

The night was bright as day under the pillar of fire going up from New House, which was far from being the youngest part of the complex. Even at that distance, the heat of it was unbearable. Despite the stablemen's efforts, several horses had panicked and broken free; now they were stampeding madly around the yard, endangering everyone. Behind her

the Great Hall exploded in a huge cloud of flame, balls of
fire bursting from every window, spewing debris.

"This way!" She grabbed at the man who was carrying
Frederik, and clutched his arm tightly as they all ran for the
Lesser Barbican. At times they had to flatten themselves
against the wall while the terrified herd went thundering by.
The ground was littered with glowing and smoking debris.
She held up her hems with her free hand, frightened of being
set alight.

"Stop!" someone screamed. "There it is! Freeze! The fly!
Don't move."

The men ahead of her stopped instantly and she bounced
off their backs.

"Go! Go! Go!"

"No!" Captain Aldea roared. "Everyone stand still. Don't
even talk."

"What madness is this?" Johanna yelled. The fugitives had
all frozen into statues around her. Frederik was sobbing. She
tried to squeeze through between two men, and Aldea's steely
fingers closed on her arm again.

"Stand still!" He sounded as if he were trying to speak
without moving his mouth. "It's the firefly."

She looked where everyone else was looking and saw . . .
a spark? A star? Whatever it was, it outshone even the great
blaze of New House behind it. Its glow was so intense that
it hurt the eyes, circling above the bailey as if it were being
spun on an invisible rope. It was hard to track, scrolling lines
of brightness on her retinas. Was it alive? Living fire enjoying the mayhem it had created?

"How do you kill that thing?" a trooper muttered.

"You can't," Aldea mumbled, not moving his lips. "Baron
says they don't live long."

They didn't need to. For no apparent reason the firefly
went spiraling down to the horses, which had trapped

themselves in the corner by the servery and were plunging and kicking madly. It spun over them as if taking aim, then plunged into the herd. A horse exploded in jets of steam and fire, and a shower of burning flesh. Where it had been the firefly danced again. It struck at another, with similar results.

"Move!" Aldea snapped. "Slowly. Don't run. We have to get out of here."

That remark needed no repeating. The smoke and heat and falling debris were becoming unbearable. There was no air. Johanna edged in close to Frederik, who was still screaming inside his blanket, as the whole party crept along the wall, all watching the terrible massacre of horses. After five or six had been destroyed, the firefly seemed to tire of the game. It rose, hovered, and then circled into the servery, straight through a wall. All the windows lit up.

The roof of the Great Hall collapsed, sending enormous clouds of sparks sailing to the stars.

"Now!" Aldea barked, but everyone was running already. They jammed up in the postern, then let Johanna and the man carrying Frederik go ahead. She staggered out into darkness and crisp, clean air. There she reclaimed her son, hugging him and muttering comfort to soothe his terror.

"Come, Highness," Aldea said. He wasn't holding her anymore, but he was staying within grabbing distance. "We're still too close."

He and his five supporters closed in around her and shepherded her over the grass to the road. No one else went with them. A row of fruit trees beyond the road was lit up as if caught in a brilliant sunset. Many people were standing there, watching the death of Fadrenschloss, although flaming fragments were falling even at that distance and the trees lacked enough foliage to provide shelter.

When she reached them, she turned to stare back at the

disaster. The ancient tower stood within a forest of flames. Had she stayed in the foxhole, she would have been baked like bread, even if it did not collapse, which it probably would. The whole of Fadrenschloss was ablaze, and now more roofs were falling in, each new collapse sending fiery clouds of sparks skyward in the night.

The Baron must be around somewhere, and she shrank from the thought of trying to offer sympathy for such a crushing disaster. It was fortunate, in a way, that he was so old and had no heirs.

"You swear this was not your doing?" Johanna demanded.

Aldea glanced down at her—he was a very tall man. "You saw the firefly, Your Highness."

"And where do fireflies come from?"

He twisted his mouth in a strange sort of smile. "From conjurers, so they say."

"Lord Volpe, perhaps?"

"Didn't say that."

"I say that! And whose orders do you follow?"

"Grand Duke's, Your Grace." His eyes narrowed with suspicion, perhaps just because he found her question puzzling. *Crack!* Aldea said, "Huh?" and fell over.

A ragged tattoo of crossbows, a couple of cries, and six men lay on the ground, some of them sporting bizarre quills of death. Frederik had his face in her collar, so he had not seen and would not understand if he had. Johanna knew vaguely that she ought to be shocked, but she was numb from too many shocks.

One of the victims was struggling to rise to his hands and knees. The Baron stepped forward with a two-handed broadsword and struck off his head as neatly as any headsman.

"They were only obeying orders!" Johanna protested weakly.

"And they would have continued to obey orders!" The Baron was a wild, hatless figure, half dressed in mismatched garments. His wispy white hair and beard stuck out in all directions; his eyes glowed madly in the firelight. "They would have followed us. We must go. Vamky will have seen the fire. Go now!"

"Go where? They will be watching the roads."

"They have roadblocks set up," von Fader snarled. "They were smoking you out. But no one catches me in these woods! Manfred, bring the child. Gunter, put these bodies in the fire somewhere. Come, Johanna, we rescued clothes that should fit you."

III

From a Check to a View

• 1 •

A panicky moth swooped around a candelabrum and came within reach of Ranter. His hand flashed out and caught it, crushed it. "I never heard of fireflies," he said.

"Why would you?" his ward asked wearily. "You are not a soldier."

She was courageous and determined and honorable, and now Bellman could add patience to her catalogue of virtues, for this was at least the sixth time Ranter had interrupted her story. The others had seen that she preferred to tell it in her own way and had respected her right to do so, but not Ranter. Subtlety worked no better on him than Ringwood's threats did.

The windows were still dark, but morning was near. Bellman's eyelids felt as heavy as boots; even the Blades looked as if they could use a rest, and Sister Trudy was limp and unfocused. Ringwood took advantage of the break to rise and attend to some smoking candles, snuffing them and replacing them with new ones.

"If you were a king or a prince, Sir Ranter," the Duchess said, "besieging a castle, your best option would be to hire the Vamky Brotherhood. It has many secret military conjurations. One of them is the firefly. How could any stronghold withstand fireflies?"

Ranter said, "Oh. And that's what shadowmen are for, too?" He was not stupid, just thoughtless. "How do they put shadowmen inside a castle?"

"We don't even know how they got them into this place," Ringwood said. "Please carry on, Your Highness."

Bellman thought of being shut up in a besieged fortress haunted by shadowmen and then tried not to. Castles had dungeons and cellars where the wraiths could lurk forever. As for a firefly, that would work like a ferret in a rabbit warren, sending defenders leaping out of every window. He wondered how much the brethren charged for their deadly services.

"We are tired and the hour is late," Johanna said. "I just wanted to take the chance while the Baron was not present to explain why you must not suspect him of betraying me. Sometimes he still treats me as a child, but that is just his way. He is very old, remember. He has lost everything. Dispossessed, exiled, and proclaimed a traitor after a lifetime of honorable service! I forgive his little tantrums." She smiled. "I have talked too much and you have listened too long. Later today I'll tell you about our journey from Krupina, and we can discuss how I can get back there."

"Don't bother," Ranter said. "You are not going back there."

Bellman had been waiting for something like this.

The Duchess's smile thinned and then vanished. "You will not speak to me like that, Sir Ranter!"

"If I have to I will. Ringwood and I are sworn to keep you safe. We won't let you go stumbling back into that snake pit."

Johanna rose to her feet, face flaming. "You will do as I say."

Bellman stood also. Ringwood turned from the candles. Ranter just leaned back on his chair and smirked.

"No, you will do as we say! Our loyalty is to our King, not to you. We serve the Pirate's Son by keeping you safe. Didn't Grand Master explain that?"

"Be silent, Ranter!" Ringwood said. "This is neither the time nor place."

"It's as good a time as any!" his ward snapped. "Understand that being a duchess brought me no joy and my husband is almost certainly already dead. Volpe can have Krupina so far as I am concerned. But my son lives. I left him in a safe refuge and my first duty now is to go and recover him. My second is to see that he comes into his inheritance, for he is either the rightful heir or already the lawful Duke. For his sake, the traitors must die. That is my mission and you two will assist me. I will accept no argument on that. If I must ask King Athelgar to issue you the necessary orders, then so be it!"

"Blades don't take orders from anyone," Ranter said before Ringwood could speak. "Your baby is not our concern. Send Bellman to fetch him if you like. We'll ask the Pirate's Son to grant you a small pension and find you a safe cottage somewhere, and that will be that. The Baron and his two flunkies can go boar hunting blindfolded if they want, but you stay here in Chivial. Incognito."

She turned to Ringwood as if expecting him to deal with this insubordination. Bellman wondered which of the two he pitied more, ward or Blade, both of them bound for life to that oaf. Poor Ringwood had been growing more and more gloomy and hangdog as her story unfolded. He must have known from the start that he was a boy being sent on a man's mission, but now he knew he needed an army, and what army in Eurania would be willing to challenge the fearsome Vamky Brotherhood on its home ground? If he were years older, if he had completed his Ironhall training and commanded a team of a dozen first-class Blades who all fenced like Sir Cedric, the odds would still be impossible. The Duchess was deluding herself.

Then she looked to Bellman for support, making him want to howl—in sorrow and frustration and rage. He wished desperately that he had some comfort to give her, but everything Ranter had said was correct. Even if her Blades personally wanted to help her with her quest, their bindings would probably force them to block it. That was a problem for another time, when they were not all so tired. Meanwhile the best he could do was to distract her.

"I have some questions about the Baron, Your Highness, which I'd prefer to ask while he is still absent. These previous attacks on you, after you left Fadrenschloss and before you came here, to Chivial. Where did they occur? Were they all made by shadowmen?"

She frowned, puzzled. "One was—in Blanburg. In Brikov, Cosanza, and Château Bellçay they tried other methods. Why?"

"You said earlier that those attacks were sent from Krupina, implying that the conjuration was being performed in Vamky. Master of Rituals told me he had never heard of spirituality being effective at such a distance; it's almost always confined within the octogram, as you know. Most likely somebody nearby was responsible, he said. They might have brought a conjurement that they could activate, but someone would have to release it close at hand."

"You are an expert in conjury, Master Bellman?"

"No, Your Highness. But the weather is not the same everywhere. Starkmoor can suffer a blizzard when the sun is shining in Grandon. So how could Lord Volpe or his helpers back in Vamky have known the sky was dark enough for shadowmen that night, here in Chivial? Who suggested to you that the attacks were being *sent* from Vamky?"

She hesitated before saying, "I don't remember." That meant she was defending the Baron. "You mean someone's been following us?"

No, he did not mean that. "Did you not try to cover your tracks?"

"Of course we did."

"On your travels, how many rulers have you asked to help your cause?"

The lady had not been born to wear a coronet, but she had learned not to expect interrogation by her own servants. She flushed. "What is the purpose of these questions?"

"I'll show you in just a moment, Your Grace. Believe me, they are very important. Let me rephrase the last one. How many times did you receive a sympathetic hearing, and where?"

She flinched, confirming his suspicions. But then her doubts were suddenly directed at him, and even Ringwood was eying him darkly.

"Who have you been talking to?" the Duchess said. "Answer me!"

"No one, Your Highness. It was only a guess. One thing that surprised me was how readily you accepted the imposter's story when he came barging into your bedchamber in the middle of the night."

"Master Bellman! . . ." She reined back her anger and continued in steadier tones. "I told you that the Baron had warned me that very day that such a coup was possible."

"Yes, you did," Bellman said unhappily. "And without his warning, how would you have reacted? Another thing. Manfred found a locket. The baron identified it as a conjuration. How? Did he try it on in front of a mirror? A woman might do such a thing; why would a man? Does he suspect everything he sees of being enchanted?"

"What are you implying?"

"You told us the Baron fancies himself as an herbalist, but that he is no conjurer."

"*He isn't!* And neither are you. A little knowledge is a dangerous thing."

"Yes, Your Grace."

For a moment it seemed she would not answer that veiled accusation. "Ernst is well informed about spiritualism," she admitted. "He had two younger brothers in the Brotherhood. They both died on faraway battlefields, long ago. Just because he's an aristocrat and a soldier does not mean he is ignorant! He lost one of the finest libraries in Krupina when his home burned. He's a clever, educated man. He is *not* a conjurer."

"But someone close to him is, Your Highness," Bellman said. "Wasn't it curious that the coup came so soon after you had been warned? And even more curious that the report reached you at all—via the Baron? That the imposter's body disappeared but the locket was conveniently torn off his neck by a bush just as he fell? That the Baron thought to check the locket for enchantment? Who knew about fireflies? Was that him, too? Was he the someone who has been encouraging you to believe in long-distance conjuration? You almost admitted that every time you found a ruler willing to listen to your story, like King Athelgar, you were spiritually attacked. Coincidence? Or betrayal?"

"No!" The Grand Duchess's shout startled Trudy, who was having trouble keeping her eyes open.

"I am truly sorry, Your Highness," Bellman said, truly meaning it, "but there are too many flies in the soup. One or two I could swallow, but not so many. Someone close to you is working for your enemies."

"That's obvious," Ranter said. "Tomorrow we'll get the inquisitors to question all three of them—Baron, Manfred, and Harald."

Ringwood flashed Bellman a smile. "Well done, brother! Tell us about Manfred, please, Your Highness."

"*Manfred?* Oh this's ridiculous!" She spun around and stalked over to the dais, as if to mount the throne. Then she turned again. "Manfred is devoted to the Baron, devoted! He's worked for him all his life. He told me his family has served the von Faders for four generations. He left his wife and—"

"And?" Ringwood prompted.

"He left his wife and family behind." She looked around the worried faces. "But his children are grown . . ."

"Harald, then?"

She sighed and looked down at her hands. "If it has to be anyone, then it must be Harald. His father is the Baron's seneschal, as his father was before him, but Harald is one of many sons, all of them huge. He was a novice in the monastery, following his older brother, Radu. Harald told his father about the plot, and Priboi told the Baron. When Fadrenschloss burned, the fire was visible from Vamky, but the brethren were forbidden to ride over and help. Discipline is so strict in the Order that a knight may not even adjust his stirrup without permission. The first thing a novice does is swear absolute obedience. Harald learned later that there had been brethren at Fadrenschloss already, blockading all the roads out, and they had done nothing to help. They just waited, hoping to catch me. Harald was so upset that he walked out of the monastery. He quit."

The Ironhall men exchanged glances. "That's allowed?" Ranter asked.

"It's quite common," the Duchess said. "Very few recruits make it all the way to knighthood. Once Harald had made sure all his family were safe, he came after us and caught up with us at Brikov. The Baron took him on. He's educated, well-spoken, and strong as a bull. I've rarely seen him without a smile on his face." She glared around at the accusing faces. "You think he was sent to spy on us, don't you? Well, I don't! The Baron would trust him with his life."

"Frankly, that does not seem wise at the moment, Your Grace," Bellman said. "Did he arrive at Brikov before or after the attack on you there?"

She hesitated, considering the implications. "Before."

"Harald must be questioned, but we won't need to bring in the inquisitors. If the Sister here is willing to help and . . . Sister Gertrude?"

Trudy was holding one hand against her neck as if she had frozen solid in the process of rubbing it. She was staring fixedly across the room at a tapestry of a lutist and a dancing woman. So far as Bellman could see, there was nothing wrong with the tapestry. Beyond it, on the far side of the great stairwell, would be . . . the Baron's room. And the servants' room next to it.

"Trudy?" Ringwood said. "Sister!"

"Death," she whispered. "And fire! Fire, fire, fire!"

The Blades jumped like crickets. Ranter bounded from his chair to the wall and grabbed a heavy tapestry of peacocks and flowers as if he wanted to climb up it. Ringwood yelled, "The locket!" looking ready to grab his ward and shake her. "Put on the locket!" Bellman was already unlocking the door.

He peered out, resisting a temptation to draw his sword. No fire in sight. He emerged on the gallery and blinked in the dimness. No emergency. Below him, Blades were rolling dice in a pool of candlelight, but they had heard him and every face looked up. False alarm? Everything seemed very innocent.

"Fire!" he yelled. "Probably deliberate." He began running around the gallery to reach the far side. "If you see a bright white . . . dancing flame . . . don't move! Just freeze. It's alive."

A thin sliver of light showed under the Baron's door, shining through trails of smoke trickling out. He slid to a halt. If there was a firefly in there—or even just a burning room hot enough to glow like that—then he would die if he opened the door. The fire would explode the moment it was given air. But if only the medicine chest had burst into flames and the Baron was still asleep, then there might just be time to rescue him. Sir East was supposed to be in there, too, guarding the chest, and he would not be asleep.

Bellman's momentary hesitation saved his life, because it gave him time to realize that the door itself was about to fail. The panels were starting to glow faintly red, becoming transparent, with spreading streaks of fire shining through. Sir Valiant was coming up the stairs at the double with three other men at his heels. Before the wood dissolved completely in a gush of ash and smoke, Bellman yelled a warning and dived into the room adjoining, just in time to escape the unbearable rush of heat. For a moment he could see nothing except the afterimage of that ghastly brilliance, but the roar of flames was obvious now. Smoke bit his lungs, made him cough.

The room seemed dark compared to the brightness outside. It held four servant beds—just cots, not the fourposters of gentry. Manfred lay on the floor, wearing only breeches. A window stood open. Smoke was streaming in under the connecting door. This was no place to linger.

Shouts of alarm made him spin around. Ringwood and Ranter had just emerged from the audience room with Grand Duke Rubin between them, wrapped in a tapestry. If necessary, they would throw a fold over their ward's head and carry him out like a parcel, but they had stopped at the sight of the tiny white brilliance hovering above the stairs. Valiant and the others must have understood Bellman's warning, because they had halted also.

Then the heat became too much for them. "Back!" Valiant shouted. They all turned to run—and the firefly swooped.

Bellman turned away in time to avoid witnessing the results. He closed the door and surveyed his immediate problem.

Manfred was alive, with a swelling bruise on his chin and a cut on his head still oozing blood, suggesting he had been knocked down and had struck the corner of the bed. A rope tied to the bed led over to the open window, showing how the killer had made his escape. The trees and shrubbery of the park were illuminated by the glare, meaning flames already had broken through the roof. Where were the Yeomen who supposedly guarded the place? Bellman could feel heat from the wall and connecting door. Quamast House would collapse in ashes in a very few minutes.

The window was too high to risk dropping an unconscious man, but he pulled up the rope and confirmed that it had been knotted at intervals to make a crude ladder. He dragged Manfred close, tied the free end around his chest, and heaved him up on the sill. Then he sat down, braced his feet against the wall, and nudged Manfred out. It was fortunate that Manfred was small and Bellman well above average Blade size. On his first day as the Brat he had been taller than anyone in Ironhall except Master Armorer, and he had grown meat on his bones since then. Even so, he could not have managed without the knots, both to grip onto and to ratchet over the sill, braking the descent.

By the time the rope went slack, his hands were cramped and he was choking in the smoke. He scrambled out and began to climb down.

Halfway down he pushed free and dropped the rest of the way to the lawn. He cut Manfred loose and dragged him a safe distance from the inferno just moments before a blast of fire from the window they had left rained debris over the ground beneath.

Bellman made sure the forester was breathing, then sprinted around to the far side of the building. Everywhere seemed bright as day. He arrived in time to see Ringwood jump and land safely in the outspread tapestry being held by a rescue team of Yeomen and Blades. He was the last. Ranter, Trudy, and the Grand Duke were all safely down already.

Bellman went to the closest Blade, who happened to be Silver, and poked him in the back. "How many?"

Silver turned and gave him a sick look. "Valiant, Yorick, East, and Clovis."

"There's an unconscious man around the far side. He needs a healing right away."

Silver said, "Done!" and started shouting, no doubt glad of something to do.

Unwilling to let their ward stay close to the inferno or be silhouetted against its light, Ringwood and Ranter were hurrying the Grand Duke over to a decorative gazebo. It was an ugly latticework thing containing a bench and a marble table. The Duke flopped down on the bench and doubled over, sobbing. Trudy was there already. Bellman joined them.

Ringwood looked a question at him and he shook his head.

"Your Highness," he said, "I regret to inform you that Baron von Fader must be counted among the dead. Manfred had been stunned, but he is safe and will be all right, I am sure. I saw no sign of Sir East or of Harald, except that someone climbed down from the window on a rope. I suggest that the Watch be informed right away and every effort be made to find Harald Priboi. He should be described as very dangerous."

The Grand Duke straightened up and wiped his eyes with the bank of his hand. "Dangerous? *Harald* dangerous?"

"I believe we must issue that warning," Bellman said. It did not feel right to him either, though. "He is big and he does have military training."

"Do that, then. Sir Ringwood, will you, please? Warn them he does not speak Chivian." As Ringwood ran off, Rubin gasped a few times, as if breathing had become difficult. "How did it happen?"

Bellman told what he had seen. "I assume Manfred woke up and saw him at his foul work," he concluded. "I do not know how he killed the Blade on watch, but he must have done so. And King Athelgar will certainly want to know how he climbed down a rope and ran away without the Yeomen seeing him."

"Conjury?" Trudy said angrily. "It is my fault! If I hadn't been half asleep I would have sensed all that happening. I could have given more warning."

"You were not asleep," the Grand Duke said. "You saved all our lives, for if you had not been there we should have had no warning at all. But your King was right. I do need a White Sister or two with me on my—" He looked at Bellman. "Do I have a quest?" he asked softly. "Will my Blades let me go back to my son?"

Ranter was standing in the doorway, apparently intent on watching the fire, but possibly eavesdropping as well. Walls were cracking. The last of the roof went down with a roar. Trudy moved over to the doorway to see better.

Bellman sat down beside the Grand Duke on the little bench. "You still have a quest, Your Highness," he said quietly. "Now, if your Blades balk, I can talk them into it."

"Thank you. His Majesty will be eager to see the last of me after this."

"I fear so." The toll was mounting—four more guardsmen dead made six, plus three Yeomen and the Baron made ten, and a mansion destroyed. Also a desperate killer on the loose. *Good-bye, Duke, and good riddance!*

"You will come with us, or do you want to be released from your promise?"

"I'm with you all the way, sire," Bellman said. It was his memory of the Duchess that sealed his loyalty, though.

Ranter wrapped an arm around Trudy and hauled her close. "You're sort of cute," he said.

◆ 2 ◆

It was almost noon before Trudy located the Krupinese contingent, and by that time she was ready to strangle someone. She had been interviewed three times by teams of inquisitors—an even worse experience for her than most honest folk, because she sensed the snoops' enchantment as a nauseating stench of week-old fish. She had done battle with Mother Evangeline, who maintained that Sister Gertrude should have called for immediate inspection of the suspect medicine chest instead of waiting until morning, should not have stayed on in Quamast House, and should not now be refusing to answer questions about what she had learned from or about the Grand Duke. A tour of duty on the west coast of Nythia would be arranged to encourage her to mend her ways.

Trudy had refused to be made scapegoat for the latest tragedy and the Fellowship's overall incompetence. The battle had continued with Mother Tranquility, Reverend Mother

Meadowglory, Very Reverend Mother Lettice, and other ancients up to and including Mother Superior. In the end Trudy had given that worthy lady very specific instructions on what she could do with her antique robes and stupid pointed hat. As a result, Sister Gertrude was no longer Sister anything, nor was she employed.

Since even a career in cadging or turnspitting would be preferable to going home and having her brothers tell her they had told her so years ago, she had decided to seek a position with the Duke. He might be pompous and fleshy, but he was also his own charming and admirably tough-minded wife. That personal ambiguity seemed an excellent arrangement, offering endless possibilities. The poor woman could certainly use Trudy's talents. Her *considerable* talents. No one had ever accused Gertrude of modesty, especially her brothers, and she had always known she far outshone her classmates at Oakendown, but one of the bleating crones that morning had let slip just how high she scored on the Sisters' rating. It had surprised even her.

Besides, the Duke-Duchess was now accompanied by two shiny new-minted Blades and the intriguing Bellman, who would not be distracted by ward problems as Blades were. A long journey with that threesome should prove educational.

Trudy's first problem was that she was no longer authorized to dress as a White Sister and was required to leave the palace forthwith. Fortunately those edicts cancelled out, because she owned no alternative costume. What could they do about that?

The second problem was finding the ducal person. Quamast House was a stinking ruin, still oozing smoke. The Krupinese had been moved to parts unknown and were being held incommunicado, no doubt with inquisitor troubles of their own—her inquiries were met with blank stares or smiles of apology, although she did learn that her quarry was still within the Nocare Palace complex. Searching that would be a lifelong task without something to go on, but she had lots to go on. Although the Duke's seeming was not especially detectable, a Blade's glow was, and Blades in large numbers glowed brighter still. Inquisitors likewise showed up well when they swarmed, or clotted, or whatever the correct expression was.

Even so, she walked the corridors for an hour before she detected a constellation of Blades. Homing in on that spiritual signal, she climbed two flights of stairs to an area she had never visited before and there found a room full of them, a dozen or so sitting around a table rolling dice. They looked her over with interest, as Blades always did. The one who rose and came to the door to speak with her was Sir Tancred, the Deputy Commander, which showed how seriously the Krupinese affair was now regarded around Nocare.

He was too old for her, and married, but he had a lovely smile. "A pleasant surprise, Sister Gertrude. How may I help you?"

"What?" Baskets of rolls and cheese on the table were shouting reminders that she had not eaten all day. "Oh—I came to see the Grand Duke."

"May I ask on whose business?"

"His business. I work for him now. Didn't you know?"

That was hardly a fair question when the Grand Duke himself did not, but it worked. Tancred led her to an inner room, where Mother Violet was reading poetry to Mother Giselle. Trudy wondered how they could stand the reek of inquisitor, for the snoops must have been using the place very recently. Perhaps these two could not detect that residual taint. They looked up suspiciously as Trudy's cheerful smile went by, but they obviously had not yet heard of her dismissal.

Tancred rapped on another door. A moment later it was

opened by Bellman, looking extremely dapper in a gold and green jerkin, with cap, hose, and short cape in darker green. His eyes lit up gratifyingly at the sight of her.

"There has been a mixup," Trudy explained hastily. "The Guard has not yet been informed that I work for the Duke now."

"Paperwork takes forever here!" Bellman said. "I'm sure I told Sir Florian. His Highness has been waiting for you. Come in."

"In" was yet another anteroom, empty of people this time, but the far door did lead into the ducal presence. A typical palace bedroom of tennis court size, with windows on two walls, a garderobe door in one corner, and too much flesh tint on the wall tapestries and ceiling frescoes, had been furnished with a long table and high-backed, gilded chairs to make a council chamber.

The first thing she noted was food on the near end of the table. A heap of clothes occupied the other, and Manfred sat unobtrusively near the middle, munching a bread roll and a chicken leg, wearing the bemused look of someone who had recently been through a healing. She could sense it on him. The Grand Duke stood in a window embrasure, staring out. Ringwood, in crisp new blue and gray, was buckling a shoe. Ranter, stripped to his shirt and hose, was pulling yet more garments from a bag. Clothes were heaped everywhere.

She went to the Duke and curtsied. He . . . yes, it had to be *he* when they had a beard. They turned his head and smiled at her.

"No ill effects I hope, Sister?"

"None, Your Highness. You wanted to hire a sniffer? I can recommend myself highly."

"Indeed I do." His face looked tired and worried, even baggier than usual. "At least, I think I do. In fact your arrival is very timely, because we have just seen off the inquisitors and the tailors and now I must decide what to do next. I have an audience with His Majesty very shortly, so the matter is urgent. If Sir Ranter is going to carry out his threat and lock me up in a cell in a swamp somewhere, then no, I don't require your services. I hope I will, though." His smile was smarmy, nothing like his wife's. "Mother Superior has agreed to lend me your services?"

At last sight, Mother Superior had been fain to swoon, but the details were unimportant.

"I am a free agent."

Grand Duke Rubin noticed her evasion but did not waste time on it. "Your professional skills will be invaluable, of course, and I would enjoy having another woman in my party." Unconsciously, he fingered his beard.

"Are you nearly done, Sir Ringwood?" he asked over his shoulder.

"I am, sire. Ranter isn't."

Trudy looked around just as Ranter hauled off his shirt and then pretended to notice her for the first time. He puffed up his chest. "Oh, beg pardon, Sister! I hope I don't shock you."

"Not at all," she said. "I used to have a sheepdog with a coat like that." Had she been honest, she would have said his glow was blinding and the scar over his heart shone like the sun, but Ranter needed no encouragement.

"Make yourself respectable!" the Grand Duke snapped, leaving the window. "Gentlemen, and you also, Sister. This morning I lost my closest friend. He was a second father to me, as you know, or grandfather, and also my most trusty councillor. I rely on your advice now, although I intend to make the final decisions myself." That was an obvious slap at Ranter. "Always tell me what you truly believe, not what you think I want to hear." He pulled a chair nearer to the door, but behind it, where he would not be visible from the anteroom.

Ringwood looked fatally worried. He was going to be the one who made the decision, however much the Grand Duke and Ranter might pretend otherwise. If Ringwood insisted that Rubin stay in Chivial, his views would almost certainly carry the day. Whichever way he decided, he might regret his choice for the rest of his life. He caught Trudy's eye and smiled wanly. "Have you eaten, Sister?"

"Not today." Grateful that somebody had thought to ask, she said, "Nice outfit. I like your hose."

Apparently this was not a judicious compliment to offer a young man. Ringwood blushed scarlet and turned his attention to the food, taking a platter and loading a whole roast duck on it. If men didn't want their legs admired, why did they flaunt them so?

"Please help yourselves!" the Grand Duke said. "We have no time for formality. One thing I have learned on the road is to eat whenever I can."

They all gathered around the table. Still buttoning his doublet, Ranter sat himself next to Trudy.

"Don't you know men with hairy chests make the best lovers?" he asked in a coarse whisper.

"Not in my experience." True! There were no lovers in her experience. She reached for the bread basket and pulled out her belt knife to attack the butter.

"Counselors!" The voice was that of Grand Duchess Johanna. She had removed the locket and all the men perked up. "I am sure His Majesty is furious at these new deaths. I fully expect him to evict me from his realm as fast as possible. Assuming this will be my last audience, what do I ask of him?"

Trudy glanced around at all the worried, drawn faces. None of them had slept. Without the seeming, Johanna looked much more exhausted than before. She was also mourning a lost friend.

"I am sure the Baron was a wonderful counselor." Bellman's lie clanged like an iron bell in Trudy's ears, shocking her, but no one else seemed to notice. "Your Highness will feel his loss forever. We, though, need some additional information if our advice is to have any merit. We know nothing about your adventures between the fall of Fadrenschloss and your arrival in Chivial. Where else were you attacked and how? Where is your son, the Marquis? Who—"

"I will not tell you where Frederik is," she said, flashing anger at him. "He is safe. Let that be sufficient. Nor have I time to relate an adventure saga."

Bellman laid big swordsman hands on the table and stared down at them. "As I am ignorant of the dangers involved, I regret that I am unable to advise Your Grace."

She did not like that. "Very quickly, then. The Baron knows the forest around Fadrenschloss as no one—"

Knuckles rapped on the outer door. Murmuring an apology, Bellman rose and went out, closing the anteroom door behind him. In a moment he returned, leaving it open again.

"The Guard is ready to escort you to the audience, Your Grace. I asked for more time, but they cannot allow us much."

Trudy started eating even faster, although no one had said she would be going to any audiences.

Johanna nodded, thin-lipped. "We escaped the brethren's attempts to catch us, with Manfred's aid." She added something in a foreign tongue for Manfred, who had heard his name mentioned. "And another of the Baron's men, Bogdan. We made our way up into the hills, to a place called Brikov, the seat of Count János. Officially we were still in Krupina, but few Grand Dukes have seriously tried to impose their rule in those mountains. János made us welcome because he is a lifelong friend of Ernst von Fader. That was where Harald caught up with us. We seemed to be safe there, but after three days the brethren struck at us. The house where we had been given sanctuary was suddenly invaded by vermin—rats, mice, flies, fleas, spiders, roaches, snakes, centipedes. They came in everywhere, under the doors, down the chimney, through the thatch, and they seemed to multiply while we watched. We were driven out."

Snakes and spiders, six- or four-legged things never bothered Trudy, but *centipedes*! Yug! Did everyone have a weakness like that, a private horror?

"The Baron told me," Johanna said, "that this was a weapon the brethren had used to good effect decades ago, in his own campaigning days. They called it a 'swarming,' and it will turn a military camp into madness. The only cure is to burn down the infected buildings."

"But it isn't really dangerous?" Ranter said. "Not like shadowmen?"

"It can be if you have enemies waiting for you outside. Snakes can be dangerous. Could you sleep if your bedding and pillow were infested with creepy things? We were fortunate that only one house was struck, not the whole settlement. It was a warning, or so we took it. Count János begged us to stay, but not convincingly, and we wanted to bring no more trouble upon him.

"From Brikov we went by secret ways through the mountains to Blanburg, for the Prince there is a cousin of Rubin's. It was at Blanburg that the first shadowmen attack came. Bogdan was killed, also four of the Prince's guards. Again we fled. We visited many, many places, too many to list now. At Cosanza, in Ritizzia, and at the Château Bellçay in Isilond, we were again attacked by swarmings. As Master Bellman guessed yesterday, the attacks seemed to come whenever I gained a sympathetic hearing. So we were being betrayed. Harald would not have needed to know the details, even. Our faces would have told him."

Her Highness sighed. "I cannot imagine why we did not suspect treachery!"

Trudy could. The traitor had convinced the Baron, the Baron had been too old to let facts change his thinking, and Johanna had trusted him too blindly. Bellman had seen that right away.

"There are still too many loose ends," Bellman said. "Even if Harald is working for the usurper, the attacks themselves do not make sense." He was interrupted by more knocking and went to answer it.

Ranter spoke up, with his mouth full. "Why'd you go around pretending to be your husband? You got looks and a nice body. You ought to be able to twist men 'round your little finger."

Trudy considered stunning him with a wine bottle. On the far side of the table, Ringwood closed his eyes and shuddered.

"But a woman is accorded much less respect than a man," the Grand Duchess said straight-faced.

Ranter shrugged. "Suppose so."

"And I will have more of it from you, Sir Ranter, or you will sing for your supper."

"Just trying to help," Ranter said sullenly. "I know I say the wrong thing oftentimes, Your Highness. Don't mean to give offense. I've tried to change, but it never helps."

"Try harder!"

He should start by learning to think before he opened his mouth. Trudy could see a dozen reasons why the Duchess had chosen to take advantage of the locket. A sovereign would receive a better hearing than a lowborn consort. Lord Volpe's assassins might hesitate to kill a head of state, whose death would attract much attention. Women's clothes put them at a horrible disadvantage on horseback—the White Sisters regularly masqueraded as men when they traveled. A woman wandering around without her husband was a social pariah, anyway. It was indecent behavior.

She said, "May I ask Your Grace what Manfred was able to tell you about the Baron's death?"

"Nothing," the Duchess said. "He was asleep. He heard strange noises, started to get out of bed, and the next thing he knew he was in the elementary, being healed. His assailant must have been Harald. Anyone else would have had to break in, and the house was tightly guarded. The Blades were watching the doors."

But even Blades could die. Sir East had been guarding the suspect box in the next room.

Bellman ran in and resumed his seat, this time closing the inner door. "Highness, we have only a few minutes. Please tell us what you know of the present situation in Krupina. Has Lord Volpe proclaimed himself duke yet?"

Trudy watched in fascination as the Duchess wrung her hands. Real people actually did that? Not just characters in romances?

"It is very hard to find anyone who has ever even heard of Krupina, let alone had recent news of it. Births, marriages, and deaths in the ducal family attract some attention in aristocratic circles, and that is all. The latest word I had was no word. I must assume that Volpe continues to masquerade as my husband and the rest of the world sees nothing wrong. That is why I have had so much trouble being believed."

She was meeting that problem again now. Trudy watched the men exchange glances. The Duchess was telling no lies, but she could be honestly mistaken in her story.

"The murders confirm your tale, Your Highness," Bellman said, and only a faint doubt shadowed his words. "Someone is persistently trying to kill you, cutting down bystanders like thistles. But with all respect, you offer no proof that Lord Volpe is the culprit!"

"He has the motive!" Johanna said hotly. "He has the means, for he controls the conjurers who made the locket. Vamky men were blockading Fadrenschloss when it burned. Are you suggesting that my husband tried to kill his own son? Explain how he obtained the conjurements or the knights who set up roadblocks around Fadrenschloss!"

Bellman opened his mouth, and then a thunderous knock on the outer door stopped whatever he had been about to say.

"Your Highness asked my counsel," he said quickly. "I think you are in grave and immediate danger. The swarmings, as you called them, were not designed to kill you, but merely to deny you help from those who might have supported you. They also served to drive you far, far away from Krupina, and I suppose Chivial was always a logical destination for you, the realm of your husband's cousin. There is nowhere farther for you to go. Now, suddenly, the traitor has turned vicious and people are dying again. In one sense this is encouraging for you, because if your husband and son were both dead, you would—pardon my putting this so crudely—you would be much less important. It does seem that the chase has ended, you cannot run farther, so it is time for the kill, and the killer escaped last night. We must assume he still has some devilish conjurations to use."

Again the Guard thundered a summons.

"Put the locket on, please," Bellman said. "My counsel is that you disappear immediately, this very day. Ask His Majesty for funds and a trusty guide who can see you safely aboard a ship. Your first priority must be to elude Harald. We are fortunate that he cannot speak the language and has no accomplices."

That was not quite a lie, but Trudy sensed reservations. They *thought* Harald could not speak Chivian and he had no accomplices *that they knew of.*

Hooking the amulet around her neck, Johanna became Rubin again. He stood up, so everyone else did.

Ringwood was pale but happy. "I agree with Bellman, Your Highness. We sail away."

Ranter sneered. "Sail away where? If you're planning to run home to unmask Volpe or whoever is behind the killings, then you're out of your minds. All of you are. If you're going to hide, then hide here in Chivial where the King's on your side."

"Cowards' thinking!" Ringwood said. "Caution is good, but Blades aren't jailers. If the Guard thought that way it would keep the King locked up in a dungeon."

The door opened. Sir Tancred peered in, furious. "His Majesty is on his way to the audience chamber, Your Highness."

"Coming!" the Duke said. "You are outvoted, Sir Ranter." He hurried out with his two Blades at his heels.

Bellman perched on the edge of the table and said, "Whoof!" His face could never be called handsome, but his smile was honest and reliable.

"Whoof to you," Trudy retorted.

"Manfred, this is Trudy. Trudy, this is Manfred."

The wizened forester smiled and muttered, *"Viel Glück!"*

"Good chance to you," she responded. "I think you're right," she told Bellman. "We must go, but where to?"

"To wherever she left her son." He grimaced. "We need to know if the kid's really safe or if the killers found him after she left."

Trudy found that possibility too nasty to think about, but poor Johanna must be thinking of little else. "I need clothes. Who negotiates wages around here?"

Bellman laughed and reached for the pouch on his belt. "Nobody. We don't talk about money at all. I think Her Nibs knows nothing about it and is terrified of the subject. She did give me a purse for expenses, but most of her funds were in the Baron's keeping and got melted this morning. How much do you need?"

"Who paid the tailors?"

"Nobody yet. We haven't finished choosing. 'Sides, Grand Duchesses are notorious for skipping town. Here, take the lot and give me back what's left." He handed her his purse. "Another thing, Sister . . ."

"I'm not a sister. I told Mother Superior to climb a tall tree and lay eggs."

He smiled. "Interesting image. I just wanted to tell you that I don't intend to spend the rest of my life in Krupina. We may all die there, of course, but I'm not bound like the Blades. Whether this thing has a happy ending and Her Nibs is restored to the bosom of her dear husband or everything falls apart, I intend to come home to Chivial in a year or two. I'll be happy to escort you if you feel the same."

"That's reassuring. Thank you." *Very* reassuring. She hadn't thought that far ahead yet. And Bellman had no ulterior motives that she could detect.

Then she sensed a glow and looked to the anteroom. Bellman took her cue and stood up.

A distinctive mustache peered in from the corridor. Seeing that he was noticed, its owner followed it in and strolled toward them. Trudy had been warned about the notorious Sir Hazard on her first day in the palace. He knew more scandal than the Dark Chamber, the Sisters said.

"Good chance to all!" he proclaimed. "I hear you are leaving." That was a lie to start with. He was fishing. "Heading home to Krupina?"

"Skyrria for the bear hunting," Bellman said. "What real news have you heard?"

"I have heard some you will find *most* interesting." He eyed Trudy speculatively. "Am I telling the truth, Sister?"

"Why ask me?" she said, angry that he had put her on the defensive so easily.

"Because most Sisters can truth-sound as well as inquisitors and you are the first eleventh-rank Sister to come out of Oakendown in forty-two years. Now, do I lie to you?"

"Keep talking." How dare he know what she had learned only an hour ago! Forty-two years, mm? She was also annoyed to see that Bellman had edged around behind Hazard so he could make faces at her over the smaller man's hat.

"I might be prepared to trade," the Blade said.

"Trade for what?" she asked, knowing she shouldn't.

He shrugged with exaggerated indifference. "Maybe a hint or two on the Trudy Stakes?"

"Manners, Sir Blade!" Grin vanished, Bellman gripped the back of Hazard's neck, putting his thumb threateningly on the pressure point below the ear.

Hazard ignored him. "Well, if you don't want to trade, sweet Sister, you don't have to trade. Pity. It is important news. Truly, Trudy." He was not lying. "How about a short list? The top three contenders, maybe? One-third my winnings at no risk, pay half my losses if you change your mind at the last minute."

Now Trudy knew what the Trudy Stakes were and felt her face blush madly. "Who are the favorites?" she asked, curious in spite of herself.

Hazard leered. Bellman released him with a shrug.

"Ansel, Hector, and Bloodhand."

"Bloodhand? That blowhard?" Trudy made a noise not approved in Oakendown. "I assure you that it will be none of those three." She was going away, or Ansel would certainly have been in the running.

"Sir Silver?" Hazard asked quickly.

"No comment."

He chuckled. "And when do you anticipate awarding the prize?"

Behind Hazard's back, Bellman raised a clenched fist, looking to Trudy for a signal to use it.

"Soon. I have narrowed the field to a short list."

Hazard rubbed his hands. "Thank you, thank you! Do remember I am available if you decide to put skill ahead of youth."

"The news?" Bellman demanded.

The Blade turned to him, eager to spread his latest scandal. "You know that even a bonfire as hot as Quamast cannot destroy bones. And you know that five men died there—four Blades and the Baron? Wrong! The coroner's men have turned up six skulls. Who was the sixth, mm?"

It had to be Harald, didn't it? Who else could it be?

"I don't know," Bellman said coldly. "I can't see how an intruder could have sneaked in through the Yeomen cordon, but then I couldn't see how Harald had escaped unseen. Was he found in the same area as the Baron?"

"That I do not know."

"I expect the King will tell His Highness. Have you any new news?"

Hazard pretended to take that question as an insult and huffed off, no doubt eager to hedge his bets on the Trudy Stakes.

Trudy had lost all appetite for lunch. "But if Harald was not the traitor, who was?" Everything connected with the Krupinese seemed absurdly obscure.

Bellman sighed. "You tell me. The inside and outside of that suite were being watched. If an intruder flew in or made himself invisible or disguised himself as a bat, you would have sensed that much spirituality, wouldn't you?"

"Likely."

"Then the bones were Harald's. He arranged the rope for

his escape and killed himself loosing the firefly. That would be possible, wouldn't it?"

"I'd think so."

"Or perhaps Sir East killed him, but too late. I'll ask Grand Wizard's opinion. I have other things to ask him for Ringwood. Can you direct me?"

"I'll take you there," Trudy said. "I must find a dress-maker."

Manfred was working his few remaining teeth, frugally scavenging the duck that Ringwood had not had time to fin-ish. Bellman turned to him and indicated in mime that he wanted the forester to stay and guard the clothes. The old man grinned and nodded, gesturing that he would continue to look after the food, too.

Bellman offered Trudy his arm and they went out together. She must not let Hazard see her like that, although she would be long gone from Nocare before the Trudy Stakes were de-cided. The winner would not be a member of the Guard. Even odds he would not even be a Blade.

◆ 3 ◆

The open road! With a strong horse between his thighs and *Bad News* slung at his saddle, Sir Ringwood, Commander of the Grand Duchess's Guard, was thundering along a country trail and loving every minute of it. There had been trouble and there would be more trouble, lots of it. One day he would die, because everybody died, and it might be soon in his case, but today he was alive and young, and life was very sweet.

Ahead of him the trail wound through the ripening late-summer countryside. It carried little traffic, which was why they had chosen it, but a few minutes ago their cavalcade had swept past a tinker and a skinny boy leading a donkey. Ringwood's eyes had prickled as hard as the poor man's would when the dust settled on him. *It's me, Dad! I'm a man now, a* gentleman, *and what I'm doing is important.*

He was doing it quite well so far, he thought. Better than most people had expected of him, he suspected. Certainly better than he had feared. It could not last, of course. He was good enough with a sword, but he lacked all the strategy training Blades normally received. Sooner or later he would make some monumental blunder.

The Grand Duke rode at his left, although now he was merely Sir John Schale and would revert to being Mistress Johanna Schale as soon as they got rid of their guide. Their guide, riding on Johanna's far side, was Sir Rivers, recently released from the Guard and hired by Leader to help out the greenhorns. No doubt he was competent and would see the Krupinese party safely to Brimiarde and aboard a ship, but there was something about Rivers that rankled. Although he was not such an all-over scrag as Ranter, he was smarter, so the way he put people's backs up seemed more deliberate.

Behind them rode Ranter and Trudy, who was a surprisingly convincing boy, and then Manfred, who was obviously an expert on horses. *Must learn from him.* Bellman was bringing up the rear, leading a pair of sumpters. *Remember to spell him off.* Remember, too, not to let Ranter monopolize the best company. And here came a chance, for the trail ahead narrowed to cross a cornfield; unkind to trample the crops by riding three abreast.

Ringwood dropped back. "Take over the string from Bellman, please, Sir Ranter," he said sweetly.

Ranter scowled and reined back without a word, which was both relief and surprise.

Ringwood smirked at his new companion. "That's better. Much better!"

"Are you telling me or asking me?" Trudy said.

"Telling you. I wouldn't dare ask." *He won a smile!* "I just can't tell you how happy I am to have you with us, Sister. You saved our lives last night, I'm sure, and you will again. Or I'll come back and haunt you!"

"Don't call me Sister," she said. "And yes, you are a welcome change. What is it about Ranter? He seems to have wasps in his doublet all the time."

"Ranter is always the lowest bat in the cave. He's sore because he had older brothers who dumped him in Ironhall to cut him out of the inheritance. It wasn't very fair." Ringwood did not want to talk about Ranter.

"I had older brothers, too. I don't go around irking people, do I?"

He gave her a soulful look. "Oh, *no,* my lady!" Big sigh. "Quite the *reverse,* my lady!"

"Idiot!" She was amused! She filled that male jerkin in interesting ways.

"Yes, my lady." Be businesslike, now. Stop smirking like an idiot. Manly. "I do have a query, my—"

"Call me True."

"Yes, True! My friends call me Ringworm and I hate it. In Brimiarde we're going to be conjured to speak Fitainish and probably Isilondian. I just wondered . . . I know some Sisters can't stand conjuration. Will you be all right?"

"I'll tell you when the time comes and I know what it smells like."

"Is that true, True? Do you smell spirits, sniff them?"

She had a lovely smile. Her face was not remarkable normally, but her smile made him think of stars and blossoms and violins. "Depends on the conjuration and the sniffer. I can smell an inquisitor at fifty paces. Like bad fish."

"How about Blades?" he asked carefully.

"For me Blades glow."

"Really?"

"Really," she said.

"You can see us in the dark?"

"Certainly. Ranter's pale yellow. You're sort of bronze."

She was teasing him. She must see him as a mere boy compared to Ranter. Ranter had muscles and fur on his chest—as he had been careful to show her that morning.

"Could be handy if you ever wanted to read in . . ." Oh, *horrors*! ". . . bed."

Why, why, why had he said that?

"I doubt if you'd be bright enough unless you took all your clothes off."

"Happy to oblige," he said quickly, but it was no good. She had done it to him again. What sort of swordsman *blushed*?

They spent two nights at the home of Sir Martin, another former guardsman. He had married so well that he owned two villages, but both he and his fox-faced wife were discreet, asking no questions. A royal courier caught up with them there and delivered passports, bankers' drafts, and letters of introduction that the King had promised Johanna. Most of the documents were genuine, but some were Dark Chamber forgeries. Kings were handy friends to have.

The next day they reached Brimiarde and put up at the Sign of the Turtle, which just happened to be run by another former guardsman, Sir Panther. Brimiarde's elementaries had a reputation for language conjuration, as would be expected in a major port. Sir Rivers handled the negotiations, with Bellman watching, and successfully haggled one group of brothers into including Bohakian at no extra charge. Trudy declined Bohakian and Isilondian, accepting only Fitainish, but even that put her to bed for two days with headache and nausea.

Then everyone could speak with Manfred and include him in the group. He turned out to be taciturn, with a cynical view of the world and a dry sense of humor. He mourned the Baron deeply, and admitted he was happy to be going home to his wife and family.

By good chance a suitable ship was in port, a squat little cog named *Conqueror* that specialized in shuttling back and forth across the Straits and had facilities for passengers. As soon as terms were agreed and entered in the log, with Bellman's signature alongside Captain Howie's, Sir Rivers had completed his mission and could ride off with good wishes ringing in his ears. He did, but no one was really sorry to see him go. Trudy just wished he had taken Ranter with him. Ranter fancied himself as front runner in the Trudy Stakes. He was certainly trying hardest. Very trying.

Conqueror needed another four days to finish loading her cargo of wool, pickled fish, and cider. After that the weather was reluctant to let her go, but one morning the sun rose in a clear sky and the summons came. Six men left the Turtle; four men and two women boarded the ship.

♦ 4 ♦

It is wonderful to be a woman again!" the Grand Duchess announced dramatically.

Trudy was not so sure. The two of them were standing on the aft castle near the helmsman, staying out of the way of the crew as Captain Howie bellowed orders through a speaking trumpet. *Conqueror* leaned before the wind, heading for open sea. Landward the view was spectacular, with hills showing the golden tints of harvest and morning sun gleaming on the roofs of Brimiarde, but the ship itself was cramped and shabby and stinky, as Sir Panther had promised them it would be; all ships were. With luck they would reach Isilond in a couple of days; without it they might take weeks, or drown. Every sailor wore at least one good-luck charm to rattle Trudy's teeth whenever he came close; she wondered if she would ever be able to sleep in the midst of so much spirituality.

"You have been deprived of that pleasure much longer than I have," Trudy said tactfully.

Grand Duchess Johanna had good reason to celebrate her true appearance. She was a spectacularly feminine woman, slender and golden, even if sorrows had shadowed the fine-cut lines of her face. With the wind tugging her burgundy gown tight over her breasts and often whipping up the hem to reveal her ankles and calves, she was a shipping hazard. Captain Howie and the helmsman could not keep their eyes off her. At the far side of the deck, Bellman, Ringwood, Ranter, and Manfred were all leaning on the rail, but they had their backs to it so they could savor the view in this direction.

Trudy secretly preferred the freedom of being a man. She *looked* like a man. No classical aristocratic beauty she, just a big-boned country wench with too much jaw and not nearly enough nose. Years of milking cows as a child had given her oversized hands and forearms like a blacksmith's. The Mothers at Oakendown had always been after her to keep her elbows in and stop walking as if she were wearing boots.

Johanna would probably have made a good White Sister, because an eye for people was usually a good clue to sensitivity. She caught Trudy's reservation and looked quizzically at her. "You have another freedom, one that I lack."

"I do?"

"You can let the moths circle your flame. I am a married

woman and must behave as one." She was almost certainly a widow, but no one said that.

"I just wish my flame burned as brightly as yours," Trudy said.

"Nonsense! It is fortunate that my Blades' bindings force them to behave, or they would be at each other's throats over you. I would be down to one bodyguard." Undertones of deceit jangled like bells. Johanna was after something.

"With respect, mistress, I believe you are mistaken. They only notice me when you are hidden by your locket."

"Oh, no. I have seen how they look at you." Johanna chuckled, pretending to be playful, which she was not. "Leaving Manfred out of consideration, how do you rank the others?"

"For looks? Ringwood is the best looking. No argument. Then Ranter. Bellman's jaw's too big."

"I would agree with that ranking." *Clang!* A lie.

"Below the neck," Trudy said, knowing she would never shock Johanna as she so often managed to shock Ringwood, "the reverse. Ringwood's a stripling, Ranter's much too meaty, but Bellman's about perfect, wouldn't you say?"

"Perhaps," Johanna sighed, love elementals caroling like larks. "But as enjoyable company? Poor Ranter would come last on any woman's list, and most men's, too, I fear. Ringwood can be witty, but he lacks confidence. Bellman? Do you find him amusing?"

"Dependable."

"Is that a fault?"

"Dependable at twenty will be a bore at thirty."

"Shame! Cynic!" The Duchess's laugh tolled Trudy's alarm bell again. "And what do you care what he will be like at thirty? We are talking flirting, not marriage."

"We women must be practical. How do we rank their financial prospects?"

Johanna sighed. "None of them has any real prospects at all. Ranter and Ringwood are bound to a penniless exile, so even their lives are at risk. Bellman has a much better chance of being alive a year from now than they do. He has considerable talent. He should do well in the world."

Now Trudy saw the problem clearly. "But he is so homely."

"Not at all. Bellman may not be strictly handsome, but there is a rugged strength to his features." No clangers. The love elementals soared to a crescendo.

Bellman was bewitched by her, and she knew it. Just what did she think Trudy could do about that? Bellman was not the type to be distracted by a heifer like her throwing herself in his path with a dahlia in her teeth. He had his heart set on Johanna, and Johanna's own response was driving her close to panic.

Crossing the bar, *Conqueror* began to roll and pitch. By the next day she was bucking like a mad horse, with the wind still rising and the largest swells coming aboard amidships, washing through the waist. The world was gray, filled with mist and spume-flecked waves. Bellman, Manfred, and the Duchess had disappeared below to the cabins. At least a third of the crew hung over the rail on the forecastle.

Trudy was gratified to discover that she was quite immune to this fashionable distemper. She wrapped herself up warmly and stayed on the aft castle, where the air was at least fresh, even if present in excessive amounts. Unfortunately Blades were immune to anything, and guarding their ward at sea did not require two of them. Ranter had Trudy to himself.

"Your body really excites me," was one of his better lines, although "Girls can never resist Blades," came close. "Blades make the best lovers," was reputedly true, if you believed

Blades. And, "You know you cannot refuse me much longer," was horribly credible. Even in oilskins, Blades glowed for her, and she kept remembering how he had blazed without his shirt. If she leaned back against the rail he stood in front of her, cutting her off from the rest of the ship. If she faced the sea he put an arm around her and squeezed.

"Is your Leader feeling seasick?" she asked, meaning, *I wish you were.*

"No, he's looking after Her Nibs."

Trudy already knew where Ringwood was, because she was standing directly above the poky cabin the two women shared. Ringwood and his ward were certainly not doing what Ranter had in mind, not while the Duchess remained the bright green color she had been an hour ago.

"So he's busy," Ranter added. "Me 'n' you can go down to our cabin and not be interrupted."

"Why does he have to stay with her? No one's going to hurt her here."

Ranter scowled. "He holds the bucket. She might choke."

"I didn't know Blades were nurses."

"For our wards we're anything we have to be. For pretty girls we're great lovers."

She hoped desperately that help would arrive soon. Bellman would intervene if he saw what was going on, but Bellman was prostrate, too. The sailors would not intrude on a Blade.

"Sir Ranter, it is midmorning in a howling gale. I am not in the mood for romance."

"Come downstairs with me and I'll put you in the mood real quick, I promise. You'll love it. The girls in Brimiarde all said how good I was."

"No!"

"You don't know what you're missing." He was genuinely puzzled by her refusal.

"Yes I do. I'm a farm girl."

"There's hay in my mattress."

For Ranter, that was a very good line indeed, and she laughed.

Error! He leered. "Then you agree?"

There were no love spirits caroling around Ranter. Red flames of lust, yes.

"I need time to think about it."

"Let me help." He tried to kiss her.

She doubled over backward to avoid him. She considered screaming. She was starting to wonder if this fight was worth the effort—give up, let him do it, and maybe he'd leave her alone for a while. But that was just the binding conjuration eating away at her resistance. Next time surrender would be even easier, and in a couple of days she'd come running if he wiggled an eyebrow at her. No woman ever could resist a bound Blade. Why else would men consent to be bound? Why struggle?

Ringwood! His glow had moved, left the cabin.

"Stop!" she said. "Your Leader's coming."

And so he did, emerging from the hatch and staggering across the deck in the teeth of the gale. Ranter's scowl should have hurled him overboard all by itself.

Ringwood grabbed the rail. "Take over for a while, brother. I need a break."

Ranter stamped away, cursing into the wind.

"Good chance," Trudy said with feeling. She was shaking. About one more minute would have done it.

"What's wrong?"

"Nothing." She turned away, looked out at the waves.

"Tell me. Please, True?"

"Nothing."

He laid a hand on hers where she held the rail. Nothing like Ranter's savage hug for him and no fires of lust, either. Not even birdsong, just a very distant, plaintive note like the cry of a curlew on a moor. "Is there anything I can do?" His hand was warm on hers.

"Ranter was coming on a bit strong."

Ringwood thumped his spare fist on the rail. "I'm sorry, True! I had him under control in Brimiarde, but I have no hold over him out here."

"Don't worry about it. If I didn't know I could take care of myself, I'd have stayed up a tree in Oakendown. There's worse around than Ranter."

"But most men will take no for an answer. No woman can resist a Blade."

She thought she'd done very well these last few days, even if she had come to the end of her tether now. "That's true of all Blades, is it?"

"So they say," he muttered, staring out at the ocean.

It was no use dropping hints, because he invariably started blushing, which just made the problem worse. In that wind it was hard to tell if he was blushing now, but the curlew's call grew even fainter, even sadder.

"I think what Ranter's doing is despicable," he said.

Try it and see how it goes, sonny. How did one handle a shy lover? If she came right out and asked him, he would be utterly humiliated. The curlew refrain showed that there was interest there. He was suppressing it, denying his longing, afraid even to dream.

"Just how did you keep him in line in Brimiarde?" she asked, knowing perfectly well. "He was almost civilized most of the time."

Ringwood grimaced. "If he could get through the day without making a fool of himself, he got time off and money to go out and buy, you know, a few drinks."

"I thought Blades didn't drink much."

"He wouldn't be drinking them. Death, True! You know what I mean!"

"Your ward told me and I couldn't believe it. It is the most childish thing I have ever heard of. I stopped being bribed with cookies when I was about five years old."

Ringwood looked surprised and then grinned at the ocean. "I suppose it is." He had been thinking of himself as the child, not Ranter. She sensed him bracing himself. "What do you like being bribed with now, mostly?"

"Sweet talk."

He turned to stare at her. She stared right back. The curlew's cry swelled to lark song. Whatever he was seeing, the pupils of his dark eyes were growing enormous. She wondered if hers had dilated, too. Bellman and Ranter had both taken themselves out of contention for the Trudy Stakes, but she had no regrets. She knew the one she wanted now. He was just proving a little more work than she had expected.

"That's all?" He was surprised. He hadn't known.

"That's often all it takes."

Suddenly nightingales were screaming love songs right overhead—he was a swordsman, trained to act instantly. There were even hints of red flames in the vicinity, too, but he was not ready to admit that yet.

"You mean like I tell you I love you? Would that be sweet talk?"

"If it's true it would be." The elementals were deafening her. Maybe some of them were hers.

He drew a deep breath. "I suppose I could tell Ranter you're my girl and he's to take a long walk."

"Why don't you?"

His pinkness was not from embarrassment now, just a fine healthy desire. "Then I would have the right to kiss you." His grin was almost a leer. "It would be an obligation!"

She'd heard of Blade reflexes, but *wooo!* "It certainly would be."

"I'm freezing out here." He put an arm around her. He was blazing like a furnace, and she was astonished at how catching his excitement was. "You want to come below, True, and I'll tell you how much I would like that?"

This was what she had wanted, wasn't it?

"Love to!" she said.

Love, too? To love? Two love? True love? Love True?

◆ 5 ◆

𝕿he storm took them to Furret. *Conqueror* had been aiming for Boileau, but Furret would do. Bellman flashed King Athelgar's passports and dropped coins on palms presented. That took care of the formalities.

Over the next few days, Manfred bought horses, with help from Trudy, who could signal when dealers were lying, even though she knew no Isilondian. The cost horrified Bellman. Six mounts, six spares, three sumpters, and the required tack ate up much of King Athelgar's donation to his destitute cousin. They would have to travel fast if they wanted to keep eating all the way to Krupina. Days were growing shorter, soon there would be weather to worry about, and there was a war on—Dolorth had invaded Bohakia. Although hostilities so far were reported only in the north, not close to Trenko or Krupina, ripples would be driving up prices and making people suspicious of strangers. They must press on with all possible speed, yet still husband the horses.

Whenever possible they traveled with merchants or other honest wayfarers who welcomed the company of three well-spoken young swordsmen. They stayed in inns, barns, or cottages, anywhere a few coins would buy them shelter. Four times they were able to claim hospitality in the homes of rich persons to whom they had been given letters of introduction. Three of those were designated Chivian consuls and one of those three was not only a Chivian himself, but a knight in the Order, the legendary Sir Beaumont, who had won the King's Cup five years earlier and still gave such fine instruction that the swordsmen insisted on tarrying there for days—to rest the horses, they said.

Commonly they rode in pairs, most often Ringwood and Trudy out front, then Johanna and Bellman, and Manfred and Ranter bringing up the rear. Manfred was the only one of them who could stand Ranter for long. The old man just chuckled around his tooth stumps and said, "Had a horse like him once. Nip? All the time! Take your eyes off him for a moment and he'd nip you. Curry him, give him oats, be as nice as you like and he'd nip. No warning. Hitting him did no good. Just had to put up with him. But spirits, he was a strong 'un! He'd run forever."

After that they called Ranter "The Strong 'Un" behind his back.

Similarly, "The Lovebirds" meant Trudy and Ringwood, who could barely keep their hands off each other. Usually it meant them. Soon Bellman realized that sometimes the term was used otherwise.

Three days out of Furret, one baking hot afternoon, when he was riding alongside Johanna . . .

"Stop looking at me like that!"

"Like what?" he asked, startled.

"Like you are in love with me!" Then she blushed and looked away.

He said, "Surely you realize I'm just reacting to my release from Ironhall? I've been let out into the stud pasture at last. I have to fall in love with the first woman I meet. It's inevitable. I'm just rutting. Pay no attention."

He had already decided that this hurt too much to be that. If his agony was mere lust, would he not chase after all women equally, as Ranter did? Why pick on one who was already married? She was practically a queen, probably one of the greatest beauties in Eurania, and he was nothing at all.

"You're very unkind," she said.

"I am your servant, Your Grace. If I offend, dismiss me and I will go away."

Silence.

"Johanna," he said, "I swear to you that I will do everything I possibly can to help you recover your son and restore him to his rightful place. If your husband is still alive, I will likewise do all in my power to reunite you with him. Then I will ask to take my leave, for I cannot live in torment forever."

It felt as if several years went by before she whispered, "And if Rubin is not alive?"

"If you are ever so desperate that a penniless, homeless lover is of use to you, then you will at least have one of those. He will be true."

"And in the meantime?"

"We do nothing," he said. The words did not come easy. "We must not, for Frederik's sake."

"What is Frederik to you?" she said angrily.

"Nothing, except that he is everything to you and your happiness is everything to me."

She said, "Thank you," and did not speak again for a long time.

A couple of weeks later, in a crowded, raucous tavern reeking with tallow smoke, Bellman went to the bar to refill his beaker and there met Ranter with his arm around a blowsy woman. Ranter was as close to drunk as a bound Blade could get, which wasn't very, but in his case was enough to reduce his already tiny social skills to absolute zero.

"Bellman!" he said. "Bellboy?"

Bellman eyed him with disgust. "What do you want?"

The Blade laughed. "Same as you do. Difference is I'm going to get it and you're not! I get it every night and you never do. What's the matter with you, Master Jack? Bellman no ball man? My ward *wants* you. Talks in her sleep about you. Maybe I'll have to give her what she needs, if you can't. One word from you and she'd have her clothes—"

Blades were superhumanly fast. Bellman was not a Blade, but only his sight had failed him, not his reflexes. His fist impacted Ranter's jaw with an audible crack, and only a bulwark of a dozen men behind the Blade stopped him from sprawling flat on the spittle-spotted floor. No one could knock out a Blade, of course. "Unconscious Blade" was an oxymoron. The men behind him crumpled under the impact, but Ranter himself bounced back upright instantly, with *Invincible* in his hand.

A score of throats screamed in alarm and the crowd exploded away, leaving an open space around the combatants. Bellman reached for *Bravado*—and froze . . .

"Stay away from Blades and Sabreurs," Ansel had warned him. He had meant, *Stay away from fights*. Bellman should not be armed at all, but experience had quickly taught him the difference it made. Without a sword at his thigh he was only a clerk or servant; with one he was a gentleman, accorded respect and thus better able to serve Johanna. Now he was trapped. He had begun the fight; if he drew, Ranter could kill him and claim self-defense.

Then Ringwood was between them. "Put up your sword!" he screamed at his deputy. His voice lacked mature sonorous authority. In fact, it was positively shrill, but he prevailed.

Ranter complied because he could not endanger his ward by committing public murder.

Shamed, Bellman slunk away.

"Coward!" Ranter shouted. Now that the crisis had passed, the onlookers jeered in disappointment.

Later, when his blood was off the boil, Bellman sought out Ringwood and apologized. By then Ringwood had put Ranter on duty, leaving himself free to wedge Trudy in a corner and feed her sugarplums he had bought. He shot the penitent a dark glance.

"It won't happen again?"

"No, Leader," Bellman said. "It won't happen again."

"All right." The Commander went back to his foreplay.

* 6 *

From Isilond they cut south into Ritizzia, and from Ritizzia northeast into a patchwork of petty principalities, most of them nominally parts of Fitain, all of them capable of making Bellman's purse bleed at their borders. He was seriously worried about finances by the time they came to Blanburg. He still hoarded the bankers' letters Grand Master had given him as return fare, but now he knew that they would not be enough to see everyone back to Chivial, if that was ever required.

Most days they took a break at noon, to rest the horses and themselves, and that day they settled in the shade of some oak trees on a knoll carpeted with shrubs and close-cropped brown grass. The golden valley was hazed with the smoke of burning stubble. Grapes and grain had been harvested; herds were being driven down from the hills for culling. The war had not come here yet, but the clouds were no longer the clouds of summer, and early snow had dusted the summits that towered ahead of them. To the north, on a hillock not too far from the river, stood a castle with a walled town draped around it like a skirt of lime wash and terra cotta.

Trudy and Ringwood lay side by side, almost indecently close. Ranter, too, was stretched out on his back, although strategically so, blocking the approach to his ward. Bellman and Johanna were sitting with very little space between them. Manfred chewed steadily off by himself, keeping an eye on the horses. Bees bumbled and hummed in the undergrowth.

Johanna gestured vaguely. "That is Blanburg town, capital of Blanburg the principality. The palace is the seat of Rubin's cousin, the Prince."

"So finally," Bellman said, "we should be able to find out some news. We'll learn what's been happening in Krupina if we have to go and ask the Prince himself." Not that they would, of course.

There followed a thoughtful silence, almost nostalgic. A chapter of their lives was about to end. They were all lean and brown as peasants, and in the case of Ranter and Johanna, weeks of sun had bleached their hair to silver. The fancy clothes they had chosen so hurriedly that last morning in Nocare were faded and threadbare—except for Ringwood's, because he had grown out of his originals and almost out of their replacements, too. Back in Ironhall, Master of Rituals would have hauled him off to the octogram and conjured him to stop sprouting.

Manfred, who had worked miracles with the horses, was grinning toothlessly at the thought of being reunited with his family soon. The swordsmen were silent. Now the feinting was over and they might have to die. The Grand Duchess, sometimes Duke, who had curried her own horse and done her own laundry without a word of complaint, might very soon be reunited with her husband. It was not impossible. The very absence of news about Krupina suggested that Rubin had hung onto his coronet after all. Then Bellman would have to bow low and withdraw, leaving only his heart behind.

Or her husband might be dead, but he refused to torment himself with hope.

"How far to Krupina?" Trudy asked sleepily.

Johanna shrugged. "Depends how we go. South and around the Siril Lakes to Zolensa would take at least a week. Or we can continue north from Blanburg to Trenko and come in by Pilgrim Pass. Maybe five days, yes, Manfred? I'd rather not go past Vamky. Straight in through Brikov would be quickest, if Manfred can find the way for us. Can you, Manfred?"

He chuckled. "With my eyes shut, my lady."

"You see," the Duchess continued, "there are only two real possibilities. One is that my husband still rules, in which case I collect our son and go home to him. More likely he is dead, Volpe is Grand Duke, and Karl is Marquis of Krupa. In that case I collect my son and go back to Chivial to accept the sanctuary Queen Tasha generously offered."

This was the best of all futures for Bellman. Johanna had finally accepted that she could not overthrow a usurper singlehandedly, and that a dispossessed son was better than a dead one. The dark side of that future was that she was still nominally a duchess, and Queen Tasha might cut costs by marrying her off to someone.

"What if Duke Rubin is alive and in jail?" Ringwood asked, rising to one elbow.

Johanna shrugged. "Or if the nobility rejected Volpe's usurpation and civil war is brewing? Every possibility, however unlikely, requires me to visit Brikov, because that is where I left Frederik. Count János is an ally and he will know what has been happening these last seven months."

"I can tell you that," Ranter told the sky. "Talked with a band of merchants from Krupina last night. Got all the news."

Ringwood said, *"You what?"* and sat up. "Why didn't you tell me?"

"Telling you now. If you want to hear."

"Where did this happen?" the Duchess asked sharply.

Ranter yawned, still prone. "In the cathouse. Bunch of us were sitting around in our—"

"Ranter!" his leader shouted. "Tell us now!"

"Yes, Leader." He sat up, smirking. He counted *one* on his fingers, glancing around to watch reactions. "Grand Duke Rubin still rules." *Two.* "Grand Duchess Johanna died in an accident last spring." *Three.* "Three days from now, Grand Duke Rubin is going to marry Lady Margarita, daughter of Margrave Ladislas of Trenko."

"If this is your idea of a joke—"

"He speaks the truth," said Trudy. "Doesn't mean the merchants did."

Bellman took Johanna's hand. She was shaking.

"A stepmother for my son?" she demanded. "Where? I mean the wedding. In Trenko?"

"I asked that," Ranter said smugly. Somehow he was even more obnoxious when he was right than when he was wrong. "In Krupa."

"Weddings are usually held at the bride's home."

"But there's going to be an enthronement right after, see? The last duchess never got enthroned, so the Margrave insisted on it this time, they said. I think they were just gossiping about that, but the big affair's in Krupa on the fourth of Tenthmoon. That's three days from now, isn't it?"

"Three days!" Johanna whispered.

"Say!" Ranter said. "Wonder what'll happen if you turn up at the wedding?"

Ringwood groaned. "Idiot! It would be over our dead bodies. Good report, but you should have told me the moment you got back last night."

"Too tired." Leer.

"We'll discuss that later."

Silence. Bellman deliberately said nothing. He had been leader ever since they left Chivial, mainly because Johanna deferred to him, but from now on Ringwood must carry the burden, whether he wanted it or not. They were in the battle zone. They had just gone on war footing.

But it was to Bellman that Johanna turned. "Was I wrong? Was it Rubin who came to Fadrenschloss after the accident, not Volpe? Has Rubin been trying to kill me all this time?" Her voice rose shrilly. "And kill his own son? Is that it? If he has no heir, he's a better marriage prospect for Ladislas's girl, so she can breed him another? Is he such a monster? Did he plot to put us both on that coach and then drive it off a cliff? With two other people? Just to marry that . . . child?"

"Shush, love! You were married to him for years. Is he such a monster?"

"No! Never. I know he has faults, but he's kind, and gentle, really."

"And," Bellman said, "even if he did murder his first two wives, he wouldn't dare risk killing you as well. Three in a row would be too much. And his own son as well? No, Volpe's the family killer. Volpe had the motive and the means. I still think he's behind it all."

"Then why is he still masquerading as Rubin?" Ranter demanded. "You saying that's *Volpe* marrying the child bride?"

Bellman said, "I don't know. I do intend to find out. The Margrave was said to want a love match for his child, so he would hardly agree to marry her to a serial wife-killer. We know things he doesn't, so what does he know that we don't? And Volpe is forbidden to marry while wearing his own face. It would make more sense if Volpe pretended to be Rubin and gave himself permission to marry again, but that isn't what the merchants said." Or the margrave might be in on the deception. The news was another clue in the most fascinating puzzle Bellman had ever encountered, but so far it led in too many directions. He looked to Ringwood. "What do we do now, Leader?"

"Suggestions welcome." Ringwood was learning.

Ranter yawned and stretched. "Sounds to me like now we have to start fighting for our supper. Where is this Brikov place?"

"Other side of that." Manfred pointed east, at the wall of rock holding up the sky.

"You're joking!"

"No, he isn't," Johanna said. "We came over that pass in springtime, didn't we, Manfred? I swear we forded a thousand freshets. Officially there's no pass there. Maps don't show one. But there is a smugglers' road, which is held on the Krupina side by Count János, and on this side by a brigand named Sigmund, who usually cooperates with him, but may just cut our throats to get our horses. Manfred knows the way now and can get us through, can't you, Manfred?"

Ringwood squeaked. "Wait a second! How many men does this Sigmund have and what's his price going to be?"

"We ignore Sigmund," Manfred said. His wrinkles multiplied into a grin. "His men are miners and charcoal burners, a few herders. A village he does not have." The forester leered at all the worried expressions. "They live far away." He spread his arms. "Given time he can bring in many men. But smile and wave as we go through, yes? Then he has no way to object."

"And we have no time to waste," Johanna said, reaching for the boots she had shed. "Three days! There's a cave, a shelter. Manfred can find it. We'll overnight there. If we start from there at first light, we'll reach Brikov by nightfall. Right, Manfred?"

The old man turned and studied the western sky. "I worry more about the weather than about Sigmund."

"It looks fine to me," Ranter said.

"Sigmund will not catch us. He uses mules."

Ringwood pulled a face. "Shouldn't we use mules, then?"

"No time to arrange that!" Johanna said, pulling on her second boot. "We ride for Brikov immediately, Commander!"

"I hear your instructions, Your Highness." Ringwood looked around the group. "But Brikov sounds like a trap—a thwarted brigand behind us and a murdering enchanter ahead of us. I wish I'd taken some of Grand Master's strategy lessons. What sort of person is this Count János?"

Johanna sprang up. "Short of stature, but big in everything else. Loud. Cruel, because he rules a harsh land. Loyal to his liege, the Grand Duke, but determined to defend his own rights first. He hates the Brotherhood because it is the only possible threat to his independence. I trusted him enough to leave Frederik there, didn't I? If Volpe came looking for my son, János said, he would hang him from the ridgepole."

"How many men does he command?"

She gathered up the blanket she had been sitting on. "I'm just a little woman, how should I know? Stop wasting time!"

Ringwood looked to Manfred for an answer.

"Fifty would answer his war horn," the forester said. "Two hundred within a couple of days. One hundred for operations outside his borders."

"And Frederik is in Brikov?"

"He is in the Count's territory," Johanna said, "not at his court. Come!"

Ringwood sighed. "All right. The expedition will now move out and make tracks for Brikov. But if I say we go no farther than Brikov, Your Royal Highness, then we go no farther! Is that agreed?"

Nothing was agreed so far as Johanna was concerned. Still muttering, "Three days!" she saddled her horse, mounted, and might well have ridden off alone had Bellman not caught hold of her bridle.

"Steady, Your Grace! We have to overnight in this cave of yours. A few minutes sooner or later getting there won't make any difference."

That seemed to calm her, although she continued to mutter, "Three days!" while she waited for the others. She was still muttering it when they were trotting along the road and only he could hear her.

In just three days the torture might be over. Either she would be restored to her husband or Bellman would claim her for his own.

They left the Blanburg road and continued east by a maze of local tracks, climbing through vineyards that a few weeks before might have bustled with harvesters and carters, but were now deserted. Above those they emerged on bare hills, grazed by goats or sheep. Although the old forester had come this way only once in his life, and going in the opposite direction, he seemed to know the path he wanted, following the dry streambeds and never hesitating when they divided, as they did constantly.

Few of their present horses had been with them since Furret. Any that weakened or needed a rest had been traded off for better, and some of the present string were not going to cope with the next two days' exertions. By choice, Bellman would have exchanged them all for mules in Blanburg. At one of their rests he suggested some be set free, and called for a vote on which were the weakest.

Manfred disagreed. "Chance rules in the hills," he said. "A strong horse with a pulled tendon is good for eating, naught else. We may need them all." His view carried the day.

By late afternoon the expedition was back under trees, but Manfred continued to lead the way confidently. Although every oak or beech looked much the same to city-bred Bellman, he could recognize trees that had been pollarded or coppiced, and knew that this was cultivated woodland, not primeval forest. The climb grew steeper.

Manfred began hunting something. He pointed to tracks, droppings, wood chips, and eventually even the others caught a faint odor of smoke. Heading upwind, they located a clearing where a group of charcoal burners were plying their trade. They were probably all one extended family, about a dozen people from elderly to toddlers, and without exception they were black. Their clothes were black. Their mule, their tools, and even their hysterically barking dogs were black. Spectacularly white eyes in black faces stared warily at the newcomers.

Their homes were makeshift tents of branches. Their mound was a giant beehive, covered with turf and soil to contain the fire within, drifting wisps of white smoke into the evening air. It looked simple enough, but Bellman knew that its construction called for real skill and that it would not burn properly without constant attention.

Manfred hailed them in a dialect that baffled Bellman's conjured comprehension. He gathered only that trading was in progress. In the end the forester exchanged a horse for information about who else was in the neighborhood, a load of cut firewood that would save the travelers much labor later in the day, and a haunch of "goat" that was certainly illegal venison. In monetary terms, the burners had the best of the bargain, but both sides were happy, which was all that mattered.

"It's a life, I suppose," Bellman said as the travelers resumed their climb.

"They are good people," Johanna agreed with surprising emphasis.

"They were not afraid of us."

"They do not fear thieves, for they have nothing worth stealing except their mule, and few brigands would stoop to stealing a charcoal burner's mule, because charcoal is a necessity for many things. They are proud folk. They value their freedom." She had recovered her good humor

"I sense a story."

She smiled for the first time since she had heard of the forthcoming wedding. "I have a sister, Voica, older than me. She ran off with a charcoal burner, much against my father's wishes. She visited me sometimes at Fadrenschloss. She was there for my wedding and I promised her I would find her man a better job. She refused, saying that they enjoyed their liberty too much to leave the hills."

This was the first time she had ever mentioned family. "Do they live in the demesne of Count János, by any chance?"

Johanna laughed. "You are *too* clever, you hear me? Yes, Voica is strong and her husband is a bull, yet they have no children. The spirits can be cruel! So I loaned her Frederik. Who will look in a charcoal burner's camp for a marquis?"

And who would recognize him with his face all sooty?

The cave served them best by hiding their fire. It would be invaluable if the weather turned bad in the night—as Manfred still stubbornly predicted, although he could not or would not explain his reasons. Since the weather remained fair and generations of smugglers had fouled the shelter with their refuse, old bedding, and probably vermin, everyone elected to sleep under the sky. The Blades kept watch, as always, but there was no evidence that followers of the sinister Sigmund were on their trail yet.

Bellman lay and watched stars and clouds for a long time. He had spread his blanket a respectable distance from Johanna's, but not so far that he could not hear her soft breathing. He heard much heavier breathing for a while from Trudy's direction, while Ranter was on watch and Ringwood was not. He envied the lovers their happiness.

Was the bridegroom-to-be really Rubin, or was he Volpe in disguise? Had Bellman come all this way just to return the woman he loved to her husband, who might or might not have tried to kill her? Would Rubin even take her back? Six months' absence would ruin any wife's reputation, let alone a Grand Duchess's. What then of Frederik? Would he still be dispossessed? The problems outnumbered the stars. What was young Karl up to all this time? If Frederik was presumed dead like his mother, then Volpe's son was heir presumptive again, and would not approve of his cousin's remarriage. Karl, it was worth remembering, had always had motive but no means. Abbot Minhea had means but no motive.

Johanna wakened at the first trace of brightness and roused everyone else. Breath smoking in the predawn chill, the wayfarers gulped a hurried meal and prepared for a hard day. Obsessed with the need for haste, Johanna would rather have skipped the meal, and yet she would not say what she thought she could do at Brikov. There might yet be time for her to go on and reach Krupa before the wedding, but her Blades would be crazy to allow it.

The road offered no easy warmup. Within minutes they

were forced to dismount and lead the horses. They went up
unstable screes, through dense pine woods, along boulder-
strewn streambeds. After an hour or so they emerged on
stony slopes naked to the sky, with ice-clad peaks glaring
down at them, seeming almost overhead. Bellman knew he
was not the only one wondering if Manfred truly remembered the way or was simply guessing. They were mites
doomed to creep over the face of the world forever.

Around midmorning Ringwood suddenly shouted,
"Look!"

He was pointing at a band of a dozen or so mounted men
in the very far distance, two or three ridges back. Yes, they
might be pursuing some perfectly innocent business of their
own. It was much more likely that they were pursuing the
trespassers. Johanna shouted for more speed, but they were
already going as fast as they could.

Manfred started taking shortcuts and, incredibly, the
going became even worse. They tied tow ropes to the sad-
dles so the horses could pull them up screes that looked fit
to baffle a goat. Twice a horse slipped and lamed itself and
had to be slaughtered. Ranter was appointed butcher, since
the task did not seem to bother him, but a couple of unfortunate animals actually fell to their deaths, rolling helplessly
down the hillside, out of reach. The pursuers were closing,
albeit very slowly.

Bellman dared not wonder what would happen if Count
János did not make them welcome. They would have no way
back and no money to replace the missing mounts and baggage. A more assertive Blade than Ringwood would have
kept his ward out of such a trap.

Soon it seemed that they had no way forward, either, for
the forester was leading them up a nearly impassable talus
slope to the base of a vertical cliff. There, surprisingly, he
mounted his horse again. When the others arrived, they

found a faint path winding around a spur to enter a canyon like a saw cut in the mountain. The made trail was now more obvious and quite passable. So Manfred had not been guessing after all. This, he explained with his toothless grin, was the divide, the boundary, and Sigmund's men would not follow them into the domain of Count János.

And so it was.

The canyon widened into a narrow valley, and that joined a wider. At the first open water, Manfred called a halt to rest the horses and let them drink. High peaks towered all around them.

"How far to Brikov?" Bellman asked.

The old man shrugged. "Should do it by nightfall." He glanced at the sky. "If the weather holds."

So they had a long way to go yet, but at least they could now travel on four feet, not two. The range's eastern slope was less steep than the western, and drier. The trail descended to rocky moorland, then sandy valleys dotted with bristly pine trees, and by midafternoon the travelers were back in pasture and cultivated woodland. Manfred pointed out traces of herds and game, even of humans, but it was late in the day before they were challenged.

The young horseman who accosted them was hardly more than a boy, but he did not seem as nervous as he should be if he were waylaying armed intruders all by himself, and the flat they were traversing was well provided with cover. His dialect was even murkier than the charcoal burners', but he and Manfred were soon jabbering away incomprehensibly. Satisfied, the boy waved an all-clear signal to the bushes and copses. After that he accompanied the group to Brikov, chattering to Manfred all the way. If there were archers in the shrubbery, they remained out of sight.

*   *   *

The sun had slid behind the hills when Johanna said, "This is Brikov!"

"This?" Bellman had expected a small town or at least a castle, but here he saw little more than a bare and stony valley, with cattle penned in dry stone walls and cottages scattered along the hillsides. Being much the same color as the landscape, the houses were hard to make out in the dusk.

"Why?" he asked. "I mean, why here?" Settlements should have a reason for being where they were: a ford, tillable land, or a good harbor.

Johanna smiled faintly. She was drooping with fatigue, as they all were. "Mining. Ernst explained it to me. They built their homes from the tailings tipped out near the tunnels. The hills are honeycombed with old adits. No one's ever tried to conquer Brikov, Ernst said—it would be like invading an ants' nest."

And as pointless, Bellman thought. Cattle were the only wealth in sight, and they could be moved elsewhere readily enough.

The trail the guide had chosen angled up the side of the valley, going close by some of the cottages and letting Bellman see that they were mere kennels, walls of stones and roofs of turf. Indeed, some of the men watching the visitors' arrival stood taller than their own houses. Many were armed and looked like another good reason for not trying to invade the valley.

The lord's residence was a group of several larger buildings, more like a fortified farm than a traditional fortress. The one-story walls were mortared and the roofs tiled. Guards with halberds stood by the main gate, but it was not clear whether they were guarding the house or the three workmen busily erecting a gallows.

• 7 •

ℐf János called in his two hundred mountain men, Ringwood decided, it would be standing room only in his baro-
nial hall. With glazed windows, a timber floor covered with
sawdust, and woollen weavings on the wall to keep out the
winter chill, it was more like a wealthy farmer's dining room
than a heroes' hall or a mess for a castle garrison. That
evening it was almost empty—no oxen on the spit above the
bare hearth, no plank tables and benches for feasting, just a
chair for the Count himself and one for his guest, Frau
Schale. The massive walls still held the day's heat, although
now the light was fading fast.

Spirits! It had been an exhausting day. Ringwood's
knees trembled with fatigue. He wished he had been given
a seat and was much annoyed that True had not. The travelers were filthy and starving, yet Johanna had refused all
offers of refreshment, insisting on an immediate audience
with the Count. Ever since Ranter had told her of the forthcoming wedding, she had been behaving oddly, muttering
to herself, scowling at her Blades. Ringwood worried that
she was going to ask János to give her an escort so she
could attend the ceremony. If János agreed, two Blades
were going to be in serious trouble, arguing with two hundred mountain men.

The Count's throne was ornately carved, had once been
gilded, and was high enough to require a footrest. Perched
up there, János could look down on the Duchess, whose
chair was too low for comfort. "Short of stature," she had
called him, but his legs must be the problem, for his shoulders were a league wide and his head as big as a beer keg.
He had a beetling brow with ferocious eyebrows, a bald
scalp, and a beard like a bushel of tangled iron wire. Jewels

glinted on his thick, hairy fingers, yet his clothes were homemade leathers, plain and well-worn.

Johanna's insistence that her three swordsmen would not surrender their weapons had resulted in delay until three of the Count's sons were located and brought in to stand behind their father and match the Ironhall men. They were shorter, wider, and much older than the Blades, but Ringwood had only contempt for the mighty broadswords they bore. He would gamble *Bad News* against one of those any day. Although they could not manage to emulate their father's fearsome glare, they made it plain that they did not approve of this upstart Frau Schale who brought armed men into their father's hall. Clearly János had not taken them into his confidence enough to explain who she was.

After the bare minimum of formalities, she said, "How goes Krupina, my lord? Duke Rubin still reigns, I hear."

"It seems so. But where is my friend Ernst?" His voice rumbled and echoed.

His glare grew ever more fearsome as she described von Fader's death and the various attacks made upon her since she left Brikov. It softened only slightly when she mentioned the King of Chivial's hospitality and his grant of expert swordsmen—he looked over the expert swordsmen with undisguised scorn. The three woodchoppers in the background were wide-eyed. Probably they had never been outside Krupina in their lives.

János made only one comment. When Johanna mentioned that Harald had turned out to be a traitor, he grunted and said, "Not surprising!"

Ringwood found that surprising. The Baron had trusted Harald and had taken him on right here in Brikov. If János had considered the man unreliable then, why had he not said so?

Of course, Johanna had one paramount question to ask,

but it was a tricky one when the meaty sons were unaware that their father was hiding the missing Marquis.

"And my darling . . . sister? And her family?"

"I assume she is well. But I do have disturbing tidings to pass along." János turned his oversized head. "Enough of these games. Off with you all. Go and be useful. See to the skinning."

"Father—" one began.

"*Go!*" the Count roared. "And send in a bench for our guests. And wine."

The three bears trooped out like banished children, scowling. János hunched his great shoulders and looked over True and the swordsmen. It did not take a White Sister to know that he was seriously worried.

"These boys are in your confidence, Highness?"

"Absolutely. *What is wrong?*"

"Many things, frankly. Many, many things. First, your husband reigns in Krupina and is about to marry the Margrave's daughter."

"I heard that."

"But he is not your husband. He is an imposter, just as you told me. Frankly, I did not believe you. Even Ernst I did not really believe. I thought that locket of yours was a mountebank trick. Well, there must be another like it. I was wrong."

That changed matters!

Johanna's voice jumped half an octave. "You know this for a fact?"

"Almost a fact." János sounded evasive and looked shifty. "I have an independent witness, although I do not believe everything he says. You can talk with him if you like, but it is fortunate you arrived today. I'm going to hang him in the morning."

"How is my son?" the Duchess demanded.

The Count was saved from having to answer by two men bringing in a long bench, which they placed alongside the chairs. The others sat down gratefully, with Ringwood claiming the place next his ward.

Meanwhile, their host could talk of safer things. "You are aware that our beloved Grand Duchess disappeared in tragic circumstances last spring? It became a considerable scandal after a wrecked carriage was discovered not far from Fadrenschloss. The driver was identified as a palace coachman and one of the passengers as the Marquis's nurse. Both of them dead. Much of the wreckage had fallen—"

Servants brought in wine and goblets and a table to put them on. Ringwood needed *food,* not drink.

"—witnesses agreed that she entered the carriage voluntarily, taking the child. Nobody was able to identify her male companion—"

The servants closed the door. Instantly Johanna was on her feet, level with the little man on his elevated chair.

"Where is my son?"

He screwed up his ugly face. "I warned you he should be left here, right here in the valley, under my eye." His great voice boomed even louder, drowning her out. "But no! You insisted on hiding him away in the woods with no one to protect him."

"Where is he?"

János pouted. He did not admit failure easily. "I don't know. About a month after you left, a troop of brethren came and got him. They took—"

Johanna leaped at him and might have clawed his eyes out, had she not run into Ranter's arm. Ringwood was annoyed to be a tiny fraction slower.

"Easy, Your Grace!" he said. "That won't help." The two Blades pushed her back down on her chair.

"Give her some wine!" János growled and took a long draft himself. "They took your sister and her man as well. I didn't hear about it until it was all over and they'd gone. They were taken to Vamky."

Johanna accepted a sip of wine. Her face was so pale it seemed to glow in the gathering gloom.

"If it helps," the Count added, "I have the man who did it. Tomorrow you can watch him dancing ten feet up on a three-foot rope."

"So officially Frederik and I are dead?" she muttered, not looking at him.

Frederik more than just officially, Ringwood suspected.

"You are. Officially. Rubin held a public inquiry. The evidence was very convincing. Some of your effects were found a league downstream. The only thing not known for certain is the identity of your presumed lover. The Grand Duke himself was at a birthweek party in Zolensa that night, a very respectable affair with lots of witnesses."

Silence.

Bellman said, "My lord? Who ordered the coaches made ready in the middle of the night?"

János scowled at the upstart flunky. "I don't know. I have better things to do than attend inquiries packed with tattling scandalmongers. I imagine there was a forged note, or something. If you want to conclude, as the inquiry did, that the Grand Duchess and her son perished in a tragic accident, there was plenty of evidence that way. If you prefer to believe that she was running off with a man not her husband, that's all right, too. All loose ends are well tied. Only the identity of the hooded man remains a mystery."

"Who," Bellman persisted in the quiet, deadly voice he used when he was in this mood, "do the scandalmongers say it was? I'm sure they put a name on him."

János snorted. "Guess?"

"Prince Karl?"

The Count nodded and took another drink.

Johanna looked up in surprise. "Why do you think so? Who told you that?"

Ringwood had never considered the possibility. If Rubin and Volpe had *both* had sons in that coach, then who had forced it over the cliff?

"You did, Your Grace," Bellman said. "Or your son did. From what I remember of my sisters, the last thing you do to calm a screaming baby is hand it to a stranger, especially a man. Yet you told us the imposter took Frederik and he stopped crying. I assume Karl has not been seen since?"

"Obviously," János said. "Hints were dropped at the inquiry that he had been observed making advances to Her Highness, that she had been leading him on, and so on. Those remarks were struck from the record, of course."

"Of course." Bellman glanced at Johanna, but she did not look up or speak. "You said earlier, my lord, that you believed that the man posing as the Grand Duke is an imposter. Why do you believe that, and when do you think the switch was made?"

"You ask a lot of questions, sonny."

"He's asking them for me," Johanna told her hands. "Bellman will ask them faster and more clearly than I can. You owe me answers."

"Do I?" the Count growled, reaching for the wine bottle. "As to when the switch happened, I don't know. If it happened. You told me you thought the Rubin who turned up at Fadrenschloss was actually Lord Volpe wearing one of those lockets. I didn't put much stock in that then. I'm not sure I do now, but a week ago one of the brethren walked in here looking for sanctuary. Said he was never going back to Vamky. Offered to swear fealty to me—which takes nerve when you've just confessed to breaking one oath of allegiance. The reason he gave was that he'd seen Grand Duke Rubin locked up in a dungeon there."

Nobody commented. Probably everyone was too busy trying to make sense of this. Ringwood couldn't even start. Only Bellman had enough brains for such conundrums. Why should Volpe lock up the Duke and take his place? There would never be a safe time to release him, so why not just kill him right away? And why go through a marriage ceremony pretending to be the rightful duke? Someone was being either incredibly devious or incredibly stupid.

The Count chuckled, a sound like bouncing rocks. "And it's pretty hard to explain how he can be rotting in chains in Vamky at the same time as he's dancing around Krupa organizing his wedding, now, isn't it?"

"Tell us about the wedding!" Bellman used a tone gentry rarely heard from the lowborn, but János was now enjoying himself too much to notice.

"The day after tomorrow, at sunset. In Krupa. Lady Margarita, the Margrave's daughter."

Marrying Volpe. Believing he was Rubin. Ringwood felt a thumping headache coming on. If the Marquis and Karl had both disappeared, then the only heir left was Lord Volpe and he, if their theories were correct, was masquerading as the Grand Duke. No matter. Whoever's butt was on the throne needed an heir, and the Margrave's daughter would inherit all Trenko. A child of theirs could rule both states. Wearing a conjured locket in bed would be kinky but not impossible. (Which father would the baby favor?)

"Has Lord Volpe also disappeared?" Bellman asked.

The Count shrugged and drained his goblet. "Not my job to keep track of the Provost. If he has a conjured locket like Her Highness's, he can come and go as he wants. You planning to take in the wedding, Your Grace? I must attend. I have no choice, but it'll be a lot more interesting if you show up."

"If the Duke is locked up in Vamky," Bellman said, "is his son there also?"

The room was almost completely dark now, which Ringwood considered a fitting symbol of his own mental state, but not good for ward protection. He waited for a break in the talk so he could ask for lights.

"Told you, sonny," János said. "Brethren took him there, and that was the last anyone heard of him. His arrival in Krupa was never announced. Sounds bad, mm?"

"But they also took his aunt and her husband, you said," Bellman countered. "That doesn't sound as if they intended to kill him."

The Count scoffed again. "If I wanted to terminate a cute little curly-haired brat like that, sonny, I wouldn't tell the men I sent to fetch him. I'd attend to it personally—later, when no one was watching. There's such a thing as morale, you know. Not the same as morals, but one affects the other. Auntie may be dead in the woods or at the bottom of the Asch.

"And don't assume that the knight-brethren work only for Volpe. Their oath is to the Abbot, who takes orders from the Grand Duke, so it says in the book. Abbot Minhea always struck me as a slimy fish. Not as cold-blooded as Volpe, though."

"But this—" Bellman began. He glanced over to the Duchess. "Sorry, Your Highness . . . Frederik's disappearance is one more reason to believe that the present Grand Duke is an imposter. If he is the real Rubin and did get his son back, surely he would have announced it? He wouldn't have to explain *where* the boy had been found. 'Wandering in the woods,' would do. It would be more evidence that Her Highness was dead and he was free to remarry."

"I think he's Volpe," the Count agreed, and emptied his goblet.

"Yet you're going to hang the man who told you so?"

János glared. "That's not why I'm hanging him. He betrayed the boy."

"Who did?" the Duchess asked.

"Radu."

"Radu Priboi?"

"That one. The old man died here about ten days ago—never really recovered from the burning of Fadrenschloss. A few dozen sons turned up for his funeral and one of them was Radu, knight-brother in the Vamky Brotherhood, family hero. When everyone else went home he stayed behind and asked me to take him on. But he confessed that he'd hunted the boy down right after you left. He knew what he looked like, he said. Not many of the brethren did."

"It's possible," Johanna said hoarsely. "Volpe came to the palace often enough and he always had a retinue."

"He knew your sister, too, Radu said. So he found the boy and fetched a squad of brethren. How many knights in armor does it take to arrest one two-year-old, I asked him? Now he knows what we think of sneaks and thieves. He stole a boy who was under my protection. His brother Harald was a killer, you tell me, and he's a spy and a turncoat. That's why he's going to hang tomorrow. You come and watch."

"No!" Johanna struggled to her feet. "I want to talk with him."

Let's leave it until after supper, Ringwood thought. How hungry could a man get and still live?

"Talk to him in the morning," János said, "when we put the collar on him. Cheer him up."

"No!" Her Highness was wearing her stubborn look. "I knew Radu before he went to Vamky."

"Doesn't mean a thing once they've taken their oath," János said. "Look how Harald lied!"

"I still wish to question Radu."

The Count shook his big head like an angry bull. "He's

been well questioned, very well. He can't stand much more. Don't want him to die before we get the rope on him."

Belying her exhaustion and distress, Johanna unleashed her Grand Duchess voice. *"Sister Gertrude! Has the Count spoken the truth?"*

"Mostly, Your Highness," True said calmly. "He did go to the inquiry."

"You call me a liar?" János roared.

"Sister Gertrude has the power to detect falsehood. Try her. How many sons do you have?"

"Six."

"Not true," True said. "Do you even know how many sons you have?

"Certainly!"

True sighed. "Wrong again. When you went to the inquiry, did you speak with the Duke, or whoever was pretending to be the Duke?"

"No."

"That's true! Did you try not to be recognized?"

"Of course not."

"Untrue. What—"

"All right, you've convinced me." Unwilling to take more risks with his personal secrets, János slid down off his chair. "You can see the prisoner."

Ringwood's stomach rumbled disapproval.

Two of the lord's sons led the way with lanterns; János and Johanna followed, with her Blades treading close behind; Bellman, Trudy, and two other men brought up the rear, carrying more lanterns. The Count's house was a strange, rambling affair, some parts of which held delicious food odors that Ringwood dearly wanted to investigate but couldn't. When their way began slanting downward, he realized that they were underground. No natural cave could be so regular, and the walls were clearly man-made. The air was cool and stale.

Johanna stopped. "Can't you have him brought to us?"

"No," the Count said. "You want to see him, you go to him."

"Lead the way, then," she said reluctantly, but she looked around for Bellman. He slipped past the Blades and took her hand.

If the house was a maze, the mine was a warren, branching and sloping, damp in places and dry in others. Some branches were closed off by solid timber doors, others were littered with ancient junk. The guides brought them to a waist-high wooden barricade, a few steps back from a rocky wall marking where excavation of that particular adit had been abandoned.

"Priboi!" János bellowed, and his great voice echoed eerily.

Squeezing in beside his ward, Ringwood almost tripped on a wooden ladder lying on the floor. When he peered over the barrier, he saw down into a pit, a shaft about ten feet deep and barely wide enough for a man to stretch out. The walls shone wetly in the lamplight, but the floor was shadowed.

Gaining no reaction, János bellowed again, and still nothing happened.

"Radu?" the Duchess said. "It's Johanna Schale. I need you to tell me about my son."

Ringwood could feel her shaking. He sympathized. He, too, disliked confined places. He added the light of another lantern.

Something down there twitched, slowly began to move. It gasped a few times, the sort of noise a man may make when he is suppressing cries of pain, but eventually he managed to look up and raise an arm to shadow his eyes from the light. Chain rattled. To Ringwood's horror, the prisoner seemed to have no clothes except a blanket and only straw for bedding. He could be Harald's brother or anyone else's brother, for that matter. His own mother would not have recognized a face so battered.

"Your Highness?" he croaked. "You are safe?"

"So far I am. I am sorry to hear about your father. He was a very kind man."

There was a pause, then the prisoner mumbled, "Thank you." The words seemed incongruous, almost illegal, in such a place of horror and pain.

"I am told that you were the one who took away Voica and my son."

"I am sorry."

"By whose orders?"

"My superiors'."

"Tell me about it, please. I want my son back."

"I was sworn to loyalty, Your Grace." Radu had a memorably tuneful voice, a clear tenor at odds with his wretched appearance. He must be frozen in this dungeon.

"So you bear no guilt. I understand. But I beg you to tell me of my son."

"I was told you had left Krupina, but had left the boy somewhere, probably in Brikov. I was asked if I knew where you might have taken him, and I thought of Voica . . . If I am to talk I must have water."

Water was ordered. One of the servants hurried away, his light dwindling along the tunnel.

"Open this gate!" Bellman said. "I'm going down there."

"More fool you," János growled, but he opened a section of the barricade. Bellman and Ringwood lowered the ladder into the pit, being careful not to land it on the prisoner. Bellman went down, taking a lantern. He gagged a couple of times.

The light showed Radu's arms and shoulders black with

bruises and welts. His hair was cropped short and his beard little longer; both might have been originally golden like Harald's but were too caked with blood and filth to be sure. An iron collar around his neck was chained to a staple in the wall. He tried to sit up, but even with Bellman's help the effort was too much for him, and he sank back on the straw.

"Who ordered you to look for Frederik?" the Duchess said.

"The Provost, Lord Volpe."

The water arrived and was handed down. Bellman held it to Radu's damaged mouth.

The prisoner continued his story, pushing every word painfully through broken teeth and swollen lips. "Lord Volpe told me your son was in worse danger than you had realized and he could find a safer place to hide him. I was to find the boy and bring back word of where he was. He said he knew that this might not seem like honorable work. It didn't, Your Highness, but I had to obey him, just as he must obey the Abbot, and the Abbot His Highness. His Highness had ordered this, the Provost said. I said I would obey."

"And did you lead the men who abducted my sister and my son?"

"I guided them there, Highness," he mumbled. "I told your sister that she had to come back with us and bring the boy."

"Or?"

"Or we would use force."

"And where did you take them?"

"To Vamky, Your Grace. I don't know where they went from there." Again he drank.

"Radu, I fear I have more bad news for you. I am almost certain your brother Harald is dead."

It was impossible to read expressions on the prisoner's face. "He died well?"

"I don't know. He seems to have been trying to kill me. Could he have been doing that?"

"If he was ordered to do so."

"So when he swore loyalty to the Baron, he perjured himself?"

"If he was ordered to perjure himself, he would. The oath has no limits."

"And when you told the Count a week ago that you were leaving Vamky? Were you also lying?"

The prisoner tried to shrug and gasped at the result. "No, I meant it. I was a fool to expect him to believe me."

"Why would you break this irrevocable oath?"

"Because I saw the Grand Duke in a dungeon in Vamky. The Provost has broken faith. He is a traitor."

"Count János refused you. Will you swear loyalty to me instead? And will you mean it?"

"Gladly. I will mean it. I fear my service will be brief."

Ringwood knew he was witnessing a feat of rare courage. The Count's brutality would have broken most men. Radu was apparently still capable of making a joke.

"You are not going to die, not tomorrow. The oath I demand is lifelong. Do I have it?"

"I swear. Willingly."

"I need you to help me rescue my husband."

"Your Highness!" Ringwood said, and heard Ranter mutter an obscenity.

"Be silent! Sister Trudy?"

"The prisoner speaks truth, Your Grace."

"You would be insane to trust him." János's voice rumbled like thunder. "How can he break an irrevocable oath and expect you to trust him?"

"I do trust him," Johanna said wearily. "I will take you into my service, Radu, if you will pass a test. Reveal a secret for me . . . How do the brethren create shadowmen?"

For a moment it seemed the turncoat would not answer. Then he shivered and said, "With a flea, Your Highness. A conjured flea. Just one will start the death-beyond-death."

"Trudy?"

Ringwood had heard True's gasp and knew what she would say.

"Truth."

"Very good. Count János, get this man out of here. See that he is tended and taken to the octogram for healing. You will not hang him. Tomorrow he will tell us many things we need to know."

◆ 8 ◆

$\Re$adu strode along the dark corridor, going fast but not running, for the summons had been *exigent,* not *instant.* If he arrived out of breath, he might be disciplined for exceeding orders. He still had the vulnerable, hollow feeling that came from being shaken awake in the small hours, but a man grew used to that in Vamky. His hood was raised, and the sword at his side hung on a shiny new brown sword belt. He was a belted knight, and that felt very good.

In effect he was navigating by stars, for burrows stretched endlessly ahead, level or sloped, lit by solitary lamps at the hubs, placed high so that their glow would not be blocked by other people. At that hour there were no other people. Once in a while he would pause to run his fingers over the numbers on a door and confirm that he had not gone astray.

When he located the door he needed, he drew a few deep breaths, then pounded the pommel of his sword against it three times. *Boom, boom, boom.* The wood was battered to ruin where generations of swords had performed the same task.

Only a minute or so crawled by before a voice bade him enter. He closed the heavy door behind him, took two steps to the simple plank table, threw back his hood, and waited to be acknowledged. Without moving his eyes, he could see that the cell was no larger or grander than any other. It included the standard bed, table, and chair, and a shelf where all personal belongings must be exposed to view. The muniment chest was extra, a mark of high rank in the Brotherhood, as were the two oil lamps that made it all seem bright as day to him.

The resident set his quill in the inkwell and looked up from his papers. He set back his hood to reveal a hard, scarred face and a silver-streaked beard.

Radu saluted. "Sir! Junior Knight-brother Radu reporting to Banneret Dusburg as commanded."

"At ease, Radu. Congratulations on your belting."

"Sir! Thank you."

Both men replaced their hoods. Radu felt naked without his now.

"Less than three years?"

"Sir! Only one month less." Two years as novice, three as squire. It was a good record.

"Better than ten years over," Dusburg agreed. "You enjoyed your trip to Trenko?"

"Sir. It was memorable and most gratifying." As junior knight in the ducal escort, Radu had seen more of the Margrave's stables than his court, but it had been a welcome celebration of his new status all the same.

Dusburg went back to writing. The man was something of a puzzle in Vamky. A banneret commanded military groups in the field, but Dusburg was clearly well into his forties and too old for that. He had not made the usual transfer to the conjuring arm, nor the rarer one to administration, so his duties were mysterious. There was even doubt as to whether he was an Abbot man or a Provost man, a distinction rarely in doubt. Radu had never spoken with him before.

After ten minutes or so, a sword boomed against the door, just once. Novices were normally left waiting—it was not unusual to see three or four of them lined up outside a door—but the banneret shouted "Enter!" right away. Radu heard the door open and close but did not turn.

The man who sank to his knees alongside him was unusually large. Dusburg ignored the interruption and continued writing, so Radu risked a downward glance to confirm that the newcomer was indeed Harald, although he had guessed that just from his size. Their father always claimed that he had gotten better with practice, and Harald, the youngest of his sons, had been the largest of them all before he was sixteen. He was eighteen now and still growing. Radu saw him around the monastery sometimes, but they rarely had a chance to speak.

Harald was panting like a dog, with sweat shining on his shaven scalp, as well it might if he had sprinted all the way up from the novice cells wearing a broadsword. Radu hoped his brother's summons had been *instant,* but it probably had, because Dusburg had called him in right away just to see that sweat.

Suddenly he laid down his quill, still ignoring the newcomer. "Radu, I have a disciplinary problem to put to you."

Radu snapped, "Sir!" but his heart sank. His own conscience was clear. What had the kid been up to? It would break Harald's heart to be thrown out, as so many recruits were. Novices were the workhorses of Vamky, drudges doing all the menial work in kitchens and stables that kept the monastery running. Some men remained novices all their lives, some were expelled, some gave up. Very few displayed the absolute obedience, dedication, and self-abasement required for promotion to squire, the first step up the ladder. Every one of Priboi's sons had tried to achieve knighthood, and Radu was the first to succeed since Fritz, the eldest, who had done so many years ago and then died on his first campaign.

"A certain novice," said the banneret, "qualified for visitation privileges and his father came to see him. The novice passed on to his father an item of gossip alleging that certain members of the Brotherhood were plotting treason. You know that to repeat such a story to anyone except one's immediate superior is cause for disciplinary action from the third list. What do you feel should be done to this novice?"

The question was so easy that Radu dared to smile, knowing his brother would not look up. He kept the amusement out of his voice, though. "Sir! A few weeks in solitary would teach him the virtues of silence. Unless, of course, he had been ordered to pass on that information." It was six months since Harald had enlisted, so he would have been due for his first visitation.

Dusburg nodded. "He was so ordered."

"Sir, I believe he should be congratulated on passing a test."

"But this information was false, Radu. He knew it was false. He lied to his own father, and we have evidence that his father was deceived. Is he not a nasty sneak, an ingrate, a foul-mouthed liar?"

"Sir, he did even better than I thought. Especially if the father in question was anything like my own father, who is an extremely skeptical and sharp-witted old man."

The banneret's hard eyes twinkled. His voice stayed icy cold. "Then you approve of his deceit?"

"Sir. Wholeheartedly."

"Then consider the following mission. The Abbot needs a

man who will pretend to leave the Brotherhood and rejoin the laity. He will be required to tell lies to explain why he has apparently reneged, also to perjure himself by swearing loyalty to an outsider with the firm intention of betraying that oath in any way required by his fundamental loyalty to the Order. He will also have to undertake certain operations that could result in death to other people and certainly his own death if he is caught. It will be a solitary mission, lonely and dangerous, and entirely outside the normal bounds of honor as the world judges. What would you say to such a mission?"

Radu felt nauseated and ashamed because of it. *A warrior does whatever is required to win.* "Sir! I should be honored to be assigned such a mission." Honored but horrified. Surely they would not put a youngster like Harald through such an ordeal?

"Why?"

"Sir. Because a solitary mission is always a great honor, and one so taxing would imply that the council puts enormous trust in me, a man who has been a knight-brother less than a month. Also, because I know that the Brotherhood does not cause death without reason, this mission must be important for the welfare of us all. Sir."

Dusburg thought for a moment. "The perjury would not bother you? The betrayal?"

"Not if I was obeying orders, sir."

"And if your orders were to avoid detection at any cost, would you willingly break the rule of our order? Would you steal, kill, even fornicate if necessary?"

"Sir. I will obey any order, as I swore on the day I enlisted." That day he had been told the Brotherhood's three requirements—obedience, obedience, and obedience.

The banneret nodded. "The novice may rise."

Harald stood up. And up.

"At ease. The novice may greet his brother."

Harald turned to look down at Radu with an eight-horse grin. "Sir! Permission to congratulate you on your belting?"

"Granted," Radu said. "And congratulations to the novice! If he really pulled wool over the old man's eyes he's a better man than I can ever hope to be." He gave his brother a hug and instantly wished he hadn't. He thought he'd lost half his ribs.

"The novice will be pleased to hear," Dusburg said, "that his promotion to squire will be announced at the midday meal."

Harald gasped, looked at Radu with disbelieving joy. Then he fell into the age-old trap and reached up to raise his hood.

"The promotion will be effective when announced."

"Sir!" Harald dropped to his knees again. The back of his neck was pink with excitement, though.

Radu hoped that what he was feeling was amazement, not jealousy. Squire in six months? Incredible! Surely that did not happen every century?

"The novice will open the shutters and report what he sees." Dusburg picked up his papers as if to read over what he had written.

Harald jumped to obey. "Sir. Just the dark."

"He will look to the left."

He leaned out. "Sir! A fire! A huge . . ."

"Can the novice judge where it is?"

"I think . . . Sir! I think it must be Fadrenschloss, seat of Baron Fader."

"Radu, go and see if you agree."

It was, of course. And there was worse to come, when the shutters had been closed, when the brothers were back before the table, one standing, one kneeling.

"Radu, Fadrenschloss was your childhood home?"

"Sir."

"You still have family there?"

"Sir."

"Radu, there are presently contingents of brethren on every road leading in and out of Fadrenschloss. They have been there since sunset. They have done, and will do, nothing about that fire. What say you to that?"

Cold as a corpse's, the banneret's eyes stared up at him. There were questions he could ask, of course—had brethren started the fire? They must have known it was coming, or somebody had. Were they stopping people going in, or people going out? But ill-judged questions brought harsh discipline, second list.

"Sir. I fail to understand the question."

"You do not wonder why they are there or what they are doing?"

"Sir. It is not my place to wonder."

Dusburg nodded as if satisfied. "Dismissed."

Radu saluted and went away, leaving his brother still there, on his knees.

He did not see Harald around anymore, but that did not mean the boy had accepted the solo mission. He might have refused it and been expelled in consequence. Or locked up in solitary if he had learned too many secrets.

It was less than a week later that Radu was again summoned in the middle of the night, but this time he was sent for by the Provost himself, which was an astonishing experience for a junior knight-brother. Furthermore, Volpe assured him that the orders he now issued had originated with the Grand Duke himself. Even granted that Radu had unique qualifications for this particular duty, it was a breathtaking honor for a mere junior to be assigned a mission so vital without supervision. He was amused to wonder if Harald's skillful lying had given the family a good name.

Radu did not go back to bed after that interview. He went straight to the quartermaster's store, where the pass the Provost had given him let him draw all the supplies he would need. He dressed in forester's leathers on the spot, replacing his gown over them, then went across to the stable to requisition a palfrey and a down-at-heel packhorse. He turned his pass in at the gate, taking careful mental note of the operation name Volpe had given it, *Jewel Case*. He rode out at first light, followed by a squire from the guard. A furlong or two down the slope, Radu reined in. Keeping his back to his companion, he removed his robe and dropped it. Then he rode away, leading the sumpter. The squire would return the garment to the quartermaster, but even he had not seen the face of the man he had escorted out.

Radu resisted a gnawing temptation to visit the shattered shell of Fadrenschloss on his way, but only because he might be recognized, which had been forbidden him. Comforted by the knowledge that he would have heard by then if any of his family had perished in the blaze, he headed up into the hills, along trails familiar from his boyhood, heading for Brikov. He avoided the settlement itself, though, for Lord Volpe had warned him that many of the Baron's people had sought refuge with Count János, including his own father.

How to locate one particular charcoal burner? If the Count's servants noticed him wandering the Count's lands, they would have questions to put and rough ways of putting them. Fortunately, the younger Radu had learned his woodcraft from Master Manfred, Baron Fader's forester, and left no more trail than a trout.

In practice his task was not so hard. Burners had no interest in tall timber trees or inaccessible mountain slopes. Woodlands were harvested on a cycle of about eighteen years, so Radu could concentrate on areas where underwood had grown up again from the coppiced stumps. The sound of axes carried a long way. In a few days, he located a man chopping down branches and recognized his companions—a woman and a toddler, who screamed with merriment as he ran from her on very short legs. None of them saw Radu, yet he could easily have been an enemy seeking to do the child harm! Lord Volpe had not been mistaken when he said that there were safer places to hide the heir apparent.

There was no sign of a burners' mound yet. The man was still constructing shelters, obviously preparing for a larger group to arrive. The sooner the child could be seized the better, but Radu's orders did not allow him to try.

He walked out to where he had tethered his horse and rode off, reaching Vamky at midnight. The name of *Jewel Case* won him admittance. He reported his return to the Provost's adjutant and within minutes was standing in front of Volpe himself, who looked as if he had just been wakened, although the blanket on his cot was neatly folded.

"Well done indeed, brother. I agree that haste is advisable. Can you manage a night without sleep?"

Radu said, "Sir." What other reply could there be?

Two hours later he rode out with a troop led by Senior Knight-brother Báthory. At dawn the cordon of grim mounted knights closed around the burners' camp, although there were still only the two adults there with the child. Radu dismounted and approached. The woman Voica snatched up the boy and sought refuge close to her man, who was not far short of Radu himself in size and had an ax, although he was letting the blade rest on the ground and being careful not to raise it in threat. Pale eyes stared out of soot-black faces.

"I know you, Voica," Radu told her.

"And I know you, Radu Priboi," she retorted. She must have recognized his voice, for his helmet's face plate, cheek pieces, and bevor concealed all his face except his eyes.

"My name does not matter. I know the boy also, for I have seen him at Krupa. He is not safe here. Others may find him as easily as I did. We will take him to a safer hiding place. You are welcome to come with him." Seeing her eyes flicker to her man, he said, "He, too, if he wants. You will all be well treated."

"You swear that?" the man growled.

"I swear it."

"And if we refuse?"

That was what Radu dreaded. These rootless hill folk cherished their freedom fiercely. Would they be insane enough to defy the Brotherhood?

"We *will* take the boy. Whatever else happens is up to you." And he exceeded orders by adding, "Please don't resist. If we must use force, we will leave no witnesses."

"We will trust you, Radu," Voica said.

So the mission was accomplished without violence. That afternoon Radu saw the boy and his two guardians enter Vamky, but where they were taken or what happened to them he had no idea.

He had barely dropped onto his cot that night before he was again summoned to Banneret Dusburg.

"Excellent work, Radu. You are promoted to senior knight-brother, effective at once. Congratulations. You are making fine progress."

Radu could only gasp, "Sir!" Of course, he had been lucky, but chance played a part in every man's career. Now he was two ranks ahead of his spectacular young brother again. He doubted he would hold that lead very long.

"Deliver this letter," Dusburg said, "with all reasonable haste—'reasonable' in this context meaning you are not to injure the horses and preferably not yourself, either. Banneret Catavolinos has been advised. Check with Operations regarding your route." Before Radu could say a word, he added, "Dismissed."

The letter was addressed to Preceptor Oswald, on assignment at the court of the Tzarina Regent of Skyrria, but Radu knew that the real message was intended for him, and was simply that he must not talk with anyone around Vamky before midsummer at the earliest. Kiensk, the Skyrrian capital, was far to the east, at least a month away.

For a lively young knight, such a mission was both reward and good training. He could see the world, perfect his horsemanship, and experience something very close to freedom for the first time in five years. He wore half armor with the Brotherhood blazon on his surcoat, so honest wayfarers saw him as a welcome companion, a deterrent to footpads and highwaymen, and the dishonest were not inclined to interfere with him. Furnished with expense money and protected by conjuration from travelers' flux and hostelry vermin, he met with few troubles. The worst were the tavern girls who enjoyed mocking a man forbidden even to notice them. He had only his willpower to defend him against them, and many times it was severely tested.

He had to detour around Bohakia and Dolorth, since both were negotiating with Vamky for knights and battle conjurers and he might have found himself stranded on the wrong side in a war. He arrived in the Skyrrian capital of Kiensk early in Sixthmoon and reported to Preceptor Oswald. Two hours later, the Preceptor handed him a letter addressed to Banneret Valentin, presently commanding brethren on campaign in Gevily. Radu saddled up and rode west, across the entire width of Eurania.

Valentin refused Radu's plea to be allowed to share in the fighting, but did have the grace to ask if there was some land he particularly wanted to visit. Radu chose Distlain and wondered why the onlookers grinned. He discovered the answer a few weeks later when the southern sun almost cooked him in his cuirass.

He duly delivered the letter Valentin had given him and was given another, but his Distlain visit was not entirely wasted. Riding alone through an orange grove one fine morning, he was shot at. One quarrel missed him and another went through his shield, but was slowed enough to do no worse than dent his breastplate. He drew his sword and charged the highwaymen without even thinking to count them. Fortunately there were only three of them, and he gave them no time to rewind their crossbows. He left their bodies for the crows and took their horses to sell in the next town. The honor of the Brotherhood was upheld.

After a six-month tour around Eurania, Radu homed in at last on Vamky. Seen by moonlight high on its ridge, the monastery was ethereally beautiful, towers and walls of dream and cobweb, so insubstantial that he looked for stars showing through them. And yet, riding his horse up the long incline, he could not deny that this felt like returning to a prison. He should have overnighted in Krupa, but honor had impelled him to press on and complete his journey instead of loitering and making two easy days out of one hard one. However weary, he might be sent right back out again if the Marquis's whereabouts were still so great a secret.

He had often wondered on his long trek whether Volpe and Dusburg really believed he was an untrustworthy blabbermouth, or were merely withholding information from someone within Vamky itself, someone so high in the Brotherhood that he could compel Radu to talk. Minhea, maybe? Gossip was a list three offense, but it was common knowledge that Abbot and Provost did not always agree.

Vamky never slept. He gave his password, *Heron Flight,* and the clerks found his card as fast as if he had been gone only a day, not half a year.

He rode over to the armory to shed the steel he had worn for so long. The squire who helped him emitted a quiet whistle when he saw the dent on the cuirass, but knew better than to ask who had paid for that and how much. Radu stripped from the neck down, donned the white robe he was given, then turned his back to remove his helmet and pull up the hood. Faceless he left and faceless he returned.

Men from the stables and quartermaster's arrived to relieve him of everything else. He walked into the monastery proper with only his robe, sandals, and sword, and even those were not his to own. The guard would inform Banneret Dusburg that his minion had returned, and Dusburg would either send him out again or advise Banneret Catavolinos that he could have his subordinate back. Radu's only immediate duty was to deliver the letter he had brought from Meistersinger Groningen in Ritizzia to Cantor Samuil and get a receipt for it. Cantor was the lowest conjuring rank, outranking banneret within the monastery. Radu did not know the man, but would be very happy to drag him out of bed. Six months' saddle sores cried out for satisfaction.

He went next to Housekeeping, a dusty, musty room where novices stood at writing desks all day, copying lists into enormous tomes. Like all brethren, Radu had many unpleasant memories of this boredom. He asked for Cantor Samuil's cell number. The solitary novice on duty, who looked both sleepy and stupid, fumbled back and forth through the directory for a while, then disappeared out a back door. Just before Radu exploded and started breaking rules by going in search of him, he returned with a man wearing the brown sword belt of a junior knight-brother, who lifted down another volume and consulted that.

"Sir. That information is not available."

"Brother, I have urgent business with the cantor."

"Sir. I do not have authority to release his whereabouts."

"Brother, I killed the last three men who tried to stop me completing this mission. I order you to tell me."

"Sir. I have my orders," the man said sullenly. He sounded old to be only a junior and not nearly arrogant enough to be sure of his ground.

No doubt the dispatch Radu bore was of no importance whatsoever, but his duty was clear and an inquiry would uphold him. Following procedure, he threw back his hood and drew his sword halfway from its scabbard. "Brother, I will see your face!"

The novice went chalky white, perhaps imagining himself being sent to drag very senior officers out of bed to adjudicate the conflict.

His superior capitulated. "Blue 1, A 5."

"Say that again?"

"*Sir!* Blue 1, A 5."

"Brother, I didn't think there was a Level 1 in Blue Hub."

"Sir. It says here to go to a door marked 'Brooms' in Blue 3, J 6. You will need a lantern," the junior knight added in a belated frenzy of cooperation.

There were seven hubs in Vamky, and Blue was as far from the main gate as it was possible to go, where the monastery abutted the mountain. Radu knew Blue 3 quite well, because that was where squires received basic conjuration training. Octograms must be sited at ground level, where air and earth elementals met, and the ridge rose steeply there, so Level 3 rested right on bedrock. Hence his surprise.

When he arrived at Blue 3, he found the J corridor dark, with no guiding star at the far end. All Vamky lanterns were the same, a glass bottle constricted in the middle to a waist narrow enough to hold. He removed the chimney and raised the lantern itself to the hub lamp to light the wick. As soon as the flame was steady, he replaced the chimney and set off in search of J 6. He found the big eight-sided room empty and silent, creepy with remnant spirituality like odors of ancient cooking. What seemed to be a cupboard door opposite opened to a staircase descending into the rock. The only staircases he had ever seen in Vamky were up in the towers, so curiosity tempered his fatigue as he began his descent. No doubt he was trespassing in territory reserved to the conjuring ranks, but he had an excellent reason to snoop and that was always a pleasure. Straight and dangerously steep, the stair eventually brought him to a hub where three corridors met, and there the walls were of ashlar again, not living rock. Numbers on the walls confirmed that he was on Level 2 and this was still Hub Blue. Another stair, even steeper, went on down.

Vamky was enormous. Even in winter, when most of the expeditionary forces returned to base, the monastery never ran out of space, so why was Cantor Samuil quartered so far away from everyone else? By the time he came back from the mess hall it would be time to eat again.

The second stair cut through a spur of bedrock and back into masonry, turned sharply to the left once, then twice, and continued down to end at a barred gate, beyond which there was light, much light. It would seem that Blue Hub Level 1, Corridor A, was a jail, and it was certainly not the hoosegow used for errant novices and squires. Radu knew that one only too well, and a busy, nasty place it was.

Standing on the bottom step, he peered through the grille in growing astonishment. The extravagant lighting was the first surprise. Oil was never wasted, yet a dozen or so hanging lamps made this place almost dazzling. It was apparently the end of the road, with no obvious way out. Six doors arrayed along the right-hand wall looked like entrances to standard monastic cells, similar to Dusberg's Red 7, A 17, or his own Green 5, F 97. He was too far away to read the numbers burned into the wood, but if one of those was A 5, then Cantor Samuil was a jailer required to live close to his charges.

The opposite wall held four doors of metal bars, dungeons for prisoners. If one of those was A 5, the idea of handing the letter to Samuil personally was devilishly tempting and utterly stupid.

Most surprising of all, a plank table in the center of the long room held a few books, two arms, and a head, the body parts belonging to a white-gowned swordsman whose buttocks rested on a bench alongside. He was snoring vigorously. There was enough light for Radu to make out that the man's sword belt was violet, meaning he was a preceptor, no less, but what sort of prisoner required a senior master to guard him? Knight-brothers caught sleeping on watch were summarily executed. If Radu reported this offence, he would put the sinner in grave danger, but he might compromise himself also. He knew he had stumbled into matters that did not concern him.

He backed up the stair until he was out of sight, then coughed. The snoring continued. He stamped his feet, but sandals made only wimpy noises. Giving up, he went down again and clinked his sword hilt against the bars. The snoring never wavered, but the gate moved.

He had assumed it was locked, and no doubt it was supposed to be locked. Did loyalty to the Brotherhood require him to report this sloppiness? Giving the miscreant one last chance, he pushed the rusty door wide. He had expected the hinges to squeak, but in the subterranean silence they shrieked like banshees, making him jump.

The guard stopped snoring . . . snuffled a few times . . . and started again.

This was ridiculous! Radu was nearly asleep on his feet and would be lucky to catch two hours' hay time before he had to start writing a report or take up weapons training again or undertake whatever torments his superiors could imagine. He marched into the jail, swinging his lantern. The first solid door was A 1. So Samuil was a jailer, not a prisoner, and his door would be right along here: . . . 3 . . . 4 . . . Three thunderous impacts on those timbers ought to give the sleeping guard a heart attack.

"Brother!"

Radu spun around, almost dropping his lantern. He knew that voice from somewhere. Only one dungeon was occupied, and the prisoner was standing just inside the gate, clutching the bars and peering out. Radu strode over to him, and for a moment the two of them stared at each other in silence. Faces were a rare sight in Vamky, and that face in this place was beyond imagining.

"Radu!" the prisoner whispered. "Help me!" He was tethered to the back wall by a long chain attached to a heavy brass collar.

"Your Highness!" This was madness! Why would the Grand Duke be—

"*Death and fire!*" roared another voice. "*Who the pus are you?*"

The shout came from a newcomer, a large, flabby man, very likely Cantor Samuil, because he was standing in the doorway of A 5 holding a sword. The sleeping guard grunted, sat up, and grabbed for his own sword. Samuil moved toward the entrance to cut off the intruder's escape.

Radu shot past the table like a crossbow bolt and up the precipitous stairs as fast as he could go. Angry shouts behind him warned that pursuit was on its way. Elementals of pure terror drove him on, around the first corner. Rubin a prisoner in the monastery? High treason! Abbots and Grand Dukes had been known to quarrel in the past, but never in all history had it come to open revolution like this. Heads must roll.

Around the second corner . . . He was a dead man if the conspirators caught him. And who could be behind this but Provost Volpe? Possibly Abbot Minhea, but it had been Volpe who had sent Radu to find the Grand Duke's hidden son. The memory hit him like a kick in the stomach—Volpe had claimed to be speaking for the Duke, authorizing the kidnapping of his own son! So the Provost was the chief traitor, and Radu was now witness to two acts of treason, accessory to the abduction and no doubt murder of the infant Marquis.

He stumbled onto the Level 2 landing and stopped. He glanced at the stairs going up and the three corridors leading spirits knew where. Then he turned and hurled his lantern back down the way he had come. Glass shattered, and a chorus of oaths turned into screams as burning oil splashed over Samuil. Radu hurried through the darkness, waving his arms before him. To run up the stairs would be too obvious. Where the corridors led he had no idea. The novice barns were on Blue Level 2, as far from anywhere civilized as possible, but the fact that he had been directed to come via Blue to 3, J 6, strongly suggested that this section did not connect with them. Besides, nobody would put a secret like that jail within reach of nosy novices.

He walked down the central passage of the three, running

fingers along the wall. When he reached door 2, K 1, he decided he had come far enough.

A few bladder-testing moments later, three men carrying lanterns and swords scurried up from Level 1 and on toward Level 3. If one of them was Samuil, he had taken time to dress. Radu fumbled his way back through the darkness to the hallway—ignoring a faint stink of burned wool—and started up the long stair to the broom cupboard. He had no way to rescue the Grand Duke; rescuing himself would need all the wits he owned.

From octogram Blue 3, B 6, he knew where he was going, even in the dark. Where had the others gone? One to find help, almost certainly. Another to report to the Provost, likely. One to fetch a stretcher for the burned man, maybe. Radu cut through octogram B 5 and took the ramp to White. He walked at a standard knight-brother pace, head down, one hand on his sword. If he were seriously challenged, he would fight, he decided, but the few other men he encountered paid him no heed. Lamps were glimmering, faint light showed around the shutters, but all thoughts of bed and sleep must be discarded. He had to get out of the monastery and out of Krupina before he was cut to pieces.

How, though? Nobody left Vamky without a pass, and those came down from the highest levels. Every window in the place looked out over a fatal drop. You couldn't let a horse down on a rope, anyway, and without a horse he would be caught inside an hour.

Would denial work? Suppose he destroyed the letter so there was no visible connection between him and the spy? If Dusburg asked about the trip, he could say that Meistersinger Groningen had just told him his vacation was ended and he could go home, period. No letter. Would Dusburg believe that? Had Samuil heard the Duke say his name? Could they beat it out of the Duke? The clerk brother in

Housekeeping would not voluntarily tell anyone that he had given out a confidential address, and why should the traitors think to ask him? They had no way of knowing that the spy they had so nearly caught had just returned to Vamky that night.

Radu had reached about that point in his thoughts—his feet were climbing the ramp from Red 4 to Green 5—when he realized he no longer had the Groningen letter. He remembered holding it when he pushed the barred gate open. He had tucked it in his belt to free up a hand when he was about to knock on Samuil's door. That was the last he remembered of it. They would find the letter—might have already done so—and run down to the gate to ask who had come in that night. They might very well be waiting for him already in Green 5, F 37. He was dead.

Lacking other instructions, his feet kept walking on the same path, and his mind revolved in the same terrible circles, like a moth around a balefire. His fingers located his cell number. No guards were waiting in the corridor. They might be inside. He had no real reason to go in there, no possessions beyond a comb, and there might be a death squad lurking inside, and yet this was his home until the day he died, which might well be already dawning out there in the world. Somehow it felt like a refuge, which it most certainly was not.

He raised the latch and went in. Nobody put a sword to his throat. There was nobody there, no change in six months except a list-three layer of dust. His blanket lay neatly folded on his mattress exactly as he had left it when the novice bringing Dusburg's summons thundered on his door. He opened the shutters and let in the light and fresh mountain cold. He was dead, dead, dead.

Three letters lay on his bed. They had been opened, of course. Letters were always read and not always delivered.

No, only two were letters. One was a note from his father congratulating him on his birthweek, five months ago. The other was from Franz saying the old man had died and they were going to put off the funeral until the twenty-fifth to let the family gather. At Brikov, of course. And hope-you-can-make-it-he-was-so-proud-of-you.

The twenty-fifth of *what*, you big, dumb farmer?

The third document was a pass, *Westering Song*, for ten days' leave, signed by Banneret Catavolinos and dated the twenty-third of Ninthmoon. He was a straight sword, Catavolinos. Few commanders granted leave for any reason at all, and he must have brought this pass here personally and left it on the bed just in case Radu returned in time. After a few minutes' counting and recounting, Radu decided that today was the twenty-fourth. The pass was still valid. If he went now, he might just make it out of Vamky.

IV

from a View to a Death

• 1 •

"**Y**ou have no doubt that the man in the dungeon was my husband?"

"None, Your Highness." Radu's voice was raspy after so much talking, but he was a new man since the healing, nothing like the battered derelict they had rescued the previous evening. Ringwood could see a likeness to Harald now, Radu being darker and not as huge. Still big, though. And he impressed. He did not need True's testimonial to be a convincing man. Even his throwaway mention of the three highwaymen had been believable.

Fed and rested, Ringwood felt much more cheerful this morning, and so did the Count's hall, with a log fire blazing on the hearth, sometimes puffing smoke when the wind gusted. Rain hissing in the chimney fulfilled Manfred's prediction of bad weather. The travelers could not have made it over Smugglers' Pass today.

They were gathered on two benches before the fireplace—Ranter, Johanna, and Bellman on the left, Radu, Ringwood, and True on the right, with János on his throne between them. They had all been spellbound by the glimpse Radu had given of the inner workings of secretive Vamky. Now the questions were starting as people mulled over what he had said. The big one was going to be, *What do we do now?* but no one had gotten to that yet.

Bellman said, "Tell me how the Grand Duke knew your name."

"When he visited Trenko last spring," Radu said, "I was junior knight-brother in the escort, so I was assigned to be his custrel. His Highness is invariably courteous to subordinates."

"He is," Joanna said, "but he's notorious for not remembering names." She frowned. "And his attendant was someone else. A longish name . . ."

"Knight-brother Nickolaus on the outward journey. I inherited the honor for our return."

"I do not recall seeing you on that trip at all!"

Radu smiled. "I saw you, Your Highness."

"I expect it was the beard. And I used to be taller than you, too!"

He laughed. "You're thinking of Franz."

"Oh? Maybe. I can't keep track of you all."

"Franz dreamt of kissing you as soon as he wouldn't have to stand on tiptoe."

Johanna flickered him a smile of the sort that Ringwood had learned to avoid. She looked up at the Count. "When do you leave for Krupa, my lord?" Here it came.

"Soon." He had a great face for scowling with, had János. "In summer, on dry roads, I can do it in one day. In this storm, I'll overnight at Donehof and go on in the morning."

The wedding was tomorrow at sunset and no one had forgotten that, least of all the Grand Duke's wife.

"And where will you be staying in Krupina?"

"I rented a house for the week of the festivities. My bursar thought I'd bought it when I told him the price."

Ringwood noted that no offer of hospitality followed. János was probably skilled at avoiding trouble. He chose his battlefields, and squiring the previous Grand Duchess to the enthronement of the next one would greatly displease his liege lord the Duke.

"When did you do that?" she asked, and the tension in the room tightened a notch.

János could have said he had sent his steward, but True might have called him on it. "When I went to watch the inquiry into your death. Your first death, Your Grace."

"Did you see Rubin at that time?"

He nodded. "Not to speak with."

"Was he limping?"

"Not that I noticed, but I wasn't looking for it."

"Well?" she demanded of the whole assembly. "I think he's a fake! I believe Radu, and my husband is a prisoner in Vamky. How are we going to rescue him?"

The Count made a derisive noise.

"He is your liege lord!" Johanna's words cracked like whips. "You will not go to his aid?"

"Get him out of *Vamky*, girl? You're out of your mind!"

Everyone else was shooting wary glances at Ringwood, but he just smiled. He had already warned his ward that she could organize any sort of rescue she liked, or any sort of disruption of the wedding, but he would not let her become personally involved. She and her Blades were going no farther than Brikov, where they were now. End of journey, end of discussion.

"Why bother?" Ranter asked. "Why would you want him back?"

Even the Count winced.

Johanna dug in her claws, arched her back, and spat. "Because, you thick oaf, Volpe stole my son and I will see him chained on the rack for it! I will gladly turn the screw until I get Frederik back, or forever. The louder he screams the louder I sing."

"The kid's dead. You know that."

"*I do not know that!* Keep your mouth shut. My lord, today I will come with you as far as Donehof."

Ringwood yelped. "Your Highness! You agreed—"

"Don't be an old woman!" Johanna said. "I suppose that's your job, being an old woman. It doesn't suit you."

"Why do you want to go to this place, wherever it is?"

"For safety! Smugglers' Pass is impassable in this weather, isn't it, my lord? So Brikov is a dead end and very dangerous for me if Volpe has any more spies around here, and I'm sure he does. Donehof will be much safer."

"What's Donehof?" Ringwood asked, knowing he had lost this battle. She had found the only argument he could not ignore, security.

"A place I own not far south of Fadrenschloss," János said. "One of Radu's brothers runs it for me. It's time I got started." He edged forward on his throne.

"It's on the west road," Johanna said, "so if there's trouble you can spirit me out to the north or south as you please. Much safer than here."

"Why do you want to go there?" Ringwood asked, knowing her answer would merely eliminate one possible lie. Why had chance not given him a nice, malleable ward, one he could bully?

"So I can wave when the bride goes by! When does the dear child arrive, does anyone know?"

"She was due in Krupa three days ago," János told her.

"Oh, well." If Johanna had really had plans to disrupt the bridal procession, she showed no signs of disappointment. "Radu? You know the situation in Vamky. How can we rescue His Highness?"

The knight-brother shook his head. "I am your man, Your Highness, and will be loyal to the end of my days. After the crime I committed against your son and sister, the least I can do is to dedicate my life to your service. But I cannot see how what you suggest can be done. No nation in Eurania would attempt a siege, and storming those walls is unthinkable. The security on the gate has worked perfectly for centuries, so we cannot hope to sneak in. And if we did, how in the world would we get him safely out again? I couldn't think of a way of escape for myself alone, one man, when my life depended on it."

Ringwood's ward was nothing if not stubborn. "You implied that the Brotherhood was divided into Abbot's men and Provost's men."

"So I did," Radu admitted. "Historically that is true, and historically the dukes have always played off abbot against provost and vice versa. We humble serfs were convinced that Minhea and Volpe detested each other, but we were guessing. We had no evidence. I have been gone half a year, remember, so I am not up to date. It may be that I should have run to the Abbot to report what I had seen, but . . ." He shrugged. "I couldn't believe such a prisoner could have been kept secret from him. His aides and Volpe's must spend half their time keeping watch on each other. Would I even have been given a hearing? The Provost himself sent me to capture the boy, so the Abbot's faction must regard me as one of his."

"You don't think the Abbot and the Provost may have ganged up on the Duke this time?" Bellman asked.

"Even that's possible." Radu was clearly suspicious of this flunky who sat so near Johanna on the bench, too close for a servant or even a social equal.

Bellman pondered for a while, and everyone else waited expectantly. The Count frowned but did not interrupt. Johanna's eyes were bright as she studied her lover's profile. It was quite obvious how those two felt about each other, yet Bellman could never have shared her bed without her Blades being aware of it. Knowing how crazy he felt if he was away from True for very long, Ringwood marveled at their self-control.

Then came Bellman's next question. "You said, Knight-brother, that you thought the gate on the guardroom should have been locked. I assume the dungeon door *was* locked, since the prisoner did not try to come out?"

"He was tethered, chained by the neck."

"Yes, and that's curious. Are the locks in Vamky like the locks here in Brikov? Just ordinary old iron locks? Not conjured?"

"I haven't noticed . . ." Radu peered across at the hall door. "Nothing special that I know of. There are almost no locks in Vamky. Nobody owns anything except the right to food and clothing. Why?"

"His father's a locksmith!" Johanna announced triumphantly.

Bellman nodded without taking his eyes off Radu. "Is your pass still valid, Knight-brother?"

"It may be." Radu looked at him incredulously. "Issued on the twenty-third. Um . . . odd month, odd days . . . this is the third?" He counted on his fingers. "It's good until midnight tonight."

"We could make it to Vamky by then, couldn't we? What's written on these passes?" Bellman rushed on without waiting for an answer. "The date issued, commanding officer's signature, an operation name? What else? Expiry date?"

"The number of men leaving. Not an expiry. Mine had 'Ten days' written on it, but that was an instruction to me, not the guard. Nothing else. Vamky is very concerned about security."

Vamky sounded like a total madhouse to Ringwood. Give him Ironhall any day. And hold the celibacy.

"The idea is that the men on the gates don't know who's doing what or why or going where," Bellman agreed. "Likewise the men coming in. There must be a way to take advantage of that."

Radu stared at him. "You are *raving!* In centuries nobody has ever broken the Brotherhood's security!"

"How many have tried? I gather you can ride out in full ceremonial plate mail or half armor or peasant rags, depending on your mission, but indoors everyone wears those white gowns?"

"Yes." Radu was openly contemptuous now. "I hope you're not suggesting we try to sneak an army in on my password?"

"Just you and a prisoner," Bellman said.

"Men on leave do not go around collecting prisoners."

"That's my point—the guards don't know what you've been doing. You could have been on leave or serving with an army somewhere, they don't know. How do they process prisoners?"

"They would give me a receipt for you and march you away in chains. Catavolinos would be told about you when he was notified of my return." Radu shook his head. "It *won't* work! There may even be a note on my pass that I'm to be arrested on sight."

Bellman grunted, looking angry and baffled. "I doubt that. With this obsessive secrecy, they wouldn't want the guards wondering *why.* If you do return you can't get out again, so why should they worry?"

"Exactly." Radu's smile indicated that the conversation was over and that the smarty young foreigner should stop trying to second-guess the Vamky Brotherhood.

"So you need two passes," True said.

"Of course!" Bellman cried. "Why didn't I see that?" He looked angry, not grateful.

"See what?" Ringwood, Radu, and János demanded with one voice.

Bellman gestured that True could have the honor.

"Truth-sounding," she said. "If Her Highness was right when she suggested that Vamky has spies here in Brikov, then I can ferret them out for you."

"No time for spy hunts," János said uneasily. "My men are ready to leave."

"I'd almost swear that the Brotherhood will have an informer here, my lord," Radu said. "Some man who's arrived since Her Highness passed through in the spring, I'd guess. Or some Fadrenschloss man who moved here, because I'm certain Vamky kept watch on von Fader. Any man who's ever served in Vamky, even briefly? Remember, they turned my brother into an assassin in half a year."

The Count scowled ferociously. "Wolfgang Webber, the wheelwright's oldest. Three years in Vamky. Gave up about five months ago because he couldn't get past novice grade."

"I'd bet a ducat he's a squire or even a knight-brother, my lord."

"That's the first thing to ask him," True said. "Even if he just answers a simple, 'No!' I will hear a falsehood."

"Then we beat his password out of him!" Ranter said with zest.

"You, boy, pull on that bell rope," János told Ringwood.

"You have a locksmith?" Bellman asked. "I'll need lock picks."

"Blacksmith does that," János said. There was excitement in the air now.

"Stop!" Johanna said suddenly. "Stop! Stop!" She jumped up. "This is far too dangerous! I forbid it."

She should have changed her mind sooner, Ringwood

thought. It was too late to call off the chase when the hounds had scented the game.

Trudy and Johanna were hastily packing in the bedroom, stuffing dirty clothes in with others not yet dry, when they were interrupted by a thunderous hammering on the door. Trudy opened it and discovered four large men and a boy, a slight, fresh-faced kid who looked understandably alarmed and much younger than she had expected.

"Fraulein Gertrude?" said a monstrous red beard. "This is Wolfgang Webber. Count says you have some questions to ask him."

Feeling ill already, Trudy forced herself to meet those innocent eyes. "I understand you spent two years in Vamky."

Angelic smile. "Nearer three years, fraulein."

"And why did you leave?"

He was easy—his pupils contracted. "Because they wouldn't promote me."

"That's a lie."

"Right!" said Red Beard.

"No, wait! Wolfgang, I know when people tell lies. You want to give me the truth now, or wait until these men hurt you?"

"You're wrong!" he said shrilly. "I am not lying."

"Bring him," Red Beard said. "We'll call you when he's ready, fraulein."

Trudy closed the door. Her hands shook so hard she could barely lace up her saddlebags. She struggled to put on the fine kidskin rain cloak and hat that Ringwood had given her.

"Don't feel guilty!" Johanna said harshly. "They kidnapped my son. They killed Bernard. They're spies and murderers and traitors. What you are doing is right."

That was easy for her to say—she hadn't sensed the death spirits already closing in on young Wolfgang. Trudy followed her downstairs, escorted by the Blades, who had been standing guard in the corridor. Having sent porters to fetch the baggage, they plunged out into the rain, which was falling in solid sheets, misting the ground, cascading off eaves, winding in rivulets over the ground. Men made room for them in the stables. There they stood and shivered, listening to the rain roaring on the slates. Out in the yard, two dozen or so men in helmets and breastplates were saddling up. When that confusion ended, with all the escort mounted and the packhorses laden, bedraggled boys still held a few unclaimed mounts. Thunder echoed through the hills, on and on.

Bellman appeared in half armor, wet as pondweed. "What're we waiting for?"

"Wolfgang," Johanna snapped. "He must be tougher than he looked."

"Do you think a daffodil would last three years in that madhouse? A question, Trudy—was Radu telling the truth when he said he was present on the Trenko expedition?"

She said, "Yes. Why?"

He managed to shrug his breastplate. "I don't know why. That seems to have been the start of this affair. What happened to the first groom, Nickolaus?"

Johanna chuckled. "You are the most infuriating man!" she said fondly. "I haven't the faintest idea! How can that possibly matter now?"

"I don't know," Bellman said, "except it feels as if it may. It's sort of like picking a lock—poking around until it makes sense. I'll ask Radu."

A helmet with a thick red beard appeared in the doorway. "Ach, there you are, fraulein! He's ready for you now."

Sick at heart, Trudy went with him. Rain pounded on her hat and shoulders. Sensing red flames behind her, she twisted around to peer out of her hood. It was Ringwood, of course.

"You stay here, love," she said. "You'll distract me." Why had she ever volunteered for this?

Wolfgang was a muddy heap against the rough stones of the rear wall of the barn. She could have found him just by homing in on the death elementals that were feeding his pain and terror. His guards' hatred was palpable. They would not be feeling like that if they had enjoyed what they had done, but they had done it. One of them held an iron bar.

"On your feet, spy!" one said, giving him a kick.

The boy whimpered and struggled to rise without using his arms. Trudy turned her eyes away, but not soon enough to avoid seeing what they had done to his face. Count János was there, looking like a very big man kneeling.

"How long where you in Vamky, Wolfgang?" she asked over her shoulder.

"Thirty-three months, fraulein." He had trouble speaking.

Could she detect lies in all this spiritual racket? She needed to make him lie again so she could judge the levels. "You're going to tell me the complete truth now, no matter what I ask?"

"Yes, fraulein."

That would do nicely. "What rank were you?"

"Junior knight-brother."

"When did you get that promotion?"

Pause. "The day I left, fraulein."

"You were sent here to spy?"

"Yes."

"To learn what?"

"To look out for the Duchess, the Baron, or the Marquis."

"That's all?"

"Anything else I thought might interest . . . them."

"Who gave you these orders?"

"Preceptor Oswald." *Clang!* went the first wrong note.

"Think again."

A man in a helmet and cuirass said, "I met Preceptor Oswald in Skyrria." She recognized Radu's voice.

She did not see what happened then, but the boy started screaming. Her stomach knotted so tight she thought she would vomit. Why had she ever suggested this atrocity? Why hadn't she stayed in Chivial? But then she would not have Ringwood's love. Could he still love her after this?

The screaming died away into sobs. Someone told the prisoner to stand up.

"Don't make them do that to you again, please!" she said. "Who was it?"

Came a whisper, "Abbot Minhea."

Bellman's voice said, "Aha!"

"And what is your password?" Trudy asked.

"Cobweb watcher."

She shuddered. "No, it isn't."

"Twist both of them," said the Count.

Trudy put her hands over her ears, but the spy could guess why they wanted that information, and it took many terrible screams and pleas for mercy to drag a true answer out of him: *Spinning wheel.*

"Is that all?" she asked. *Please let it be all!*

"Not quite." Radu stepped forward. "Who's your commanding officer?"

"Cantor Samuil," Wolfgang mumbled. His teeth were chattering, and Trudy could sense the despair and cold drowning his will to live. If they didn't get him to a healing soon, he would die of shock.

"His cell?"

"White 5, D 21."

Radu glanced in Trudy's direction, but that was the truth as Wolfgang knew it, so she did not speak.

"And yours?"

"Green 2, G 55."

"How did you know what the Duchess looks like?"

"Saw her when she came to the monastery. Fetched writing paper for her."

"How many other spies are there in Brikov?"

Silence.

"Don't be a fool!" Radu barked. "There's lots worse things they can do to you. Answer."

"None I know of."

Everyone looked to Trudy, who nodded. It was close enough to truth.

"So when you saw Her Highness here yesterday, who did you tell?"

"No one."

"Hit him some more," said the Count.

Trudy yelled, "No!" as Wolfgang shouted, "It's the truth!"

"Why not?" Radu asked. "Who were you supposed to tell and why didn't you?"

"Carter Franhof. I give him notes to deliver. He's not back yet. He's not Brotherhood, just does it for money."

The Count's wordless snarl boded ill for the carter.

"And what did you write about me?" Radu asked.

"I can't see."

"Senior Knight-brother Radu."

"Traitor Radu?"

Radu raised a hand to stop the man with the iron bar. Wolfgang cowered, waiting for more pain. The rain was washing the mud and blood off him and what it was uncovering was even worse than Trudy had imagined. She turned away again.

"Just answer the question, brother," Radu said. "And don't bother lying."

"I wrote that you came for a funeral and the Count put you in a cell." The spy's voice rose from a hoarse whisper to a croak. "So they'll come to rescue you and rescue me instead! You'll all pay for this."

Radu shrugged and turned away.

"Too late for you, scum," the Count said. "But at least you'll get out of the rain. The gibbet won't be wasted after all. Hoist him."

Trudy started back to the stable, then sensed Ringwood walking at her side. She stopped and grabbed him in both arms. He crushed her tight and held her as she added tears to the rain running off his shoulder.

"You did right," he said in her ear. "Very important things are often the hardest to do. You may have saved all our lives with that information."

She couldn't stop the sobs long enough to get words out.

"He's as guilty as the rest of them," Ringwood said. "He killed Bernard and the others. He wasn't looking for Her Nibs's baby just to play patty-cake."

But now she was just as bad. She hated herself. How could Ringwood possibly love her?

"He knew what would happen if he was caught," he persisted. "He swore that terrible oath knowing it might cost him his life."

Was it any worse than the Blades' oath? Ringwood might be next.

◆ 2 ◆

Armor was terrible stuff. Ironhall owned some examples, even plate mail, and all candidates had to try fighting in it a few times, but Blades were duelists, not warriors. Bellman's protests having been overruled, he rode inside a cuirass like a barrel with rain dribbling steadily down his neck; steel tassets rested heavy on his thighs, and hardened leather sleeves pinched every time he bent an arm.

Rain blotted out half the world, too, driving in clouds over the bare green hills. The entrance to the valley was a nasty canyon. The counts had held this pass for generations against all comers, Radu told him, but conversely, it was a fine place for an ambush. Everyone seemed to breathe more easily when the cavalcade emerged onto open moor. Bellman cantered forward to where Johanna rode alongside the Count.

"My lord, Manfred says this is where we leave you. Radu begs you to keep in mind what Wolfgang said about a Vamky attack. Not to rescue Radu, but to silence him. It's amazing they haven't come for him already, since they know where he went."

"Think I haven't thought of that?" János said grumpily. On horseback he looked big. "Means the traitor's first message got through. They think I already solved their Radu problem for them. No fear, I'll keep eyes peeled when I get back from the wedding."

Bellman drew his sword to salute. "By Your Highness's leave?"

"You're not doing this for me, you know!" Johanna said, too loudly. She'd already tried tears, terror, derision, martyrdom, intimidation, appeals to reason, and outright bribery. She was not making a hard job any easier.

"Yes, I am," Bellman said. "You are never going to be safe while the killer is at large, so I want to stop him. But also I hope to help a mother find her son."

"Truly?" The agony in her eyes was only hope.

He shrugged. "I do think he's alive, love."

"Why?"

"Just something that was said. And don't worry about us. Radu and I have hours to talk this over on the way. We've agreed we won't go in unless we're sure it will work."

Leaving her and knowing it might be forever was purest torture, but Bellman could see the Count's sneer in the background. He had already said too much, and he dared not embrace her in public. In a day or two she might be reunited with her husband, and scandal would be deadly for both her and himself. He kissed the icy fingers she offered and turned his mount aside.

Manfred led Radu and Bellman over rocky uplands in a blinding storm as if he knew exactly where he was going. They could have ridden with the Count down to the plain and followed the highway north to Olden Bridge, but Bellman had sought out the wiry old forester, who had agreed he could show them a shortcut. "Happy to," he'd said. "My saddle sores are healing too fast."

The weather was appalling, cloudbursts mixed with downpours. They had hours to go yet and the only part of Bellman still dry was his head, inside his helmet. He would freeze to death before he saw the notorious monastery.

At first they went in single file, but eventually better terrain let Radu pull alongside Bellman and ride knee-to-knee. The two men eyed each other curiously. They had met only a few hours ago and already they were partners in a mission that seemed close to suicidal. The man was impressive and Trudy had vouched for his veracity, but he had changed sides once. How far could he be trusted?

Radu was obviously wondering much the same of Bellman. "If you'll pardon my saying so, Her Highness is not good at disguising the way she feels about you. I would not pry, but I am curious to know why you would risk your neck to try and rescue her husband. This would seem to be contrary to your personal interests."

Bellman's laugh emerged more strident than he intended. "So it is, but duty drives me. I originally agreed to serve her because I have friends to avenge. The personal interest came later, and I do not deny it. Mainly, though, I want to untangle this web of evil and make the killers pay for their crimes."

That wasn't all of it. There was also arrogance. Puzzles fascinated him. The temptation to try and bring the monster or monsters to justice had been irresistible, and now the thought of outwitting the Vamky Brotherhood had become almost an obsession. He knew this was folly and could not resist it. Curiosity killed more than cats.

"And you, Knight-brother? Your former brethren are more likely to embrace you with a hempen noose than open arms. May I ask you to name your own motives?"

Radu nodded, making water dance off the brim of his helmet. "I am horrified at what the Brotherhood has become. The power it wields must be ruled by honor if it is not to be perverted into evil. Ultimately its loyalty must go beyond Provost and Abbot to the Grand Duke of Krupina. I obeyed orders to kidnap a child because those orders came from the child's great-uncle and he told me they had originated with the boy's father. When I find that the father has been imprisoned and an imposter wears the coronet, then I feel my oath and loyalty have been abused. My conscience forces me to try to make amends as best I can."

Which was what he had told Johanna, but it was a weak reason. He had been indoctrinated for years to put obedience ahead of everything else, and had done so repeatedly, by his own testimony. He was probably sincere now, but a man who rats once may rat twice. His estrangement from the Brotherhood had been an accident; he had discovered a dangerous secret and panicked. Offered a pardon and a welcome back, he would fold like a collapsing tent.

And he would have good reason to do so if he discovered that Bellman was not being completely honest with him. Which he wasn't.

The road dipped into a hollow and a pine forest, forcing them to ride in single file. They picked up the conversation on the far side.

"Also, like you, I seek revenge," Radu said. "My brother died. Those who ride the warrior's road know that slaughtering and slaughter may be their lot, but this was no honorable war. My brother was perverted into a murderer. Where is the honor in that?"

"I don't think he was the monster Johanna described," Bellman said. "I hardly knew him, just a few hours. After the fall of Fadrenschloss, he came to Brikov and persuaded the Baron to take him on. He must have capitalized on your father's long service, and he must have deceived your father as much as he deceived the Baron. He certainly concealed some dangerous conjurements in the Baron's medicine box. None of that is honorable behavior. Yet I do not believe Harald was a killer. You told us the shadowman conjuration was carried in a flea. I assume that the one that attracts vermin, the one called a 'swarming,' is equally easy to conceal?"

"I believe so," Radu said guardedly. "My training had not proceeded into the higher realms of military spiritualism." Meaning: *Do not pry!*

"It is hardly a murderer's weapon."

Radu frowned. "Harald used a *swarming* against her Highness? It is said to be effective against towns under siege. What purpose did it serve for him?"

"It kept her moving. As well as being a revolting experience, it was a warning that her enemies knew where she was. It drove her out of Brikov, and of course Harald went with her. As soon as she showed signs of settling in one place for more than a few days, he would send another plague of vermin and her hosts would panic and force her to move on. You see, Knight-brother, there is more than one villain in this affair. You believed you were saving the boy, Frederik, from possible future harm. Your brother was performing that service for the boy's mother. Other men sought to kill her. They came close in Fadrenschloss with the firefly. She fled to Brikov, but before they could attack her there, Harald evicted her. She went on to Blanburg. Not only was it the closest town, but Duke Rubin's father's mother was of the House of Blanburg, and she could appeal to the Prince for aid. Her enemies struck at her there with shadowmen, killing Bogdan. She fled again, but after that they lost her, which may have been Harald's doing. It was certainly his purpose. Remember that your brother was in her confidence! Had murder been his intent, he would have had a thousand opportunities. He could have snapped her neck with one hand."

Radu rode on for some time in silence, then said, "Thank you for telling me this. But surely he could have just warned her?"

"Not if she would have refused to believe whoever sent the warning," Bellman said. "Tell me this. A swarming is not especially dangerous. Shadowmen are deadly unless you know to stay in a good light. Fireflies are utterly fiendish. Would a man of Harald's experience have been allowed to train with those?"

"Of course not. A firefly could destroy Vamky itself."

Which confirmed Bellman's guess that the Brotherhood must do its spiritual experimentation somewhere else. "So only very senior brothers are allowed to use them?"

Radu studied him for a moment. "Normally no man below the rank of cantor is trusted with lethal conjurements. You do not believe that Harald was slain by his own firefly when he lost control of it?"

Bellman was both enjoying himself and despising himself for showing off. If he could impress his partner with his cleverness, he would have more success steering their joint efforts the ways he thought they should go, but he could see that Radu Priboi was a man of action with a limited appreciation of mental agility. Also a pompous jackass.

"I guessed that fireflies were dangerous to the user, because Johanna's story of the destruction of Fadrenschloss suggested that the conjuration had been planted and set to take effect some hours later. Am I right?"

"Probably," Radu conceded. "The conjuration is called the 'egg.' In theory the hatching may be set for hours later or even days. I have heard that it is unpredictable and hazardous to the user."

"So Johanna escaped from Blanburg in Thirdmoon and the villains lost her. In Fourthmoon, Wolfgang Webber was posted to Brikov to keep watch in case she returned that way. Someone else was sent ahead to Chivial, because Rubin was also related to the royal family there. The relationship was more distant, but King Athelgar is a potent monarch and has much less reason to fear the hand of Vamky than rulers of petty states like Blanburg do. She duly arrived there in Eighthmoon, and the other attackers loosed their shadowmen against her again."

"Does Her Highness know all this?" Radu asked.

"No. I was never sure enough of my reasoning until we heard Wolfgang Webber's confession this morning. He said he was told to look out for Johanna *and* Frederik, but that was in Fourthmoon. You had captured the boy in Thirdmoon. There must be at least two factions in the Brotherhood!"

"That could have been just a careless briefing."

"Does the Brotherhood brief spies carelessly? Giving an agent an impossible task must increase his chance of detection. Male strangers investigating children invite suspicion."

Radu grunted. "You are right. I apologize."

That was another point to Bellman, but it might be a point against him if Radu played him false. He might regret taking the man so far into his confidence.

"After the shadowmen attacked, Johanna rode off to Iron-hall to bind Blades, leaving only Manfred and Harald in Quamast House. The residence was very tightly guarded when she returned, but may not have been so while she was away. After Johanna's return, Sister Trudy detected more death elementals in the medicine chest than she had sensed earlier. How could that have been Harald's doing? That box held his store of conjurements, so how could he have increased it? Clearly someone else managed to gain entry and meddle!

"Harald did not understand that, but he did know that the box was to be inspected the next day, and he had learned that Chivian inquisitors can detect falsehood, so he would be exposed. He tried to escape. He probably had no money, could not speak the language, and must have been truly desperate. He knocked out old Manfred when he awakened, to stop him raising the alarm. Again, as with Johanna, your brother could have killed the old man with his bare hands. He didn't. He did the minimum necessary. He very nearly did get away. So why didn't he?

"The Baron and a Blade, Sir East, were in an adjoining room. Harald's strength would have been useless against a Blade. The only thing that could have killed East before he could even raise an alarm was the firefly itself, so he must have been sitting close to the box and died instantly when the firefly hatched. Harald heard it or saw it and rushed in to try and save the Baron. I do not believe your brother was an assassin."

Radu transferred his reins to his left hand and reached across to offer a handshake. "I am much in your debt for this. You are a clever man, Herr Bellman."

"I may not seem so by this time tomorrow."

"And who is the villain who seeks to kill Her Highness? Who is behind it all?"

"We are on our way to find out, are we not? With these conjured lockets around, anyone may seem to be someone else. You say that Lord Volpe himself gave you orders to abduct Frederik. You cannot be certain that the man you saw was the Provost."

Radu nodded. "I have thought of this ever since I heard the Duchess's story. And Wolfgang may not have been dispatched by the Abbot."

But whoever was locked up in the dungeon knew the truth, if he was still alive. They rode on in silence for a while, until the knight made an admission that was a surprising concession from him.

"I have never heard of these lockets. They must be a devastating military conjuration, as long as their existence is kept secret. To be able to impersonate your enemy's commander-in-chief, say!"

"Difficult to apply in practice. In Grandon I asked Grand Wizard about them. He had seen examples of similar enchantments, but nothing so effective, nothing that would create a likeness capable of deceiving anyone. He grew quite excited! He did point out that it was the necklace that carried the conjuration, not the locket—it works when you close the necklace around your neck. And he said that such an enchantment would require the original to be present. Both locket and Grand Duke must have been inside the octogram, in other words. I cannot see how one would go about arranging that in a war."

"But why . . . ?" Radu thought for a moment and then laughed. "From what I have heard about our Grand Duke, he probably had it made so he could send a double to represent him at boring social occasions and be free to go about his private business. A dangerous contrivance if it were stolen."

Or if the conjurers had secretly made two lockets, not just one. "Tell me about Knight-brother Nickolaus."

Radu said, "Death and fire! I cannot see that he is any business of yours!"

"Nor can I. I am merely playing a hunch, but if we two cannot trust each other, then we had better turn back now."

Radu sulked in silence for a while, but eventually said, "There is nothing to tell. He and I are friendly rivals—class-mates, you could call us. Men never talk of their back-grounds in Vamky, but Nickolaus is obviously gentle born. He's popular, competent . . . He was sworn in a few days be-fore I was, but I was belted a week sooner, so I had the edge in seniority. On any assignment the low man gets the menial tasks, like watching over the horses."

Bellman chuckled. "And mothering the Duke?"

"Especially mothering the Duke. As soon as we reached Trenko, Nick was assigned some other duty, so I inherited the currycomb and bootlicking. I have not heard of him since. Of course I have been away for months, and even if I had not, there would be absolutely noth   unusual or sinis-ter about that! Are you satisfied, Your Ne ness?"

"It feels relevant. You came back one man short?"

"Yes, we did. So?"

"So nothing. All I can do with hunches is let them hatch in their own good time. Thank you."

This one was chipping its shell, though, and what was emerging looked very much like the truth at last.

The track descended a rocky slope to a rivulet now swollen by the rain. Manfred, a tiny, swaddled shape in the saddle, was letting his horse drink.

"You're here, my lords," he said hoarsely. "Follow this and you will meet the Asch just below Olden Bridge. I am going home to enjoy a nice bout of pneumonia."

They laughed appropriately and thanked him. He rode back up the hill, vanishing into the murk. The swordsmen turned downstream and Bellman switched to practical matters.

"We have planning to do," he said. "You must have seen keys in Vamky. I want to know exactly what they look like. How big are they?"

"As long as my finger, maybe longer. A handle, a shaft, and a sort of flag on the end."

"Bow, shank, and bit. Are the shafts hollowed? Do they have holes in their ends to fit over a pin?"

"Not that I recall."

"Then describe the bits. That's what I need to know."

"You're not doing very well, you know, Squirt," Ranter said.

"What do you mean?" Ringwood countered, although he had been thinking the same thing.

"As Leader. To start with, Blades have to know the terrain, we were told. You got any idea where we are right now?"

They were on horseback. They were following directly behind their ward and the János brigand, with a dozen or so armed men riding ahead and about as many behind. Apart from that . . . No, Ringwood had very little idea where he was beyond "Somewhere in Krupina." Rain had been falling steadily all day, and now dusk was falling, too. Donehof was said to be halfway between Fadrenschloss and Krupa, and they had ridden past the charred ruins of Fadrenschloss some hours ago. They were still on the highway, which was a long, thin swamp of mud today, but if he understood the geography correctly, which was doubtful, they should be turning off to the west very shortly.

"We're about an hour from Donehof."

"You're guessing. And why are we here anyway? You're supposed to keep our ward out of danger, Squirt. You're not doing well there, either."

Because Ringwood had been upbraiding himself for this

all day, he did have a few answers ready. None of them were very good. "And what would you have done differently if you were Leader—other than locking Her Nibs up in Chivial somewhere?"

"I wouldn't have let her leave Brikov. You know spittin' well that she's going to try and gate-crash the wedding tomorrow."

"She won't. We'll see to that. And we couldn't stay in Brikov. She was right. With only one way out, any peabrain could see it was a trap."

"I wouldn't have let her get in there in the first place," Ranter ranted. He was wet and tired and frozen and scared, with Ringwood his only available target. "Charging in over that Smugglers' Pass, losing horses, making the local robber baron mad at us. That's burning bridges, that is."

Ringwood, too, was wet and tired and frozen and scared. Also hungry. "The reason we had to go over the pass, *brother,* is that you went and spewed out the news of the wedding. If you'd reported it to me in private, as you should have done, I wouldn't have told her. We could have taken the slow, safe way around by Zolensa, not going through Brikov or Trenko, and by the time we got here it would have been too late! She'd have given up and we could have escorted her back to Chivial to live." Not a bad rant, he thought, and some of it was true.

"Bah! Second-guessing! And she'd have insisted on going to Brikov to collect her brat. The Brotherhood would have heard about her being there and come and got her. And if they hadn't she'd be running around screaming looking for him, 'cause he wasn't where she'd left him."

"Now who's second-guessing?" The trouble was, Ranter's complaints were all justified. Ringwood had blundered, just as he had always feared he would. He had let his ward slip ever further into danger until now he could see no way out. His most recent and worst mistake, which Ranter had not discovered yet, was that in the rush to leave Brikov that morning he had forgotten to ask Bellman for the money. He had no money. The Duchess never carried any. They were entirely dependent on Count János now, until Bellman came back, and the odds that Bellman would ever come back were not much better than the odds that Count János would prove to be a generous benefactor.

The vanguard was turning off the so-called highway. "Here's the Donehof road now," Ringwood said.

"So now we'll have the rain right in our eyes and the wind's getting up. The going will be even worse than this, and I expect we'll arrive at a cold house with no food ready. Let's just hope we get there soon. It's going to be a very dark night."

Yes, it was, Ringwood agreed. A very dark night.

Daylight was fading on the peaks, and down in the gorge it was already night. Still the rain fell. Radu reined in at Olden Bridge. Bellman halted beside him, and the two peered at each other.

"A good night for shadowmen, Herr Bellman?"

"I don't recall ever being wetter or colder in my life, Knight-brother."

"This has been a better day than some I spent in the Count's dungeon," Radu said, "but not by much. Now we must choose."

"I thought we had already chosen."

"There is no shelter between here and Vamky. If we wish to turn back, cottagers near here would give us shelter for a copper or two. Tomorrow we could hasten to Donehof and rejoin your lady. You decide."

Bellman shivered and patted his mare's neck. The poor brute would be lucky to escape bronchitis after such a day, but her rider might have much worse problems even sooner. "Answer me one question, Knight-brother. I can see ways around almost any pitfall we have discussed except a few of the extremely unlikely ones, and those I will dare when the stakes are so high. I see only one exception, just one, and you first suggested it yourself. When the doorman pulls your pass out of the box, will it be tagged for your immediate arrest? Will it ring alarm bells, or will it be dealt with by standard procedures? You dropped the letter, so the traitors can have no doubt that you were the intruder who discovered their secret prisoner. They cannot seriously expect you to return, but will they have taken precautions in case you do?"

"You rest your decision on that alone?"

"I do. If you will take that risk, then I will brave all the rest." Bellman was determined not to be first to quit. He desperately hoped that Radu would do that for him.

"You are a fool, Chivian," Radu said harshly. "You expect to outdare a Vamky knight?"

A *renegade* knight? Bellman was tired of the man's airs. "Well, yes. We locksmiths' apprentices have our pride, too."

"I should cut out your tongue for that."

"The light is poor for surgery. If you want to run away, say so, otherwise move your ass out of here before mine freezes to my saddle."

Without a word, Radu dug in his heels and rode forward, onto the bridge.

Bellman followed. *See what you just did, idiot?*

The horses knew when they were close to Donehof, whinnying and picking up the pace. Soon the expedition passed under the walls of a high, drum-shaped tower, barely visible in the last shreds of daylight. Close beyond that stood a mansion with lights glowing in upper- and lower-story win-

dows. Already it was a much more imposing residence than
János's seat at Brikov, and surrounded by numerous outbuildings, workers' cottages, and livestock paddocks. Ringwood was impressed and Ranter must have been, too,
because he turned sarcastic again.

"Why does he live up there in his mountain squalor if he
owns a palace like this?"

Probably the Count felt safer back in his ancestral stronghold than he did down here on the plains within reach of his
ducal overlord. Ringwood did not say so, because János was
still alongside the Duchess close ahead and might be
listening.

The visitors dismounted gratefully, then gasped and
blinked as they followed their host indoors, into a blaze of
many candles and seductive warmth. Fires crackled on two
great hearths, and high walls hung with hunting trophies
soared up to galleries and hammer beam ceiling. Ranter's
fears proved unfounded, for the seneschal had been expecting the Count and had everything ready. Flunkies came running with steins of spiced ale to take away the chill.
Ringwood managed to down a surprising amount of his before his binding turned it to lye in his mouth; the heat flowed
straight into his veins and raised goose bumps all over him.

Max Priboi, the seneschal, was presented to Frau Schale.
He was an older, balding, and much bulkier version of
Radu, with an easy smile reminiscent of the turncoat Harald. He bade the visitors welcome and conducted them upstairs in person to show them their quarters. Those were
close to perfect—a large and imposing chamber for the
women, reached through an anteroom that would house the
Blades nicely.

Bucket-bearing servants were already filling an oaken tub
with hot water. Johanna and True waited impatiently while
Ringwood hastily inspected the accommodation. Hasty did

not mean slipshod to a Blade, though, and he hunted duti-
fully for potential trouble. He emerged from peering under
the bed convinced that there was none. He opened his mouth
to say so, then took a second look at the love of his life.

"What's wrong?"

True frowned. "Nothing's . . . Well, there's something. I
haven't tracked it down yet."

"What sort of something?"

"Ask me again when I'm warm and dry and well fed."

"True!"

She nodded, tight-lipped. "True! Now go away."

Unhappy, Ringwood went out to the guardroom to towel
off and change. She was tired, as they all were. Worse, he
hadn't been able to spare her any time all day. Not that True
was jealous or anything! She understood how his binding
worked. But a Blade should never fall in love, especially a
Blade bound to another woman.

They dined in a small, elegant room: Duchess, Count,
seneschal, two Blades, and True. Servants hurried in and
out, bringing a collection of mouth-watering roast meats,
fish, stews, soups, cheeses, hot bread, poultry, vegetables,
peppery sauces. Ranter overate as always, and Ringwood
topped him handily, but the other men were close behind.
Even the women tucked in well, sampling one dish after another, so there was very little conversation for the first half
hour or so. Meanwhile a man sitting in the corner played
the viol and sang sorrowful Krupinese songs. When he had
finished, János praised him highly and sent him off clutching gold coins. That was a surprising view of the barbarous
chieftain who had so callously tortured and hanged a man
that morning.

By then the dishes were being removed and a second
course brought in, offering a similar variety, with eels and
salmon instead of loach, pork instead of beef, and so on.

With the sharp edge of his appetite blunted, Ringwood could eat while returning to his duty, which was to worry about everything imaginable—what had True detected that had bothered her, and was that what was still making her squirm now? He had never seen her so fidgety. Did the seneschal's odd glances at the Duchess mean that he had guessed who Frau Schale really was? And what was going to happen tomorrow when János rode off to the wedding and there was no sign of Bellman and the money?

Chivian inquisitors had a conjuration called the Question, which forced the victim to confess everything. Even if the brethren had no similar means of interrogating prisoners, they could always resort to thumbscrews, and then they would come straight to Donehof to find the lost Duchess. That was assuming they managed to take Bellman alive, of course. Ringwood was starting to appreciate how much he'd come to depend on the man's good sense.

Talk sprang up. For a while the Count cross-examined the seneschal about farm accounts, the output at some mines he supervised, and other business matters. János had been drinking steadily, so his ugly face was now very flushed, but the wine had not dulled his wits yet. Then the conversation turned to tomorrow's wedding, the enthronement ceremony right after, and the days of festivity to follow.

"Krupa's never seen anything like it," the seneschal said.

"You mean the Duke didn't celebrate his other marriages so lavishly?"

"I'm too young to remember them."

"Or do you mean the gentry approve of this wife more than they liked the last one?" János *was* drunk.

Big Max waited until a last footman had left the room, then said with great deliberation, "I do remember the late Grand Duchess Johanna, my lord. The old man and I rarely got along, as you know, but I did visit Fadrenschloss once when she lived there. She was incredibly beautiful and universally adored."

Johanna exploded in laughter. She had been drinking, too. "I told you he'd know me! It is good to see you again, Max! How are your family?"

His family, he said, were all well and visiting at some place called Werfurt. "And they will be honored to hear that Your Highness asked after them."

Ringwood shuddered. Why not send heralds with bugles to Krupa and Vamky to proclaim that she was here now, come and get her, and this time kill her properly? How many other people in this house had recognized her? This was all his fault. He must be the most incompetent Blade in the history of the Order.

"Of course," Max said, "if in 'family' you include my brothers, sisters-in-law, nephews, and nieces, Your Highness, then I would have to go on all night. Almost all of us managed to meet in Brikov at my father's funeral last week, and we saw him off in a style he would have approved. We even have a fully-fledged Vamky knight-brother in the family now! Radu? You remember him?"

"Yes, I do," Johanna said with a sideways glance at the Count.

Was János about to admit how he had treated his seneschal's brother?

No, he wasn't. He said nothing.

Max missed the sudden tension. "And even Harald, our teeny baby, is a squire already!" he said proudly. "It is wonderful to see that the terrible stories of your death were untrue." And so on.

After a while Ringwood realized that everyone else had finished eating. Regretfully he wiped his knife on his sleeve and tucked it away in his belt. He caught Trudy's eye and she nodded. He pushed back his stool.

"By your leave, Your Highness, my lord?"

The Count interrupted himself to turn and glower. "Where you think you going?"

"A brief look around the house, my lord."

"Don't trust my hospitality, huh?"

"My lord, if I did not trust you completely my ward would not be here, but I am required to inspect security."

"Required by who?" János was turning puce with anger.

"By my oath, my training, and my binding. I did no less in King Athelgar's palace when there were a dozen other Blades on guard duty."

"Sit down! Max will show you around later."

When Ringwood's ward did not speak up in his defense, he sat down. Blades should be seen and not heard, Grand Master said, and if possible not seen, either.

The principals continued their chatter. Max was given most of the Duchess's story. Told that Harald had tried to kill her and was almost certainly dead, Max just frowned and shook his head sadly. He did not ask what the resurrected Duchess intended to do about the wedding, although he must be wondering. Did Johanna herself know? And what could Ringwood do to stop her? He let the conversation trickle along in the background while he went back to worry and guilt.

It was late. Suddenly János yawned. With a clumsy attempt at subtlety, he inquired if he would find his bed warmed the way he liked it, and Max assured him he would.

"Sleep well, ladies," the Count said and waddled out the door.

Johanna frowned, True smirked, and then everyone rose to follow him. The house was quiet and dark. Most of the servants had gone to bed; fires were banked. Ringwood escorted the Duchess to her room. He told Ranter to inspect it and then stand guard.

Now, at last, True could hunt down whatever had been bothering her all evening. Carrying a lantern, she wandered along the upstairs corridors, with Ringwood and the seneschal following. Max must have a vast capacity for liquor, because he showed no ill effects from the ale he had been quaffing all evening. He watched True curiously, but spoke of other things.

"I've heard of the Blades. Bound by enchantment?"

"Yes."

"For life?" He was not as tall or broad as Harald had been, but he would have outweighed him. Ringwood felt like a child beside him.

"In our case, yes. The King can release his own Blades. And you? Radu said all his brothers had joined the Brotherhood."

"Except a couple who died in childhood. You want to look in the attics, fraulein?"

True had reached one end of the house and was retracing her path. "No," she said, smothering a yawn. "Servants sleep up there?"

"You finding anything?" Ringwood asked. That was what mattered.

"Only the usual good luck charms and what my former Fellowship politely calls 'family-planning conjurations.' "

Max chuckled. "In there?" He pointed at the Count's room.

"Yes."

"I loaned her one. Don't tell his lordship, because he still has ambitions to outdo my old man. Downstairs, then?"

They headed for the stairs.

"So how are the brethren bound?" Ringwood asked. "Or rather, how are the brethren *un*bound?"

Max took a moment to answer. Treads creaked under his weight. "You do not trust me, Sir Ringwood?"

"I'd like an answer."

"The useless are kicked out. Those that want to give up—
novices, mostly, and some of them quite old men—they go
to their commanding officer and declare that they consider
themselves unworthy to belong to the Order. They're escorted to the gate and sent away."

Following True through to the kitchen area, Ringwood
said, "So you never are formally unbound?" Bellman had
suggested this possibility, months ago. "Once a brother, always a brother? Does the Brotherhood ever come calling in
after years, bidding you to start honoring your *irrevocable*
vows again?"

"It has happened." The seneschal smiled. "Never to me,
though."

"But the Count cannot rely on your allegiance absolutely?"

"Count János never trusts any man absolutely."

That evasion was confirmation: Once a brother, always a
brother.

"How are the brethren sworn? Is your oath backed up by
conjuration as ours is?" That was another of Bellman's suggestions.

"I will not answer that question, Sir Ringwood. Yes,
fraulein?"

A few skivvies were still cleaning up in the kitchens, but
True had gone by them, into an area of larders and pantries, a
realm of bales, barrels, and boxes, bedecked with dangling
hams and strings of onions. There she had come to a halt just
short of what was obviously the back door of the house, heavily bolted and barred at this time of night, but her attention was
on another door close to it, an imposing barrier of iron-
strapped timber.

"Where does this lead?"

"To the cellars, fraulein."

"I need to look down there." Perhaps it was only a trick of the light from their lanterns, but she seemed so tense that Ringwood wrapped an arm around her. She was shivering.

"No, fraulein," Max said. "That door is boarded up, as you can see."

"You have shadowmen down there!"

The big man sighed. "Let us go to the hall and talk about it."

Hand in hand, Ringwood and True followed him to the great hall that had greeted them when they first entered Donehof. Max led them to benches alongside a fireplace and settled wearily on one. They sat opposite him. Ringwood had one arm tight around True, but his other hand kept taking hold of *Bad News*'s hilt all by itself, no matter how often he told it to let go. His binding was screaming at him to get his ward out of there as fast as possible. *Shadowmen!*

"When you arrived, did you see the keep?" the seneschal said.

"The old tower?"

"Yes. It is very ancient, pre-Imperial. Private fortresses are forbidden in Krupina, so it has been blocked up for centuries. To occupy it would be an act of rebellion."

"So why was this house built so close?" Ringwood asked.

Max chuckled. "It makes a good windbreak, maybe?" He was an infuriatingly likable man. "You're thinking that a tunnel through to the castle cellars would be a good escape hatch, son? That if the Grand Duke ever plays him foul, János could take refuge in the keep and wait until his mountaineers come to his rescue? That is the way he thinks, certainly, and his brother before him was worse. It was his brother, Luitgard, who bought the land and started building the house. János completed it."

"Where do the shadowmen come into this?" True asked, still shivering.

"The point is that they don't come in, fraulein. Luitgard did tunnel into the crypt under the keep, and shadowmen were what he found. Or they found him. Only one of the miners with him escaped, and he later died of his wounds. Luitgard and the rest are still in there."

"Who were they?" Ringwood asked. "These shadowmen?"

The big man shrugged. "Who knows? The last garrison of the keep, possibly. There are also stories of barons who kept *schattenherren* in their dungeons as unpaid executioners. They are reputedly not dangerous as long as you are forewarned and have a good light. Since there is no light down there, they cannot pass through the door to attack us. And if the Count of Brikov is ever seriously threatened here, he could still seek refuge down there and dare his foes to follow him."

"That's crazy!" True said.

Max gave her a fatherly smile. "No. Anyone as rich as János cannot be crazy, just eccentric."

"If shadowmen aren't dangerous, what killed Count Luitgard and his men?" Ringwood asked.

Max Priboi shrugged. "I do not know, Sir Ringwood. I never met a shadowman. I hope I never will. Fraulein, I was afraid you would discover our *schattenherren*. I did know about them, I swear. I have lived here almost ten years with my wife and children, and I assure you that they are not a danger. It is late. Please, can we go to bed and forget about gibbering wraiths in the basement?"

"One last question, Seneschal," Ringwood said. "Have you told me any lies this evening?"

Max's face darkened. "Not that I recall. No. Why?"

"No offense intended. It's just that we Blades always double-knot our laces." Once a brother always a brother, but True wasn't shouting foul. Apparently Max Priboi could be trusted.

* * *

It was an insane venture Bellman had embarked on, and only its very insanity gave it a chance of succeeding. Mosquitoes might bite where wolves could not, and it was possible—just barely possible—that Vamky had failed to take adequate precautions against a two-man suicide mission. Also, Bellman reminded himself for the millionth time, the raiders were not up against the entire Brotherhood. If worst came to worst and they were apprehended, they could always cry treason and hope that their captors were not in on the conspiracy. Radu had not been pursued to Brikov, which suggested that the traitors' power might be limited within the Order.

By now many senior masters would have left to attend the ducal wedding, and anyone of rank would be abed and asleep. That might help, too.

Good shadowman weather indeed! Radu was a superb horseman, even by Blade standards. Bellman had given up wondering how he found the road and was relying on his mare's ability to follow. The hill grew steeper and rougher, where rain had eroded it. It went on forever. Once in a while he jerked awake just as he began to slide out of the saddle. At such times his mind threw up strange fancies.

"None I know of."

None what? Who had said that? He worried through his memories until he remembered Radu's question to the doomed Wolfgang: "How many other spies are there in Brikov?"

"None I know of."

That, he saw now, had been an evasion. Trudy had not cried foul, but the word pattern was wrong. Speaking at all had been an effort for the poor kid, and all his other answers had been more direct. *None I know of, but I suspect . . .* Suspect whom? Many factions within the Brotherhood might have spies in Brikov. Wolfgang had failed to report that the

Grand Duchess was back from her travels, but the unknown other might have done so.

Bellman wished he had thought of that in time to warn Ringwood.

A faint clinking from one of his saddlebags was a constant reminder of the lock picks that János's blacksmith had reluctantly contributed to the cause. John Eastswine of Camford would have spurned them as clumsy junk, and it would be nice to think that all Krupinese locks were as primitive as those Bellman had seen so far, but the wealthy, distrustful Vamky Brotherhood might have higher standards than backwoods Brikov. Radu's descriptions of keys he had seen had been vague, for he knew nothing about the mechanics of locks. Back in Quamast House, the keys had been burglars' nightmares, with cuts for seven or eight intricately shaped wards. Bellman would need hours of uninterrupted concentration to open such brutes, even if the picks he had with him would fit, which he doubted. Tonight he would be lucky to have a few minutes without a knife at his throat. He was also four years out of practice.

It felt as if four more years went by before he saw two misty lights in the distance and Radu outlined against them, turning to wave him forward. He urged the exhausted mare alongside.

Radu said, "Last chance to change your mind, *Spinning Wheel*."

"Last one in's a big fat hen, *Westering Song*."

"Then we ride together, talking of nothing important."

"Unless you say, 'Scarper!' "

"Don't even think it," Radu muttered, staring at the archway looming ahead.

"Scarper" was their signal to run. They had planned everything they could think of, everything except sheer terror like icy hands in the belly. Bellman's teeth were chattering, but they had done that all day. The wonder was that he had any teeth left. His hands were so numb that if he tried to fight, he would probably drop his sword and cut off his own toes.

The lights were two great lanterns flanking a high arch. Beyond it stretched the barbican, a tunnel lit by smaller lights. Hooves rang on paving. It was a great miracle to be out of the rain at last, into sudden peace. Instinctively glancing up, Bellman saw a dark gap spanning the barrel roof from side to side and knew that the slightest suspicion of anything wrong would bring a portcullis slamming down. He noted loopholes high in the walls, where bowmen might lurk. Run by the finest soldiers in Eurania, Vamky was probably the best-held castle on the continent. And he was hoping to crack it!

Straight ahead, a seeming very long way into the trap, the road ended at a massive timber gate. It looked about a furlong thick. Radu reined in just before it, where a faint light showed through a lancet window, tall and narrow.

"*Gate!*" he bellowed. "No, brother, black olives and green olives come off the same tree."

Bellman tried to keep his voice from quavering. "Is it the pickling that changes their color, then?"

"Password?" The voice came from far away, beyond an immense thickness of wall. A head obscured the slit of light.

"*Westering Song,*" Radu said. "Yours, brother?"

"*Spinning Wheel.* And we're frozen. Be quick or I'll file a complaint."

The face disappeared. Radu continued to babble. "Wine is quite different. Red grapes make red wine and black . . ."

This was the moment of life or death. More than a moment . . . several minutes. The highest demonstration of courage, Grand Master had once remarked, must be to die of fright. Curiously, that remark now began to make sense.

"*Gate!*" Radu bellowed again. "*Are you all dead in there?*"

Were they dead out here? When it was his turn to babble, Bellman found his mind blank on wine. "What do they do with the ordure?"

"Novices take it out in wheelbarrows and put it in wagons to be sold to farmers. Why?"

"Just wondered." He had wondered whether he had over-looked a way to pass in and out of the monastery unseen, but evidently the Brotherhood had thought of that one, too. All supply wagons were unloaded into hand barrows outside, Radu had told him. "Why such precautions in a land at peace? Who do they fear?"

"It is training for other places. Talk of lesser matters."

More agony. Surely it should not take so long to find two cards in a drawer?

"In Isilond they have a delicacy called 'truffles,' " Bellman said. "Dug up by hogs—"

Radu's nerve broke. "Too long! Scarper!" He wheeled his horse, but he took the exhausted beast by surprise and it almost stumbled.

At that point Bellman had to decide whether to go with him or stay and try alone. They had agreed on that—the decision whether to run or stay and play a lone hand would be his to make at the time. But he was so startled that he reacted like a Blade and whipped out his sword. That committed him. "What's wrong?" he yelled. He turned the mare, but held her back from trying to follow. "Where are you going? Come back here!"

Radu had his mount moving and was raking it with his spurs, but it could not rise above a trot, which was not fast enough. With a thunder that shook the monastery and the mountain, a wall of timber crashed down across his path, sealing off the exit.

✦ 3 ✦

It was a bad night, full of rain and wind and worry. Ringwood kissed Trudy good night and told Ranter about the danger downstairs. Then he left his deputy on guard outside the bedchamber and took himself back downstairs to keep watch there. Max had assured him that even in this weather a night watch was patrolling the grounds with dogs, so no intruders could sneak in undetected. Fine, but a Blade took nobody else's word for anything where his ward's security was concerned.

The drudges had finished their labors in the kitchen and disappeared, so he had the house to himself. He walked through the great hall a few times, but mostly he stayed close to the back door and the cellar of horrors. The thought of what lurked behind that door oppressed him. It was hinged to open into the corridor and barricaded by balks of timber bracketed to the frame. It seemed secure enough, yet why would anyone keep such a danger in his house instead of bricking it over? The slim chance that the Count would ever be desperate enough to use the haunted cellar as an escape route seemed trivial by comparison with the risk that some busybody would decide to go treasure-hunting.

The next door in, a few paces along the corridor and on the opposite side, led to a large pantry holding barrels and large crates, heavy items stored near the entrance. There Ringwood laid in a supply of candles and lanterns, preparing to make a night of it. There he could keep watch on both cellar and back door, which was a more likely target for an intruder than the front. He realized after a while that a would-be assassin could break into the keep instead, come through the tunnel, and just shine a light on the far side of the door. Then the shadowmen would do the rest. All

Blades are slightly mad—that was one of Master of Rituals' homilies.

Nights were bad, all nights except the great ones when he and True could have time alone. Otherwise he had no company except Ranter. At least tonight he was spared that. He explored the various pantries, but could not force himself to stay away from that ominous door very long. He did have an unlimited supply of snacks available—seven different types of cheese, to start with. He had tomorrow to worry about, which must be today already. He and Ranter would have to keep their ward chained up, which would need careful planning and cooperation from Count János.

János? János, who was totally unpredictable, who had completed this magnificent house but preferred to live in a barren mountain valley? János, who had barred the way to the cellar where his brother died and yet not gone so far as to brick it up. János, who could torture a man and appreciate music. János who had inherited his lands and title from his brother, Luitgard.

Oh, cesspits!

Ringwood resisted a temptation to charge a stone wall with his head. Why hadn't he seen that right away? The Duchess herself had told him that nobility put younger sons into the Brotherhood. Once a brother, always a brother. János was the last person he should be trusting! János was one of *them!* Now Ringwood had trapped his ward here in Donehof, with dogs patrolling the grounds, with no money for an escape; with no way, even, to reach the stables. Failure, failure, failure! Why had he been such a stupid, arrogant imbecile as to *volunteer* for this mission? And then allow his ward to appoint him Leader? Ranter could have done no worse than this. Ranter had been right when he said Johanna should stay in Chivial.

His torment was interrupted by a crash of breaking glass

and an impact that shook the house. Before the echoes died, he was on his way to the great hall, lantern in hand.

The hall was dim, but there was enough glow from a few candles and the banked fires to see that one high leaded window lay in ruins. Wind wailed through the gap, stirring tapestries, bringing rain. The rock that had shattered it was the size of a bushel basket, far beyond the means of any man to lift. It had smashed furniture as it rolled.

As he started up the stairs, another window exploded and another missile shattered flagstones and ricocheted into a fireplace. Paintings and stag heads tumbled from the walls. A ballista was not accurate enough and could not be rewound fast enough, so this was conjury at work. The Vamky equivalent of Chivial's Destroyer General was assaulting Donehof. A trumpet blew outside. This was no sneak attack.

The door to the women's room stood open and Ranter was in there, shouting. Other voices were raised in the corridor, and footsteps drummed overhead. Ranter came out with a bundle of cloaks over his arm. Ringwood told him what he had seen. The trumpet blew again, fainter here.

"Dogs?" Ranter said. "Guards?"

There had been no barking. "Dead, I think. Or chained up. We've been betrayed, brother."

Lights showed in the corridor as doors flew open and men stumbled out. Count János appeared, roaring furiously, clutching a naked sword and almost naked himself, seemingly clad only in boots and a fur cloak. Then Max's great bulk materialized out of the shadows, shouting orders.

Johanna and True were next, dressed but unfastened, trailing laces. The Blades wrapped cloaks around them and shepherded them downstairs within a torrent of János's guards, a mob of half-dressed, sword-waving maniacs. Somewhere beyond the shattered windows someone was bellowing through a speaking trumpet. The words were indistinguishable, but Ringwood could guess that the terms offered would start with the surrender of the Duchess—perhaps not by name. "Women and children" would suffice. There was one person who must not be allowed near the state wedding and enthronement.

Crossbows and halberds had mysteriously appeared. János climbed onto a table and began screaming orders. He probably had a nasty hangover, but he knew what he wanted—everyone to assemble here in the great hall, around the fireplace, and lots of light.

Ringwood worked it out and understood. "Quick!" he said. "This way."

"No!" Johanna protested. "The Count wants us to stay—"

"*This way!*" Ringwood grabbed her arm and dragged. "You *never* argue with your Blades, you hear me?" (Not even a Blade who had never finished training and made mistakes?) He ran his shocked ward into the corridors that led to the back of the house, looking back only to confirm that True and Ranter were following. They had only one light between the four of them, but he led them through the kitchens to the pantry where he had set up his stock of candles and lanterns.

"Light!" he said. "We must have lots of lights, too."

"Just what do you think—" the Duchess began.

"Quiet!" He leaned close, so they were eye to eye. "Do not speak a word! János is a traitor and there are killers out there looking for you. Say nothing and do exactly what I say." Johanna recoiled in amazement. True grinned at him as if this were great fun. Ranter was lighting lanterns, not arguing at all.

They were all depending on Sir Ringwood of the Blades to keep them alive, and so far he had failed their trust miserably. He had better do better this time, or he would never get another chance.

He placed himself by the door, keeping it open a crack so he could see along to the other door, the cellar door. He wasn't totally blocking the light behind him, but the Count would certainly bring lights with him, and would probably not notice the knife-edge of brightness coming from this door.

Ranter whispered, "Who's attacking?"

"Vamky," Ringwood answered, just as softly. No one else would be using military conjuration on that scale.

"And whose side is János on?"

"His own. He's Vamky, too, but this is a double-cross."

Another impact shook the house. Muffled battle noises from the great hall suggested the attackers were starting to move in, so if János was planning what Ringwood thought he was, he would have to move soon.

And he did. Two voices arguing came first. The darkness of the corridor began to brighten, slowly at first, then suddenly, as the source of the light turned a corner.

Ringwood pushed the door to and turned to smile encouragingly at the others' frightened faces. He said "Draw!" and Ranter blinked in surprise at seeing *Invincible* in his hand, as if she had jumped there all on her own.

The argument went past and ended. The Count had won, of course. Ringwood opened the door just enough to peer out with one eye. They were not opening the back door, which he had expected them to do first. Max was standing in front of it, a lantern in each hand, two more at his feet, while the massive, low slung János worked on the cellar door with a crowbar. Wood creaked and splintered.

"I wish I knew where Johanna and the Chivians went!" Max said.

"They can fend for themselves!" With a mighty heave, János snapped off the last of the bars. "Ready?" He jerked the door wide and at the same time moved backward to the safety of the lanterns. The shadowmen must have been packed in on the other side, because they came pouring out of the cellar like smoke.

"Stay where you are!" Bellman roared, pointing his sword at the would-be fugitive. His voice echoed through the barbican. "And dismount." Drawing a real sword on horseback was strictly forbidden in Ironhall. The irrelevance of that thought made him want to giggle, and he realized he was balanced on a knife edge of panic. He drew deep breaths.

"Put up your sword!" said a voice from overhead. "Both of you dismount and move away from your horses."

Bellman slid *Bravado* into the sheath on his saddle and dropped clumsily to the ground, almost falling. He hobbled to the far side of the barbican, feeling the usual illusion after a day on horseback that his legs had shrunk. Must be how Count János felt all the time.

Metal clattered, hinges squeaked, and a postern gate began swinging open. It was high enough and wide enough to admit a man on horseback, but the squad of men-at-arms who entered came on foot. They wore padded cotton armor and carried halberds with evil, shiny points. The gate closed behind them.

They took Bellman first, perhaps just because he was nearer, but hopefully because he was not the one who had triggered the alarm. Their leader consulted a card in his free hand.

"Password?"

"Spinning Wheel."

"Signed by?"

"Cantor Samuil."

"Cell?"

"White 5, D 21. And don't bother asking me the date because I don't remember exactly. Early in Fourthmoon."

"Do you know the man you rode in with?"

"No. We met on the hill."

"Then welcome back, brother. Excuse the delay."

Was the man a "sir" or a "brother"? The badge on his helmet must denote his rank, but Bellman couldn't read it. Fortunately his own rank was a mystery, because he was wearing no insignia. "It's been that sort of day," he said.

Without a backward glance, he led his horse to the postern, which opened to admit him. Almost certainly he and Radu would be reunited in adjoining dungeons before very long. Radu had briefed him for this disaster as well as he could, but he must have overlooked many, many things.

Beyond the barbican is the bailey and you ride over to the quartermaster's store . . . to your right . . .

It didn't look like a bailey and he was already dismounted, standing bewildered in an arcade where a few lanterns burned, shedding light on bare stonework and arches curtained by rain like shimmering white lace. The yard was out beyond that. How far did he have to go? Should he remount or lead his horse?

A man in an ankle-length white gown came running— an adolescent, face and scalp shaven. *Hood down and white belt mean he's a novice. Call him "Novice" or nothing at all.*

"Sir!"

"Take her," Bellman said. All he had to do then was follow. They went to the right, came to a big door with lantern light inside, obviously not a stable. He hoped it was the quartermaster's, not the bakery or the apothecary's. "Wait a minute!" He began to fumble at the saddlebags with frozen fingers.

"Sir! I will bring them for you."

He could overrule a novice—assuming this was a novice and not some higher rank sent to watch over him. "I need something out of this one, is all. But I want that sword." *You can ask to keep the same sword. You're allowed a favorite sword unless your commanding officer doesn't like the look of it.*

The novice said "Sir!" and opened the bag for him. "I will bring the sword, sir."

"Do that." Bellman lifted out the bulky wallet of lock picks. In Chivial a man could be hanged for owning those without good reason. The kid led the horse away. What sort of sadist made stablehands work in white gowns?

The hall was large and dim, rows of shelves visible at the back, open-fronted cubicles to the left. This was the right place. By the time he reached the nearest cubicle, two more novices were running to help.

"Sir. Towels, sir?"

About to begin by removing his helmet, Bellman recalled the rules about not showing faces and left it for last. Eager hands unfastened his cuirass and lifted a ton of steel off of him. If they noticed his trembling they would attribute it to the cold. It was a great joy to chafe himself with the rough towels.

He was handed a white gown. His sword was laid on the bench. "Sir. What color?"

What color what?

"Er, orange." He donned the gown, removed his helmet, pulled the hood forward. "Oh . . . Novice! I need a lantern."

If the powers were watching over him, he had just signed his own death warrant, but the lad *Sirred* him and ran. Obedience, obedience, obedience.

He accepted an orange sword belt and girded on *Bravado,* which he had certainly not misnamed. The sandals fit quite well. He remembered to keep his head lowered as he walked out of the cubicle and accepted a lantern, unlit. Carrying that in his left hand and the lock picks in his right, Senior

Knight-brother Bellman strode out of the store to begin his hunt for the mysterious prisoner.

And nobody challenged him.

He found the start of the ramp Radu had described and took his time walking up it, letting his eyes grow accustomed to darkness again. *There are seven hubs, roughly in two rows back from the entrance—Red, Green, White, Blue to the north, Yellow, Orange, Violet on the south, but they cross-connect. Mostly they do. They can have up to six levels. You go from one hub to another by a ramp, usually. And usually from one level to another by going across to another hub and back. Corridors are level. But it's a lot less regular than I've just described.*

He retrieved Johanna's conjured locket from the wallet where he'd placed it, fastened the chain around his neck, and tucked the locket itself inside his gown. The face it gave him might or might not be instantly recognized around the monastery, but if he ran into trouble he would be able to change his appearance very rapidly.

Momentarily, something passed under the light far ahead. In a minute his heart started beating again, even faster than before. Two men were coming down toward him. They were armed, of course. *If anyone asks you anything, just say you have your orders. That even goes for your hair.* He needed to look behind him more than he had ever needed anything in his life. Two opponents might be manageable, but one against four or more was not worth the sweat.

They swished by him without looking up.

He continued shakily up the ramp to the next light. He ought to be in Red Hub now, but he did not stop to confirm that. He had a choice of one ramp up, two down, and several corridors, which were smaller and narrower. He chose the up ramp, hoping it would lead him to Green. It was steeper than the last one. At the top he walked a few paces along a corridor and stopped to wait.

Nobody came after him. A follower would have to stay close, very close, but there was no one. He ran his fingers gently over a door as Radu had described, and found "G 2, C 1," which made sense. He headed for what he hoped would be White.

It wasn't. It was Orange 4, which confused him. The only comforting thing about this labyrinth was that they would never find him before he starved to death. Next hub ought to be Violet 3.

It was White 3. He had a choice of two upward ramps.

Blue 4. Back to White 3 and try the other. Violet 4.

Now he understood why the brethren hid their dirty secrets on Blue 3—there was no Blue 3. He went back to White 3. Then Blue 4 again and a down ramp. Violet 3. Keep going . . .

Blue 3! Got it. Corridor H and Corridor K. No Corridor J. Playing hard to get. The maze was even less regular than Radu had said. H and K were dark, no speck of light at the far end. He was about to light his lantern from the wall lamp when he heard voices and light appeared at the far end of K.

He fled along H as fast as he dared go in the dark, trailing one hand on the wall, until he came to a dead end and stopped in panic. He had passed several doors. There were two beside him now, but he had no idea what lay behind them—harmless old books or insomniac knight-brothers. Lanterns turned the corner into Corridor H, shining on white gowns. He was just reaching for the nearest latch when they stopped and the first man opened a door.

He counted them going in—two brethren, Radu with his hands tied, four more brethren. The guards on the gate had been relieved of their prisoner, who was too important to be entrusted to low-ranks.

They had left the door ajar. Bellman sprinted. It was door Blue 3, K 1, and it led into an octogram with another door

open at the far side. The outside of that one was numbered
B 3, J 5. Perhaps this maze was a smartness test for novices.
He saw the last of the escort vanish into what he assumed
was the fake broom cupboard, opened B 3, J 6, opposite, and
found the octogram Radu had mentioned, dark and empty.
He left his lantern there, but kept the wallet of lock picks.
Hoping he would be safe enough following the brethren as
long as he could keep their lights in view, he started down
the stairs.

He reached the hub at the bottom without breaking his
neck, but then he was in pitch darkness. This would be Blue
Level 2. He tried to remember Radu's story—another stairway and several corridors? He found the stair the hard way,
wrenching an ankle but saving himself before he pitched
headlong. He thought he could hear voices now, so he
worked his way down to a landing, found a turn. From there
he saw light, filtering around another corner.

Just as it had been described, the second flight descended
to a barred gate, which presently stood open, and the room
beyond it was so bright that Bellman hesitated to go any
closer. He could hear voices beyond, many voices, but he
could not make out the words. Six guards had delivered
Radu, and the other prisoner would not have been left unat-
tended. There might be a dozen brethren down there, all
warriors trained to use the swords they bore. Even a Durendal would not take on those odds. And if anyone else came
to inspect the spy, Bellman would be trapped with nowhere
to go.

He retraced his steps to Level Two and explored the hub,
confirming the two stairs and locating three corridors. He
walked along one until he thought he would be invisible
from the stairs, then flopped down and leaned back against
the cold stonework. Exhaustion sifted over him and engulfed
him like a wagonload of sand.

How many hours until the monastery awoke to a new day? People would come trooping along this corridor and find an intruder snoring on the floor. That would certainly attract suspicion. He didn't think he could stay awake any longer.

To sleep was to die. He dragged himself upright and began staggering up and down the corridor just to stay awake. His whole body ached and quivered with fatigue. Physical exhaustion he could deal with, for about another hour maybe, but he needed his wits now as he had never needed them before, and he knew they were failing. If he had Radu with him they could find a safe place to rest, keep watch by turns, find food and drink to sustain them—and that thought gave him a raging thirst. By himself he was close to helpless as long as Blue 1 A was held by so many brethren.

Voices and lights . . . men coming up the stairs . . . grumbling as if their sleep had been broken for no real purpose . . . carrying on up to Level 3, not noticing the watcher in the dark. Six of them. Silence and darkness returned. Radu remained below with however many guards had been there before. On the night he had discovered the prisoner there had been at least four, possibly more. When no one else appeared, Bellman went to the stairs and started down.

The Count and seneschal were well illuminated and hidden behind the flap of the open cellar door. Ringwood, similarly, had only one eye showing and even more light behind him. The walking dead ignored them all and went scuffling and shuffling along the corridor in search of easier prey. Solid and lethal in the near darkness, they emitted foul odors of corruption. There were more than a score of them, some bearing weapons or tools, a few clad in antique armor, others ragged or almost naked, and even a couple of women. Many showed death wounds horrible enough to turn Ringwood's stomach.

"That must be all," the Count said, emerging. "No, wait. I can hear something else coming."

"Leave it! Why bother?" Max demanded.

"Because I want them all out and then I'm going to shut the door so they can't find their way back in. Daylight kills them, or didn't you know that?"

"This is a terrible thing you have done!"

"I am defending my house!" János roared. "Those brigands attack me by night, without warning? Smash my property, slay my dogs, my guards—"

"You don't know that!"

"Then why did I get no warning? Serves them right. Listen! It's started."

Distant screams echoed faintly through the mansion as the attackers discovered their peril. However perverted the Count's strategy, Ringwood had to admit that it was worthy of the Brotherhood. János had ordered his own people into a well-lit area and loosed the shadowmen on the attackers, who were outside in the darkness of this especially black night. The cellar of death had never been an escape route, only a secret defense.

"Come, then!" Max said. "We must make sure people don't panic. And we must find the Schale woman and the Chivians."

"Why bother? Dead is dead."

"Not always!" Ringwood threw the door open and emerged with *Bad News* in his hand. Ranter was at his back and the corridor grew brighter as the women followed with more lanterns.

The Count's pry bar lay discarded at his feet. He was still wrapped in nothing but a fur cloak that displayed his hairy chest and forearms. He wore his broadsword on his left and his right hand held a lantern he would have to drop before he could draw, giving Ringwood plenty of warning. The big seneschal was unarmed. The back door behind them was barred and bolted.

Ringwood had the upper hand for the moment. Could he keep it against two Vamky men?

"Oh, there you are, Your Grace!" the Count said. "We were worried. Put that sword up, sonny. It's bad manners to draw on your host."

"It's worse to sell a guest to her enemies." Ringwood walked closer. Insectile rustling and clinking sounds from the cellar indicated that *something* was still scrabbling up the steps, but he ignored that. "Did you hang Wolfgang Webber, or just pretend you were going to?"

Lamplight shone back from the Count's eyes. "What filthy business is that of yours?"

"Just tell me you didn't leave orders that he was to be taken to the octogram and healed after we left."

"Sir Ringwood!" the Duchess protested at his back. "This is absurd. I told you how Lord János helped us after Fadrenschloss burned. He has been a loyal friend to me, and he was a lifelong friend of Ernst von Fader."

Ringwood kept his eyes on the Count. "He's also an apostate Vamky knight, Your Highness. He left the Order after Luitgard died, but that didn't free him from his oaths. Yes, he helped you and the Baron. Then Harald arrived with orders for him. That was why János recommended Harald to the Baron, and why he hinted you ought to leave before Harald loosed any more swarmings on him. And he got other orders later, didn't you, my lord? When Radu turned up for his father's funeral you arrested him. Why? You said it was because he'd left the Brotherhood, but that was exactly what you'd done yourself."

"He kidnapped a child who'd been left in my care!"

"And who told you that? Was Radu so stupid? He took care not to be seen, he said."

"What business is this of yours, sonny?"

Ringwood was almost enjoying this. Bellman would be proud of him. "It certainly concerns your seneschal here. Did you tell him how you battered Radu to jelly and caged him in a pit like an animal? He knew no secrets you cared about. You were told to interrogate him because Vamky wanted to hear how much he'd discovered. Then they told you to hang him. And you would have done so if we had not arrived in the nick of time."

Max made the sort of "?" noise a bear would make on being kicked awake in midwinter.

"And when Her Highness showed up two days ago," Ringwood persisted, "you sent word to Vamky and promised to bring her in, as you had been instructed. Max knew we were coming, didn't you, Seneschal?"

Max said carefully, "I knew he would be bringing guests."

"So his lordship sent two messages he didn't tell us about. Unfortunately his friends didn't go along with his plan. Or they got impatient. They decided to drop in this evening and help themselves. What went wrong?"

"You tell me, lad," János said in tones that would scare off a wolf pack. "You're the one spinning yarns. Why would friends of mine wreck my house, kill my dogs, kill or disable my guards?"

The sounds of tumult were growing louder. Were the attackers outside fleeing into the house to find safety from the shadowmen? If so, the Count might have outsmarted himself.

"That I'm not sure of," Ringwood admitted. "Were you asking too much for her?"

"And why," the Count inquired, as he casually shifted the lantern to his left hand, "would I have turned on Wolfgang, if I am still loyal to the Brotherhood?"

"I didn't say you were loyal. I said you take orders, and

I'm sure you were furious when you realized that Wolfgang was spying on you. Besides, what harm did it do? The boy had a nasty hour or so and his arms were smashed so badly they may never heal properly, but a knight-brother must expect to suffer a few hard knocks for the cause, yes? Did you hang him, though? In my Order that would be seen as going a little too far. Tell me you know he was hanged."

"I will not. Now stand aside while I see to my house and my people." János advanced a pace and halted when the glinting point of *Bad News* did not budge. He knew of True's truth-sounding skill and had been very careful to speak in questions, avoiding direct statements. So Ringwood still could not be absolutely sure.

He was pleased how steady his sword was, though, and the Duchess had stopped arguing. "I will let you pass and apologize, my lord, if you will state that you have received no orders from Vamky in the past year. That you hanged Wolfgang. And tell us why you tortured Radu."

"I will do no such thing! Stand aside!"

"Drop your sword," Ringwood said, watching the Count's eyes.

The Count threw the lantern at him with his left hand and drew his broadsword with his right. He swung a cut to kill his impudent tormentor. His sword clanged to the ground and he screamed in pain.

Much, much too slow! Ringwood had appealed for assistance with a quiet "Starkmoor," batted the lantern aside with *Bad News,* and parried inward. Steel screeched. The old man's power in engagement was incredible, but Ringwood turned to his right, throwing all his weight into it, and that opened room on his left for Ranter to step in and crack the Count's elbow with an upward blow of the flat of his blade. The broadsword fell. Match over.

Felt good.

Very, very good! First real fight. (The less blood you shed the better, Grand Master said; lawyers feed on it.)

"Thank you, brother," Ringwood said. "Seneschal, I do think you should go and see what's happening out front. If I were you, I'd be worried that the attackers will set fire to the house. The rest of us are going out through the cellar and we will take your lord along as hostage."

Max Priboi, former Vamky novice, was staring very hard at him, as if seeing him for the first time. "There may still be shadowmen down there."

"Quite likely. But I know for certain that there are two living factions up here who wish my ward no good, and they are more dangerous. If you are still alive and in control in the morning, you may be able to ransom this creature with some horses and a light breakfast."

János roared, "I am not going down there for all the—"

Max's great hand slammed him back against a wall. "So that's why Radu disappeared right after the funeral without saying good-bye to anyone?" Again he hurled the Count back, shoving with two hands this time. "Beat him to jelly, huh?" Obviously he would switch to fists, given any excuse.

"Until the sun turns to water and the moon burns!" János roared.

The seneschal growled angrily and backed away. The second fight was over.

"What does that mean?" Ranter demanded.

"Part of their oath, I'd think," Ringwood said. "They're both Vamky men."

"No more!" János shouted. "I spared Radu, didn't I? I did *not* report that the Duchess had come back. Am I telling the truth, girl?"

True nodded. "He is, dear."

"So he ratted again?" Ringwood said. "He turns like a weathercock. Seneschal, you are excused." No need to make any more enemies right now.

"You're crazy to go down there, lad. At least wait here until . . ." Max paused to listen.

Voices were shouting not very far away.

"Quick!" Ringwood shouted. "They're coming."

"Sir Ranter," Ringwood said loudly. "We'll send Count János ahead with two lanterns. Follow him. You may need to prod him along with *Invincible,* and he doesn't understand gentle. Take a lantern, too. Your Highness, you must trust me. Follow Sir Ranter, True. I will bring up the rear."

"If you think," the Grand Duchess said, "that I am going down those stairs under any circum—"

"You think lights will protect you?" János yelled. "Then what killed my brother and the miners?"

"Ignorance or panic," Ringwood said. "Move him, brother."

Ranter had years of practice at bullying and had been lugging *Invincible* around for months without a chance to use her. In no time he had the Count yelping with pain and starting down the steps, a lantern in each hand and minor flesh wounds in his buttocks.

"Let me past!" Max said.

Taking no chances, Ringwood backed into the pantry to let him go by.

The big man raised a fist in salute. "Good chance, Sir Blade. If I'm still in charge in the morning, I'll try to help." He sighed. "But if that's Vamky out there, then you'd better not trust me."

"Thanks. I understand. Better hurry." The sounds of battle were coming closer.

True retrieved the Count's broadsword. "Onward and downward!"

"You can't use that!" Johanna protested.

"Oh, can't I? You think I don't have the muscle? I can take

Ringwood two falls out of three. Let's go." She disappeared into the stairwell with sword and lantern. Wonderful woman!

Fortunately the Duchess did not seem to have noticed True's brag, which was untrue, if not totally without basis. She was staring in horror at the gloomy doorway. "This is madness!"

Ringwood handed her a lantern. "It is necessary. We have to get you to the wedding, Your Grace."

"You do? But you were arguing—"

"—the other way yesterday. But now they know you're back, they're out to kill you. Attacking a count's house in the middle of the night? They're desperate!" He gave her another lantern. "We have to display you in public as soon as possible to show the world you're alive. Or very soon you won't be. Please, Your Grace! I can't carry you and fight off shadowmen at the same time. Which is it to be?"

Obviously his ward had an unreasoning dread of darkness or underground places or something similar, but he knew she had courage, and now she proved it again by doing as he asked. He followed her in, awkwardly pulling the door closed behind him. He doubted anyone would come after them. It would depend how desperate the enemy were, whoever they were. Fine Blade he was, not even knowing the identity of the foe who had been trying to kill his ward for half a year!

Four steps down Johanna cried, "*Eek!* What's that?"

"Just a shadow-thing," True said cheerfully. She had waited below the obstacle. "Hold your light low and walk right through it."

"It" had once been a man who had died in chains. It had no legs, which was why it had taken so long climbing the stairs after its fellows. In a good light it became transparent and immaterial, so its efforts to grab ankles were ineffectual.

"Wait for us, Ranter!" True shouted. "Don't get too far ahead. We're coming." Her voice echoed down into the cellars.

◆ 4 ◆

$\mathcal{B}$ellman crept down the stairs until he reached the second corner, and from there he could see down to the barred gate, which was shut. He could hear voices and something else: *Crack!* And then again, *Crack!* He went on, one fearful step at a time. A man spoke. Someone laughed. Then a voice he knew—

"Stop that!" Johanna shouted.

His heart jumped, but that was only her voice when she was wearing the locket. Someone growled a reply he could not make out. It sounded like a threat.

He went on down until he could peer through the top of the gate below him. The room was much larger than he had imagined, but otherwise just as Radu had described: bright lanterns, six timber doors on the right, a heavy table in the center with two benches (one tucked in close, one pulled back), and four barred doors on the left.

And five men.

One of them was heavyset, almost portly, clad in a shabby, dirty robe, and if it was not Grand Duke Rubin himself, it was his exact double. At the moment he was standing inside the second dungeon, holding the bars of the door and shouting at what the other men were doing. As Radu had described, he was also restrained by a long chain attached to a metal collar.

Another man was crouched on his knees in front of the third barred door, with his wrists tied to it. His gown had been pulled down below his waist and one of his captors was swinging a whip. *Crack!* Another bleeding cut joined the weave across the prisoner's back. Two more brethren were watching.

No. If Bellman just crept away and let that go unchallenged, his conscience would torment him for the rest of his life. No matter that the alternative would probably reduce the rest of his life to a matter of minutes, he must do something to stop that. Three against one? To a real Blade those were frightening odds, but not impossible. Grand Master in his youth had once overcome four, but Bellman was not a real Blade; his hands shook with fatigue; he had never finished training; he had only one good eye . . .

Stop that! It had been the candidates in Ironhall who had consistently bested him. He had beaten plenty of Blades from the Royal Guard at their first or second attempt. It was only when they discovered how to come in on his blind side that they had made him look like a turtle. The brethren could not know about that.

"I said stop it!" Rubin shouted. "You are disgracing the Brotherhood! This man has not been tried or convicted of anything."

"And I said to keep your mouth shut or I will push your balls in it and nail it shut!" said the larger of the two spectators. "We are interrogating a spy."

"He is a knight-brother, entitled to a trial."

Bellman chose a couple of picks, rolled up the wallet again, and moved down to the gate as quietly as he could.

"I have already told you everything I know," Radu said, his voice unsteady.

"Tell us more!" the larger spectator said. "Achim!"

Crack!

Radu gasped. "I dropped the letter somewhere."

"You dropped it *here*! Again, Achim."

Crack!

Bellman applied pressure and confirmed that the gate was locked. He slid the pick into the lock, working by feel, keeping his eyes on the brethren. Fortunately the lock was on his right, so if one of them looked his way they would see someone waiting to be admitted, or just a nosy parker spying. Unfortunately his hands were shaking. He found a ward . . .

Crack!

Radu cried out that time. "No! I couldn't find this place. I dropped it somewhere else. I knew someone would find it and see it was delivered. Then I learned my father had died, so I went to his funeral."

"You are lying. You were identified."

Crack!

"Identified by me!" the Grand Duke shouted. "At first sight I thought it was Radu, but I made a mistake. It was another man. I was wrong."

"And I told you to keep your mouth shut!" said the large man. "What are you waiting for, Achim? Keep laying them on until I tell you to stop."

Crack!

Radu choked down a scream. "Would I have come back if I had done anything wrong?"

"You will pay for this, Samuil!" the Grand Duke shouted.

So the big one was Samuil. The lock was simple enough, with only two wards to circumvent. Bellman could touch the bolt now, could even make it move slightly, but the pick was too short to push it far enough. He tried the other.

Crack!

Radu cried out. "Please! Oh, please stop!"

"Sir," said the other spectator. "It is true that the prisoner is a knight-brother, so under the rule of our order, he is entitled to a trial. He should not be interrogated without—"

"Shut up, Gerlach!"

Crack!

"I've told you everything!" Radu yelled.

Crack!

Either Bellman was overlooking something, or this pick was still not long enough. Or was the bolt set too heavily in the detent? If he applied more pressure and broke the pick, then he would have lost any chance of opening the door.

"I don't care if you have told us everything, Brother Radu," Samuil said. "You have not paid for my eye yet. Get on with it, Achim! Or paid for these scars on my face. We have a long night ahead of us."

Crack!

Radu moaned.

Click! The gate was free.

But both Samuil and Gerlach had heard. They turned to look. Bellman waited, keeping his head lowered as the brethren did, his face shadowed.

Gerlach strode over. "Who are you? What you want?"

Bellman gave the first name that came into his head. "Knight-brother Harald delivering a package for Cantor Samuil."

He held up the leather roll holding the picks, but he kept it outside the bars. Gerlach reached through for it. Bellman grabbed his wrist with his free hand, heaved Gerlach forward, and slammed his arm down on a crossbar, throwing his weight on it in an effort to break it. Judging by the resulting scream, he had at least come close.

He shouldered the gate open, taking the unfortunate Gerlach with it, and jumped through, drawing *Bravado*. Two more swords hissed from their scabbards. Three against one, six eyes against one and a bit. The moment of surprise had worn off. Samuil advanced to meet the intruder, but he came cautiously, so maybe Ansel had been right when he said Bellman *looked* like a swordsman.

Achim, the torturer, instead of blindly following his superior into the fray, started around the far end of the table. He clearly hoped to take Bellman from behind and that was soldier's thinking, a reminder that these were trained fighting men—not Blades, but sure to be good. They would want to take the spy alive. That did not mean uninjured. This was going to be very dicey.

Bellman ran forward and kicked over the bench in front of Samuil, making him jump back. No, only five eyes! One of Samuil's was milky white, and his face was patched with white scar tissue. Healings could not heal everything, especially flesh destroyed by burns.

Leaving the one-eyed man for later, Bellman ran back around the table to meet Achim. Gerlach was still upright, struggling to draw his sword with his left hand, but a fast slash at his neck in passing put him permanently out of the fight. No quarter asked or given . . .

Achim was big, but in spite of that and his floppy white robe, he moved like a skilled swordsman. Having been appointed torturer, he was probably the youngest and strongest of the three. He brandished a bastard sword, a hand-and-a-half broadsword, which he swung in a wide slash that would have cut Bellman's head off had he waited for it. Bellman parried it with the pick bag he still held in his left hand—he would lose fingers if he tried that very often—and raised his head. Achim saw the Grand Duke's face inside the hood. Distraction! *Bravado* struck his left wrist, sending the broadsword clanging to the floor.

"Behind you!" roared the Grand Duke.

Bellman spun around and recovered, parrying a cut from Samuil. He recovered again, backing away from a murderous series of slashes until he was almost pinned against the timber doors. He slipped away to his left and recovered back the way he had come. The one-eyed brother was good, but he was going to wear himself out very soon. Bellman was almost back where he had started, near the door, and just as he remembered that Gerlach's body was somewhere there, he stepped on an arm and almost stumbled. Samuil followed, teeth bared in a grimace of hate. The traitor was fighting for his life, too. Only the winner would survive this battle for long.

Right! The brethren were warriors, not duelists. They were edge men, trained with longsword or saber against armor or on horseback. *Bravado* had an edge, but she was lighter, more nimble, and had a point as well. Bellman went on the offensive, lunging and thrusting, keeping his distance as much as possible. Samuil deserved credit for trying to fight at all with only one eye, for he could not know his opponent was in almost as bad a shape. He was also aging, already out of breath, but there could be no mercy or surrender in a treason case. Bellman deliberately turned him and drove him along the line of cells, jabbing *Bravado*'s deadly point at his face.

When he had put the Grand Duke in the dungeon, Cantor Samuil should have chained his ankles as well as his neck, because Rubin was now sitting on the floor with both legs extended through the bars of the dungeon door. Unaware of this trap behind him, Samuil tripped and lost his balance. Bellman killed him with a thrust through the heart. Before he could free his blade, the Duke yelled, "Look out behind!" and Bellman leaped around, parrying Achim's scythe stroke. *Clang!*

The big kid had followed him and was whipping that bastard sword about almost as well with one hand as he had with two. Now it was Bellman recovering, being steadily forced away from the door, trying to catch his breath and measure this opponent. The last of three was bound to be cautious. And desperate. Achim's left arm was running blood, but he would need a long time to bleed to death. He was still the best of the three. He had Bellman level with the fourth dungeon and was about to drive him back against the end wall. *Clang!*

Bellman knew he was very close to the end of his strength. "You're good, Brother Achim!" *Clang!* "Drop your sword—" *Clang!* "—and I'll give you a—" *Clang!* "—royal pardon."

Achim laughed. *Clang!* "I'll give you a state funeral."

"My jailbird twin will confirm—" *Clang!* "—the offer! Won't you, brother?"

Rubin said, "Absolutely."

Clang!

Even Radu was into the fight now. He had scrambled back on his knees, pulling the dungeon gate with him until it stood wide. In a last desperate spurt, Bellman rushed Achim, whirling *Bravado* in a silvery mist to drive his foe into the trap. Achim recovered—one step . . . two . . .

And Radu hurled himself forward as if to close the gate, swinging it at Achim's back. The brother heard the squeak of hinges, or just sensed it coming. He managed to dodge but he was too distracted to parry the thrust that went through his eye and into his brain. He fell with a thud and thrashed a few times, but it was all over.

The silence was broken only by Bellman's desperate gasping for breath and some quiet clapping from the Grand Duke in his cell.

◆　5　◆

The stairs descended about twenty steps between damp stone walls to end in a wide blackness. Ringwood, coming last, found his companions standing in unhappy silence, holding lanterns high and peering around. The air was dank and fetid, but it told of vegetable rot, not animal; it held no trace of bad meat or rodent-hunting cats. Square stone pillars marched in rows ahead, to left, to right, every one branching upward into four arches, but there were also many stubby small pillars, of uneven height and spacing. This was an incomplete cellar and those were piles of flagstones waiting to be laid. The existing footing was uneven, wet, and rubbly. Shadows lurked everywhere, as did junk, at least here beside the exit—upturned wheelbarrows, rotted baskets, masons' trowels, hammers, shovels.

Lanterns could illuminate only so far, but he could see walls in the distance. Certainly there was a masonry ramp off to the right.

"Where does that go?" He pointed with his sword.

"Barrel ramp," Ranter suggested. "To the yard?"

"Bricked up." János seemed as lost as the others, but he had probably never been down here before, either. "I'm going to see you hang for this, you Chivian scum. And that's nothing to what my sons will do to you if I die."

"Naw, they'll be too busy fighting among themselves," Ranter said. "Which way to the secret passage?"

"Find it yourself."

"When did your brother die?" Ringwood asked. "How long ago?"

"Ask him. He's still around here somewhere."

Thirty years? Longer. János had sons older than that, and they must have been born after the disaster.

The Duchess whimpered. She looked frozen, although the air was not especially cold, just damp and rank. She needed Bellman to comfort her. The big fellow would comfort them all, or he might have seen the trap sooner and saved them from having to be here. Ringwood mostly wanted to hug True, but hugging was not an option when every hand held a sword or lantern.

"Don't let him scare you, Your Grace," he said. Only a fool would not be scared here. Things kept moving in the corner of his eye, making tiny shuffling noises. He felt a million dead eyes watching him, could see a million places where shadowmen might be hiding from the lanterns. It would be folly to assume that they had all been waiting by the door. "You're in this with us, your lordship. Which way to the keep?"

János answered with an obscenity, yelped when Ranter jabbed him.

"Keep that for when it's needed, brother," Ringwood said. At least he need not worry about their hostage running away. János must be as scared as the rest of them, just more experienced at disguising the fact. "Let's go exploring. This way first."

He headed over to the abandoned barrel ramp and a conical hill of rubble beside it. Also more rotting wheelbarrows.

"There's one!" True yelped and everyone turned to stare where she was pointing. There was nothing visible by that time.

"Can you sense them, love?" Ringwood asked.

She shivered. "Oh, yes. They're around. I can't pinpoint them, though."

"We're safe enough. We have lots of light. Don't let the Count get too close to you." He wished she had not brought the broadsword. If the former knight-brother grabbed it away from her, things might turn nasty.

Oh, they're not nasty now?

The heap was mud and pebbles, not builders' waste. "I think this," Ringwood said, "is what they dug out when they were tunneling over to the keep. They piled it here so other men could take it up the ramp to wagons in the yard. But if they weren't able to complete the tunnel, they'd just put most of it back. Does that make sense?" Would Bellman have agreed?

Ranter kicked at a pile of rotting timber. "This was to shore up their diggings?"

"Good man! Of course." But was that tunnel still open?

The builders would not have installed permanent walls and roof until they knew their efforts would serve some purpose. There were no stacks of building stone waiting. Work must have stopped the moment they broke through to the castle crypt, and how big a hole did a shadowman need? Would the air be so stale here if there was open access to the keep?

"Here's the trail," True said. On the far side of the tip the floor had been paved, and muddy tracks showed where the barrows had come forty years earlier. "This way!"

"Wait!" Ringwood said. "The Count first. Stay in order. And keep together."

Menaced again by Ranter's sword, János stumped off along the ancient trail. At the first pillar, a figure lunged out at him, hands clawing for his face. He screamed and staggered back, dropping both his lanterns as he tried to defend himself. Glass shattered, darkness surged in. János went down under the attacker's weight.

Ranter roared and attacked the wraith with light and sword. He would have done better with one or the other, not both. *Invincible* passed harmlessly through an apparition. Fortunately he had stabbed horizontally, for a downward cut might have killed János. Other lights arrived; the mirage scuttled away on all fours, joining a collection of other shapes at the edge of darkness. The enemy was in view now, a lot of them.

The intruders' seven lanterns were down to five. Ringwood tried to count the watching shadowmen, but they kept shifting. More than a dozen, certainly. Their silent hatred oppressed him. If they would moan or shout abuse they might seem less dangerous.

"You all right, my lord?" Johanna asked, going down on one knee.

János was huddled in a heap on the flagstones. He didn't look all right. He looked big, because he wasn't standing, but he was mumbling, gasping, almost sobbing. A man of his age could die from a shock like that.

"Did you see what I saw?" Ranter said. "Youngish lad, old-fashioned clothes, tattered but originally quite fancy, I'd think. Those others out there, see? Most of them are half-naked workmen. This one was special. And his legs—"

"That's enough!" Ringwood barked. His legs were short? That had been Luitgard himself. Or *itself*, now? Poor old János had been attacked by his brother of forty years ago. Ringwood shivered. "On your feet, Count! We have to find a way out of here. Give him a light, Your Grace. One lantern for each of us. You lose it, you do without. Hurry!"

Johanna helped the old man rise. He wasn't the bully boy of Brikov anymore; he had shrunk and aged. His beard had lost its bristle.

Two more pillars brought them to a wall with alcoves in it, and in one of those alcoves some ashlar blocks had been removed. As a doorway, it was small, barely head high and only just wide enough to admit a wheelbarrow. Here the long-dead Luitgard had begun his illicit tunnel over to the keep.

"We'll take turns looking inside," Ringwood said. "The rest of us must keep light around the entrance."

He waited until last to make his inspection. The tunnel sloped down gently, no wider than the entrance, with a shadow at the limit of his sight that might be a branching tunnel. The roof was framed with timber, but some of the planks had sagged badly, and the props looked unsafe. In places the shoring had collapsed, heaping debris on the floor. What a pathetic, incompetent Blade he was to bring his ward to this!

He emerged to consult the others. They stood in a half-circle, facing the shadow-infested darkness.

"Don't say you wouldn't go in there if your life depended on it," Ranter said cheerfully, "because it does."

"It slopes down," Ringwood said, "and the floor's wet. Seepage."

"Wood's all rotten," the Count growled. He kept rubbing his throat as if it hurt. His brother's corpse had tried to strangle him.

"Yes, but there must be drainage somewhere. I know it may be no bigger than a mouse hole. We just can't be sure unless we go and look."

"I can't go in there!" The Duchess was hugging herself, as if she felt very cold. "I just can't."

"Nor I," János said. "I won't. I'm going back and you'll have to kill me to stop me. I think you should all come. Let the boy go if he wants to."

Commander Ringwood faced his first mutiny. "Tell us the truth, then, my lord. You sent word to the Brotherhood that you had Her Highness in your power and would sell her for a suitable price?"

The Count's attempt to shout emerged as a painful croak. He coughed. "Fool boy!" he whispered. "No. And you don't bargain with Vamky! Yes, I was a knight-brother until . . . this." He jerked a thumb at the tunnel behind him. "Forty-four years ago I left the Order. For forty-four years I never heard a word from them. They left me alone. Then orders came. Not by Harald. You were wrong there, too. After he'd gone, about Fifthmoon. Obey or else!"

"Else what?" Ranter asked, as if really wanted to know.

"Else anything you can imagine. I was ordered to lock up the Duchess or any of her companions if they showed up. I was to send word to Vamky."

Ringwood said, "But that was months after she'd left! Why did they wait until then?"

"I *don't* know!" the Count yelled. "I didn't *ask*! Finally, *last* week, I was told to arrest Radu and question him about what he had seen that he shouldn't have. I did. I reported. I got orders to hang him."

"But you didn't," Ringwood said. "You waited, hoping he would do the decent thing and die quietly in the hole so you wouldn't have to hang a brother. You freed Radu when Her Highness turned up. You didn't lock her up, either."

"Because you convinced me he was telling the truth," János said. "Volpe is engaged in high treason, him and the Abbot. I want none of that. I hold my lands from the Duke, not Volpe. So I defected. I didn't report that Her Highness was back. Well, girl? Am I lying?"

True said, "No, my lord," and shot Ringwood a worried glance.

Ringwood's laugh startled even him. "That was why you were so hard on Wolfgang! You hadn't realized he was spying on you. Did you hang him?"

The Count shook his big head. "I told them to heal him and leave him in the pit till I got back. I agree with you on that, kid. Brother shouldn't hang brother."

"Who's your handler at Vamky, my lord? Who did you send the message to?" Why did that matter? It didn't. Ringwood just needed time to think.

"Dunno. I write to a cell number. He knew the password they gave me when I left, that's all that mattered."

"And now someone's smashing your windows? Who? And how did they learn Her Highness was here?"

"I dunno."

"That may be my fault," True said. "Wolfgang said he didn't know of any more spies in the valley. He didn't say there weren't any. I think he suspected someone, maybe even the Count."

"It doesn't matter!" János roared. "They're on to us. We have to get out of here before they burn the house down on our heads, and there's nothing for us in the keep. We go back."

"We'll take a vote," Ringwood said unhappily. "Go back or explore the tunnel. True?"

"I vote with you, love."

He'd sheathed his sword, so he had one arm free to hug her.

"We go back!" the Duchess said. "I'm choking down here. There's no air!"

"Brother Ranter, you have the deciding vote." And would probably have the command from now on, too, if the Duchess had lost confidence in the present Leader.

Ranter shrugged. "You're Leader. I'm with you."

"Then I . . . You *are*?" Ringwood wondered if he'd misheard.

"All the way. You think I want to be in charge of this disaster? You got us in, brother, you get us out." Ranter could do the right thing sometimes, he just could never say it.

"Thank you, brother."

" 'Sides, I don't think we'd make it back to the stairs alive."

János said, "That's the truth," and disappeared.

He lay on his back, spread-eagled, while a rock the size of a baby's head rolled away into the passage. A sizable dent had appeared in his forehead. His lantern, amazingly, had not shattered.

"Inside!" Ringwood roared, and grabbed the Duchess. She screamed and struggled, but he wrestled her into the tunnel over the Count's body. True followed with the Count's lantern. Ranter came last, dragging the Count himself, who was no mean burden in such a confined space.

Rocks came flying in after them. Why had they never realized that the shadowmen could use real weapons? Even if everything they had with them when they died—like the Yeomen's halberds—shared in their curse and faded away in brightness, shadowmen were solid enough in darkness, and a stray rock remained a rock. That must be how they had destroyed Luitgard and his workmen. Another miscalculation, Sir Ringwood, and probably a fatal one!

"Don't jostle the pit props!" True shouted. "Keep going, love."

Ringwood led the way along the burrow, stooping and stumbling. The floor was littered with pebbles that had fallen from the walls. Those would make perfect missiles for the shadowmen if they followed. In places the sides had crumbled, spilling heaps of clay or sand as well. Ranter, being rearguard, was holding a board up as a shield, and Ringwood could hear rocks rattling off it like hail. They reached the branching he had noticed earlier and it was merely an alcove where two barrows might pass, not deep enough to provide shelter. He could see the ancient wheel tracks.

He paused there, though, to take stock and fight down a rising panic that said he was going to die now and his ward with him. The barrage of rocks had slackened, most likely because the passage did not offer enough room to throw things.

"Where's the Count?"

"He was turning transparent, Leader," Ranter said in a small voice.

So Boy Commander had now lost a man, caused a death, lost his innocence, proved himself a useless dung beetle. He should have stuck to mending pots. What's the use of doing something with your life if it's the wrong thing?

The barrage had stopped. "Are they following us?"

Ranter peeked around his makeshift shield. "Yes, Leader. Lot of the buggers. Creeping closer all the time."

"Then let's keep going. Can't be much farther. They wouldn't be following us if there wasn't a way out." Ringwood didn't *really* believe that, but perhaps someone would. Five lanterns and four people left.

As he stumbled along, he wondered what made the shadowmen so aggressive—were they jealous of the living? Did they seek revenge for a violent death? He decided it must just be the way the spiritualism was concocted. One of the Yeomen at Quamast had cut his own throat. They didn't want revenge; didn't want to make you suffer; just wanted you dead like them.

Suddenly his feet were splashing in water and there was no more passage.

The pool was shallow, ten or twelve paces long, filling the space from wall to wall. It ended in a sandy slope. This was the end of the road, and stones were still pinging off Ranter's shield. Once in a while he would curse as if one had hit him instead.

Glass shattered. "Oops!" Ranter said. "Need another lantern! *Quick!*"

Four lanterns left. Here we stand and fight. Here we die.

The shoring stopped short of the tunnel end and some balks of timber lay at Ringwood's feet unused, so this had been the active face of the mining operation, not just a later collapse. In forty-four years the unsupported stretch of roof had crumbled, dumping sand and clay into the pool. The pool was seepage collecting at the low point of the tunnel. How far underground were they? Ringwood waded forward and raised his lantern to see if there might be a way out overhead, but there wasn't, just a dome going nowhere.

Why had the workmen stopped here?

Why didn't the whole tunnel fill with water?

"Hold this!" He thrust his lantern to True and started in on that sandy slope like a dog digging for rabbits, hurling muck through between his legs. In moments he found clay and pebbles that tore his hands. "Give me that!" He took the broadsword from her and began using it like a pick, digging away the detritus. It was strenuous work, but he drove himself hard, still hearing those vicious rocks bouncing off Ranter's shield. *I don't want to die down here in a rathole*.

The sides of his dig became unstable and collapsed. He kept on digging. True came to help him with a scrap of plank to use as a shovel. They dug side by side, ferociously. Above them loomed the unsafe roof of the cave, trickling sand.

"They're coming closer, Leader!" Ranter said calmly.

In a few minutes Ringwood would have to change places with him. He couldn't keep this up much . . . *There it was!*

"We've found rock!" he shouted. "It's a wall." Ashlar blocks, rough and unfinished on this side, set in mortar. Now he had to dig lower and his narrow trench kept trying to close up. "This is the wall of the crypt! Chisel marks! The opening must be here somewhere." Down near the water, of course.

"Back, vermin!" Ranter shouted. He was striking at shadows and a little more than shadows, for Ringwood could hear faint metallic sounds.

But the opening was in view now. The workers had smashed a block completely, but only one, and the gap was plugged with sand and clay. Ringwood tore at it with his bare hands, scooping it out. Could a living person squeeze through that? Shadowmen had come through, but they might have had light to make them intangible.

He drew *Bad News* and dropped on his belly. His shoulders were too tight a fit, but he wriggled his head and one arm into the gap, so his chest rested painfully on a surface of rough mortar studded with sharp fragments of rock. There might be legions of shadowmen on the other side. Suppose something grabbed hold of his arm and pulled? . . . He waved his sword down, up, every way, and encountered nothing. There was a big space out there, but how far to the floor? There might be a lake, or a thirty-foot drop onto spikes.

But the air smelled fresh and clean.

He squirmed back into the passage. Trudy and Johanna were standing in the mud and even Ranter had retreated into the pool now, fighting off swords and pikes. The shadowmen were much closer than before, and horribly visible, a mass of writhing giant cockroaches, mummified wraiths, filling the tunnel to the roof. Most of them were ragged or naked, and the first dozen or so were transparent. Only the narrowness of the tunnel kept them from swarming all over Ranter. They were trying to smash his lantern, but its light turned their weapons to nothing; if they tried to strike with planks their hands faded out and the planks fell to the ground. They should just move back into darkness and throw rocks again, but Ringwood wasn't about to tell them so.

He tossed a pebble through to the crypt. It hit something and bounced. The drop did not sound very far. There was still hope.

"Lantern!" he said. "I can't find a floor. True, you go and look. We'll pull you back."

She didn't argue, wonderful woman! She said, "If I get stuck halfway I'll never forgive you," but she flopped down in the mud, put both arms and a lantern ahead of her, and wriggled headfirst into the nasty, rough space. Ringwood gave her a few seconds, then grabbed her dress and hauled her back. He heard her dress rip.

She howled. "Ow! That hurt! But it's not very far. I can do it."

"You first, then," he said.

"This will not be dignified," True said, but she was already covered in mud from her chin to her toes. She kissed him. "I want no fancy heroics from you, my lad!" she whispered. Again she heaved herself into the opening face-down, but now feetfirst. Her gown bunched up; her hips gave her trouble. She swore, squirmed, and then swore again as her legs flailed helplessly and her shoulders were crushed against the top of the gap. When only her arms were visible, Ringwood gave her a lantern and she pulled it in with her.

Then even that vanished.

"True!" he screamed, and hurled himself down to follow. He stopped when he saw the glow of the lantern coming from below the opening.

"All right, love!" she said, and her voice reverberated in a larger space. "Nothing here but me. Wait a minute, though." The glow faded away and his heart began tying itself in knots. Then a horrible shriek.

He screamed in panic and banged his head against the top of the gap. Almost before he stopped seeing stars, he heard her voice.

"That sounded bad, didn't it? It's a door. Just making sure it would open. Send Her Grace through. I want to see it done gracefully."

A door? But how many other doors were beyond it? Would there even be a way out of the crypt and the keep when they got there?

Ringwood wriggled out of the hole and then back in again, still one-armed, so he could pass True another lantern. She could not quite reach it standing on tiptoe, but he dropped it to her and she caught it without mishap. He had a brief glimpse of an apparently empty chamber and the door she had mentioned on the far side. The keyhole opening was grating him like a carrot.

Then Johanna. She said nothing and he noticed she had her eyes shut as she lay down to get in position, feetfirst, facedown.

"It's all right," he said. "Trudy can help you."

Still without a word, Grand Duchess Johanna went squirming into the sewer and disappeared. That must take tremendous courage from someone with her dread of being underground. There were only two lanterns left, so the corridor was dangerously dim. It was time for fancy heroics.

"Right!" Ringwood said, drawing *Bad News*. "You next, brother. My turn to hold off our admirers." Oddly, saying it was easier than he'd expected.

"No," Ranter said. "I won't fit through that. You go."

The attackers had found some poles long enough to threaten his lantern. He was chopping at them and stamping on them. Some were so rotten he could break them. Others weren't. It was hard work, and he was dancing around so much that Ringwood couldn't squeeze past him to take his place.

"No!" he said shrilly. "I'm Leader and I'm ordering you to go!"

"I won't fit. Stop wasting time."

"At least try! If you really can't fit, then I'll go, but you *must* try."

"No! Take the other lantern and go, Beanpole. You rapier types have all the luck. Us saber men make better lovers. Now get in there and look after our ward!"

The thought of Johanna down in the crypt with no protection and possibly shadowmen prowling threw Ringwood into near-panic. No heroics, True had said, but he was Leader, it was his *duty* to be last out. It made things no easier to know that Ranter was right. The big oaf would never squeeze through that tiny gap. Ringwood was not at all sure he could make it himself.

"Please!" he screamed. "At least try!"

"Fine pair of onions we'll look if I get stuck in it with you on this side."

"You won't know until you try."

"I'll try, I promise. Now go," Ranter said. "Quick! I can't hold them much longer."

A faint, distorted scream echoed out of the hole in the

wall. Then two screams. The women were being attacked. No! No! No!

Whimpering, Ringwood sat down, put the third lantern close to hand, and slid his legs into the burrow. He sent *Bad News* through ahead of him, hilt first so he wouldn't kill anyone. Then the broadsword. He rolled over on his face and started. Assuming he didn't castrate himself, his hips would be the problem. He had to twist and struggle to force them through, and the rocky claws seemed to be cutting him to the bone. Ranter swore loudly, as if he'd been hurt, but at that moment Ringwood thought he was permanently stuck and could go neither forward or back. His shoulders were wider than his hips, but more flexible. Then he was through, his legs were dangling, and he had to hang on while he got a grip on the lantern.

Hands gripped his legs, and he suppressed a wail of fright, frantically trying to convince himself that they were trying to help, not drag him through to his death.

"I'm gone," he said. "You come now!"

"Be right there," Ranter said.

Ringwood slid agonizingly over the edge, tearing belly and shoulder blades both. He wanted to bring the lantern with one hand and hold onto the edge of the opening with the other and didn't succeed. Trudy was trying to take his weight on her shoulders and she failed, too. They collapsed together. He hit the flagstones hard enough to knock all the breath out of him. The lantern shattered.

He struggled to sit up. "You all right?" Nothing seemed to be broken.

"Yes, yes!"

They had been lucky. "What's wrong? Why were you screaming?"

"Nothing's wrong," she said.

"We could hear you arguing, Commander," the Duchess

said, "doing the manly thing, and we had to get you moving. We need you, both of you."

He stood up shakily, smelling his own blood. "You all right, Your Grace?"

"I've been better, but I'm not injured."

He was surprised to see how far he had dropped. The hole was a rectangle of faint light. He could just hear Ranter swearing at the shadowmen.

"Ranter!" he roared, and the chamber reverberated. *"Come now!"* He turned to give True a hug. "Any shadowmen here?"

"I don't think so. Very faint. But I've been sort of numbed by their stink, so I may be wrong."

"Ranter!"

The light winked out.

"Ah!" the Duchess said. "He's coming!"

Ringwood looked at Trudy. Trudy looked at Ringwood.

"I don't think so, Your Highness," he said hoarsely. "I think they broke the last lamp."

Silence. There was no noise from the tunnel.

"Ranter?"

More, terrible silence.

"If I climbed on your shoulders," True whispered. "And held a lantern to the hole?"

Ringwood put an arm around her again. And then the other one round Johanna. All three of them hugged for a moment. If Ranter were alive, he would be telling them so.

"He wouldn't have been able to get through the hole," True said. "Would he?"

"I don't think he would." *I wish I was certain. I wish he'd tried.*

So Ranter's name would be added to the *Litany of Heroes* in Ironhall, and it would be Ringwood's duty to write the citation: "Abandoned by his leader, he fought on undaunted against impossible . . ."

Some other time. His own name was still heading in that direction. Just as well, perhaps, that there would be nobody to write about him. Neither *Bad News* nor *Invincible* would ever hang in the sky of swords.

Now they must go. To stay and mourn would be folly and a betrayal of Ranter's sacrifice. Running would not be cowardice, only brutal common sense. He was bruised, abraded, and exhausted, and the women were in no better shape. Three people and two lanterns. He looked down at the one he had dropped and was dismayed to see how little oil there was in the splash of broken glass.

"Let's move our lanterns away from that opening," he said. "I don't think the monsters can get through there in the dark." But he didn't *know* that, and he had underestimated the shadowmen before. "Let's go and see the sunrise." The first ray of daylight would make them safe.

The chamber was muddy, but not littered. It had no windows, only a small and rusty iron door in it.

"This looks like a jail," he said, heading for the exit. The others followed, bringing the lights.

"I was thinking that," Johanna said. "Chain someone up in a place like this with a few candles and let him watch the shadowmen for a while. Then you come back when the candles start to run out and ask if he's ready to talk yet." That was the longest speech she'd made in hours. Her voice held a hysterical brittleness, but at least she was talking.

"That's not a nice thought, Your Highness."

"Unless the someone was Lord Volpe," True suggested. No one disagreed.

She had managed to push the door open a handsbreadth. Leaning on it, Ringwood was surprised by the effort he needed to move it farther. She must be even stronger than he had realized. The hinges screamed again. When all three of them had squeezed through the gap, he and Trudy between them managed to shut it, and once again the crypt rang with the cry of tortured iron.

There was a lock, but no key. He didn't mention that.

"I can smell rain!" True whispered.

"I can hear it!" the Duchess said. "And the wind!"

They were in a corridor, facing a similar door that probably led to a similar room. To their right the corridor ended, so they set off to the left to find the source of the fresh air. Trudy still carried the Count's broadsword. The flagstones were carpeted with soft loam where dirt had washed in.

Very soon they came to a rockfall. Huge masses of masonry blocked the corridor from side to side and as high and far as their pathetic puddle of light could reach. The keep was a ruin, fallen in on itself, and stored in its own crypt. There was no sky, but rainwater was trickling and dripping in somewhere. Fungoid vegetation lurked in corners and tree roots twined between mossy relics of arches and pillars.

True said wistfully, "I could use that rain. Be nice to get rinsed off."

"Morning must come soon," Ringwood said. "We'll find a way out of here as soon as there's some light." He did not believe that. Only mice would ever find a way through that heap.

Whether the others were deceived by his bravado was not established, because at that moment a groan of rusty hinges echoed in the corridor behind them. True raised her lantern and peered back along the passage. Whatever was coming was not visible . . . yet.

"I think the trumpets have sounded for the third passage of arms," she said.

With the score at Shadowmen two, Humans zero.

Ringwood said, "Find a niche to hide in. I'll hold them off." He had no Ranter to help him now. His turn, and soon he would be fighting in the dark. How long would the oil last?

"We can do better than that, I think," True muttered, moving closer to the rock pile. "The shadowmen have a way through this. I can smell it."

Miracle woman! She meant White Sister smelling, of course, not real smelling, but he didn't care. "Lead the way, then. Quickly!"

True scrambled up the heap and wriggled into a badger-sized gap under a slab. After a moment her voice echoed back out: "All clear ahead."

"Your Grace?"

This was going to be much worse than the tunnel or the hole in the wall had been. Even if True was right and could find the road of the dead, there was no reason to believe that living bodies could follow. The Duchess knew that. She had her demons back, but she said nothing, just followed where True had gone, tracking the glow of her lantern. Ringwood went close behind her, ready to lend a hand if she had trouble, staying close to her light so he did not get lost. He kept expecting icy hands to close around his ankles.

Progress was terrifyingly slow. The tunnels and cracks seemed to get smaller and smaller as they climbed higher. At one point, when True had been forced to backtrack and was hunting for a way through, he found himself jammed in a very awkward bend, not at all sure he would be able to get past and unable to try because his ward's feet were right in front of his eyes. He could hear her breathing. It was too fast, too irregular. She must be close to panic.

He said, "I am deeply sorry, Your Grace, that I have been such a disaster as a Blade. I have failed both you and my Order."

After a painful silence she said, "I think you have done marvelously, Sir Ringwood. You saw through Count János. I'm sure he would have turned me over to Lord Volpe if you hadn't spirited us away. You and Bellman and Ranter were all wonderful, and I am not ready to give up yet."

"You are very brave!"

"If women were cowards, there wouldn't be babies, Sir Ringwood."

Silence again. Ringwood was listening to tiny noises behind him and trying to convince himself they were only his imagination, or rain dripping.

Johanna laughed harshly. "It isn't difficult to be brave when you have no choice. I don't mean that I do not appreciate Sir Ranter's sacrifice. He had no choice but to defend both himself and the rest of us this night, but he made that decision back in Ironhall. I saw him overcome his fear on the night he was bound, and that memory has given me courage to do what I have had to do this evening. He was not an easy man to like, but he had some admirable qualities."

"Yes," Ringwood said. "He supported me tonight when he could have settled an old score. He gave me a chance to live when he knew he must die. Above all, he did his duty. If I survive this I will report his heroism to his brothers in the Order."

"If I do I will raise a statue to him."

Then Trudy called down an all-clear, and the Duchess resumed the climb. At the cost of some more skin, Ringwood wriggled past the tight place and followed.

A moment later a cry of triumph came echoing down. "Moss!" And then, "I'm at the top!"

Soon he emerged beside the women in a rockbound hollow. Cold, wonderful rain drizzled from the blackness overhead and pattered on leaves of shrubs and spindly trees that had sprouted amid the tumbled and mossy masonry. The sky remained as black, but a very faint glow from somewhere illuminated the enclosing curtain wall of the keep, an empty drum pocked with blind black windows.

"There's a light up there!" True pointed. Why was she whispering all of a sudden?

It was firelight, not daylight, a star twinkling through the foliage.

"Should we shout?" Ringwood asked.

"No, love! Let's have a better look first." True led the way up a long, canted slab, still using the Count's sword as a staff, for the mossy surface was slippery. Shadowmen might not be the only peril around, but the lanterns would give them away soon enough. At the top they had a better view, but the source of the firelight was still hidden by trees.

Ringwood pointed to the left. "Can you see what I see?" The others could not, but Blades' night vision shamed cats. "That's a staircase!"

They had more rock climbing to do to reach it, but now they were under the sky and not squirming like worms in a sand-pile. The staircase clung to the curved curtain wall of the keep; once there had been a wall on the inner side of the staircase also, but little of that still stood. The narrow steps were well worn, surprisingly clear of rubble, certainly easier going than the jumble of precariously balanced masonry the fugitives had just left. This might be the answer. Ringwood could hold a stairway against a whole army of shadowmen if they had to come at him one at a time.

"Onward and upward?" he asked, instinctively whispering.

"Certainly," Johanna said. "Freezing to death is no improvement."

"True?" Ringwood asked. "What's wrong? Can you still sense the shadowmen?"

"Yes." She turned to stare up at the fire. "And something else up there, too. Don't know what."

Unidentified conjuration meant Vamky.

"You lead," he said. "You next, Your Grace."

The ancient treads were worn and cracked—half fallen

away in places—but someone had cleared the debris off them. That unknown obsessive housekeeper must have lived long before his time, Ringwood decided, for many treads had since collected enough leaf mold to sprout grass.

After a short climb they topped the trees and paused to study their first real view of the nightmare terrain they had just left. The center of the stronghold had collapsed into a jumble of shattered stone, now inhabited by vegetation. The great curtain wall itself was almost intact, with remnants of the interior structure still clinging to it like shattered honeycomb—fragments of floors, walls, even rooms. The fire burned in one of those dollhouse half-rooms, up in what had been the uppermost story. Its glow threw a very faint illumination over the inside of the keep, and now Ringwood could almost persuade himself that there was a trace of sky showing above the jagged upper edge of the wall. It was not yet bright enough to dissolve shadowmen, though. The only safe place to be was close to that fire.

The Duchess's lantern flickered and went out. She gasped in dismay.

"I'll carry it," Ringwood said, thinking it might make a missile. "Onward?"

"Follow me!" True said unnecessarily, and resumed the climb.

The footing was tricky, and soon there was a very long drop on the right-hand side. Once Ringwood heard a pebble roll behind him and spun around so fast he almost fell off. He could see nothing down there.

"Pigs' blood!" Trudy said, and stopped.

Lacking any sort of railing, the steps were strictly one person wide. The Duchess peered around her, and Ringwood struggled to see past both of them.

They had come to the end. The stairs stopped, cut off cleanly with its top step level with a long-lost timber floor, for the curtain wall beyond it showed a horizontal line of holes that had once supported beams.

Eight or ten paces away—but as utterly out of reach as the moon—a squarish ruined tower remained adhered to the curtain wall, a column of chimneys that had stood when all else rotted away. Fragments of floors and walls still stuck to it, creating the illusion of small rooms. The uppermost of those held a great stone hearth, facing the watchers at the top of the broken staircase and level with them.

Beside the cheerful blaze crackling there, two men sat on stools. They seemed comfortable—warm, no doubt, and protected from the drizzle by a canted overhanging fragment of slate roof. One of them wore a white robe emblazoned with the blue V of Vamky, his face hidden by his hood. The other, resplendent in fur and brocade and cloth of gold, was Grand Duke Rubin of Krupina.

♦ 6 ♦

Seniors at Ironhall often fenced without padding or masks. While practice weapons did have dulled edges, they were capable of inflicting injury, and every week or so someone would be rushed to the octogram for a healing. The risks could be justified because a dangerous profession required rigorous training, and the prospect of sudden pain was a strong incentive to develop a strong defense. But even that tough apprenticeship had not prepared Bellman for a real fight against real foes trying to mutilate him with real weapons. He had no binding to inspire him, either.

He was amazed at the reaction that followed. He shivered so violently he had to lean against the table to stay upright, his breath rasping in his throat, and dark flames swirling behind his eyes. He had been driven very close to his limits. *It was over!* And it had been a worthy battle for a man with half an eye missing. Even a real Blade would not have been ashamed of that one, and he would hold his head higher because of it. Better than carrying it under his arm.

"A remarkable display of swordsmanship, young man," said the person in the cell. "I have never seen a finer."

Bellman nodded thanks. He could detect real authority in that calm remark, as if the speaker knew exactly what the battle had cost him.

He took control of his breathing. "You know, Your Royal Highness, I do not recall having a twin. I believe one of us must be a fake."

"You think you are acting in character?"

"I wish I'd had a better seat for the show," Radu said, reminding them of his predicament.

Bellman wiped the shockingly red blood off his sword with the hem of his gown, which was already bloody, and knelt to cut the thongs holding Radu to the gate. "You ought to stay away from dungeons, my good man. They are bad for your health."

"I'll try and remember that." The knight swayed when Bellman helped him stand. His face was ashen with pain, and when he clasped his rescuer's hand with both of his, they were icy cold. "My apologies if I belittled you, friend. You made a legend here tonight."

Bellman set the bench on its legs again. "Sit. We'll get you to an octogram as soon as we have tidied up a few other matters."

He went to face his mirror image inside the bars. They studied each other for a moment, then Bellman removed his locket and looped it around his belt for safe keeping.

"I don't know you," the prisoner said. "You are not of the Brotherhood."

"No, I'm just a locksmith's apprentice. Radu told me you had some lock problems hereabouts." Foolish humor could warn of hysteria. "Who has the keys?"

"Samuil," the Duke said. "Most of them."

Bellman removed a bundle of keys from the corpse's sword belt and returned to the cell door. "Jack Bellman is my name, my lord." He chose a key and held it up thoughtfully. Fatigue was washing over him in waves, yet he must stay alert for the toughest negotiation of his life.

"He's one of the King of Chivial's Blades," Radu said.

"Ah! Then their reputation is not overblown after all."

"Don't judge them by me, my lord. I failed the course." Bellman tried the key in the lock. He knew it wouldn't fit.

"So she made it as far as Chivial, did she?"

"There and back again, my lord." Another wrong key? "Tsk! It was she who sent me, so you know who to thank for your deliverance. Where did you say her son was?"

Long pause. Bellman tried and discarded three more keys. "Mm?"

"He is safe."

"You may trust him," Radu said, and added uncertainly, "Your Highness?"

Bellman frowned at the key ring. "I am sorry to take so long, my lord. I seem to be having trouble finding the right key." Was it wise to provoke a tiger just before releasing it?

"The boy is in the care of the Dowager Countess of Bad Nargstein."

Click!

"There it is!" Bellman said cheerfully, opening the door. "Now let's see about that collar." He should perhaps have asked for an oath on the information, but instinct told him that trust would work better with this man. Assuming he was who logic said he must be.

"Samuil did not have the key for that," the prisoner said.

"Then I shall have to pick the lock. If you would be so kind as to sit on the bed, my lord. Excuse my familiarity, but it will be easier if I sit beside you. I'll be as fast as I can." He spread the battered remains of the wallet beside him.

"I am grateful to the Duchess for sending you, if indeed she did, but my debt is still to you. What reward may I offer?"

"I am sure I will think of something soon, my lord," Bellman muttered, concentrating more on finding his way around inside the lock. He feared the Brikov tools were too coarse for it.

"Why do you call him that?" Radu asked. "You do not believe he is the Duke?"

"Oh, no," Bellman said. "Never. He recognized you when you first saw him in here, or so you told us. Duke Rubin has a poor memory for names, his wife said, and he would not address you as 'Brother,' would he? Surely he would call you 'Knight-brother' or 'Brother Radu'? Ah! There." *Click!* It was an absurdly simple lock.

The brass collar swung open and he lifted it from the prisoner's throat. The face above it blurred and transformed. Radu gasped.

Happily Bellman said, "Lord Volpe, I presume?"

The solid, bony face was just as Johanna had described, strong and monumental, except that the scalp and heavy jaw bore several weeks' graying stubble. Prison had not lessened the ferocity of the extraordinary, perpetually staring eyes.

"You really guessed who I was just from that?"

"That and some even wilder guessing, my lord. The divisions in your Order had to go right to the top, so there were not many people you could be. Radu told us you were chained by a collar but you could still reach the door of your cell. That is an inefficient way to secure a prisoner, a waste of chain, so I suspected the collar might be there for some other reason. The conjuration to make a necklace like the one I was wearing must be difficult and very secret, but it might be possible to enchant two of them at the same time. I wasn't quite certain, because I could see no reason why the conspirators should have chosen to make you look like the Duke instead of some anonymous peasant. Why did they?"

"It is not so crazy as it seems," the Provost said, rubbing his neck as if he was glad to have it back, "if you know the Brotherhood. Granted, our rule is based on absolute obedience. There is no republic. The brethren never vote. But the Abbot's powers stop short of throwing the Provost in jail without a trial. If Radu had seen my face in that dungeon he would have rushed off to tell his commanding officer or his friends. The news would have been all through Vamky in no time."

Volpe rose and stretched. He was a big man, and his dirty robe no longer suggested it was concealing flab. "As for why the Duke's face. Well, several of the men involved, like that Achim brute, believed I was who I seemed to be, so they thought they were committing treason. They obeyed, but they were very careful, and they did not go around blabbing about it! Besides, Minhea had the conjurement to hand, the illicit copy of the one he had made for the Duke. It would have taken time to make another. I want to know how you did this. How did Radu even get you in? Come along."

Bellman followed him out of the cell. "We learned a valid password by very foul means. No matter how we got *in*. The question that matters now, my lord, is whether you can get us safely *out*. Even better, can you regain control of your troops in time to block the marriage?"

"Has Abbot Minhea gone to the wedding?" The Provost looked from Radu to Bellman and back, but both shook their heads.

"Sir. We do not know."

Volpe examined Samuil's sword and chose Gerlach's instead. "Then let us find out! And yes, we must stop that wedding at all costs." He clasped Bellman's hand in a rock-crushing grip. Their eyes were level. "I thank you, Herr Bellman. I owe you my life. But saving my life was not your motive."

Bellman was having trouble focusing, let alone thinking. His tongue weighed so much that even talking was an effort. "I have friends to avenge. And you have a worse loss than that. Can you call the killer to account now?"

"I must," Volpe said. "I should have done it years ago."

Johanna reeled back in amazement. Ringwood caught her to steady her. The lantern he had been carrying shattered on the rocks far below.

Hearing the noise, Rubin turned to peer across the gap. "Johanna, my sweet! You made it at last. That is you, isn't it? That really is her, isn't it, Kuri?"

And that really was her husband. What a fool she had been!

The hooded knight-brother glanced down at something he held on his lap and nodded. He had his back to the fire, so his face was invisible inside his hood.

"Kuri's been tracking you, you see, my dear. When we discovered you weren't in the house, Kuri located your baggage, all full of things with memories of you. He has a cunning little contrivance to track you from that. When we saw you were going along the Luitgard tunnel, we decided to come on ahead and make sure you arrived safely. You lost János, I see. No great loss there. And one of your boy swordsmen? Ditto, I'm sure."

She found her voice. "Are you *you*?" That bizarre perch in this dangerously haunted ruin seemed such an infinitely unlikely location for the husband she remembered. "The real Rubin? Not another imposter?"

He laughed erratically. She had rarely seen him drunk, but perhaps he was merely very tired. It was almost dawn, after all, with traces of brightness in the sky above the jagged coronet of the keep. Or maybe she was the one who was crazy. Certainly she was ready to drop with fatigue.

"Of course I'm me, my sweeting! Who else did you ever think I was? You, maybe? Kuri tells me you've been playing at being me all summer, running around Eurania. I hope you didn't damage my reputation *too* much, my dear, mm? Did you have fun? Was she having fun, Kuri?"

"Great fun, Your Highness," the other man said.

"Oh, that's good." The Grand Duke sighed. "Because the fun is over now, dearest. This is Cantor Kuritsyn, by the way. He will be proclaimed Provost of the Brotherhood during the enthronement assembly this evening. My nephew met with a serious accident. I am grieved you must miss all the festivities, sweeting! You would have enjoyed them so much."

"But you are going to rescue us, aren't you?" Johanna said. "Get us out of here? That was why you came?"

Her husband sighed. "No, my sweeting, I'm afraid not. Quite the reverse, in fact. My wedding is just too important to me. You simply cannot imagine how I've suffered all these months while you were gadding about the continent having fun. The waiting! The burning desire! It's very unhealthy for a nation when its head of state cannot concentrate on his work properly. I pined until half my wardrobe doesn't fit me anymore. But that's all over now. Tonight she will be mine. I've set aside an hour between the enthronement and the state banquet for the deflowering."

"He's mad," Trudy muttered. "Raving, foaming, gibbering crazy."

Johanna ignored her. "So what are you going to do with me?"

"Me? Nothing, my love. Didn't János explain about the

keep? Maybe he didn't know! What do you think, Kuri? Did János know?"

The hooded man shook his head and said something whose only audible word was "Luitgard."

"Yes, he must have," the Duke agreed. "It was virtually suicide. You see, my dear, the keep at Donehof belongs to me. For centuries it has been a convenient solution for embarrassing problems, a private midden where the Grand Dukes can dump their refuse. I've never had need of it before, and my father not often, I think. My grandfather was a rogue, though. Anyone who peeved him at all was shipped out here to the Keep. The *schattenherren* did the rest. Very convenient, very economical, never any awkward bodies to explain. They don't even need to be fed."

She had been wrong all along. That was Rubin, not Volpe. Volpe would never speak in that mincing, gloating fashion. He wouldn't sully his honor by pretending to be Rubin at all. She should have seen that half a year ago. It had been Rubin all the time and she had been a blind fool, refusing to believe the unbearable obvious.

"You're just going to leave me here to die?"

"I have no choice, my dear. I can't have you making a scene at the wedding, embarrassing everybody. You have been very lucky, you know. Kuri here is the most successful assassin since Silvercloak and you escaped him not just once but three times!"

Trudy was peering at her . . . or past her. "Don't look around, Your Grace," she said softly. "Just keep the madman talking until Ringwood gets there."

Only now Johanna realized that her one surviving Blade was no longer at her back. Gets there? Gets where? Past the shadowmen? The keep was still dark. He would never make it.

"Keep him talking!" Trudy repeated in an urgent whisper.

"That wasn't luck!" Johanna shouted. "If that man's your hired killer, then he isn't capable of stomping earthworms."

"No! No! No! You were lucky, that's all. Chance playing absurd tricks! Tell her how lucky she was, Kuri."

Cantor Kuritsyn stood up. "We should leave, Your Highness. We promised to be back before dawn and we don't want men coming to look for you, do we?"

"It isn't close to dawn yet! Where are the shadowmen? You said the shadowmen would follow her."

"They will, don't worry."

"Are you so certain?" Johanna yelled. "You tried to kill me with shadowmen before, didn't you? Twice you tried. Once at Blanburg, but we had Harald with us and he knew what to do. What an incompetent, brainless way to try to kill someone!"

"They came close," Kuritsyn said. He had a harsh, unpleasant voice. "And even closer in Grandon."

"Never! You think I was fool enough to sleep in the dark? They killed a bunch of innocent men, is all, and if King Athelgar had listened when the Baron and I warned him, they would have done no damage at all." Then Queen Tasha would not have talked Athelgar into sending her to Ironhall, so she would never have met Bellman, and where was he, now? Dead or captive in Vamky? No Bellman and no Blades. Ranter dead. Ringwood . . .

The silence of the night was broken by the ring of swords in the darkness below.

The moment Ringwood decided that the fat man over there by the fire was the real Grand Duke Rubin, his binding sent him plunging headlong down the stair. On the face of it, he was abandoning his ward in the face of danger, but if Rubin was the spider in the web, the cause of all the trouble, then he was responsible for *all* the deaths, even tonight's, and should pay the penalty. More important, putting a sword at Rubin's throat was the most likely way to extract the Duchess from this trap. At least, that was what Ringwood assumed was happening. Bindings worked like instincts and had no need of logic.

Anyone with lesser reflexes than a Blade would have fallen off those greasy, irregular treads by the third or four stride, but Ringwood hurtled down them about ten times faster than he would normally have dared in daylight and dry weather. He even managed to draw his sword, which was no easy matter when the curtain wall was flying by him on his right-hand side. He had barely done so when he come to the first shadowman pursuer.

The figure loomed out of the night below, climbing doggedly and carrying a halberd in both hands. Even in the darkness Ringwood recognized the short-legged waddle of János. Trudy still had the Count's sword, but a halberd would be just as deadly in these impossible fighting conditions.

Sir Tancred had said that Shadowmen seemed to have superhuman strength but sluggish reflexes. Gambling on that and using his velocity, Ringwood leaped over the halberd and rammed the János corpse with both feet. He hit the wall with his shoulder, slid down it, and landed on his seat with a crack that seemed to lift his skull off his neck, but the shadowman pitched backward and impacted another behind him. Together they toppled, rolled outward, and were gone. The corpses themselves fell with no sound. He heard their weapons clang on rocks and could tell that the drop was still too far to risk a jump. It would be like jumping onto iron spikes, anyway.

The jolt of agony as he stood up made him wonder if he'd broken his pelvis, but he was more worried by the broadsword coming straight down at him. He parried it out-

ward with all his strength, clutching *Bad News* two-handed.
Engagement with the massive weapon gave him leverage to
push himself safely back against the wall. *Clang!* But the
corpse's strength shocked him. Again and again it chopped
at him and he parried. *Clang! Clang! Clang!* Then at last he
found enough leverage to force the broadsword outward; the
corpse lost its balance and went over the edge. Third man
down, this time with a crashing of small timber.

He started downstairs again. He'd known since the night
he was bound that the binding had improved his night vision. Ironhall had several legends of Blades fighting in pitch
darkness, although few were well documented. He wasn't
aware of *seeing* at all in this battle. He was just behaving as
if he could see. He knew where and what things were.

Like that fourth shadowman ahead, a great hulking carcass that could not possibly have come through from the
tunnel by any normal means. How many of the monsters
were there? Was he going to have to fight the entire corpse
population of the keep before he could get off this accursed
stair? And what good was he doing anyway? The monsters
could fight on after their heads were cut off, Tancred had
said, so broken bones wouldn't stop them. Only dawn. Until
then they would just keep coming back for more.

The fourth one took him with the same ploy he'd used
successfully against the third. It lunged to his right and he
was forced to parry toward the wall. The shadowman flipped
him out like a pancake.

He turned a complete somersault on the way down. He
wondered how the shadowman conjuration worked and
whether the fall cancelled out the contact in some way, or if
he was now doomed to haunt the keep through all eternity.
He even had time to hope he would land on his head and
smash his brains out, not just lie there broken and suffering
for hours or days until he died. Then someone caught him.

♦ 7 ♦

Three men in stained white robes strode through the Vamky labyrinth. Bellman supported Radu, who was in even worse shape than he was, and both struggled to keep up with the impatient Volpe. The Provost knew exactly where he was going, but it involved a long, circuitous trek. He threw open cell doors and marched in, snarling orders. Startled brethren jerked awake and hastened to obey, grabbing up sword and robe, but he had to rouse his most trusted subordinates first, and there was no system in the locations of their cells. Only when he had set his counterrevolution in motion could he spare a moment for his two rescuers.

"Cantor Isidor!"

A white-haired, scrawny man opened his eyes in bewilderment, blinked up at the Provost's lantern. "Sir!"

"Brother, I am suppressing a mutiny. Call only on men you can trust absolutely and beware of betrayal. The password is 'Morning light' and the rejoinder 'Justice and retribution.' Got that?"

"Sir." The old man sat up. "Morning light. Justice and retribution."

"You may arrest or kill anyone who does not know this. We urgently require a healing. Senior Knight-brother Radu, here, has been injured. This man is a valuable ally and the finest swordsman I have ever seen, Sir Bellman of Chivial. Both men need anklets. Then feed them, dress them in highway informals, and have them ready to ride at first light."

"Sir."

The door closed with a bang. Cantor Isidor just sat and stared after the Provost for a moment, then looked to his two guests. His scraggy mouth folded into a smile. "I hope you two can remember all that better than I can. Pass me my gown and sword, brother. Repeat what the Provost just said."

In seconds the old man was ready to leave. A cantor's belt was green. "Have you ever used anklets?"

"Sir," Radu said.

"There's some on the shelf there. Wait here until I send for you."

"Sir."

The door closed.

Radu tried to raise an arm and winced, for his gown had adhered to the wounds on his back. "Give me one and take one for yourself. Wear it next to the skin. Either foot will do."

The anklets were strips of leather with thongs at one end. Bellman wrapped one around his left ankle, above his sandal, and at once felt a pleasurable tingle spreading up his leg. He knelt to help Radu.

"Fatigue relief," Radu said. "They're good for about a day. Try to eat often, or you may need weeks to recover your strength. When the anklet starts to hurt, you must remove it. It should be destroyed then, because the power has gone out of it. And after that you must sleep. You will have no choice. That can happen suddenly, and a second inspiration before you have recovered from this one could kill you."

"I feel better already!" Also hungry. *Reeeeeeeally* hungry. Tingling all over now, Bellman began to pace restlessly. He sneezed.

The door was opened by a hooded figure wearing a blue sword belt. "Morning light."

"Justice and retribution," Radu responded. "Sir."

"Brother, I am to take you and your companion to the octogram."

The dark corridors of Vamky were busier now, with brethren running in twos and fours. Somewhere bells were tolling. Bellman waited impatiently on the sidelines while eight men chanted to heal Radu of a beating for the second time in less than two days.

After that it was Radu who set the pace. He led Bellman at a trot to the quartermaster's, where they were outfitted in fresh traveling clothes of white leather, simple in style and of exceptional quality. The breeches were supple, the jerkins hard as armor. Bellman was given a sword belt checkered in blue and white, a blue cloak of soft wool, and a shiny steel helmet. Novices and squires fussed around, brushing, polishing, checking the fit.

Then—*at last!*—Radu led him to a huge refectory and let him eat. He gorged, mostly on meat: beef, goose, sheep liver, washed down with pitchers of buttery milk. He could have eaten even Ringwood under the table. Radu not only kept up but surpassed him. Other men were hurrying in, eating hastily.

He sneezed several times.

Radu frowned across at him. "You caught a cold!"

"Hardly surprising after yesterday."

"Yes, but the anklet will make it worse. You have the choice of fatigue or a bad attack of sniffles."

"Restored, I see? Do not rise." Volpe stood at their side, shaven, shorn, and clad in much the same costume as they. He was a big man, conscious of his power and authority, although his only symbols of rank were a silver sword belt and a horn hung on a baldric. "You have only a few minutes, and you will need that food. Remember you are borrowing strength from future days. No matter how sprightly you feel, you must try not to overdo it."

"Sir," Radu said with his mouth full of pheasant, "my experience has been that consorting with Bellman leaves a man no choice but to overdo it or be utterly shamed."

"Baldertwaddle!" Bellman exclaimed. "You were the one who got me into trouble. I am ready whenever you are, my lord. Vamky is secure?"

An eagle glare warned him of his impudence, but he was still in favor. "It is," the Provost said. "Thanks to you. And justice is about to be done. The boy is safe until we need him. Where is Her Highness?"

So Johanna was now Her Highness, was she? That title boded well.

"She went on to Donehof with Count János, my lord." Bellman's euphoria faltered under the Provost's scowl. "Not good?"

"Probably not. János is a deferred brother." The Provost smiled thinly at Bellman's alarm. "He asked to be relieved of his duties for family reasons. That is known hereabouts as 'breeding leave,' but only the obligation of celibacy is withdrawn, and he may be recalled to duty at any time until the hour of his death. There are thousands of men in and around Krupina similarly bound. When the Fadrenschloss refugees took shelter at Brikov, we looked for János's file and could not find it. I sent Radu to retrieve the boy. If Minhea's men have located János's records since then, he is theirs."

Bellman wondered again how much free will the brethren had, whether their oaths were spiritually implanted, like the Blades', but he dared not ask.

"Sir?" Radu said.

"Speak."

"Sir. János knew I had been behind the child's disappearance. I hadn't told him, obviously. He questioned me very severely about that."

"Almost killed him," Bellman said.

"But he also asked why I had come to Brikov and he would not accept my father's funeral as my reason. Eventually I told him I was apostatizing, my lord, because of what I had seen . . . or thought I had seen. He . . . he redoubled his efforts after that."

Volpe shrugged. "Of course the board will ask what you revealed under torture, but expect it to be lenient about that."

"Sir? Board?" Radu lost color.

"You should have reported your suspicions of treason to your commanding officer, of course. The fact that you returned voluntarily will offset anything you said about apostatizing. Expect to be demoted and given a chance to reaffirm your oath. The Duchess may be in very grave peril, but our mission cannot become any more urgent than it is already. You ride well, Herr Bellman?"

"Yes, my lord." He wasn't as good as Radu, but he would uphold the honor of Ironhall if it killed him. He had more motive than any of them.

Lord Volpe's smile was disbelief and challenge. "You will ride on my left. I want to hear your story in detail. Knight-brother Radu, Banneret Dusburg will assign you your place. Dawn approaches!" The Provost put the horn to his lips and made the hall ring.

Ranter was not breathing. At the moment of death his eyes had rolled up and the lids were partly closed, revealing only slits of white. He stank of death and the indignities of death. He was cold. He . . . it . . . no, *he* was making no aggressive move. He was not moving at all. Not breathing.

Ringwood was breathing, gasping for breath, heart drumming like all the world's woodpeckers. He was not dead, not yet, but he was helpless as a baby in the shadowman's arms.

"Put me down, brother?"

Ranter set him down. Now it was clear that he had been stabbed and slashed half to pieces. He had several black-crusted wounds in his chest, and his throat had been cut. Blades never died easily. His hips and shoulders were abraded to the bone, cloth and flesh torn away where he had come through the hole from the tunnel, but those wounds had not bled. *Invincible* hung at his side.

A dozen other corpses stood around in the darkness,

watching, motionless. Was this sudden loss of aggression a sign that dawn was near? Or . . . like Sir Bernard and Sir Richey? *They became shadowmen, too,* Sir Tancred had said, *and we found their bodies with the others in the morning. But they did not attack the living, the way the dead Yeomen did. Perhaps they didn't get the chance, but Grand Wizard thinks their binding may have given them some immunity, at least for a while.*

Ringwood forced some spit into his mouth and pointed up at the fire. "The man up there wants to kill our ward, brother. I must go up there and kill him. Will you help me?"

Ranter turned and stepped out into space. His foot landed unerringly on a jagged boulder a long pace away and lower. The other swung over to a foothold on a jagged spike of stone, and his hand reached for a grip . . . he was doing all that in the dark, and Ringwood was seeing it in the dark. The moment Ranter's boot cleared the first stepping-stone Ringwood put his own there in a long half-stride, half-fall. There was no way to do this slowly. He must keep up his momentum just to remember the moves. He followed his dead guide across the deadly labyrinth, up and down, over six-foot gaps, under overhangs. Ranter plowed through stands of shoulder-high thistles and jumped down eight-foot drops without a care. Yet he did seem to know what his companion was doing, because once Ringwood found himself dangling by one hand and unable to find a second grip or haul himself up by the one he had. An icy fist closed on his wrist and lifted him like a trout in a net.

"Thanks, brother," he gasped, but Ranter was already on the move.

Ranter never spoke. Ranter's throat had been ripped open, after all. Ranter, face it, was very dead. Perhaps his corpse would play foul and turn on Ringwood without warning, but until then Ringwood could not refuse its help. Some of the other shadowmen were following, making just enough noise that he knew they were there.

Crossbow kept niggling at him. Even leaping out into blackness to find a toehold that he knew was there only by some sort of spiritualist faith, he kept thinking *crossbow*. He had seen no crossbows, smelled no crossbows, tasted no crossbows. No one had mentioned crossbows. His binding was sending him hunches. The way Johanna had described her husband, Rubin should not be here in person. To stay in character he should have stayed home and read about it tomorrow in the comfort of his study. No, he had come to see with his own eyes that this time she died right and died real, and he would keep her there on that staircase until there was light enough for Knight-brother Kuritsyn to use a crossbow. Johanna was at point-blank range, and even a near-miss could kill someone perched on that staircase.

When the nightmare journey ended, there was no doubt that the sky was brightening. The rain had not stopped, but clouds alone could not keep the world dark forever. Voices came drifting down in the wind, the words inaudible, Johanna pleading with Rubin. The ruined chimney block rose from its bed of rubble to tower to the sky. If one thought of the jagged fragments of former floors and walls protruding at all angles as blades, then it became a gigantic mace. The shadowmen didn't expect Ringwood to climb *that,* did they? They expected something. There were a lot of them there, standing around like thirsty men outside a tavern.

Ranter climbed a tilted slab, turned his back against the wall at the top, and cupped his hands. Shivering with distaste, Ringwood took hold of his dead friend's jerkin, placed a boot on the step offered, and climbed. When he was standing on Ranter's shoulders he was still not quite high enough to reach the doorway above him, so he reluctantly used the top of his former friend's head as one more step. The corpse did not object.

Ringwood caught hold of the sill and hauled himself up. He was on a stair landing, with one flight going up from there and another down. Straight ahead of him was a tunnel with only darkness beyond it, but he could feel wind on his face and decided it was a passage through the thickness of the curtain wall. At the end of it he found a heavy door propped open by a lump of stone. He peered out, seeing campfires with men standing around on guard. He was about one story above ground level, but there was a ladder at his toes. For the first time in many hours, he felt the siren call of hope. The soldiers were a problem, but there might be a way out of this mess after all.

He retraced his steps to the stairs. Several shadowmen were standing on the downward flight, blocking it—so he wouldn't go the wrong way, perhaps? How stupid did they think the living could be? The other had to be the route the Duke and his henchman had taken. He drew *Bad News*.

"You are going to be very bad news for somebody, my sweet!" he whispered. He had not taken two steps before a hand like an iron glove closed on his shoulder. He squeaked in alarm, then realized that it belonged to Ranter, who had followed him up. Many other shadowmen were scrambling up after him.

"What's wrong, brother?" His voice came out more shrill than he had expected. "This is the way up, isn't it?"

Ranter's dead face did not change. His grip on Ringwood's shoulder became unbearable.

"What? What's wrong? Stop! What are you trying . . ." He crumpled under that relentless weight. Even alive, Ranter had enjoyed showing off his brawn, and now he folded Ringwood small, crumpling him down on his knees and farther, until his nose was almost on the first tread.

There he spied a thin golden thread, spread across from side to side.

"Ah! This is your problem?" He had been brought here just to remove that? "Is this a sort of warding cord?" He was talking to himself. "You can't cross it?" There was no one there to answer him, only dead people, but the idea was logical, because there must be some sort of conjuration to keep the walking dead from leaving by that door he had found. "I go first, all right?" The hand did not move. He could not even twist around to see Ranter's face, but it would not tell him anything anyway. "I promise you I'll let you and your companions have them before daylight." The chill hand was lifted from his shoulder. He stood up.

He lifted the cord on the tip of his sword and nothing ill happened. Up the stairs he went, bearing it before him, and Ranter led the army of the dead at his heels.

Two flights up Ringwood heard voices and went more cautiously until he found himself looking out at the Duke's aerie; the Rat's nest. Nothing had changed. The fire had dwindled but was still a powerful blaze, bright enough to neutralize shadowmen. The two evildoers had their backs to the doorway—paunchy Rubin perched on his stool and the white-robed, sword-bearing brother standing beside him. Both were facing out into the rainy dusk, looking across at Johanna and Trudy, still over there on the stairs, but sitting now, huddling together for warmth. Still talking. The crossbow and a quiver of quarrels stood in a corner behind the fireplace, where they would not be visible from outside.

There was enough light to start shooting now.

"I assure you that I even spoke to you!" the knight-brother said. "I was dressed as an inquisitor and nobody looks very hard at inquisitors, or speaks to them unless they must. Not even other inquisitors!"

If Johanna had noticed that her Blade had just joined her husband's party, she give no sign. Yet her next question might have been designed for him.

"So that was *after* you planted the firefly in Quamast House?"

"I have already said so."

Another golden thread lay across the doorstep. Ringwood slid his sword point under that one, too, and stepped forward to flip both of them into the fire. The other men felt the floor sway and heard his footsteps crunching on the rubbly surface. They turned. The swordsman drew—fast, but not fast enough to be worrisome.

"There he is," the Duke said. "Oh, the poor thing is hurt. Put him out of his misery, Cantor."

The two swordsmen eyed each other carefully, and Kuri edged away from the Duke, giving himself more room.

"No," Ringwood said. "I am a Blade, so I am in charge here now. He slew six of my brothers and another died tonight because of him—and you, too, Duke. You are just as guilty. Now I will do the killing."

After all those hours of failure and self-blame he ought to be exulting at the smell of vengeance, but he could feel no emotion. He was an execution machine, an insentient instrument of justice. Numb, and implacable as a shadowman.

"Be careful!" True yelled across from the stair. "Kuritsyn's a conjurer. He may have tricks."

There was no room to stage a showoff fencing bout. Since Ringwood had promised these two jackals to the shadowmen, just driving them off the edge would be a breach of faith. Duke Rubin jumped to his feet and grabbed up his stool to use as a weapon.

"Don't be ridiculous!" Ringwood said wearily.

But even a stool could be dangerous. He flashed forward at Kuritsyn, feinted, parried the riposte, and swept *Bad News*

around to strike the Duke's arm. He had recovered two paces
before the stool even hit the floor or the Duke screamed. The
platform swayed unnervingly.

"First royal blood to me," he said. Kuri came for him,
saber flickering firelight in a series of fierce cuts. His was a
showy technique, not one to impress a Blade. Ringwood
played with him for a few passes, then riposted to cut his
shoulder. *"Bernard!"* He parried the next pathetic lunge and
opened a gash down his ribs. *"Richey!"*

The cantor cried out and recovered perilously close to the
edge. Ringwood needed three or four careful lunges to move
him away from it and turn him, so he could be driven back
to the door: *Clang! Clang! Clang!* For the first time he
glimpsed the face within the hood—fortyish, lean, twisted in
a rictus of terror.

Then—*"Valiant!"* That was a nasty cut on the thigh,
spilling blood like a black tide.

The knight-brother threw down his sword and raised his
hands. "Stop! Mercy!"

"Mercy? You showed no mercy!" Ringwood put *Bad
News* at the end of the wretch's nose. He could cut the man
to straw now, but there was no joy in this. "Back with you!"

Terror-stricken, Kuritsyn backed away and *Bad News* followed him, step by step, until he was at the doorway.

"You are judged guilty and sentenced to whatever you did
to my brothers," Ringwood said. "Ranter! You and your
friends can take this one now."

A dozen dead hands reached out and dragged the knight-
brother back into darkness. He screamed several times, each
cry shriller than the last. *Yorick, East, Clovis . . . Ranter.*

It had been obscenely easy! Not even winded by the bout,
Ringwood strolled over to the crossbow, carried it to the
edge, and hurled it off. He had been expecting the Duke to
intervene, perhaps rush him in the hope of overcoming him

with his vastly greater weight, but Rubin was clutching his wounded arm, trying to apply pressure with a silken kerchief.

"Take off your cloak!" Ringwood said.

"What?" The Duke looked up in terror. "I'm sorry your friends had to die, young man. It was all my wife's fault, you see, but husbands should keep their wives under better control than that, so I'm willing to pay some sort of compensation if that—"

"Take off your cloak!" The sky was getting bright. There was little time left. As the shivering Duke obeyed, Ringwood looked across to the audience. The jury, he thought.

"Your Grace, Sister Gertrude? Have you any more questions to put to the accused, or know you any good reason why I should not pass and carry out sentence?"

"No!" It sounded like both of them together.

"NO!" The Duke fell on his knees. "Killing me will solve nothing."

"It will make the world a better, cleaner place," Ringwood said, scooping up the cloak. As he walked over to the hearth, he sheathed his sword to leave both hands free. "Ranter! This one's yours, brother."

Ranter emerged from the darkness of the doorway, but his feet made no sound on the gritty floor and he cast no shadow in the firelight. The Duke screamed and scrambled to his feet. Wailing, he backed away until it seemed he would pitch off the platform.

"Do you want to do it?" Ringwood asked, just to be certain.

The wraith nodded. Its cut throat made moist noises.

Ringwood draped the great cloak over the fireplace arch and held it there to cut off the light.

Ranter solidified. He shuffled across to the Duke, took him by the neck, and forced him down, first to his knees, then onto his belly. He bent his head back until his neck snapped, then released him and straightened up.

The cloak was smoldering, so Ringwood tossed it into the hearth. The dead Blade became smokily transparent as the light blazed up more brightly. He turned and headed for the door, blank eyes and frozen features conveying nothing.

"Brother?" Ringwood's throat was so tight he could barely speak. "That was well done! Wait!" He caught the corpse's arm. It was flimsy, insubstantial, yet he could feel the chill of death through the sodden, tattered cloth. Ranter detected the contact and stopped.

"Don't go, brother! Stay here. You'll die at first light, but you're already dead. Don't go down to the cellars, please! Don't be a shadowman. Get it over with and die properly. I'll stay with you, I promise. I'll hold your hand until the sun comes up, if that will help. And afterward we'll return you to the elements with a proper funeral."

Ranter resumed his walk, pulling right through Ringwood's fingers.

"Brother! *Invincible?* At least send her home! Let me take her so she can hang in the sky of swords."

The shadowman showed no sign that he heard. Ringwood watched him vanish into the dark of the stairs. Dead Rubin went shuffling after his killer, head hung at an odd angle.

Ringwood fought back sobs. None for Rubin. Most for Ranter. A few for himself. He had won, but he should have done better. Why was victory so hollow? Had the fight, when it came, been too easy? Or was it just that killing off the evil did not restore the good?

When the women started shouting for him, he walked as close to the edge as he dared. He yelled his words to the world. "The shadowmen are gone! The villains are dead!" The keep echoed for him. "There's a way out of here below me. Go back down the stair and find shelter from this accursed rain. I'll come and get you."

"I love you!" True shouted. "You're my hero always!"

"That goes for both of us!" Johanna said.

He watched them start down, and then surreptitiously went to the fireplace and tried to warm himself, but his clothes were so wet that the heat just seemed to make him shiver harder. After a few minutes he decided that the daylight was now bright enough to banish shadowmen, and he had better leave before the soldiers outside came looking for their lost leaders. At the bottom of the stairs, he stumbled on a sheathed sword lying across his path. It bore a cat's-eye gem on the pommel.

✦ 8 ✦

When the Provost of Vamky rode out, he rode in style. Bellman was astride a black, seventeen-hand stallion that would have turned the King of Chivial emerald with envy, and every man in the company was mounted as well or better. Yet this was not an elaborate turnout as Vamky judged such things—just a standard-bearer in the van, Volpe with his Chivian guest, and fifty steely-eyed young swordsmen churning along the sodden roads like a tidal wave, other traffic be damned. Fortunately there was no other traffic in the cold dawn light. Plate mail would be more impressive, but today Volpe wanted speed, and speed he was getting.

The rain had stopped. The Duke might yet get a fine day for his wedding.

Volpe overwhelmed, irresistible as a landslide. The only man Bellman had ever met to compare with him was Grand Master, but Grand Master was a thrusting sword, with both point and edge. Volpe seemed to be pure broadsword. He began flashing questions when they pounded out the monastery gate, and by the time they crossed Olden Bridge, he knew everything Bellman had seen or done since Johanna arrived at Ironhall.

After that he fell silent, leaving Bellman free to chew on his own worries. Johanna—assuming she had not already been betrayed by János to her odious husband and murdered in the night—Johanna would recover her son, so Bellman could count his expedition a success. Her happiness was what he wanted. But Volpe was obviously determined to nullify Rubin one way or another, which would leave Volpe running the country, so then what happened to Frederik? In a sense his mother would lose him again, for he would be state property. And Bellman? Even if Volpe allowed the Grand Duchess a significant role in rearing the new Grand Duke, Krupina would never tolerate her marrying a penniless lowborn foreign adventurer. If she had to choose between Bellman and Frederik, Bellman would lose.

And that was not even the least of his worries, because he still did not know the true story of how Volpe had landed in a dungeon in his own fortress. Betrayal, was all he had said. But suppose he had been the traitor? Suppose he had tried to kill Rubin, Frederik, Johanna, and even his own wastrel son, and Rubin had imprisoned him because of it? Suppose clever-clever Bellman had intervened on the wrong side and released a monster? Rubin might be remarrying because he genuinely believed his wife and son were dead. The brief mourning might seem callous, but he was fifty and must be impatient for an heir.

"That's Fadrenschloss," Volpe said, pointing.

Bellman saw only hills and trees, but nodded wisely.

"As a child," the Provost went on, changing the subject without warning, "he was always a perfect little gentleman as long as there were adults around. But the kitchen sluts were terrified of him." Was he about to volunteer his side of the story? That would be a surprising courtesy, but he would have some hidden reasons, no doubt.

"The family married him off as soon as it was half-decent and hoped that would be the end of it. When his first wife died we could not be sure." The gathering daylight caught a rueful smile that seemed to be directed only to the road ahead. "One lesson I learned early in my military career, Jack Bellman, is that *pessimists live longer!* Good news is much easier to believe than bad. Give your enemy reason to believe that you are far away and nine times out of ten he will believe it right up to the moment you kick his door in. It is true in ordinary life, too. We all find reasons to accept sugary fables and ignore unwelcome tidings. The family did not *want* to believe that the girl's death had been anything but an unfortunate misjudgment.

"He threw the second one out a window. This time there was no doubt. One of the wineglasses reeked of poppy, so much so that he must have had to carry her across the room. He was Grand Duke and I his sworn vassal, but obviously something had to be done. I told him there would be no more marriages. He agreed. He didn't like what happened, either, he just couldn't help himself. He promised to stick to the lowborn and pay them off as soon as he tired of them, and that scheme worked for more than thirty years. Even when I was away campaigning, he kept to our agreement. Apart from that one weakness he was a good Duke—frugal, prudent, and too lazy to go looking for trouble as so many rulers do. The girls did well out of it. They had to endure degrading carnal abuse for a couple of weeks, but afterward they went off with enough money to buy a decent husband. A few days' rest and most of them were as good as new and perfectly happy again.

"Then that idiot von Fader! He knew the game but he wouldn't play. If she had been any sort of blood relation I could have understood it, but she was nothing to him. By the time I heard of it the marriage was being proclaimed. I tried to frighten the girl out of it, but that didn't work."

The Provost turned his intimidating stare on Bellman, who assumed he was expected to comment.

"Her Highness does not scare easily, my lord."

"Obviously. I underestimated her." Again that grim smile came and went. "Women are not my forte. I warned Rubin I would tolerate no more violence, but you can't reason with him when he's in heat. I arranged for the Court to boycott her and hoped he would quietly put her away when he came to his senses.

"Unfortunately, she behaved perfectly. She did as she was told, caused no trouble, never complained, even when he went back to bedroom minuet again. She dropped a son right on the legal deadline, and after that putting her away was out of the question. The commoners worshiped her because she was one of their own and they dreaded me inheriting. They certainly didn't want Karl. Frankly, I couldn't see Karl as a duke, either. Rubin never let her out of the palace. He told her he was concerned for her safety, but he just didn't want to hear her cheered, because he never got cheered. He is not a cheerable sort of duke.

"This spring the Margrave's son died and we all realized that his daughter would inherit the March. Even before I broke that news to Rubin I knew what was liable to happen. I tried to mend a fence or two with the . . . with Her Highness, but of course she wouldn't trust me.

"I suspect that Rubin had already decided to dispose of her. He was tired of seeing her around, maybe, or he just can't stand being married. I don't understand how his clock ticks, but he knew he would need something more subtle than defenestration to satisfy me.

"He began by bribing Abbot Minhea, which wasn't difficult. Abbot and Provost never get along. That's always been the idea behind the joint rule, and we two were no exception. Rubin swore he'd let Minhea arrange a vacancy and name a crony as my successor. The old fool agreed and so Rubin gained the spiritual resources of Vamky. That's where the locket came from.

"He also enlisted my no-good son, which was probably even easier. I tried to bridle Karl by keeping him on a short purse string, but he had become very skilled at sponging off women. Rubin twisted him like yarn. 'Seduce Johanna,' he said. 'Get her with child, then I'll pack her off in disgrace and that brat of hers with her, and you'll be second in line again.' The young fool accepted the challenge, of course. He didn't see that getting rid of two heirs might be twice as good as getting rid of one. He also discovered he wasn't the slick seducer he thought he was when it came to women his own age."

"You don't suppose," Bellman snapped, "that Her Highness might deserve some credit for not being deceived?"

Volpe shot a sour glance at him. "I suppose it's possible. At any rate, Rubin tired of waiting on Karl. On the way to Trenko, he arranged for the Baron to be told I was plotting a coup. He knew the old man would tell Johanna and she would hare back to Krupa to defend her child. Rubin himself went off to Zolensa that night to establish an alibi. He announced that his wife was at Fadrenschloss and of course everyone believed him. Karl, armed with the locket, did the rest. Spirits know where he was taking her."

"He told Johanna they were headed for Vamky."

Volpe grimaced. "Then I'm glad I don't know what he thought was going to happen when they got there. Minhea sent Cantor Kuritsyn to set up the ambush. The man's a virtuoso assassin. It worked well, but not perfectly. Perfection would have been all the bodies in view and identified.

"Rubin suspected that von Fader was hiding the girl . . . Duchess, I mean. So he burned Fadrenschloss to smoke her out." Volpe barked a laugh. "I'm supposed to be the warrior in the family, but I have more scruples than he does. Minhea had set up roadblocks to catch her when she tried to escape. I suppose her body and the child's would have been retroactively found in the wreckage of the coach."

The conversation was interrupted then. The standard-bearer signaled a turn and led the column off the highway onto a tree-flanked avenue. Volpe blew a warning call on his horn. In a few moments the troop arrived at a stockade set within paddocks and fenced pasture where, to Bellman's amazement, about sixty fresh mounts stood waiting, already saddled and tethered in lines. Some hands were hastily tightening girths and others were still tumbling out of the buildings to assist. The Royal Guard was never so organized.

"Take your pick," Volpe said as he dismounted.

Needing no second invitation, Bellman beelined in on a four- or five-year-old chestnut who looked as if he could run all the way to Chivial without drawing breath. A brown-belted junior knight-brother had made the same choice. They met on opposite sides of the stallion's head and for a moment there was challenge in the air. Then the knight glanced down at Bellman's sword belt, saluted without the least change of expression, and walked away.

"What do you think of that, big fellow?" Bellman asked as he reached for the stirrup buckles. The chestnut rolled his eyes and said nothing.

There was a slight delay in departing. When everyone else was in the saddle, waiting, the Provost stood deep in conversation with two men, one of whom was Radu. Checking on Bellman, perhaps?

Volpe picked up his story again as soon as the column was back on the highway. "I was taken in like everyone else at first, I admit. I believed in the accident." The big man laughed. "More wishful thinking! I assumed I had been right after all and the gold-digger commoner had run off with a lover. It even crossed my mind that he might be my idiot son.

"When Fadrenschloss burned, I guessed that Rubin was back to his old tricks. I sent Harald Priboi to investigate, because he was a Fadrenschloss boy and known to the Baron. If he found Johanna was still alive, he was to worm his way into her confidence and keep her out of harm's way until I could straighten things out in Krupina. Having been a Rubin agent first in this affair, he then became one of mine, just by doing what he was told. He did a fine job if he chivvied her all the way to Chivial."

So far Bellman had learned almost nothing he had not worked out in his head, which was dangerously gratifying.

Volpe continued, "He sent back word that she had left the boy somewhere in Brikov. Minhea had men rummaging like mad through the archives for the password that would reactivate Knight-brother János. I dispatched Radu to locate the child, and we moved the boy to safety. I've sent word to Bad Nargstein and we'll see his mother gets him back today."

"That's very considerate of you, my lord. Her Highness will be overjoyed."

"She has earned that much." The Provost fell silent for a while. Hooves beat the mud with a steady beat. "Tell me," he said at last. "One thing still puzzles me. According to Harald's reports, the Duchess has been absolutely convinced all this time that I tried to depose Rubin, or even that I had already done so and was masquerading as him. I can see how the locket might inspire such mad notions, but surely she must have had more reason than that?"

"She saw Rubin arrive at Fadrenschloss," Bellman explained, "and he was limping."

"Seven save us! That was all? His horse stepped on his toe?"

Bellman risked a smile. "Possibly it was just chance, but he may have been testing. He must have been worried that the fake Duke had been found in the wreckage. If so, and the Baron was not shouting miracle, he must know about the locket, which was damning evidence. Sure enough, the old man was deceived by the limp. The Duke detected his distrust and knew he knew. You following this? The answer was to burn the place down and hope to eliminate Duchess, Baron, and locket all at once."

Volpe muttered an oath.

"Your nephew, my lord, is a cunning man! As for Johanna, I believe your pessimist principle came into play again. Any woman would be reluctant to believe her own husband was trying to kill both her and their son. Also, you had cast yourself as the villain long ago, if you'll forgive my saying so."

"Under the circumstances," Volpe said, "I will. Ensign! Signal a trot! Of course, when the fire failed to kill his wife, he sent Kuritsyn after her. He failed to kill her in Blanburg and then lost her, thanks to Harald. Rubin has no patience when he's in estrus, and he decided to settle for second best. He unveiled the scandal he had set up. He did a good job of it, I admit—shows what a capable man he is when he can be bothered. Soon the whole country knew that the Duchess had eloped with an unidentified man and both she and her child had gone over a cliff.

"It worked. The old Margrave needed a husband for his daughter, and was greedy for a grandson who would inherit both realms, so Frederik's death made the match more attractive. He agreed to the marriage but insisted on six months' mourning for his son. Now the time is up." He looked to Bellman. "Have I left out anything?"

Conscious that the question might be unwise, Bellman said, "Margrave Ladislas doesn't happen to be another deferred Vamky knight, does he, my lord?"

The Provost's glare almost blew him off his horse. "Are you suggesting I used an oath sworn fifty years ago to force a man to prostitute his own daughter to my homicidal nephew?"

"No, my lord," Bellman said hastily.

"Then why ask?"

"Because otherwise I do not understand why Ladislas agreed. I suspect Abbot Minhea had fewer scruples than you." He knew he should stop at that, but he must know if he had the rest of it right. "I think your approach was more subtle. Trenko being right on Vamky's doorstep, Vamky would love to see another Vamky man succeed Ladislas. I think you checked through the roll and picked out a promising wellborn younger son to take with you when you went to the funeral. You would not have used any sort of compulsion, I suspect, and no threats. But you could have dropped hints that this young man would make a good military advisor or aide-de-camp or something. Knight-brother Nickolaus, my lord?"

The predator eyes studied him as if measuring him for a larder. "You are a *dangerously* astute man, Herr Bellman."

"Thank you, my lord," Bellman said uneasily. Had he overdone it? He wanted to impress the man, not antagonize him.

"How did you find out about Nickolaus?"

"Talking with Her Highness, and with Radu. All I know is that he stayed behind in Trenko and is of gentle birth. The rest was guesswork, truly."

"Originally Prince Nickolaus, third son of the King of Microsia. Now personal equerry to the Margrave's daughter. What other secrets have you pried out of Vamky in the last two days, Herr Bellman?"

"None, my lord. I do have one more question—how you came to be locked up in your own castle."

The mercenary's face darkened. "I waited too long. I couldn't be certain that Karl had been the fake husband in the coach, and I was frightened he would turn up alive and make a fool of me. I waited for Rubin's inquiry to convene, hoping I'd glean some more evidence from that. Before I made my move, I was betrayed. Rubin thinks I'm dead, by the way. I look forward to seeing his face when I turn up at the wedding. Minhea told him I was dead, but kept me alive as insurance. I was his hold over Rubin, partly because I'm officially his legal heir now, partly because I know where the real heir is. Naturally I wouldn't say. They worked on me a bit, but they could afford to be patient. Any man will talk eventually."

They rode on for a while thinking their own thoughts. The fields were steaming in the sunlight. Autumn trees shone like beaten gold. Somewhere ahead was Donehof, but was Johanna still there? Had János taken her into Krupa with him? Or had he betrayed her to Rubin? Was she even alive?

"So what will you do now, my lord?" Bellman asked.

Again Volpe studied him, taking time to plan his words. "I don't know. Depose my nephew, certainly. Have him certified insane, most likely. Possibly execute him. Proclaim Frederik and declare myself regent, maybe." Again that sinister, craggy smile. "And certainly find out what you're up to, Herr Bellman."

If you sat perfectly still in wet clothes, the parts that touched you eventually became warm. The trouble came when you moved and rediscovered all the other parts. Johanna and Trudy had found a nook near the bottom of the staircase and huddled there, close together for warmth, trying to keep still and not even shiver. Waiting for Ringwood.

Daylight was seeping into the keep, a new day. A very strange new day it would be. Johanna was now a widow. She had watched her husband killed by one of the shadowmen his own evil had created. Volpe was also dead. Frederik, if he lived, was Grand Duke, so who would run Krupina for the next fifteen years or so? Most certainly not the daughter of Erich von Schale—not if the aristocracy had anything to do with it. She would be very lucky to be allowed any access to her son at all. Where was Bellman? Who was the prisoner he had gone to rescue, if not Rubin? And inevitably doubts crept in. Rubin visiting a haunted ruin in the middle of a stormy night was a mind-bending improbability. Had he really felt an obsessive need to watch his wife die and know she was really dead? She struggled to believe that it *must* have been Rubin. Volpe would not have tried to fight a Blade with a stool. Did Frederik have any blood relatives left? That cousin in Blanburg? He or King Athelgar would be the new duke if Frederik was dead.

Sometime in her worrying she drifted off to sleep, in spite of her cold and hunger and the pain of her wounds, for she was an all-over midden heap of cuts and bruises. Some protector Sir Ringwood had turned out to be . . .

"Time to rise and shine," Trudy said. "I want to watch the shining bit."

Johanna started awake, bewildered. "What?"

"They're here."

The sky was bright, scraps of blue between the clouds. Three men were placing a ladder across a gap only a few feet away from her, while others stood watching in the distance—Vamky brethren and Ringwood, who was tattered and bloody and snow-white with exhaustion.

Johanna's first efforts to move discovered a million aches and cold, wet places, and she shivered violently. Ringwood laid a plank on the ladder, carried another to the middle, accepted a third from one of his helpers, and in moments had built a bridge. He stepped off the near end, bowed curtly to his ward, then grabbed Trudy in what started out to be a passionate hug and at once became an explosion of *Oo!*s and *Ouch!*es, and finally happy laughter—happy because pain is a sign of life. The dead feel nothing.

One of the knight-brothers steadied the far end of the squeaking, groaning bridge while the other followed Ringwood across. He saluted Johanna.

"Your Royal Highness, I am Banneret Helmut Schwartz, sent to help you out of this wilderness. I am instructed to extend the deepest sympathy of the Order upon your—"

She nodded. "Who is in charge?"

His eyebrows rose to the brim of his helmet. "Abbot Minhea has taken personal command." His gaze flickered over her shredded, bloodstained clothes. "If you will come with us, we shall see you receive proper care, Your Grace. We can set up a field elementary to treat your injuries without delay. You may start planning what you would like for breakfast." For a man forbidden to speak to women except in emergencies, he knew exactly what to say.

She accepted the hand he offered, a powerful soldier hand, well calloused, and he led her across the shaky bridge. Ringwood came close behind her, leading Trudy but ready to grasp his ward if she needed him. It took a long while to move the ladders and planks, leapfrogging gaps across the rock pile to the tower where Rubin had died. The men chopped thistles out of her way, steadied ladders when she had to climb up or down. They led her to the base of the chimney tower, and up yet another ladder.

At the far end of a windy tunnel she paused beside a thick timber door, looking down at a pasture where campfire embers still steamed. A couple of dozen Vamky knights were forming up as a guard of honor, and at least as many were following behind her now, their work in the keep completed. Rubin's huge eight-horse ducal coach stood ignored in the background. Beyond it lay the paddocks and outbuildings of Donehof, with a backdrop of fall hills and snow-capped mountains. The main house was out of sight, behind the tower. Although the final ladder waiting for her feet ought to look like escape from a deathtrap, she could not shake the illusion that she was leaving freedom behind. For half a year she had been making choices without having to refer them to some man for his approval; now she would be taking orders again. All the beauty of the morning could not quite make up for that.

Muttering, "By your leave," Ringwood squeezed past her to go first, as if a Blade's duties included acting as soft landing for falling wards. He was doubly laden, for somewhere in the last few minutes he had acquired a second sword. Both of them had cat's-eye pommels.

She turned around and began her descent.

Her worry-faced Blade was waiting at the foot of the ladder. "Your Grace," he murmured, eyes flitting everywhere except in her direction. "I think there may be trouble now. Insist on your royal honors."

The honor guard no longer looked much like an honor guard. A dozen men were lined up on one side, a dozen on the other, and a twenty-fifth stood at ease in the center, waiting for her. She had never seen the Abbot in military garb before, and might very well have failed to recognize that bland, unremarkable face under the helmet. He was not fat, no worse than chubby, and his features were as smooth as a boy's, their apparent youth belied by gray-flecked shrubby eyebrows. She did not trust a face without worry lines.

He smiled as she approached with Ringwood on her right and Trudy on the left, Trudy carrying the Count's broadsword as if it were a personal souvenir. Last survivors of an interesting evening, Johanna thought.

"Good chance, Frau Schale. I gather you have had an unpleasant night."

"Minhea, isn't it?" she said. Ernst van Fader had admired Volpe in some ways, disapproved of him in others, but he had never had any use for the Abbot. "Where is Lord Volpe? Has he been notified of his nephew's death?"

The Abbot's smile persisted. "Of course you have been away . . . Lord Volpe predeceased his nephew by some weeks."

Trudy coughed a warning.

"And his son, Lord Karl?" Johanna asked.

"Ah, yes. You will be asked about Lord Karl's disappearance."

"So there can be no doubt that my son is now Grand Duke. Where is he?"

Minhea's eyes seemed to glaze. "If you don't know, then it doesn't matter, Frau Schale."

Too late she saw her error. She should not have admitted her ignorance. "I am Dowager Grand Duchess Johanna and will thank you to remember it."

Minhea shook his head, sending rays of morning sunlight streaking from his helmet. Suddenly his smile seemed more genuine, as if he had discarded some trifling doubts and was free to enjoy himself. "Were there a Grand Duke Frederik of Krupina here to confirm your status, lady, then that would be so. We could see your injuries healed, provide food and clean clothes. Then your coach would rush you without delay to Krupa to attend to the formalities attendant on the death of your lamented husband, proclamation of national mourning, and so on. Absent the child or proof he still lives, you are nothing but a suspect in a sensational murder case."

Twelve men on either hand and another score or so descending the ladder from the keep forming up behind her. What odds on a Blade and two women with three swords amongst them? After all she had been through, must she accept failure now?

"All three of you are at least material witnesses," the Abbot said. "Banneret! Disarm the prisoners."

"I am a Chivian Blade!" Ringwood said sharply, too sharply. "I cannot submit to disarming. I beg you not to throw away lives by making the attempt."

Minhea laughed softly. "I have fifty lives to throw against your one, boy. Your bravado jeopardizes these girls as well as yourself. Drop your sword on the grass, boy."

"Never!"

The ground trembled.

A horn sundered the peace of the morning.

Around the mass of the keep, which had concealed their approach until that moment, thundered a column of Vamky knights. They and their foam-flecked horses were gray with mud, but their blue cloaks streamed in the wind and sunlight flashed on their helmets. As they curved around and came to a halt in a double line behind the Abbot, Johanna recognized the leader, the one with the horn.

She had never thought she would be happy to see Volpe.

The horn spoke again. The riders' swords flashed from their scabbards. Echoes died. So, perhaps, did the hopes of Abbot Minhea.

"You were telling fibs, my lord," Trudy told him.

He had his back to them now, so Johanna could not see his face, but something about the way he was standing suggested that there was no longer a smile under the brim of his helmet. When he shouted a command, his voice sounded slightly off-key, even to her.

"Troop, sheath swords! Prepare to dismount!"

"As you were!" the Provost countered. "Disregard that man."

"I have overall authority in the Brotherhood, Volpe!" Minhea screamed. "They will obey my orders. You will be brought to trial."

"You are a murderer. You confined and tortured me without authority."

In almost perfect simultaneity, Abbot and Provost pointed at each other and shouted, "Arrest that man!"

The Brotherhood stood divided.

Ringwood's hand went to his sword as if he were about to intervene. Johanna caught his wrist. "Wait!" The numbers were about equal, but a swordsman on foot was no match for one on a horse. And if it came to a battle, she was going to be caught right in the middle of it.

She heard the squelch of approaching boots and did not turn. Banneret Schwartz went tramping past her, all the way to the Abbot. In silence he relieved Minhea of his sword and carried it across to offer it to Lord Volpe. The revolution was over. Wild cheers erupted from Minhea's men, and they rushed forward to mob their resurrected Provost.

"This is starting to smell suspiciously like a happy ending," Trudy said.

"Not yet," Ringwood retorted. "We're still one man short."

"Two," Johanna said.

A chestnut-and-mud-colored stallion pushed through the throng and walked across to the forgotten Dowager Grand Duchess. The rider reined in, swung his leg over the saddle, and dropped to the turf at her feet. Dust and mud made his face unrecognizable until he unfastened his chin strap and threw away his helmet, uncovering a familiar tangle of wavy brown hair sorely in need of a barber. He took her hands in his.

"Frederik is safe," Bellman said, and the world vanished in tears.

✦ 9 ✦

ℜingwood found the Brotherhood's field healing station impressive, not least because Banneret Schwartz seemed to call on men at random, the closest seven, as if every knight-brother was an expert conjurer. In minutes they threw up a tent and laid out a small octogram with strips of canvas, and then the eight of them chanted the conjuration entirely from memory. The Vamky ritual must be designed for serious wounds, yet it banished scrapes and bruises at least as well as Ironhall's did. The brethren also handed out anklet bandages conjured to postpone fatigue. These perked up the two women, but Ringwood's gave him such violent cramps that he had to remove it and do without—apparently his binding disapproved of the enchantment, just as it disapproved of sleep and wine. No matter, he was cantering along nicely on sheer excitement.

Fresh, dry clothes were another joy, and when the seneschal produced garments belonging to his eldest son and these proved to an almost perfect fit, even the accompanying jokes about beanpoles could be overlooked.

None of those pleasures could hold a candle to eating, though, and when the women finally tired of primping and preening and paraded down to the dining room, they found that Max Priboi had laid on for them a feast as fine as the previous evening's dinner with Count János, which seemed a long lifetime ago now. Ringwood consumed a dozen schnitzels and six spicy sausages before he even finished planning the rest of his meal.

Provost Volpe had left word that they were to start without him, so only the Duchess and the three surviving Chivians assembled around the table. Johanna sent the servants away to have privacy. She offered a brief tribute to Ranter.

True summarized the shadowmen adventure and the death of the Duke for Bellman, who then recounted his adventures rescuing Lord Volpe. He obviously left much unsaid, but he was coming down with a bad cold and reluctant to speak much.

Ringwood was too busy to talk, and he was not just being greedy. Time to eat and attend to his toilet would be precious from now on, because a solitary Blade was on duty every minute of every day. Life would be much harder without Ranter to share the burden.

No one was speculating on what was going to happen next, except that Bellman repeated Lord Volpe's promise to see Johanna reunited with her son before nightfall. Only Volpe himself knew what else would happen. He was now sole ruler of the Vamky Brotherhood and also head of the ducal family until Frederik came of age. He held all the power in Krupina.

The moment the Provost walked in he dominated the room, as he would dominate any room he ever inhabited. He was a big, powerful man with a very unsettling, wide-eyed stare. Ringwood was relieved to see that the former wicked uncle was on his best behavior, bowing to Johanna, asking her leave before he joined the company. He even attempted a battle-ax joke about prison diet, yet he ate frugally and watered his beer. He wanted more details about the shadowmen and the night's deaths, so that story had to be told again. When it was done he tucked his knife back in his belt and pushed his stool away from the table.

He offered Johanna a smile that made the back of Ringwood's neck prickle, although apparently it was well intended. "Your Highness is prepared to travel to Krupa to swear allegiance to our new, small Grand Duke now?"

"If I have to crawl!"

"Not necessary. You can ride or go in the coach, as you

please. Either should get you there before His Royal Highness can arrive from Bad Nargstein." He gazed around the table as if he wanted to fight someone, before returning his attention to Johanna. "I am heading to Krupa now and my first duty will be to inform Lady Margarita that her wedding is canceled. I do not anticipate that she will die of grief."

"I never met the child," Johanna said acidly, "but she was reported to be young and flighty, not insane."

The Provost glanced at Bellman, who said nothing.

"After that," Volpe continued, "Rubin's death and Frederik's accession must be publicly proclaimed. Both wedding and enthronement will be cancelled. I fully realize that you were never formally enthroned, Your Highness, and I accept the blame for that, but now that you are Dowager Duchess, an enthronement is out of the question."

Johanna said, "I understand. I will bear no grudges, my lord, as long as you continue to recognize and respect my son's status as Grand Duke."

These negotiations were sounding very much like the making of a peace treaty, and Ringwood was able to relax a little. He took a second helping of pickled eels to celebrate.

Volpe nodded. "I will swear fealty to your son in your presence. I have never broken an oath in my life." The terrible gaze settled briefly on her Blade. "I am thankful that the spirits of chance saved me from having to take action against a nephew who was also my liege lord."

Thanks for the murder. Ringwood thought it safest just to nod. He had his mouth full anyway.

"There will have to be an inquiry into his death, of course," the Provost added.

Ringwood choked.

Bellman thumped him on the back. "Don't worry, Brother Ringwood. He won't want any public testimony about His

Late Highness's recent activities. Some fish are better left in the sea. Take a drink."

Volpe frowned. "The matter of most concern is who will rule Krupina until our new Grand Duke comes of age. I need to provide guardians and tutors for him until then. I must appoint either a regent or a council of regency—there are precedents for both."

Johanna's eyes had grown almost as wide as Volpe's. "I trust that I may act as mother to my son, my lord?"

Volpe nodded. "Certainly."

"And you will have the courtesy to consult me on these other matters?"

"I will consult you, certainly, and acknowledge you as Frederik's mother, but frankly—pray excuse my bluntness when time presses—I cannot see Your Grace as regent."

That was a nice way of saying she was a commoner and a woman. It was also a load off Ringwood's shoulders.

Johanna seemed surprised and uneasy. "I assumed you would hold that office yourself, my lord?"

Volpe sighed. "Government bores me. I will oversee from the wings, but I will find a deputy for the day-to-day trivia."

Grand Duke Rubin coughed. "May I volunteer?" he asked.

True squeaked like a trampled cat. Ringwood bit his tongue. No one had noticed Bellman putting on the locket.

"You *dare*?" Volpe roared. "You even *dare* suggest such a thing?" He leapt to his feet, sending his stool flying. "A low-born foreigner masquerading as head of state, assuming royal honors?"

Ringwood grasped his sword hilt.

"Granted it is an unorthodox solution," the imposter said mildly. He spread his hands—small, soft hands, not Bellman's. "But is it not also the simplest? It would save a lot of awkward questions. The Margrave may be upset at seeing his daughter jilted. At least he will have to pretend so in public, but in private . . . ?" He looked meaningfully at Volpe.

"Insolence! What training or abilities do you have for running Krupina?"

"Oh, none. But you said yourself, *Nephew*, that the less ruling a ruler does the better, or words to that effect. You obviously would prefer to remain at Vamky. What harm can I do? You can depose me at any time just by taking away the locket."

"It is unconscionable! Deceiving the child and the entire country?"

"People believe what they want to believe, you told me."

Volpe shot a furious glance at Johanna, as if wondering whether she was party to this blasphemy. "You would expect to sleep in the Grand Duchess's bed, no doubt?"

"Tsk!" said her late husband. "Surely Her Grace should be allowed to decide her own sleeping arrangements? Of course His Royal Highness would have to be informed eventually. Or perhaps not? We can discuss that nearer the time. Did I not warn you, my lord, that I might call in a favor sometime?"

Aha! If personal gratitude came into it, then Bellman held the high ground.

Volpe leaned on the table to shout across at him. "This is madness! How could you possibly even get through this afternoon? You would have to return to Court and announce that your wedding is canceled. You would be apologizing to hundreds of guests, people you are expected to know."

Bellman's answer was a severe attack of coughing. "My memory for names is notorious," he croaked. "And I do believe that my laryngitis is getting worse."

Volpe's rage vanished as suddenly as it had come. He righted his stool and sat down. "You are remarkably convincing," he said calmly. "And you continue to impress. Very few men retain their composure when I yell at them."

"You hadn't already thought of this yourself?" the imposter inquired hoarsely.

"Certainly not!"

True smirked from ear to ear. The others followed her example, one by one. Volpe frowned suspiciously at their unexplained amusement.

"The laryngitis is fortuitous. What do you think of this insanity, Your Highness?"

Johanna's face was answer enough. "Oh, love!" she said. "Would you dare?"

"For you I would dare anything," Bellman said gallantly.

Volpe snorted. "How sweet! I will require an oath of secrecy from each one of you. And an oath of loyalty from you, Herr Bellman, if I am to put my country in your hands."

"I will gladly swear to serve Grand Duke Frederik with all my heart and strength until my dying day." The imposter smiled at Johanna. "And his lady mother also."

"Even sweeter, but let us be practical. You are overlooking a major problem. The enthronement could proceed, I suppose, with the former Duchess in place of the new, and the other planned festivities to follow, but not the wedding. You do not expect to marry Lady Margarita as well, I hope? Whatever she may think of the news, her father and all Trenko may well see this as a grievous insult. How are you going to explain your previous wife's miraculous return from the dead?"

Around the table the smiles faded. How indeed? Ringwood chewed thoughtfully. *She fell out of the coach, landed in the river with the Marquis in her arms, and they were washed away downstream? It has taken her half a year to walk back.* But why had she been in a coach with another man to start with? Grand Duke Rubin had slyly branded her an adulteress to win sympathy for his betrothal to the Margrave's daughter. Even if she had survived, why would he take her back now? No, it was impossible.

The dream popped like a bubble.

The Duke coughed again, painfully. Unless Bellman was a much better actor than Ringwood had ever suspected, his voice was fading fast.

"It is usually best just to tell people the truth," he whispered. "Or almost the truth. Why don't we all go for a ride in that great monster coach and make up our story on the way? Are we ready to leave?"

"Tomorrow," True said fondly, "when Sir Ringwood stops eating."

After that the day broke up into a few hard peaks of wonder towering above a rolling fog of fatigue. To relax in that terrible bouncing coach was impossible—it was hard enough not to be thrown right off the benches—but Ringwood wedged Trudy in a corner for safety and comfort and concentrated on enjoying her closeness and his own digestion. He drifted as close to sleep as a Blade ever did, ignored the others' plotting, coming alert only when Trudy nudged him.

He flicked back a few seconds . . . Trudy had said, "Happy to, my lord" . . . answering a question from the Provost, "You two will witness?"

"Happy to, my lord," he said. Witness what?

Oaths: Volpe, Johanna, and Bellman swearing loyalty to the infant Grand Duke, who was to remain officially only the heir. And then, astonishingly, Bellman and Johanna were led through a brief exchange of marriage vows by the Provost.

While bride and groom were sharing a kiss, Ringwood realized that he wasn't quite a solitary Blade now. Bellman was not bound by conjuration, but love was a potent binding in itself.

"Well, that takes care of the formalities," Johanna said happily. "Except for one thing." She frowned at Trudy.

"Krupina is not Chivial. Nor is it the open road. Krupa is a stuffy, old-fashioned, straight-laced town, and only married couples share bedrooms. Sir Ringwood will be an important person at Court. You cannot continue sleeping with him unless you're married."

Trudy glanced sideways at Ringwood, then turned a deceptively innocent gaze upon Johanna. "And the problem is . . . ?"

Ringwood shied like a shooed chicken. *Married?* Shadowmen were one thing—his binding gave him courage to face them—but *marriage?* At his age? For the rest of his life?

"You haven't told him your news?" the Duchess said.

Trudy shrugged. "I thought he had enough worries." She patted Ringwood's knee. "No matter, hon. If you don't want to, you don't want to. I must have misunderstood some of that love talk."

What news? Ringwood gave up wondering why they were all grinning at him and forced his mind to be practical. Even with Bellman helping on night shift, being a solitary Blade was going to leave him no time for romancing girls. He'd never find another like True anyway. The thought of her leaving and stranding him here in Krupina did not bear thinking about. No, if marriage was what it took . . .

"I didn't say I didn't want to!" he protested. "But you threw it at me too suddenly. Marriage? Sure. Well, that's no problem. You want to tie the noose . . . I mean knot . . . that'll be great. Er, do you have any particular date in mind, darling?"

True sighed. "Yes, love. Once again, please, my lord. With feeling."

The Provost said, "Do you, Ringwood, take . . ."

* * *

The ducal coach rolled into the palace yard soon after noon, causing a mad flurry of activity and no small relief, for the wedding guests would start arriving soon. Flunkies ran off in all directions to summon court officials. The yard was already crowded with delivery carts, and the Palace Guard's efforts to line up were not assisted by the escort of Vamky knights, who innocently contrived to back their horses in the wrong direction as often as possible. Stable hands and the ducal band added to the confusion.

Inside the coach, Lord Volpe said, "You are *absolutely* sure you want to go ahead with this?" Even he looked nervous.

Bellman and Johanna smiled at each other and said, "Yes!" with one voice. Probably neither of them could believe that all this was really happening.

A guardsman opened the door. The unknown swordsman who emerged first caused some surprise. Then came Lord Volpe, who had not been seen around the palace for weeks. He turned to offer a hand to His Royal Highness. The band director raised his baton . . . and then dropped it in his amazement. A universal cry of astonishment raised pigeons from the rooftops as the Grand Duke in turn handed down the *late* Grand Duchess. He looked around the yard uncertainly, then nodded to the band. Never had the Krupinese national anthem been worse played.

The ducal party proceeded into the palace, smiling regally to the ashen-faced spectators bowing or kneeling.

"Adulation at last!" Bellman whispered in Chivian. "This could become habit-forming." Johanna did not answer. Was her hand trembling on his arm or was his arm trembling under her hand? Both, likely. Behind them walked Lord Volpe and Sir Ringwood—and Trudy, who would be hopelessly lost if she became separated from the ducal party. Behind them, in turn, a whirlwind of whispers. News of Johanna's resurrection would be everywhere in minutes.

Fortunately, the imposter had no need to ask the way or be prompted by Volpe, for every possible wrong turning was blocked by gaping onlookers, leaving only the path to the ducal quarters clear. Two guards on the door stared open-mouthed as the couple approached.

"I m-m-must go and get r-ready, my dear," Johanna said. "You will break the news to What's-her-name, won't you?"

"As gently as I can," Bellman said, raising her hand to her lips.

"Not *too* gently!" Her Highness replied icily.

Surprisingly, the Grand Duchess's quarters were not even locked—a breach of security that clanged gongs of alarm for Ringwood. He ordered his ward to stand in a corner while he searched for intruders, but she was far beyond listening to him now. She threw open drapes and drawers and closet doors with squeals of wonder.

"Is this not a day of miracles!" she cried. "All my clothes! Still here! Trudy, dear, help me choose! What shall I wear to my enthronement? Pull that bell cord, Sir Ringwood, I need help."

Why get so excited over a mere fifty or so gowns? Ringwood rang the bell and prowled off to explore the rest of the suite.

At a hastily called audience, Grand Duke Rubin and Provost Lord Volpe regretfully informed Margrave Ladislas that his daughter could not be married that evening after all. As Bellman later reported, the old man wept with joy, while his daughter screamed most indecorously and hurled herself into the arms of her dazzlingly handsome equerry, Prince Nickolaus of Microsia.

The Grand Duchess's sister and brother-in-law arrived an hour or two later, in attendance on an elderly dowager and a curly-haired toddler. Johanna went white as snow at the sight of him, so that Ringwood stood poised to catch her if she fainted. He should have known her better by this time.

"He'll need a few days," Voica warned. "It's been far too long for him to remember. Do you know who this is, Freddie?"

The small but genuine Grand Duke thought for a moment and then said, "Mommy," and all the women started weeping. That frightened him, so he wept, too. Even the stallion-sized charcoal burner did. The *former* charcoal burner—he had been promoted to woodward. Blades were not allowed to weep, so Ringwood didn't. His wife shed enough tears for both of them.

The highlight of the day would be the enthronement. Get through that, Bellman thought, and he could survive anything. People believe what they want to believe.

The first great test was his toilet, though, and he could not reasonably have Volpe around to back him up in that. It went without a hitch. Valets shaved his fake face, combed his thinning gray locks without noticing that they were in fact an overlong mop of brown waves, and pulled silken hose over calves and thighs of solid muscle, thinking they were flab. None of the dozen or so people attending him noticed anything wrong, other than a bad throat infection. None was brash enough to suggest that he trot down to the palace octogram for a healing, because they all knew that no conjuration could cure the common cold.

He refused all the grandiose brocade and jewels laid out for his wedding. Tonight was to be his wife's triumph, he explained, and he would not upstage her. He was seriously out of character there, but nobody talked back to the sovereign, and disbelief did not extend to questioning his identity. Reluctantly the dressers produced a somber, almost drab cloak and very plain, dark hose. He had to wear his gold coronet, of course, and he let the heralds talk him into the jeweled star of the Order of Gottfried the Glorious. All through his ordeal flunkies were coming and going, whispering messages, improvising a new ceremony to replace what had been planned for months. He barely had time to disgust himself with a glance in a mirror before they informed him that he was due downstairs in the anteroom.

"Lead on!" he croaked, and went out to meet his fate.

He had never seen Johanna properly adorned before, and she was breathtaking in a gown of cobalt and emerald silk with slashed and puffed sleeves and ermine trim; state jewels flashed and sparkled on her bodice and neck. His wife! He stared at her in incredulous delight. She curtsied to him; he bowed to her, and moved close to kiss her fingers.

"You look magnificent, my dear," he whispered.

Her eyes shone happily at him. "So do you, Your Highness."

At her side stood a skinny swordsman gloriously bedecked in braid and gold epaulets. How had they ever found anything to fit him at such short notice?

"Congratulations, brother," Bellman whispered. Oh, the joys of laryngitis!

Ringwood's glazed eyes came to startled focus. "What?" Then a faint smile. "On what, er . . . Your Highness?"

If even he was starting to believe, then this must be going to work. "On your marriage, of course."

Ringwood nodded and smiled uncertainly. Bellman resisted the temptation to spring his impending fatherhood on him. As Trudy had said, he had enough to worry about just now.

Volpe hurried in, apologizing for being late. His sword hilt sparkled with gems, his spurs were silver, ostrich plumes waved above his helmet.

"If it please Your Royal Highness to proceed?" bleated the chief herald in his dazzling tabard.

Bellman offered his arm to his Grand Duchess.

"We are ready," she said.

The great hall was huge and bizarre: gilt, marble, and frescoes, with bosomy ladies wafting across the ceiling and near-naked but remarkably unsweaty warriors battling all around the walls. King Athelgar's palace of Nocare had nothing that would compare to it for outright vulgarity, and that evening it blazed with lamps and all the nobility of the realm in massed finery. On the dais stood twin thrones for the Grand Duke and his consort. But which consort? The news was out, and if any of the hundreds of guests assembled had still been in doubt that the marriage they had come to witness had been canceled, they were reassured when the Margrave and his daughter entered with the other Trenkoan notables and sat beside them in the Trenkoan reserved section. The ex-bride's radiant happiness was noted by all.

Trumpets brayed and everyone rose to honor . . . who? The published order of service indicated that the bride would now enter, but the bride was already present.

Instead the Grand Duke himself walked in from the side to take his throne, but his attendants were not as listed, either. Abbot Minhea of the Vamky Brotherhood was supposed to lead the way with the ceremonial mace, but that was certainly Lord Volpe carrying the ugly thing. After him came an unidentified lanky youth in the uniform of a colonel in the Palace Guard, bearing a naked sword, and who was the woman leading the infant Marquis Frederik? None of these people was mentioned at all. And the Grand Duchess on the ducal arm was the *late* Grand Duchess, who had been officially mourned for half a year.

The last notes of the national anthem mercifully died

away. Duke and Duchess settled on their respective thrones and everyone else was free to sit down also. Almost the only one who didn't was the boy with the sword, whoever he was.

So *that* woman, the peasant, sat on the consort's throne in state at last? But Lord Volpe was there, raising no objection—not even looking displeased. If *he* was willing to accept her it would be politic to do likewise. At first glance she seemed to have quit her boudoir half-dressed, for she was hatless, unlike every other woman in the hall, and her ash-blond hair hung unbound, but that was necessary for the ceremony. The great ladies of Krupina pursed their lips.

Grand Duke Rubin began to speak and sneezed three times. He tried again, but no one could hear a word. He coughed. He waved his nephew forward.

"Your Graces, my lords and ladies," Lord Volpe proclaimed, in tones that filled the hall like a carillon of bells, "His Royal Highness is suffering from a minor throat fever and has bade me speak in his stead. He apologizes for this discourtesy. He bids you all welcome, especially his dear brother ruler, Marquis Ladislas of Trenko, and his most exquisite daughter, the Lady Margarita . . ." An excruciatingly long list of names and titles followed. His Highness nodded to confirm that he had approved this tribute.

The best view in the house belonged to Ringwood, standing alongside the Duchess's throne. He could take some small pride in the glow of happiness that his ward was radiating. As True had said, this did smell like a happy ending. He still could not quite believe that the pudgy, pompous man with the gray goatee and gold coronet was actually Bellman. How did he keep a straight face amid all this kowtowing and folderol?

"As you can see," the Provost continued, his glare defying anyone present not to, "there has been a change of plan. Her Royal Highness Grand Duchess Johanna, my dear niece-in-law"—he bowed to her—"supposedly died in an accident half a year ago. Although her body had not been found, she was declared legally dead, as was her son, His Grace, Marquis Frederik of Krupa. His Royal Highness subsequently announced his betrothal to Lady Margarita, daughter of His Grace, Margrave Ladislas of Trenko." Volpe bowed again.

You could hear a snowflake fall, Ringwood thought. When King Athelgar wore his crown—opening Parliament, say, or at investitures—Commander Florian stood beside him like this, holding his sword, *Thorn*. But Florian was quite old, probably over thirty, and Ringwood should be still a precocious senior at Ironhall, yet here he was, on display like a state treasure.

He wondered if Florian ever developed this *frantic* need to scratch.

"The reason for this deception . . ." Volpe glared at the ensuing ripple of shock. "Yes, it was a deliberate deception! The reason this deception was necessary was that the accident to the coach in which Her Royal Highness was traveling was no accident. It was contrived, and it was murder!"

Tumult.

Seeking to divert his attention from the itch that now consumed him from his knees to his waist, but mostly burned in his crotch, Ringwood meditated on being a colonel at his age. If he had done the calculations correctly, he was now earning more in a year than Dad had made in a lifetime of mending pots. And there was the small matter of a Grand Duchess kissing him right on the mouth and thanking him for making it all possible, as if he'd done something brave or remarkable. Ranter and Bellman had done it, not he. He'd made too many mistakes, just as he'd feared, and only luck had let him win through in the end.

Volpe had them calmed down again.

"Obviously whoever the miscreant was who sought to slay the Heir Apparent and his mother, his initial failure did not mean that they were out of danger. Nay! Far from it! The monster might strike again at any time! For this reason, it was deemed advisable that Her Royal Highness the Grand Duchess and His Highness the Marquis should disappear from sight. Their deaths were proclaimed so that the murderer would believe his foul schemes had succeeded. Thus might he be lulled into a false sense of security!"

Volpe ought to have made a career in epic poetry, Ringwood thought. He had the audience shivering in their corsets.

"To aid in this deception, the noble Margrave Ladislas and his daughter most graciously consented to engage in a deception—"

Bellman had invented all this foolery in the coach. Now he was sitting there in glory looking as if he didn't care *what* happened, please could he just crawl away and die? Probably a week from now he would be feeling much better and his entire dukedom would be down with the same curse.

"And only today was the killer unmasked!" Volpe's voice ricocheted through the hall. "The treacherous Abbot Minhea—"

The roar of disapproval frightened the Marquis, so Voica led him out, lucky fellow. Ringwood identified Trudy up in the balcony and wished he dared wink at her. Married! He was married! She was his forever! That was the most incredible event of this whole incredible day. What could possibly top that?

Now the ceremony could proceed, with Volpe reading out the proclamations and Bellman performing the ceremonial, prompted by whispers from Johanna. He set the silver coronet on her head, he bestowed the Order of Gottfried the Glorious on her, and finally he knelt to kiss her hand. Only Ringwood noticed how she chucked him under the chin. Everyone else was cheering loud enough to drown out the trumpets.

Now a hundred or so other people would have to come forward and kneel to her. It was going to take a long time, and no doubt she would savor every moment of it. After that would come the banquet, when Ringwood would have to stand and watch everyone else eat.

That did not feel like a happy ending.

EPILOGUE

Far, Far Away

$\mathcal{M}$ost honored Grand Master,

I greet you well, commending to your lordship the bearer of this letter, Sir Radu Priboi, personal equerry to Her Royal Highness, Grand Duchess Johanna of Krupina. The noble knight is a man of most excellent probity and discretion, charged by Her Grace to deliver this and divers other documents to you. He also bears letters to others, including their Majesties and some members of the Fellowship of White Sisters.

Yet the kernel of his mission is to lay before you in Ironhall *Invincible,* the sword of Sir Ranter, that it may hang in its proper place forever. Sir Ranter died alone and very young, but in the manner of his death his name is worthy to stand with the greatest in the chronicles of our Order. I enclose herewith a formal notice of his death for inclusion in the *Litany of Heroes.* Because this is limited by tradition to the bare facts, I do earnestly pray your lordship that you will also make known in the hall and throughout our Order that Sir Ranter with his own hands slew the evildoer who originated the deaths of Sir Bernard, Sir Clovis, Sir East, Sir Richey, Sir Valiant, and Sir Yorick. Thereby he avenged their deaths and also those of many other persons, even his own.

My ward was moved by Sir Ranter's sacrifice to consider erecting a statue to him, but on taking counsel determined that no true likeness could be posthumously wrought and such a memorial would have little value in a faraway land where our Order is unknown. When honored by a request for advice on this matter, I ventured to propose that a more fitting remembrance would be to donate funds in memory of Sir Ranter for the upkeep and repair of Ironhall, whose fabric and furnishings are in many cases suffering from age, as your lordship is aware. My ward was graciously pleased to approve this suggestion, and sends a most generous endowment by the hand of Sir Radu, with the prayer that your lordship will accept the same on behalf of our Order. The deed of gift grants your lordship and succeeding Grand Masters total discretion in the application of these funds for the benefit of all candidates in years to come.

Sir Radu also brings to your lordship in your private capacity, a packet from Master Bellman, which I understand represents certain financial instruments that your lordship made available to him, but for which he now sees no need, and which he therefore returns to your purse, being most grateful for your loving consideration, as was I upon hearing of it.

I regret that I am forbidden by solemn oaths from revealing all that I am disposed to tell you, and I do particularly caution your lordship that Sir Radu is not privy to Master Bellman's current situation. I can divulge only that he prospers, having found gratifying and meaningful employment well suited to his talents, and is most happily married to a lady of great estate and personal charm.

Sir Radu may freely disclose to you my own happy circumstances. Although the duties of a solitary Blade can be onerous, His Royal Highness has generously appointed me commander of the Palace Guard, granting me the means and authority to train assistants who are already able to ease my burden. It is no small perquisite to dwell in a royal palace! You may be surprised to hear of my own marriage, to the former Sister Gertrude of the Fellowship of the White Sisters, who accompanied us on our journey and at divers times saved us from peril, but our union brings us both great happiness and is likely to be blessed with progeny even before you read these words.

In closing, although my joy is tempered by grief at Sir Ranter's untimely end, I am content to inform your lordship that the mission you assigned to us last summer, which we undertook with trepidation and scant hope of success, has been brought to successful fruition. Our ward came safely home, although not without some anxious moments, and our efforts aided in resolving Krupina's problems, so that the land again rejoices in the rule of a sagacious and benevolent Grand Duke, secure in the prospect of the royal line being legitimately extended to future generations. Lord Volpe's part in the turbulent events of a year or so ago proved on careful analysis by Master Bellman to have been misrepresented, and I know for a fact that Provost Volpe and His Royal Highness are now on better terms than they had been for many years past.

Most honored lord,
I pray that this brief report will meet with your approval.

Done by my hand in Krupina,
this first day of Thirdmoon, 406 (Chivian style)

Ringwood,
Companion

Now available in hardcover

The Jaguar Knights
A Chronicle of the King's Blades

I

The master first lets slip his best hounds.

◆ 1 ◆

Something was up. The Royal Guard liked to think it knew all the news and heard it before anyone else did, but that day it had been shut out. The morning watch had been on duty for two hours already, but Commander Vicious had not arrived to hold the daily inspection and the graveyard shift had not yet been stood down. They were supposedly attending the King, who was meeting with senior advisors in the council chamber. Absurd! Even during the worst panics of the Thencaster Conspiracy, three years ago, Athelgar had never summoned his cabinet in the middle of the night.

Deputy Commander Lyon must have some idea what was going on, but he refused to admit it. Infuriatingly, he just sat behind his desk in the guardroom, reading a book of poetry— Lyon not only read poetry, he wrote it too, yet he was a fine swordsman, subtle and unpredictable. The half-dozen

Blades sustaining the permanent dice game under the window were doing so halfheartedly, grumbling more than gambling. Sir Wolf was polishing his boots in a corner—Wolf never read poetry, was never invited into the games, and cared not a fig what folly the King was pursuing this time.

The park beyond the frost-spangled panes was all pen-and-ink, stark white and black, sun-bright snow and cadaver trees under a sky of anemic blue, for this was Secondmoon of 395, the coldest winter in memory. Nocare, with its high ceilings and huge windows, was a summer palace, impossible to heat in cold weather. The King had moved the court there on some inexplicable whim and could not return it to poky old Greymere as long as the roads were blocked by snowdrifts. Courtiers slunk around unhappily, huddled in furs and muttering under their smoky breath.

Innumerable feet shuffled past the guardroom door: gentry, heralds, pages, porters, stewards, White Sisters, Household Yeomen. No one paid any heed until a rapid tattoo of heel taps raised every head. Blades knew the sound of Guard boots, and these were in a hurry.

Wolf went on polishing his left one.

In marched Sir Damon, still wearing his sash as officer in charge of the night watch. The kibitzers by the window exchanged shocked glances. The matter was much more than routine if Sir Vicious had sent a senior Blade as messenger, instead of a junior or just a page.

Damon glanced around the room, then bent to whisper something to Lyon. Lyon turned to Wolf.

"Leader wants you."

Wolf put foot in boot and stamped. "Where?"

Damon said, "Council chamber. He's still with the Pirate's Son."

At the dice table, eyebrows rose even higher. The Pirate's Son was King Athelgar. It was common knowledge that Vicious preferred to keep Sir Wolf out of the King's sight, so if Wolf was wanted now, it was because the King had called for him by name.

Wolf was the King's Killer.

Ignoring the rabble's surprise, Wolf strode across to the mirror and looked himself over with care. Like all Blades he was of middle height, slim and athletic, but he was invariably the best-turned-out man in the Guard—boots and sword belt gleaming like glass, not a wrinkle in his hose nor speck of dust marring his jerkin. He adjusted the feather in his bonnet an imperceptible amount and turned away. He did not examine his face. No one looked at that horror unless they must.

Exchanging nods with a lip-chewing Lyon, he strode out into the corridor, and Damon fell into step beside him. Together they marched along marble corridors, past statuary and tapestries. Courtiers stared with interest at two senior members of the Royal Guard moving at an urgent clip. Word that the King had sent for the infamous Sir Wolf would spread like fire in dry grass.

So what was up? The last time Wolf had been summoned to the royal presence, Athelgar had named him—over Leader's objections—to lead the Elboro mission, which had required him to kill two brother Blades. It had not been the first such filthy job the Pirate's Son had given him, either, and Wolf's written report afterward had let Athelgar Radgaring know exactly what he thought of his liege lord. Moreover, since Leader had not ordered him to rewrite it, it had warned His Majesty that others shared those opinions. The Guard had been shorthanded back then, else Wolf might have been thrown in a dungeon for some of the comments in that report. In the two years since, Vicious had kept him well away from the King.

What had changed? Well, the guard was up to strength

now, so one possibility was the Athelgar was going to award him the Order of the Royal Boot. That was highly unlikely. Knowing how Wolf felt about him, Athelgar was more likely to keep the King's Killer bound to absolute loyalty forever—safer that way.

Another possibility was that the Pirate's Son wanted someone murdered. Blades were bound by oath and conjuration to defend their ward from his enemies, not to commit crimes on royal whims, but defense could cover a multitude of nasty situations.

Wolf saw anger in Damon's tightly clenched jaw. Damon was a decent man, not one of those who carried grudges against the King's Killer.

"Any hints, brother?"

"Dunno anything. Huntley and Flint rode in about four hours ago."

"Ah! And Leader wakened the Pirate's Son?"

"They've been in council ever since. No one's allowed in or out except inquisitors. A *plague* of inquisitors!"

That news merely deepened the mystery. Sir Flint and Sir Huntley were typical examples of Blades who failed to find a real life after being knighted and discharged from the Guard. Both men were in their fifties, idling away years at Ironhall, instructing boys in fencing and horsemanship, yet still hankering after the sins of the city. Whenever Grand Master needed a dispatch taken to Court, men like Flint or Huntley would accept couriers' wages, knowing that the skilled young pimps of the Guard would always find them some of what Ironhall lacked.

So whatever had provoked this emergency had originated at, or near to, Ironhall. Although it was officially headquarters of the Loyal and Ancient Order of the King's Blades, in practical terms it was only a school and orphanage, a factory for turning unwanted rebellious boys into the world's finest swordsmen. Wolf could imagine nothing whatsoever that could happen there to provoke a middle-of-the-night meeting of the King in Council.

He could guess why he had been summoned, though. When the weather was this bad near Grandon, it must be mean as belly worms up on Starkmoor. Grand Master would not have sent anyone on such a journey unless the matter was supremely urgent, and he had thought the trek perilous enough to send two of them. Most likely his despatch required an answer, and Athelgar had decided to give his least favorite Blade the putrid job of riding posthaste to Ironhall over snowbound roads in this appalling cold. That would be a typical piece of royal spite.

There were Blades on duty even outside the anteroom, which was not usual. The rest of the graveyard shift was sprawled around on the chairs inside it, sulky and unshaven. They looked shocked when they saw the man Damon had fetched. Damon halted, Wolf kept going. Sir Sewald had the inner door; he tapped and opened it so the newcomer could march straight in without having to break stride.

The Cabinet Chamber was large but gloomy, newly repaneled in wood like molasses and furnished with spindly chairs from some lady's boudoir. Athelgar had terrible taste and his expensive renovations were methodically ruining every palace he owned.

Since his summons had officially come from Commander Vicious, Wolf could go straight to him and ignore the King, always a pleasure. He stamped boots and tapped sword hilt in salute. Dark and menacing as one of the bronze memorials along Rose Parade in Grandon, the Commander was standing well inside the chamber, so he had been taking part in the talk, not just being an ornamental doorstop. Vicious was notoriously taciturn, but had not always been so. The facial scar that made speech physically painful for him was a memento of the

Garbeald Affair, another of the King's follies. His vitriolic hatred of inquisitors dated from that same disaster.

Maps, papers, and dirty dishes littered the central table. Lord Chancellor Sparrow stood on one side of the crackling fire, the Earl Marshal sat bundled in his wheeled chair on the other, and Grand Inquisitor were by the window, being extra-inscrutable. Grand Inquisitor were twins, indistinguishable. All inquisitors seemed foreboding, with their black robes, sinister reputation, and unblinking stare, but to have two of them doing it at you was twice as bad. The Guard called them the Gruesome Twosome.

Sparrow was a perky, beak-nosed, little man, more of a pompous robin than a cheeky sparrow, but rated a better-than-average chancellor. He feared Athelgar not at all and often quashed his mad notions before they did too much harm. The Earl Marshal, old as the ocean and crippled with gout, was asleep. A spidery clerk crouched over a writing desk, busily wielding a quill.

Flint and Huntley were slumped on chairs in a far corner. They looked exhausted and were probably chilled to the bone over there, too. They had earned some sleep, and keeping them from it was carrying security to absurd lengths.

And the Pirate's Son . . . As always, Athelgar was wandering, restless as a dog with fleas. He was not his usual splendid self. His hose was rumpled, he wore no jewelry, and his hair—dyed a respectable Chivian brown—was badly in need of brushing. Even his goatee, which he left its original Baelish red, looked somehow bedraggled. He had just turned twenty-five and was about to celebrate the fifth anniversary of his accession.

"Sir Wolf, sire," Vicious said.

Wolf turned and performed the gymnastics of a full court bow.

"Ah, Wolf." Athelgar headed to the fire. "We have bad

news. Your brother has been seriously injured. We are distressed to impart such dire tidings."

That could not explain the emergency. The King had no interest whatsoever in the well-being of an obscure private Blade, whom he had not seen for years, who was not even a member of his Guard.

I know how you weep for him, Wolf did not say, *since you've kept him locked him up on Whinmoor all these years.* "Your Majesty is kind. Injured by whom?" Blades did not meet with accidents.

The uninvited query made the King spin around and glare. "That remains to be discovered. Three nights ago, Quondam was attacked by persons unknown. Sir Fell and Sir Mandeville are slain."

Wolf gaped, shocked into silence. Lynx wounded, two other Blades dead—there should be a dozen corpses lying around as evidence, so why was the criminals' identity in doubt? And *Quondam*? Quondam, on Whinmoor, was absolutely impregnable, a fortress that had never been taken by storm or siege. If this was not a bizarre joke, it must be the start of an invasion. Or armed rebellion. The emergency snapped into focus.

Moreover, the King was *scared*. In Wolf's studied opinion, most people could lie to ears, but not to eyes. If you knew how to look, you could learn a man's feelings more truly from the way he held his chin and moved his eyes than you ever could from his words. All really good swordsmen had some of this skill, even if they were unaware that they were reacting to the twitch of an eyelid flagging a lunge before their opponent's foot began to move; it was why Ironhall discouraged dueling masks during training. Grand Inquisitor were unreadable, of course, but the Lord Chancellor was usually fairly legible and Athelgar displayed his feelings like heraldic banners. With shoulders hunched, wrists crossed low, and teeth set, he was proclaiming worry in fanfares. Sparrow was chewing his lip. Even Vicious was not standing with his hands confidently behind his back as usual, but looking rather as if he were poised to leap to his ward's defense. If this tale was a hoax, the King and his most senior advisors were not in on it.

"A sizable force," Athelgar said. "Gone already. Their tracks led to the beach."

"Raiders, sire? Baels?"

"Not Baels!" snapped the royal Bael. "These were definitely not Baels!"

Wolf bowed and waited to hear why the King was so sure and who else could have pulled off such a feat.

The King did not say. "Baron Dupend was seriously wounded. At least a score of his men were killed, and Grand Master thinks about as many of the attackers. The Baroness was abducted." He paused to stare out the window. "That appears to have been the sole motive for the assault—to kidnap the lady."

Wolf resisted an urge to tell his sovereign lord he was out of his mind. Why should anyone storm one of the most formidable strongholds in all Eurania to carry off a woman guarded by three Blades and a garrison of men-at-arms, knowing the loss of life this must entail? Even if Celeste's stunning beauty had survived four years imprisonment, that would be carrying rape to improbable extremes, and why else should anyone want that trollop? She had no land, no rich relatives, no importance. Nevertheless, the report had come from Grand Master, and for almost a year now Grand Master had been Durendal, Lord Roland. Any Blade would accept Durendal's testimony if he said the sea was wine.

"My brother's ward was kidnapped, yet he is still alive?" That was truly incredible.

"I said so!" Athelgar was staring at him very hard. "Does this news surprise you?"

Wolf hastily adjusted to the idea that he had been summoned to answer a charge of treason. He looked to Vicious for support and saw suspicion there, too. His path and Celeste's had crossed in the past; his brother shared her captivity at Quondam. He struggled to view the grotesque news through Athelgar's snaky eyes.

Fortunately he need only speak the truth. "It amazes me. Your Majesty, I swear that I had no prior knowledge of any plan or plot to rescue Lady—" he saw warning signs "—I mean *abduct* Lady Celeste. The news dumbfounds me. I do not know who could, or would want to, remove her from Quondam, nor who could achieve it. Surely Your Grace cannot question my loyalty? Even if my binding would allow me to engage in armed rebellion against your royal peace— which I do not believe it would—I should never involve my own brother in so dastardly a plot."

"The evidence is not yet clear," the King said narrowly. "We are not certain who injured your brother, nor which side he was supporting."

"I swear I know nothing about this, sire!"

"Grand Inquisitor?"

The one on the right said, "The witness speaks the truth." They never hesitated and never spoke at the same time, but nobody knew how they did it. They did not just take turns.

The weather in the chamber changed for the better.

We are relieved to hear it," the King said, without looking much pleased. "Then you will wish to hurry to your brother's side, Sir Wolf, and we will have you investigate this crime for us."

The shocks were coming too fast. Promoted in a blink from chief suspect to chief inspector, Wolf mumbled something about being honored.

"Your first destination must be Ironhall," Athelgar said. "The casualties were taken there, for it has the nearest octogram where they might be healed. Grand Master thinks Sir Lynx will live."

Not, *will make a complete recovery*? Wolf nodded, distrusting himself to speak. Outlawed at twelve, imprisoned five years in Ironhall and four more at Quondam—his brother had never known freedom. Now this.

"And that is about all we know," Athelgar said, pacing again. "Everything else is hearsay. Go and find out the facts! The news must be kept secret, until we know who and what and why. Is that understood, Sir Wolf? Extreme secrecy! Premature disclosure will cause panic and talk of a foreign invasion. It may *be* a foreign invasion for all we presently know. The Commander recommends you as the best man to investigate. We know," he added sourly, "that you can be discreet."

And ruthless, but no doubt he was hinting that any other investigator might uncover secrets Wolf had known and kept for years. Those would make stale news now, no longer capable of raising the epic scandal they would have stirred up once, yet Athelgar would certainly prefer that his youthful follies remain unmentioned. Spirits knew he had enough others to satisfy anyone. Wolf bowed and murmured gratitude for the royal compliment.

"You will be granted all the powers you require. Go and see to your brother and then proceed to Quondam."

"Your Majesty does me honor." Wolf wondered if he was being appointed royal scapegoat for something. The King thought of him as a killer, but Vicious knew he did any job as thoroughly as possible, whether it involved killing or not.

"To expedite matters, Commander," Lord Sparrow said primly, "pray advance Sir Wolf adequate funds from the Guard's coffers and apply to Chancery for reimbursement. A representative of the Office of General Inquiry will accompany you, Sir Wolf."

"But I will be in charge?" Wolf's query created an angry

pause. It should go without saying that a Blade would not and could not take orders from a Dark Chamber snoop. It also went without saying that the snoop would feel free to ignore, subvert, or misunderstand any orders from a brainless sword twirler like Wolf. Especially Wolf.

"You will report to the Lord Chancellor," the King decreed, "and the inquisitor to Grand Inquisitor."

"Your Grace is setting up two inquiries?"

More glares.

"I do believe, sire," Sparrow twittered, "that Sir Wolf should be given overall authority."

Athelgar nodded grumpily.

Wolf said, "I will also need the help of a sniffer, my lord." This business reeked of conjuration.

"The nearest White Sisters' priory," the Chancellor said, "is in Lomouth. Your commission will give you all the authority you need. The Council expects frequent reports, Sir Wolf, but should you conclude that additional assaults are likely, you will issue a general alarm directly to the authorities concerned."

"Who keeps the King's Peace on Whinmoor, my lord?"

Sparrow pursed lips. "The sheriff is Baron Dupend himself, but you will speak with the King's voice."

"How soon can you leave?" the King barked.

"The moment I receive my writ and the funds, sire." Wolf looked to the Gruesome Twosome. "And my assistant?"

"Inquisitor Hogwood will meet you at the stable, Sir Wolf," said the one on the left.

"We will send your commission there also," said the Chancellor, peering over the clerk's shoulder at what he was writing. "Momentarily."

"By your leave, sire?" Wolf bowed to the King and was dismissed.

• 2 •

Vicious stepped out to the anteroom with him. Wolf turned, expecting some sort of explanation, but the Commander just snapped, "Move!" and went back in again.

So Wolf moved. Heads turned as he streaked along the endless marble floors of Nocare, skidding around corners. He paused at the Guardroom door long enough to shout, "Modred, pick me out a horse!" and resumed running. He reached his quarters, dressed in two of everything, topped off with a heavy fur robe, and was down at the Guard's stable with a pack on his shoulder before the groom had finished saddling up under Sir Modred's needle eye. The yard outside was heaped with dirty snow, and the horses' breath was icing up their stalls.

The haste was unseemly but necessary if he were to leave before Inquisitor Hogwood appeared, which is what Vicious had meant. Nobody liked the way inquisitors spied, lied, and pried, but the mutual dislike between the snoops and the Blades ran especially deep, and Vicious morbidly detested them. Wolf, moreover, was the Dark Chamber's least favorite Blade.

THE SERPENTWAR SAGA
FROM *NEW YORK TIMES* BESTSELLING AUTHOR

RAYMOND E. FEIST

SHADOW OF A DARK QUEEN
0-380-72086-8/$7.99 US/$10.99 Can

A dread darkness is descending upon Midkemia—a powerful and malevolent race of monsters has slipped through a hole in the dimensions. And two unlikely young heroes must take up arms in the struggle to protect their besieged world.

RISE OF A MERCHANT PRINCE
0-380-72087-6/$7.99 US/$10.99 Can

Surviving the wrath of the fearsome Sauur, noble Erik and cunning Roo have delivered a timely warning to the rulers of the Midkemian Empire, and are now free to pursue their separate destinies. But a beautiful seductress threatens to destroy everything Roo has built and become.

RAGE OF A DEMON KING
0-380-72088-4/$6.99 US/$8.99 Can

A foul and terrible thing has escaped from a world already devoured to feed on one consumed by chaos—an insatiable nightmare creature of dark and murderous nature. The final conflict is joined, pitting serpent against man and magician against demon.

SHARDS OF A BROKEN CROWN
0-380-72088-4/$6.99 US/$8.99 Can

Winter's icy grasp is loosening on the world. The Emerald Queen's vanquished army has its broken back to the Bitter Sea. And treachery is its only recourse.

Available wherever books are sold or please call 1-800-331-3761 to order.

www.AuthorTracker.com

RF 0104